P9-CJJ-139
RECEIVED
JUN - - 2019
BY:

Elizabeth of Bohemia

NO LONGER PROPERTY OF
SEATTLE PUBLIC LIBRARY

Elizabeth of Bohemia

A Novel about Elizabeth Stuart

THE WINTER QUEEN

DAVID ELIAS

Copyright © David Elias, 2019

Published by ECW Press

665 Gerrard Street East
Toronto, Ontario, Canada M4M 1Y2
416-694-3348 / info@ecwpress.com

All rights reserved. No part of this publication may be reproduced, stored in a retrieval system, or transmitted in any form by any process — electronic, mechanical, photocopying, recording, or otherwise — without the prior written permission of the copyright owners and ECW Press. The scanning, uploading, and distribution of this book via the Internet or via any other means without the permission of the publisher is illegal and punishable by law. Please purchase only authorized electronic editions, and do not participate in or encourage electronic piracy of copyrighted materials. Your support of the author's rights is appreciated.

Cover design: Michel Vrana
Maps: © Chris Brackley/As the Crow Flies Cartography/www.atcfc.ca
Cover image: "Princess Elizabeth (1596–1662), Later Queen of Bohemia" by Robert Peake the elder (c. 1606), from the Metropolitan Museum of Art: Gift of Kate T. Davison, in memory of her husband, Henry Pomeroy Davison 1951
Author photo: © Anthony Mark Photography

This is a work of fiction. Names, characters, places, and incidents either are the product of the author's imagination or are used fictitiously, and any resemblance to actual persons, living or dead, business establishments, events, or locales is entirely coincidental.

LIBRARY AND ARCHIVES CANADA
CATALOGUING IN PUBLICATION

Elias, David H., 1949–, author
Elizabeth of Bohemia : a novel about Elizabeth Stuart, the Winter Queen / David Elias.

Issued in print and electronic formats.

ISBN 978-1-77041-463-1 (softcover)
ISBN 978-1-77305-327-1 (PDF)
ISBN 978-1-77305-326-4 (EPUB)

1. Elizabeth, Queen, consort of Frederick I, King of Bohemia, 1596-1662—Fiction. I. Title.

PS8559.L525E45 2019 C813'.54
C2018-905339-9 C2018-905340-2

The publication of *Elizabeth of Bohemia* has been generously supported by the Canada Council for the Arts which last year invested $153 million to bring the arts to Canadians throughout the country and is funded in part by the Government of Canada. *Nous remercions le Conseil des arts du Canada de son soutien. L'an dernier, le Conseil a investi 153 millions de dollars pour mettre de l'art dans la vie des Canadiennes et des Canadiens de tout le pays. Ce livre est financé en partie par le gouvernement du Canada.* We acknowledge the support of the Ontario Arts Council (OAC), an agency of the Government of Ontario, which last year funded 1,737 individual artists and 1,095 organizations in 223 communities across Ontario for a total of $52.1 million. We also acknowledge the contribution of the Government of Ontario through the Ontario Book Publishing Tax Credit, and through Ontario Creates for the marketing of this book.

Canada Council for the Arts
Conseil des Arts du Canada
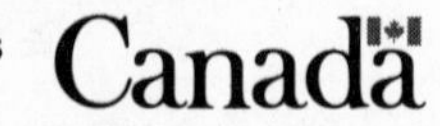

PRINTED AND BOUND IN CANADA

PRINTING: FRIESENS 5 4 3 2 1

For my sons,

David and William,

and my daughter,

Wendy.

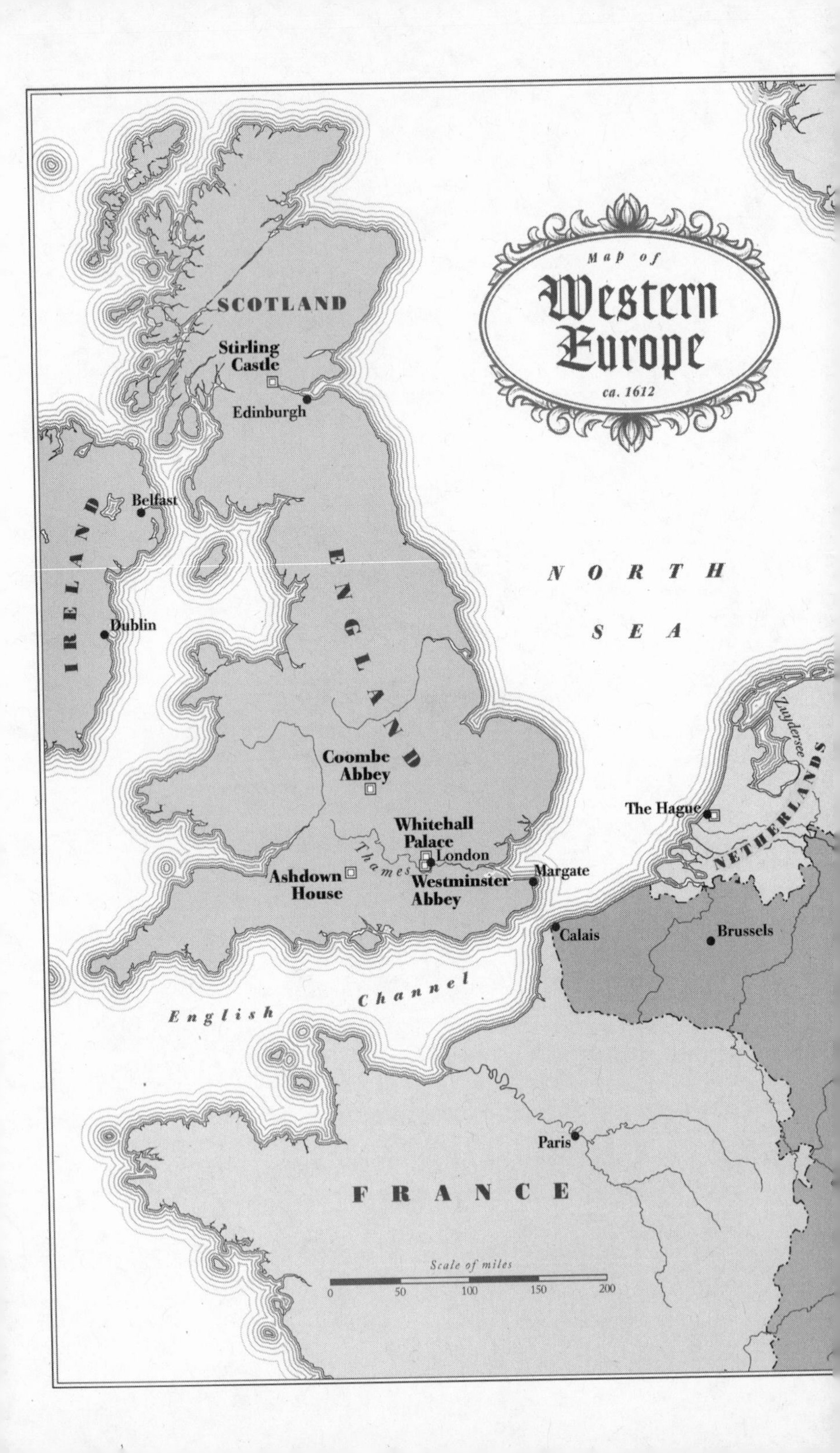
Map of
Western Europe
ca. 1612
SCOTLAND
Stirling Castle
Edinburgh
Belfast
IRELAND
Dublin
ENGLAND
NORTH SEA
Zuydersee
NETHERLANDS
The Hague
Coombe Abbey
Whitehall Palace
London
Thames
Ashdown House
Westminster Abbey
Margate
Calais
Brussels
English Channel
Paris
FRANCE
Scale of miles
0
50
100
150
200

NORWAY
SWEDEN
BALTIC SEA
Copenhagen
DENMARK
Hamburg
Weser
Elbe
Oder
Castle of Custrin
SARMATIA
HOLY
Berlin
Herford Abbey
Warsaw
Bonn
ROMAN
Prague Castle
St. Vitus Cathedral
Prague
Rhine
Frankfurt
PALATINATE
Heidelberg
Heidelberg Castle
BOHEMIA
Vltava
Neckar
SLOVAKIA
Danube
EMPIRE
Vienna
SWITZERLAND
AUSTRIA
ROMANIA
Bern
VENICE

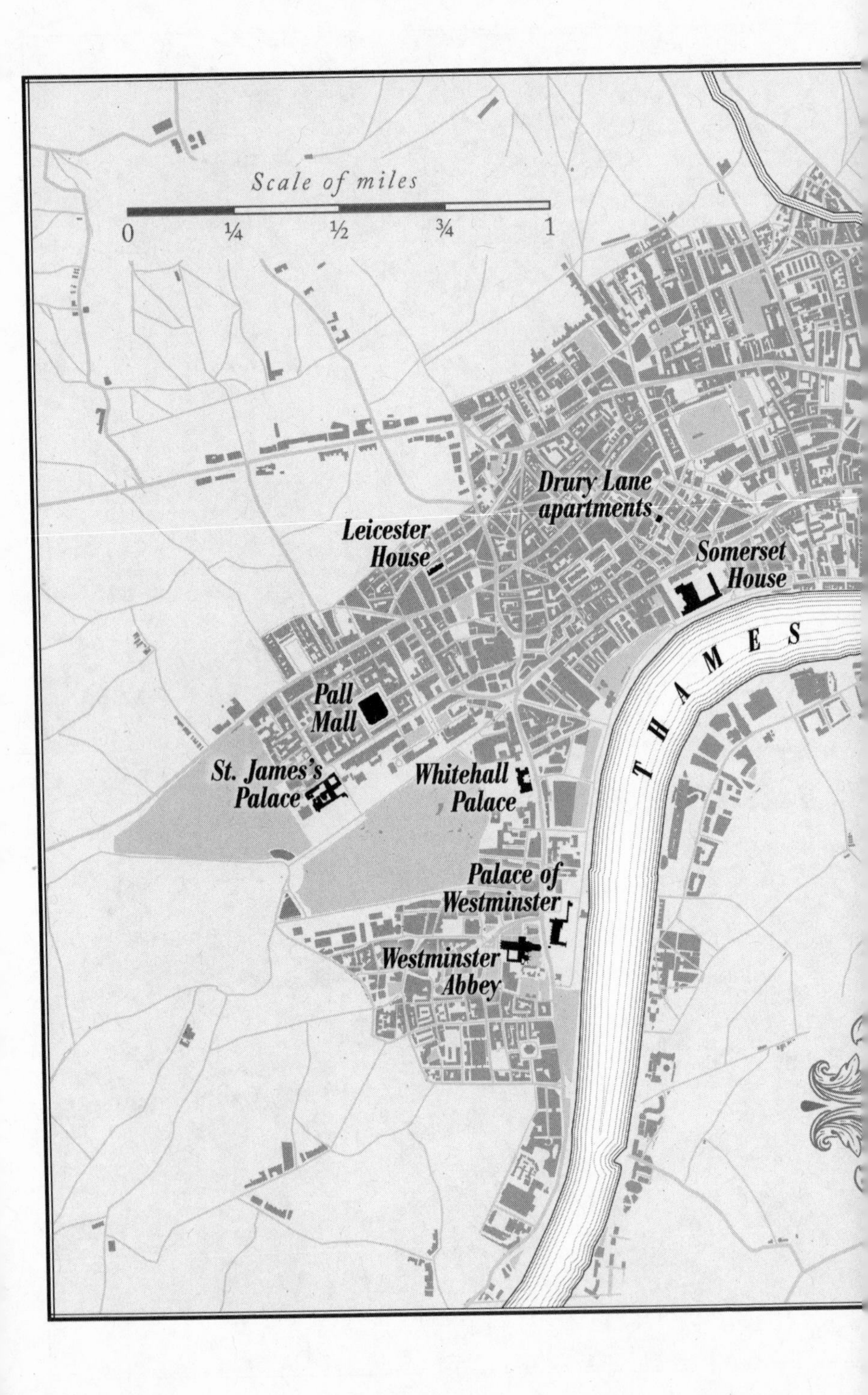

Scale of miles
0
¼
½
¾
1
Drury Lane apartments
Leicester House
Somerset House
THAMES
Pall Mall
St. James's Palace
Whitehall Palace
Palace of Westminster
Westminster Abbey

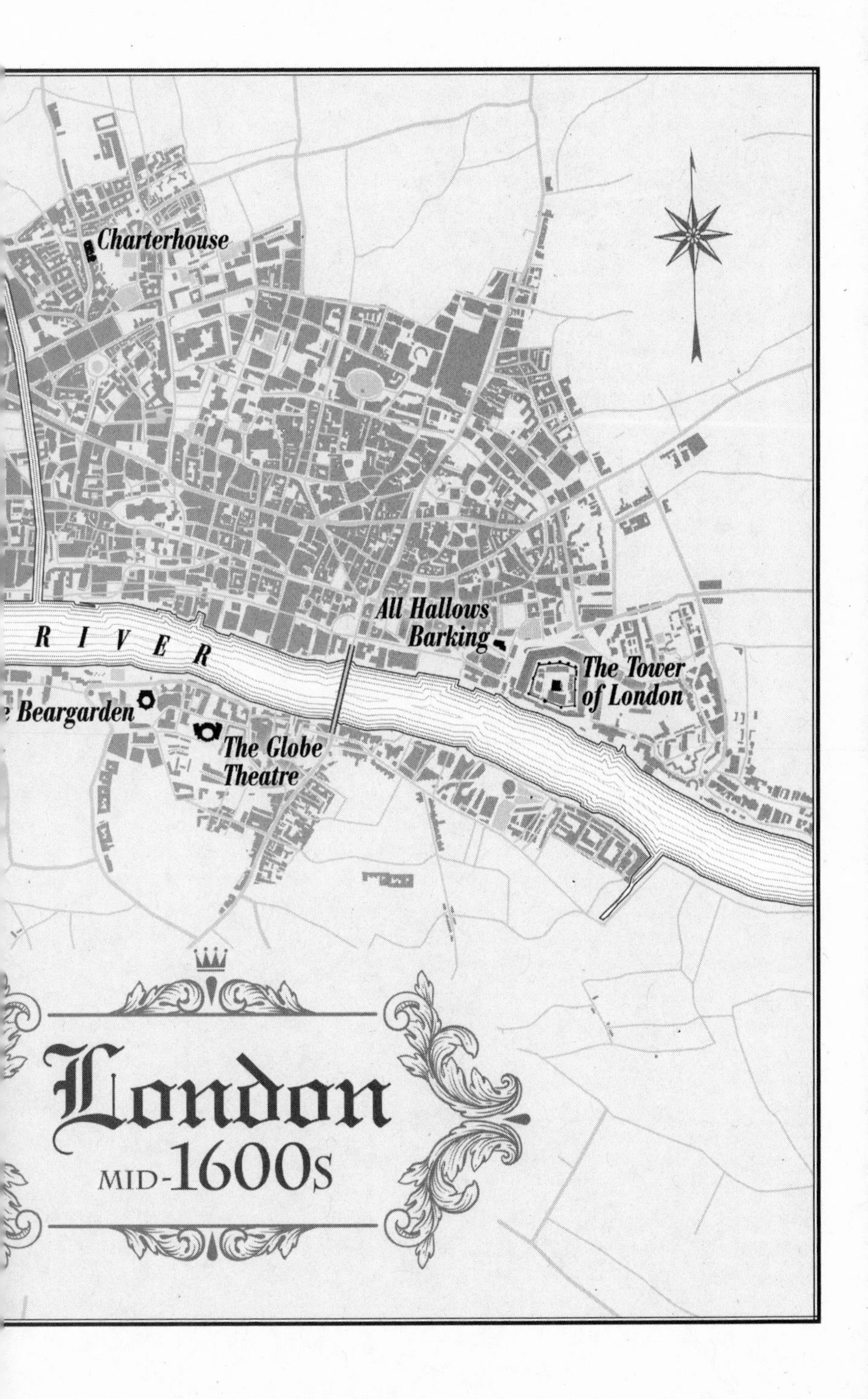
Charterhouse
R I V E R
All Hallows
Barking
The Tower
of London
e Beargarden
The Globe
Theatre
London
MID-1600s

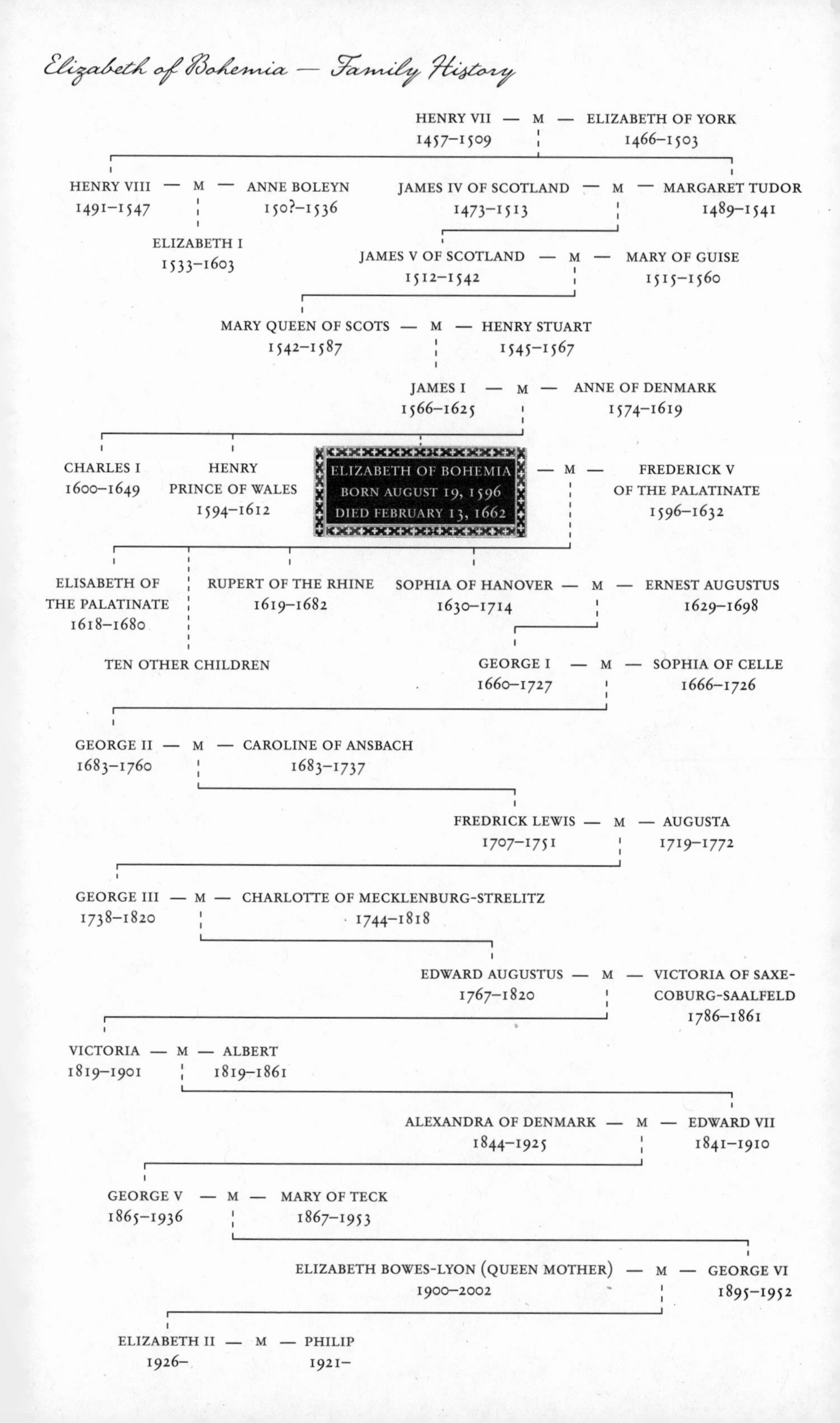
Elizabeth of Bohemia — Family History
HENRY VII — M — ELIZABETH OF YORK
1457–1509
1466–1503
HENRY VIII — M — ANNE BOLEYN
1491–1547
150?–1536
ELIZABETH I
1533–1603
JAMES IV OF SCOTLAND — M — MARGARET TUDOR
1473–1513
1489–1541
JAMES V OF SCOTLAND — M — MARY OF GUISE
1512–1542
1515–1560
MARY QUEEN OF SCOTS — M — HENRY STUART
1542–1587
1545–1567
JAMES I — M — ANNE OF DENMARK
1566–1625
1574–1619
CHARLES I
1600–1649
HENRY
PRINCE OF WALES
1594–1612
ELIZABETH OF BOHEMIA
BORN AUGUST 19, 1596
DIED FEBRUARY 13, 1662
— M — FREDERICK V
OF THE PALATINATE
1596–1632
ELISABETH OF
THE PALATINATE
1618–1680
RUPERT OF THE RHINE
1619–1682
SOPHIA OF HANOVER — M — ERNEST AUGUSTUS
1630–1714
1629–1698
TEN OTHER CHILDREN
GEORGE I — M — SOPHIA OF CELLE
1660–1727
1666–1726
GEORGE II — M — CAROLINE OF ANSBACH
1683–1760
1683–1737
FREDRICK LEWIS — M — AUGUSTA
1707–1751
1719–1772
GEORGE III — M — CHARLOTTE OF MECKLENBURG-STRELITZ
1738–1820
1744–1818
EDWARD AUGUSTUS — M — VICTORIA OF SAXE-
COBURG-SAALFELD
1767–1820
1786–1861
VICTORIA — M — ALBERT
1819–1901
1819–1861
ALEXANDRA OF DENMARK — M — EDWARD VII
1844–1925
1841–1910
GEORGE V — M — MARY OF TECK
1865–1936
1867–1953
ELIZABETH BOWES-LYON (QUEEN MOTHER) — M — GEORGE VI
1900–2002
1895–1952
ELIZABETH II — M — PHILIP
1926–
1921–

"This is precisely the moment adapted to the poet or novelist . . . that the accomplished artist has blended in her composition the strength and individuality of historical lineaments with the more touching graces of poetic expression, and breathed into the plastic forms of the imagination the glow of nature and truth."

ELIZABETH BENGER, 1825

Part One

Chapter One

October 18, 1612
Whitehall Palace
London, England

Outside the grey skies shed a stinging rain to freeze upon the crusty lawns, and everywhere the damp cold crept in through the stone walls of the palace. Autumn had come so harshly to the city that my brother Henry declared it only a matter of time before the rippling waters of the Thames must disappear under a layer of treacherous ice. I let the letter I'd been reading fall into my lap and leaned forward to take in the warmth of the flames. The groom of the chamber had just been by to replenish the hearth and the fire crackled before me, yet I felt a shiver. A rogue strand of tawny curls fell across my eyes and I brushed them aside, played a finger along the length of my neck as I pondered a future both uncertain and unwelcome. There was a knock at the door and Lady Anne Dudley stepped into the room.

"Your Highness," she said matter-of-factly, "it is time."

"Yes." I folded up the letter. "Yes, of course. I'm ready."

"You've been ready for the better part of an hour now, Madam."

Through the open door of the privy chamber I could see the ladies of the court in the anteroom beyond, swirling about in a sea of gossip and giggle, hardly able to contain their excitement. Seated and standing, preening and fussing, they were eager to get on with the evening's entertainment, giddy at the prospect of this first meeting between their mistress and the newly arrived prince, come at my father's bidding to meet his bride. They were all aflutter to think who among them might be chosen as one of a dozen or more bridesmaids for the wedding, but for all their education and erudition they were a vacuous and silly lot, and it was Lady Anne Dudley alone that had my trust and confidence.

"Another minute, if you please," I said.

Lady Anne turned to close the door behind her and stood before it, hands folded. "As stylish as it may be for a beautiful young princess to be a little late, there can be no more putting off."

"Yes, yes, by all means we must take our leave."

"That gaggle out there has worked itself into a froth, I can tell you." Lady Anne cocked her head to one side. "We must go, if for no other reason than to stop up their incessant fuss and chatter. They are worse than children."

"I envy them their anticipation, for it is of a happier kind than my own."

"You are uncertain of what lies ahead."

"On the contrary, it is all laid out for me. The evening's proceedings shall lay the groundwork for a ceremony of betrothal, soon to be followed by a wedding, after which I can expect to find myself in Heidelberg, there to bear royal children and live out my days much as my mother did when she was brought out of Denmark at the age of fourteen." I looked up at Lady Anne, who had come to stand next to me and rest a hand on my shoulder. "And none of it my own doing."

"I grant you deserve better treatment." Lady Anne's eyes betrayed a momentary depth of feeling I had seldom witnessed. "But do not abandon hope, for the fates may yet be kind." This woman, you understand, was more of a mother to me than my own, who could not be bothered even to feign interest in her daughter's affairs.

"What if it should go badly?"

"Forgive my confusion." Lady Anne straightened up, reverted to her usual business-like manner. "But have you not given me repeated assurances of your desire to see it does exactly that?"

"But if it should go otherwise?"

"You speak in riddles."

I took up the small portrait lying on the table beside me and held it up to the light. The painting had arrived some days earlier and been presented to me, along with a note I had yet to open, by the Prince's chamberlain, a man named Count Schomberg. I had hardly given the portrait more than a passing glance, but now I allowed myself to examine it more closely.

"Look here," I pointed, "at these cherubic cheeks and this tousled hair. The wide eyes and girlish lips resemble those of a school boy. It is hardly a man."

Lady Anne took the portrait from me. "And yet what if this likeness is terribly out of date, and he should turn out to be handsome and manly? What if by word and deed he prove himself to be honest and worthy? What then?"

"No matter, should he appear as charming and handsome as Sir Raleigh himself it shall not move me, for I am determined upon meeting him to be as cold as civility will allow. How could I hope to be otherwise when the offence is so great? To think he had been chosen for me as though I were a foot and he a boot. Humiliation!"

"I will say he reminds me a little of your brother."

"I don't see any resemblance to Henry."

"I meant your brother Charles."

"Then it were better to close the book on him at page one."

"You judge your younger brother too harshly."

"If during his stay the Elector Palatine should prefer to keep company with him, he shall keep less of mine."

"And yet after Henry, it is Charles who shall find himself one day seated upon the throne."

"Not so had I been born a male child." I glanced up at Lady Anne. "Do you think I would have made a good queen?"

"As good and better than even she who was your godmother and namesake, I venture."

"You flatter as those chicks and hens in the next room. At any rate, we play at idle chatter, for it shall be Henry who assumes the throne, and I am glad for it."

"Pray there may be no more unseen misfortune."

"Why say you so?"

"I hardly think you can have forgotten the events that transpired at Parliament not so long ago."

"I have done my best to forget."

It was coming on seven years ago that a group of men had plotted to seize the throne from my father and invest me as child queen. If the plan had succeeded, my entire family would have been slaughtered save for myself. Thereafter I should have been seated upon the throne of England, my rule overseen by those who had orchestrated the coup.

"You were only ten years old, I grant," said Lady Anne, "but you know as well as I do that there are yet those remaining who would take matters into their own hands."

"Indeed."

The conspirators were led by a man named Guy Fawkes, but when their ambitions were foiled at the last moment and the perpetrators brought to justice, my father insisted I bear witness to their execution. Even now the images flashed into my head of men being stripped naked, their genitals cut off and burnt before my eyes, bowels removed, hearts torn from their chests before they were beheaded, all while the crowd roared and I recoiled in horror. For months I suffered crippling nightmares.

"Here, let me see to that." Lady Anne tucked a lock of hair I had been brushing aside back into place, fussed over me as a mother might, in a manner both irritating and soothing.

"Suppose this foreign prince should declare his love for me at first sight?" I teased.

"I think not."

"You don't consider me worthy?"

"I say it is a fanciful notion best uttered by those who tread upon the boards." Lady Anne crouched to pull a rogue thread from the sleeve of my dress. "A fiction if you ask me, offered up to please those gullible audiences at the Globe."

"And yet when Romeo did confess his love for Juliet, were you not moved to see it?"

"It was not love, but mere infatuation."

"I have witnessed ladies swoon at the mere sight of a certain gentleman. Sir Raleigh, for one," I said evenly.

"Your mother was ever one to dissolve at his gaze. There are whispers it was that which sent him to the Tower in the first place."

At the mention of the Tower, my thoughts turned back to the letter I had been reading. It was from my cousin Arabella Stuart, whose unwelcome fate gave me good cause to be cautious where my father's wishes were concerned.

October 4, 1612

Dearest Cousin Elizabeth,

I hope this correspondence finds you in good spirits. I can hardly say as much for my own. I am left almost entirely without comforts here in the Tower and another winter in this cold and damp place is a grim prospect. I know I shall not be warm for even a single moment. I am afforded less and less in the way of clothing and blankets. What's left constitutes little more than rags and will be no match for the harsh elements soon to seep in through the stone walls.

Do you remember when we were children together in Coombe Abbey, how I found the rainy days insufferable and spent all my waking hours wrapped in blankets next to the fire? Oh, to luxuriate in such comforts. I shall have no recourse for that here. To think Sir Raleigh is fortunate enough to have a fireplace in his quarters, and a small stipend of wood to burn. Give me the use of such and I should better hope to withstand these dreary ramparts and desolate hours spent lying in a hard bed or perched upon a wretched stool.

I know Sir Raleigh has cautioned we must keep our exchanges to a minimum or be found out, but I simply had to write and say that I had never thought to experience both the greatest joy and deepest sadness of my life in the space of an hour. How swiftly my heart flew from bliss to anguish. And yet I dare not reveal it. I should be grateful for your company, and for the chance to confide in you, but my advice is to forgo any more visits to the Tower. Your father has spies everywhere, not to mention that the Yeomen Warders here are a drunken and slovenly lot who cannot be trusted to honour the dignity of even a princess such as yourself. And yet I almost burst with this news!

I'm sorry to be so cryptic but I just had to write in case something happens to me. I hope yet to be released from the Tower, and I know you are doing everything in your power to try and persuade your father to be merciful, but I'm afraid I have angered him greatly.

Word has reached me of a Bohemian prince come to seek your hand, and it would seem your destiny, like mine, lies elsewhere. What a precious thing a daughter is from the very moment of its birth, even though it may be destined for a life among strangers.

Yours in best friendship and true blood,
Arabella Stuart

Arabella would surely have disclosed more to me were it not that she feared her correspondence might be intercepted. I'd heard it rumoured that her husband had come across the channel in secret to visit her in the Tower, but it seemed the hints in her letter alluded to something else. I considered how I might pay her a visit notwithstanding that I had to contend with this bothersome prince. Much as was the case with me, my father had foisted various suitors upon Arabella, including his own cousin, Lord Esme Stuart, not to mention a proposal from the brother of the Pope himself. But instead of giving in to these petitions, Arabella had married the man she loved, William Seymour, in a secret ceremony. When my father found out, he had Lord Seymour thrown into the Tower and Arabella confined to her estate. Even at that, she hadn't contented herself to be held prisoner and instead hatched a plan to flee to France with William. I myself had a small hand in bringing the scheme to fruition, though thankfully my father never discovered as much. Lord Seymour managed to escape from the Tower, intending to rendezvous with Arabella at the port of Lee, where they would set sail for France together. Arabella donned an elaborate disguise, dressed as a man to elude her captors. I thought it was all so daring and romantic!

But things did not go as planned. The ship Arabella boarded left the harbour before Lord Seymour arrived, but worse, my father learned of the scheme and sent out a vessel of his own to overtake her. Arabella was recaptured, and this time he relegated her to the Tower of London, where she remained imprisoned even now. As I waited to be introduced to this foreign prince, I was mindful of my cousin's fate, and though I had no intention of giving in too easily to my father's authority, there was reason enough to fear the consequences of defying him outright.

Lady Anne gestured for me to rise. "Here, let's straighten down your skirts."

The chair I had been sitting on was more like a stool, as uncomfortable as the gown for which it was designed, but specially constructed to accommodate the impossibly wide skirt and exaggerated bum roll.

"This is a hideous dress," I said.

"It is the fashion, My Lady."

I was wearing a French Farthingale encased below the waist in whalebone with hoops that elevated the skirt behind and brought it down in front. The effect was meant to streamline my torso and accentuate its length, but it came at the expense of all practicality.

"I hope there shall be a suitable chair in the banquet hall, or I am doomed to disappear when I sit down."

"It has all been seen to, My Lady. Shall we take our leave?"

"Listen to them out there." I turned to the full-length mirror for a final inspection. "They are as full of merriment as I am of trepidation." I brushed my hands down the front of my skirt. "Would one of them might go in my stead."

"I don't doubt they should scratch and claw for the chance," said Lady Anne.

"More out of ambition than loyalty, I venture."

"Come, My Lady. We must be on our way."

"Very well, lead on."

We entered the antechamber to much fussing by the ladies-in-waiting, who proceeded to organize themselves into an entourage which, though seemingly impromptu to the untrained eye, was in fact a carefully orchestrated arrangement that took into account who should have the privilege of walking nearest behind me, who at my right and left, and so on. Lady Anne would settle any last-minute disputes among them while I tempered my disdain for all their petty intrigues. Some were eager to accompany me to Heidelberg, where their prospects for advancement might improve, while others harboured ambitions I could only guess at and had best be wary of. I found it prudent to keep them as yet somewhat in my favour, if only to mitigate their disappointment should I succeed in sending this foreign prince back to Bohemia.

With my entourage in tow we made our way through the halls of the palace, brightly lit for the occasion with hundreds of candles. It was along this same hallway, adorned with an extravagance of ornate sculpture and ornamentation, its walls hung with intricate tapestries, that my brother Henry would escort the Palatine to the banquet hall. Upon my arrival the ladies hurried to find their places while I joined the rest of my family in the vestibule. My parents and Charles stood in a trio at one end of the room. My mother, with her excess of pearls braided about her neck, bracelets upon her wrists, earrings dangling, had as usual dressed more like a costumed gypsy than a queen. My father wore his usual padded peasecod and out-of-date breeches over a pair of wrinkled pantaloons. But there, seated upon an oak Wainscot in a corner of the room, resplendent in his embroidered doublet and fashionable trunk hose, was my brother Henry. I expected him to bound over and greet me with a kiss upon both cheeks as always, but instead he remained seated and smiled over at me weakly. I grew instantly troubled.

"Your brother has fallen ill again," my mother announced.

"Henry." I hurried next to him and leaned down. "Say what is the matter?"

"Forgive me, sister, but it seems I have lost all my strength, I know not how."

At these words a great weight of dread descended upon me, that the one shining light against the darkness of my uncertain future should threaten to be extinguished. In our time at Coombe Abbey my brother and I had formed a little family of our own, raised as we were away from our parents, in the household of Lord and Lady Harrington. The time we spent together there forged in us so strong a bond as naught but death could hope to sever.

"How long has he been like this?" I looked up at the others but none made to answer.

"It came of a sudden just after I'd taken lunch," said Henry, "and I remain in hopes that it shall leave with equal haste."

"Something you ate, perhaps," said my mother.

"You should bring it all back up." Our younger brother Charles offered this advice with a hint of smugness in his tone, as it was ever he that appeared frail and sickly compared to his older brother.

"I have and more," answered Henry.

Henry, normally in the best of health, had of late from time to time been seized upon by a sudden tiredness, followed by headache and stomach pains. Even so he had always been one to keep up appearances, and as easily as I allowed myself to drift on occasion into melancholy, he took pains to remain a steady harbinger of good cheer. Where I saw fit to voice displeasure, he upheld decorum, as he was doing now, trying to disguise his discomfort, but there was no hiding it. I had never seen him so pale.

"I promised to escort your Palatine into the banquet hall," he said, his voice sounding different, "the better to take measure of him and test his handshake, but now I fear I shall have to beg off. I hope you can forgive me."

To see this same brother who loved nothing better than to be all day at swords and tilting, at golf and tennis and hunting, deprived of his boundless energy in such a sudden fashion disturbed me deeply.

"It needs no forgiveness," I assured him. "You have a slight fever." I held a hand to his forehead. "You should be in bed."

"Our daughter would be about the practice of medicine again." My mother turned to pull back the curtain and peek out at the gathered guests.

"The physicians have already seen to him," my father offered.

"I take little solace at such news."

"I suppose you will want a sample of his urine next," said my mother.

"Is that what the physicians do?" Charles looked up at her. "What do they do with it?"

"They taste it," said Henry. I took heart that he should still have humour enough to tease his younger brother, as he was wont to do.

"How disgusting." Charles made a face.

"Henry has been excused from the evening's proceedings," my father announced, "but he insists on staying nevertheless. We have seen to it that Charles shall conduct the Palatine into the hall." He placed a pale, effeminate hand upon his younger son's shoulder, who smiled ingratiatingly up at him.

"What an organizer your father is." My mother raised an eyebrow. "For my part I should be more than content to let the Palatine find his own way to the banquet."

"For mine, he can stay aboard the ship that brought him," I added.

My father grew stern. "We would be assured that these preparations have not been made in vain."

"You would have me carted off like so much chattel, I know."

"This tone is unbecoming. *Vos protestor nimium.*" Among my father's many annoying habits was the employment of Latin platitudes to bolster his claim of divine authority.

"Father says you protest too much," Charles translated needlessly.

"*Qui tacet consentire*," I answered.

"Silence is consent." Charles checked to see his older brother's reaction, eager as always to impress him.

"This borders on impertinence," my father cautioned. "I have expressly forbidden you to be schooled in Latin."

"At which, naturally, she has taken pains to study it all the more," offered my mother.

"I had expected better from a daughter," my father scolded.

"And I from a father," I spat back, my cheeks burning.

"Sister." Henry reached up to put a hand on my shoulder. "This prince shall find himself aptly judged."

"I prize your counsel above all others'." I spoke softly. "One word from you and I shall have reason enough to refuse him."

"I meant not myself but you, Elizabeth." Henry looked over at my father. "The decision must be yours."

"This Palatine is a fair and excellent prince, I'm told," said my father.

"And yet merely that." My mother made no effort to conceal her disdain. "No more than a prince."

"Enough of this." My father signalled an attendant. "We will go in."

The horns sounded and we prepared to make our entrance into the hall. Henry laboured to rise from his chair.

"I would not see you suffer in this way." I gave him a hand up. "I'd rather you went home and got straight into bed."

"And forgo the chance to see this Palatine and offer my greetings?"

"The Palatine can wait. Let me see to a carriage that will take you back to St. James's."

"I won't hear of it."

It seemed each episode of this troublesome affliction brought a new resolve to my brother's demeanour, an ever more rigid denial of such uncharacteristic frailty, which belonged more rightfully to the harvest of old age.

"Let's go in." Henry straightened himself up with a steady determination, insisted he would walk unaided to his chair, which I allowed. Charles left to fetch the Palatine and escort him into the hall, while the lesser protocols of courtly formality ran their course. I had brought the note from Prince Frederick with me, intent on handing it back to him unopened, but now I tore it open just the same.

September 28, 1612

Her Royal Highness Princess Elizabeth Stuart
Richmond Palace
London, England

Dear Elizabeth,

By now you know that I have received an invitation from your father, the King, to come to London and be introduced to your person, and that I have accepted. I look forward to the day we shall meet face to face, the better to consolidate the interests of those to whom we owe our allegiance.

I have sent along a portrait which my chamberlain, Count Schomberg, has by now placed into your delicate hand. It is a miniature of me by the Dutch painter Van Mierevelt. Do you know of him? I confess I look hardly more than a boy, but it is the most recent likeness I have on hand. I can assure you I have matured considerably since I sat for it. I have managed to get my hands on a miniature portrait of you as well, done by Nicholas Hilliard. Do you remember it? I cannot stop looking at it, especially your beautiful eyes! Your playwright, Mr. Shakespeare, has said the eyes are windows to the soul. I have seen to it that his plays are performed here in Heidelberg of late, and would be delighted to make his acquaintance when I come to London. Do you think it could be arranged?

I depart from Heidelberg on the ninth of October and hope for an uneventful crossing. Notwithstanding undue delay we expect to arrive in London on the fifteenth or sixteenth and plan to stay for a few weeks, though if all goes well it may be longer!

With assurance that I am a man of honour and a fondness for your good graces, I am,

Frederick
Count Palatine of the Rhine

Post Script: I have heard of some other suitors who seek your hand, among them Louis XIII of France. I am no king but hold prospects to become one, much as your brother Henry. I very much look forward to meeting him and hope you can arrange for us to spend some time together.

Post Post Script: By the way, you should know that Louis XIII has a speech impediment. And a double set of teeth. Also a habit of holding his tongue out of his mouth for long periods of time before he speaks. And he never blows his nose. And he sweats a lot!

If I thought there was some charm in his attempts at flattery, the reference to matters concerning the consolidation of interests gave me pause. It was obvious that my father wanted to use me as little more than a pawn, a means to advance the Protestant cause in Europe. My marriage to the Palatine would form an alliance better able to resist the Catholic interests of the Hapsburgs which dominated so much of the continent. Time and again I had seen my father impose his will upon his family for selfish and petty reasons, but this time I was determined not to make it so easy for him.

At last the honoured guest and his party made their entrance, and I recognized Count Schomberg at once, a handsome and distinguished-looking gentleman with a generous dark moustache and broad shoulders, but it seemed to me the young man walking alongside Charles could hardly be the foreign prince, for far from being clothed in royal garbs, he was wearing but a simple doublet with wings and tabs, gathered breeches, and plain leather shoes upon his feet. He was presented first to the King, where he removed a close-fitting, brimless felt cap from his head and bowed. My father offered his hand, which the Palatine took and bent to kiss. The Queen was next but suffered herself merely to be bowed to and hardly bothered to return the visitor's gaze. The Prince seemed not perturbed at this obvious slight and moved on to Henry, who rose stiffly to shake the Palatine's hand. And here was the first sign that things might not be so easily resolved, for I saw that same air of dignified civility I'd always admired in my brother now reflected in this visitor. As they chatted, their expressions softened to warm smiles and each put a hand upon the shoulder of the other.

"It's plain they've taken an instant like to each other," said Lady Anne.

"They do but greet each other in proper fashion."

"There's more than politeness there. If not first affection," she proclaimed, "then first friendship is here given birth to."

I had to admit the exchange was more like one between long-lost friends than strangers, and for a moment I thought they might embrace, but Count Schomberg seized the Palatine by the arm and urged him along. It disturbed me greatly to see that no sooner had they turned away than Henry slumped back into his chair, eyes dull with pain and fatigue. Lady Anne gave me a nudge as the Palatine now stood before me, waiting to be introduced.

"Allow me," Count Schomberg announced formally, "to introduce His Highness Prince Frederick V, Elector Palatine of the Rhine." He turned to the Palatine. "Your Highness, may I present Her Royal Highness Princess Elizabeth Stuart of England."

The Palatine bowed deeply. "Madam, I am honoured to make your acquaintance." His voice was a pleasant baritone and not so boyish as I had expected, and his dark moustache and goatee testified that he was indeed of greater maturity than the portrait had offered. I grant he was not dashing, had not the wide shoulders and piercing blue eyes of Sir Raleigh, but I found him not altogether unhandsome. His dark brown eyes and unassuming smile spoke neither of pretense nor vanity, and his demeanour gave little cause to dismiss him outright. Still, I was determined to discomfit my father, and so when the Palatine straightened and waited for my hand to bring to his lips as was customary, I made a great show of failing to offer it, at which the Palatine went down on one knee to take up the hem of my Farthingale. I promptly snatched it away. He rose stiffly and we stood facing each other for some moments.

"I beg your forgiveness," he said.

"For what? You've only just arrived."

He lowered his eyes and brought his hands to his side. "I'm afraid my attire leaves a great deal to be desired."

"I took notice of as much, and thought perhaps such modest apparel the custom in Bohemia."

"Those royal garments I had hoped to wear upon our first meeting are nowhere to be found, so that I am forced to present myself to you in these, my travelling clothes."

"You've lost your luggage, then."

"Just so." He could not hide his embarrassment. "I humbly beg your pardon."

"It is hardly my pardon you need seek, nor my favour. Carry on."

The Palatine turned to Count Schomberg, who stepped forward and held out a small case with both his hands.

"His Majesty humbly offers a token of his regard," the Count announced.

I had not counted on such an offering, and turned to glance at Lady Anne.

"It is the protocol," she assured me.

"Why wasn't I told?" I whispered.

"I thought you knew."

I took it from him, a purple velvet jewellery case, filigreed with gold and perfectly lovely.

Lady Anne's eyes were merry with sport. "You hadn't counted on being enchanted."

"You place us at a disadvantage," I said to the Prince. "We have nothing for you."

"None needed." The Palatine looked uncertain and turned to the Count, who whispered in his ear, after which he added, "Save for the gift of your good graces and beauteous company."

Lady Anne, sombre once again, turned to Count Schomberg. "If the Palatine seeks to soften, be assured this princess is no gull to flattery."

"And whom," the Count said with a smile, "have I the pleasure of addressing?"

"This is Lady Anne Dudley, my Maid of Honour," I answered.

The Count took up her hand and bent to kiss it. It was the first time I had ever seen Lady Anne blush.

"I meant not to give offence." The Palatine looked at me pleadingly.

I opened the box impatiently and lifted out a pair of magnificent drop pearl earrings.

"From the Medici collection," announced the Count.

Lady Anne and I looked at each other knowingly. "If you were looking for your chance," she said, "you've found it."

I tossed the earrings unceremoniously back into the box and gave it to Lady Anne to hand back to the Count.

"Your Highness?"

I indicated the string of pearls around my neck. "These were handed down to me from my grandmother, Queen Mary. They are part of the very collection you speak of, which consists of six pieces, all of which I have in my possession."

The court buzzed in hushed and sombre tones while Count Schomberg whispered intently into the Palatine's ear.

"But the Count assures me there must be some mistake."

My father beckoned Lady Anne over and spoke quietly while the court waited in expectant stillness. Having returned to my side, she seemed somewhat embarrassed to announce,

"The King assures us there were in fact seven sets of pearls in his mother's possession, and that a set of earrings was lost."

The Count held the box out once again.

Lady Anne took it from him.

My father had found a way to undermine me yet again, and I was determined not to let him win so easily. I had to do something outrageous, and so I straightened myself up to my tallest, stepped forward to clasp both of the Palatine's shoulders in my hands, and brought him closer so that he had to tilt his head up slightly in order to meet my gaze.

"What say we measure the prospect of consolidating our mutual interests with something more than feeble formality?" I pulled him closer still and pressed my lips upon his. Gasps rose up from the crowd, and here and there utterances of shock and amazement. When I released him, he stood before me, eyes on mine, while I tried to gauge his reaction. I had expected him to shrink back in embarrassment or scowl at me in contempt, but he did neither.

"Well," I spoke for all to hear, "what say you?"

"Madam?"

"We would know your judgment, Sir," I said with exaggerated interest.

"I can hardly say," the Palatine's voice was unsure, "but that you have caught me unawares."

"Still, we would know the verdict." I was eager to disdain whatever his answer might be.

"You press for my opinion as to . . ."

". . . the merits of this kiss, yes, yes, go on . . ." I urged.

"I would venture to say . . ."

"I wish you would." I played to the audible snickers in the crowd. "Be unequivocal in your judgment. We will hear it."

"Madam, I am nothing if not honest . . ."

The court held its collective breath.

". . . and can only . . ."

Not a sound could be heard in the banquet hall.

". . . praise it to heaven."

No sooner had the crowd breathed a collective sigh of relief than a commotion at the far end of the table brought more gasps and murmurings. I turned to see that my brother Henry had slipped from his chair down to the floor. The Palatine ran to his side, knelt to lift him gently up and cradle his head. Then I was there, cursing the dreadful Farthingale skirts that would not let me kneel properly. Henry opened his eyes as though waking from a sleep and before I could make further enquiry insisted we help him to his feet.

"I hope you can forgive this affront to decorum," he said to the Palatine, who steadied him on one side while I did the same on the other, and we helped him back into his chair.

"We shall summon a physician," said Count Schomberg, who had come to stand nearby.

"No." Henry put up his hand. "It needs none. I suffered but a moment's dizziness."

"You will take to your bed at once." I called for an attendant.

"But the banquet is hardly begun," Henry protested.

"The banquet can go hang," I said. "I'll not hear otherwise."

"Your sister is right," said the Palatine. "You were better to see to your rest."

"I'll come with you and see to your comfort," I said.

"I won't hear of it," said Henry.

"For my part it gives not offence," the Palatine assured me, "if you should choose to see to your brother. I am content."

"Nonsense," said Henry. He rose from his chair, waved off any attempts to steady him. "I'm perfectly capable of looking after myself." He took my hand. "Sister, it would give me great comfort that you not abandon this prince and these festive proceedings for my sake."

"Very well," I said, "but straight to bed with you."

"I promise." He turned and walked from the room unassisted, but it clearly took all of his willpower to do so.

I watched him take his leave while Count Schomberg led the Palatine away to join the rest of his party and continue with the introductions. The banquet proceeded with all manner of dining and entertainments, but even as I was forced to witness my parents cavorting about, taking food and drink as though nothing had happened, my eyes kept coming back to Henry's empty chair. I stayed only as long as courtesy required before making my apologies and heading back to Richmond, much to the disappointment of the Palatine and the annoyance of my father.

Later, in the privacy of my bedchamber, seen to slumber by Lady Anne as always, my thoughts harkened one moment to a possible future with a stranger I had only just met, and the next to concern for a brother I loved more than anyone in the world . . .

That was the first time I felt it. There in that unsettled bed, in the place between waking and sleeping. A darkness hovering over me. Understand, I still thought I was fine. We all do, don't we, right up to the moment we're not? I suppose I'd been expecting it, sensed that something was on its way, a vessel of misfortune come to toss me about in unfamiliar seas, carry me to distant and unwelcome shores.

Chapter Two

I woke the morning after the banquet from a restless sleep, wondering at my brother's condition, and went at the earliest convenience to St. James's to look in on him, expecting to find him still in bed, only to discover that he had long since left the confines of his bedchamber to see to preparations for a performance that evening. Henry had arranged for a production of *Hamlet*, which the Palatine was apparently very fond of, to be mounted by the King's Men. I found him backstage, consulting with the playwright over some details of the dialogue. My brother was in the process of assembling his own court at St. James's, and any number of musicians and poets, artists and entertainers were vying for appointment. The rivalry was intense and not without intrigues. In the case of Mr. Shakespeare's theatre company there were rumours that they should soon give themselves over to the Prince of Wales and call themselves Prince Henry's Men thereafter, a move sure to infuriate my father.

When Henry saw me he raised one hand to signal he would be just a moment and resumed his conversation with Mr. Shakespeare, while I used the time to study his demeanour and appearance. I thought him far from recovered, for he was pallid in complexion and clearly labouring to bring energy to his actions. Now he excused himself and came to stand before me.

"Elizabeth." He kissed me on the cheek. "What brings you here so early?"

"Surely you must know I came to see how you're feeling. I'm surprised to see you up and about. Do you really think it advisable?"

"I can't see why not. Is something amiss?"

"Amiss? Henry, you fainted last evening. Are you pretending nothing happened?"

"I'm fine, I tell you."

"You don't look fine. Have you had breakfast?"

"I shall see to some lunch as soon as I'm finished here."

"I don't like the idea that you are going to all this trouble. I hope you're not trying to impress the Palatine for my sake." I took him by both hands and inspected his features closely. "You are such a brother as a sister can only hope for, and I do not mean to bring you undue worry, but I tell you in all honesty, Henry, you are not well."

"I grant my strength is not yet entirely returned, but you must not concern yourself. I shall be fully recovered by tonight."

"Not if you if you keep this up."

"I appreciate your concern, but now I must ask that you allow me to get back to the business at hand." He hesitated for a moment. "And for your part, shouldn't you be entertaining the Palatine?"

"I intend to make myself as little available as our father shall allow."

"But why should you do so? This prince seems entirely decent, and not without considerable character." He looked past me at Mr. Shakespeare, who was beckoning to him from the stage. "Yes, yes, one more minute, if you please," he scolded, and turned back to me. "This playwright's impatience speaks to his vanity. He seems to be under the impression that an artist's talent dictates that he be treated as an equal."

"I suppose it had been better to live in Roman times," I said as we watched Mr. Shakespeare hold up the folio to

Henry and poke at it with his finger, "when they contented themselves as the hired help."

"But to the matter of Prince Frederick." Henry gave me a pleading look. "I am not asking you to marry the man, only to give him a chance. Must you be so eager to dismiss him outright?"

"You know I have my reasons."

"You mustn't let your acrimony toward our father cloud your judgment."

"If only it were that easy. But let that go. You are eager to get back to your preparations. Promise me you will get some more rest."

"I promise." He kissed me on the cheek and hurried back to the actors.

"And something to eat," I called after him.

"I shall."

I made my way back to Richmond, where I learned upon arrival that Count Schomberg was waiting for me in the antechamber, eager to convey an invitation from the Palatine to dine with him at lunch. I made my way down the hall and, finding the door slightly ajar, paused when I saw the Count seated in close conversation with Lady Anne.

"The Palatine assures me he has hardly met a fellow as splendid as your Prince Henry," the Count offered, "and admires him greatly."

"There can be no doubt the feeling is mutual. They certainly took to each other even upon their first meeting."

"They have since had a second. Prince Henry came by early this morning to personally invite the Palatine to the performance of the play this evening at St. James's, whereupon the two of them struck up a long conversation."

My eavesdropping left me unable to decide which was the greater offence: that my brother should have gone traipsing about London after giving me such a scare only the night before, or that he should have seen fit to seek out the Palatine's company and not mine.

"Prince Frederick did confide to me," the Count continued, "he felt as though he had come upon the best companion of his life, or had a long-lost friend returned to him."

"Remarkable that two people should strike up such an amiable acquaintance in so short a time. Who would have thought?"

"Tell me, Madam, what had your mistress to say about Prince Frederick?"

"Little, I'm afraid, but you will allow she was concerned for her brother's health."

"That was quite an introduction they had."

"Indeed."

"Lady Anne, may I pose a question to you?" Count Schomberg asked.

I had been about to show myself and make my entrance, but now I lingered a moment more.

"I hope it is within the bounds of my office to answer."

"I grant the matter is somewhat delicate, for it concerns the matter of a man's desire."

"A man may desire what he likes, though desire and fulfillment are two different things."

"I grant as much, but tell me, what does a man want more than anything from the woman he loves?"

"I might hazard a guess, but then, I am no man."

"But cannot a maid know a man's heart?"

"I am no maid."

"I beg your indulgence. I only meant for you to consider the question from your woman's point of view."

"Speak plainly. What is your drift?"

"I have always thought, and it seems to me clearer of late, that more than anything a man desires that the woman he loves should think highly of him."

"I will caution that My Lady's favour is not easily won."

"I meant not the princess but yourself."

"Sir?"

"How might a man hope to gain your esteem?" The Count leaned in a little and looked into Lady Anne's eyes.

At this I pulled the door wide and entered the room.

"Your Majesty!" Count Schomberg rose quickly.

"Madam." Lady Anne followed suit and the two of them stood facing me. "We were just talking about you," she added stiffly.

"You seem a little out of breath," I teased, "as though I might have caught you in some act of illicit indulgence."

Lady Anne was clearly flustered and looked to the Count to intervene.

"I have come at the Palatine's bidding," said the Count. "He wanted to enquire after your plans for the afternoon."

"I have none," I answered, "but how for you two?"

"Madam." Lady Anne became serious. "I am at your service."

"As you, Sir, must be to your Elector," I said to the Count. "Tell him thank you, but I must send my regrets, and shall at any rate entertain his company at this evening's play."

"Very well." The Count bowed, then turned to Lady Anne, took up her hand in both of his, and placed upon it so lingering a kiss that she finally pulled her hand away and offered me an awkward smile.

"I think he may be enamoured of you," I said when the Count had left the room. "Do you find him handsome?"

"I had hardly taken notice of his features." Lady Anne glanced at me sideways, and when she saw that I was utterly unconvinced, added, "I suppose he has a good moustache."

"Though not as fine as Sir Raleigh's, you must agree."

"Yes, yes, you have taken pains again and again to assure me he has the best moustache you have ever seen, but is it merely that which brings you to mention him just now?"

"He would surely have attended this play were he not confined to the Tower."

"Indeed he has languished there for too long."

"And yet my father will not relent."

"I suppose you imagine Sir Raleigh devoting all of his attention to you at the expense of the Palatine."

"It's only that I should have liked for them to meet."

"But to what end?"

"No more than for the three of us to be together in the same room."

"You suffer yet from that same girlish infatuation," Lady Anne scoffed. "The man is old enough to be your father."

"As are most of the suitors my father would have me married off to."

"And this one, this Palatine, he is too young, you think?"

"It matters little what I think, or so it would seem."

"Your brother has certainly taken to him."

"And not to his own bed, as like would have been wiser."

"At any rate," said Lady Anne, suddenly all business, "we have much in the way of preparation for this evening. Do you know what you're going to wear?"

"And how for yourself?"

"Come, we have much to do."

As much as I had witnessed Lady Anne's composure unsettled by the Count, she had seen mine undone by Sir Raleigh. I had no explanation for it except to say that it seemed entirely out of my hands. His nearness would give me to entertain such thoughts, give birth to such cravings as I had not yet experienced in my young life. Granted there had been some interludes with boys by that time, of an exploratory nature, but nothing more. And now this young Palatine had come to seek me for his bride, and me a young woman utterly smitten with the fanciful and girlish dream of being swept up in the arms of an older man.

Evening found me at St. James's, where a small audience was already assembled when I arrived with Lady Anne, and though Henry greeted me warmly, I saw at once in the tightness of his facial features, the struggle behind his eyes, that he was fighting off some intense discomfort. He was quick to dismiss my concerns, admitting only to a riotous headache that he insisted was already passing. I was soon seated between my brother and the Palatine, with Lady Anne in behind me next to Count Schomberg, and when Henry excused himself for some final consultation with the players we sat in an uneasy quietude for some moments before the Count spoke up.

"Madam, you've no doubt seen this play performed before?" he enquired of Lady Anne.

"Indeed," she answered curtly.

"Prince Henry has arranged for Richard Burbage himself to play the title role," offered the Palatine.

"One of the finest players in all of London, I'm told," the Count allowed.

"We are fortunate, then."

"And the playwright himself," the Palatine turned to me, "shall act the part of the King Hamlet's ghost."

"Even better." Lady Anne's sarcasm continued unabated.

"You've seen him upon the stage, I take it?"

"I have."

"And what say you for his acting?" the Count enquired.

"Much as I do for his writing."

"By which you mean to give him high praise?" He smiled over at Lady Anne.

"By which I mean it were better he abstained from both."

The Palatine leaned a little toward me and spoke in a stage whisper, "Your Maid of Honour is a harsh critic."

"Of playwrights and princes alike." I stared straight ahead.

Henry made his way back to his chair just as the last few ladies and gentlemen settled into their seats, while upon the stage the players shuffled about in their final preparations behind the curtains.

"I see this play is billed as a tragedy, but I confess I am not familiar with it," said the Count. "What is the upshot?"

"A young prince comes to a bad end," said Henry, rubbing at his temples. He spoke as though more to himself than the others, and there was an ominous tone in his voice that troubled me.

"It concerns a young woman who is torn between obedience to her father" — Lady Anne cast a sideways glance at me — "and her prospects for a relationship with a prince."

"A Danish prince, no less," I said.

"I dare say the Queen might know some of the history behind it, then," said Count Schomberg. "She came from Denmark, did she not?"

"Just so," said Lady Anne, "when she was yet two years My Lady's junior."

"We could ask her about it," I offered, "if she were here." My mother had not consented to sit for the play. She could not be bothered with such dramatics when they did not concern one of her precious masques.

"And the King?" the Count asked.

"Busy, as you can see," I said. My father was seated on an elevated platform at the far end of the room, more interested in cavorting with the young men that fawned over him than the company of his children.

The Count turned to Lady Anne. "And what is your opinion of this play, Madam?"

"Only that it promises to unfold much the same as any other, namely that the lines spoken to greatest import shall be uttered by men, that the lion's share of soliloquy shall likewise be so, and that those few utterances accorded the fairer sex, being spoken by lanky youths with milky voices, shall consist in the main of hand-wringing and general fretting about."

"This sounds a sharp indictment," said the Count.

"Perhaps an apt one nonetheless," I offered.

The noise of the audience died to a gentle murmur as two pages with long-handled candle snuffers made their way around the room until the light grew dim.

"Do you not think Ophelia a role of depth and character?" The Palatine turned to me.

"She does little else but rummage over Hamlet. Where he doth search his soul, she espouses naught but confusion at his alienation of her affection."

"Because he will not have her and she would know the reason."

"Sometime it may be so," said Lady Anne, "only the other way round."

"Perhaps it had been better to mount a production of the Scottish play," I said.

"The King is descended from Banquo," Lady Anne explained.

"Or so he would have us believe," I said. "Our father is wont to take from history such particulars as suit his purpose, and dismiss others."

"Much as this playwright," Lady Anne added.

Now the curtains pulled apart at last, and the stage revealed a cloth backdrop upon which was painted a scene depicting the walls of a fortress. A man clad in armour stood at centre stage while another approached from the wings.

"Who's there?"

"Nay, answer me: stand and unfold yourself."

"Long live the king!"

At this line there was a barely audible smattering of murmurs through the crowd. When the apparition appeared clad all in armour, the audience gasped, and Count Schomberg leaned over to Lady Anne.

"He speaks not," said the Count.

"He shall. Do but bide a little," said Lady Anne.

The play had advanced well into the first act when the

Palatine leaned in close to me and whispered, "Madam, what think you of this lengthy counsel Polonius would bestow upon his son Laertes?"

"He exhibits that same vanity my father suffers, which is to think himself wiser simply because he is older."

"*Those friends thou hast,*" Polonius was telling Laertes, "*and their adoption tried, grapple them unto thy soul with hoops of steel.*"

"He overshoots the mark," said Lady Anne. "This might pass better for comedy."

"There is something of the buffoon in him, I grant," said the Palatine.

"I think he gives good counsel," Henry insisted. "A man is known by his words and actions."

"Yet many a man may fall victim to his own shortcomings."

"A worthy man will overcome such," I said.

"And never second-guess?"

"As Hamlet does, you mean?"

"I say he shows conviction in his deliberations."

"Have your father spoken to you as this Polonius does?" the Palatine asked.

"I have suffered to hear him do so, yes. At the news of your coming he gave me instruction that I should offer up that which is best in a daughter, the better to become thereafter a compliant wife. Obedience, loyalty, and faithfulness: these, according to my father, are the highest virtues my gender can aspire to."

"Madam." The Palatine leaned in closer. "I do most humbly beg you may see fit to address me as Frederick, that we might enjoy some greater degree of informality."

I thought him bold to come so near, and yet there was no offence in it, for his warm breath was not unpleasant.

"And I suppose you will want to call me Elizabeth."

"If't please, I should be glad for it."

By the fifth act a troubling drowsiness had come over my

brother. I saw his head nod forward in sleep, after which he tore himself awake, only to fall again into slumber. I took up his hand in mine and found it cold as ice. When I examined it more closely I discovered an unusual greenish hue at the base of his fingernails, at which he stirred and turned to look at me in surprised exhaustion.

"Hamlet is preparing for his duel with Laertes," said the Palatine.

"They sense that tragedy is about to befall," Henry murmured.

"Horatio counsels that Hamlet shall see fit to decline this challenge."

"*You will lose, My Lord,*" said Laertes.

The audience had grown strangely quiet.

"*I do not think so,*" Hamlet replied, "*since he went to France I have been in constant practice. I shall win at the odds.*"

"I have often witnessed our Prince Henry," Lady Anne whispered to Count Schomberg, "in long and arduous practice with foil and lance."

"What think you of this Horatio fellow?" the Palatine asked Henry.

"The two are good companions," he answered. "Indeed he has been throughout the play Hamlet's closest and perhaps only ally, steadfast in's loyalty, and given to honest counsel always."

"Just so," said Count Schomberg.

"And yet am I not entirely certain Hamlet's best interests lie at the foundation of his heart," said the Palatine.

"Why do you say so?" Henry asked. "He bids Hamlet forgo the match."

"But wherefore does he so?"

"For fear Hamlet shall come to harm, naturally."

"But what reason have he to think so?"

"That Laertes is the better swordsman."

"He knows otherwise. Hamlet himself is surprised to hear he think not so."

"What is your meaning?"

"Perhaps Horatio knows more than he lets on."

"You think him guilty of duplicity?"

"Is there a man incapable of betrayal?" said Lady Anne.

"I say such a man exists," said the Count.

She turned to him. "Can you name one?"

"In all honesty, Madam, such a one is Prince Frederick."

I looked past him at Henry, who sat ill and pale but now utterly absorbed in the play. "Hamlet's about to be poisoned," he said.

"And by the man who is brother to the woman he loves, no less," I added.

"Some would argue Laertes has just cause. Hamlet did greatly wrong his sister, Ophelia, even unto her tragic and untimely death."

"Indeed, what can be more just," the Palatine added, "but that a loyal brother should seek to defend the honour of his sister?"

"It's a little late, if you ask me," said Lady Anne.

"He feels remorse," the Palatine looked at me, "and seeks to atone with revenge."

"He chided her that Hamlet's vow of love should not be trusted," I said.

"Out of love for her did he so caution." Henry's eyes remained fixed upon the stage. "In fear for her heart."

"Yet Hamlet did forsake her," I said.

"Because he thought her guilty of betrayal."

Henry spoke quietly. "Hamlet takes this duel for an entertainment."

"He knows not that the tip of Laertes's sword is poisoned," Lady Anne whispered to the Count, "as is the goblet of wine set by for him."

"Look how he stays yet a while." Henry seemed to be speaking to himself now, as much as to anyone of us. "Sits in quiet apprehension of some unknown fate that awaits him."

Up on the stage, Horatio strode toward Hamlet, knelt before him.

Hamlet lowered his head, placed his arm on Horatio's as he spoke quietly to him, "*But thou wouldst not think how ill all's here about my heart.*"

Henry leaned forward, as though the actor upon the stage were speaking directly to him, and moved his lips along with the actor's as the lines were spoken. "*It is no matter. If it be now, 'tis not to come,*" he mouthed; "*if it be not to come it will be now; if it be not now, yet it will come: the readiness is all . . .*"

I glanced in my father's direction just as Hamlet's mother drank the poison, and thought I saw there in his visage an expression not unlike that which came over the King in the play.

When the performance ended Henry came out of his trance and did his best to make himself as amiable as was ever his nature, but I was not convinced. He seemed to be in the clutches of some nagging augury that tortured him, and even as he managed to pluck up his energy and take his leave of us, it was plain to me he was putting up a false front, fighting to maintain his cheerful demeanour. Something was amiss, but even in my darkest misgivings I could never have imagined what it would come to.

Chapter Three

I had hoped my brother, having seen to the previous night's performance of the play, should see to some much-needed rest, but my mother wasn't going to allow it. She remained oblivious to such considerations and summoned him next day to Somerset, where she was making frantic preparations for another one of her hideous masques. Henry asked if I would accompany him, and so we made our way along the north bank of the Thames, seated side by side in a carriage.

"I admit I had imagined your debut upon the stage more like to occur in a play at the Globe," I said.

"A small role in one of the tragedies, perhaps," said Henry. Though he seemed somewhat restored, there persisted about him an aspect of disquiet.

"A comedy should do as well," I said.

"I could play the part of the fool."

The name of this latest production was *Oberon, the Faery Prince* and my mother had goaded Henry into playing the title role. She had commissioned the design of a suitable costume for him, and I had agreed to accompany him to the fitting to offer my opinion on it.

"I always thought you would make a creditable Hamlet."

"Indeed there are times" — he looked over at me — "I feel myself in possession of such sentiments as would befit the Danish Prince."

"And this Oberon, how are your sentiments inclined toward playing that character?"

"Thankfully I have no need to affect any."

My brother had insisted that his role in the production should amount to no more than a brief appearance upon the stage, and that he should not suffer the indignity of reciting so much as a single line. My mother had reluctantly acceded to his wishes and arranged for him to make a grand entrance dressed as Oberon himself in the finale.

"This latest masque promises to be even more extravagant than the last," said Henry, "and is sure to bring the exchequer ever closer to bankruptcy."

"Such matters are of little concern to the Queen."

"The same can be said for the King."

It often seemed to us that our parents were living in a dream world, condemned to one day find themselves most rudely roused from their slumber. They considered it beneath their station to show restraint or to heed any warnings that their profligacy would one day lead to dire consequences. We were equally appalled at their frivolous pageantry and undisguised self-aggrandizement, but soon Henry should be free to realize his own vision at St. James's Palace, where his tastes were sure to distinguish him as a more sophisticated patron of the arts.

"I take it the script has been written by Ben Jonson, as usual," I said.

Henry nodded.

"The scenery and costumes designed by Inigo Jones, naturally," I added, "and of course Alfonso Ferrabosco has composed the music."

My mother regularly commissioned those three for her masques, and they were a triumvirate to be reckoned with, an alliance of avarice and vanity, all of them invariably short of money and scheming for more. Eager to prop the Queen up as a champion of the arts, they shamelessly flattered her vanity for the sake of their own advancement, which was reason enough to dislike them.

"Now that you are starting up your own court, the three of them are doubtless among those eagerly seeking appointment," I said.

"Indeed they have presented me with all manner of entreaty, not to mention the attendant jealousies and petty insecurities so familiar to their nature."

"They know only too well that the money is bound to run out where the Queen's masques are concerned. I trust you have some other candidates in mind when it comes to court composers. Tobias Hume, for one."

"That goes without saying."

"Nothing will please the Captain more than to find himself in your employ. He has been trying for so long to obtain a position at Somerset, only to be turned away time and again by the Queen."

"She cannot see past mere appearance to appreciate his talents."

"Never were a man and his music a less likely match."

Captain Hume, as he preferred to be called, was a gruff man, not prone to flattery, and in his dress and manner the very antithesis of men like Alfonso Ferrabosco and his associates. But his music was unassailable, and my brother never tired of listening to his compositions, which the Captain often had occasion to play for him in private. In addition to being a brilliant composer he was also a highly skilled soldier, and had distinguished himself on a number of lengthy military campaigns. Though his swordsmanship was unequalled and his musicianship impeccable, his personal mannerism tended to put people off, as he exhibited a general disregard for decorum, whether it be in his attire or the language he used, and this caused him to be treated as something of an outcast by those at court, who considered him too ill-mannered and shabby to be seen with.

"Those other courtiers shall be more than a little chagrined to find you have chosen the Captain."

"I received some correspondence from Monsieur Ferrabosco regarding that very matter only this morning." Henry smiled wryly at me. "In fact I have it here with me. I thought you might find it amusing." He pulled a letter out of his pocket and handed it to me.

To His Royal Highness the Prince of Wales on this seventeenth day of August, 1612

Your Majesty,

It has recently come to my attention that you may be considering Tobias Hume for a position at the court you are initiating in St. James's. Though I had held out hopes for such an appointment, I nevertheless beseech that if there can be but one beneficiary in the matter you find in Captain Hume's favour. Rest assured I fear not for my future, neither for the recognition of my works in posterity. Though his compositions are less likely than mine to bring glory and honour to their patron, and while it is a far more precarious undertaking to pin your hopes upon the Captain, let us set aside such considerations for the moment.

I grant his works lack originality, as he is wont to filch entire movements from other works and pass them off as his own, and that your ear may not be privy to his slanderous remarks, which are numerous, but let mercy be your guide. In the unlikely event that the appointment should fall to me I ask that you offer the Captain some small gesture of recognition, a token of remuneration, if only for my sake.

I remain ever your loyal and faithful servant,
Alfonso Ferrabosco

"Do you see how they stick the velvet knife?" Henry said.

"Indeed there are those," I answered, "who would commit such acts of treachery and deceit as make this letter seem tame by comparison."

When Henry turned to look out through the window, I allowed myself to inspect his features, told myself it was only the overcast day and lack of light inside the carriage that made his complexion seem so pale.

"The very reason," Henry turned back to me, "we must both seek to remain yet in the good graces of our father."

"And I suppose you will say upon that premise stands another, which dictates that our mother must be appeased as well."

"We are neither of us in a position to do entirely as we please."

"I doubt that day will ever come," I said. "Just the same, I intend to defy them at every opportunity."

"I would bide my time yet awhile."

"You have more to lose than I."

"If by that you mean the throne, neither of us is far removed from it."

"Our younger brother Charles is closer than I," I said. "Such are the laws of accession."

"The laws are changeable."

"At any rate when the time comes the crown shall be yours for the taking, Henry. I have no wish for any other outcome."

"Sir Raleigh says a sovereign's first duty must be to the people."

"Who acknowledge even now that you will make an excellent king."

"'For though you may seem at a great remove from them,' he said to me once, 'you must rule as though their collective breath were upon your neck.'" Henry offered me an unconvincing smile.

The horses had set a good pace, following along the tree-lined avenue where here and there couples strode arm in arm. A carriage went by in the opposite direction, and as the sound of the hooves clopping faded into the distance, it seemed to me all of London was awaiting some event of unknown import.

"I doubt not the wisdom of this last," I offered, "for often enough it is the neck that must be looked to."

"Uneasy lies the head that wears the crown." Henry raised a hand to the window to pull the curtain back a little wider. "So writes Mr. Shakespeare."

"And how for the head that stands to inherit it?" I added.

"There are times when it's wise to capitulate."

Off to our right were groups of well-dressed young men and women with mallets in their hands, some of them striking at colourful wooden balls lying here and there upon the lawn.

"What game do they play at?" I asked.

"Pall Mall, they call it," said Henry. "It is all the rage in Paris. You see those hoops arranged upon the grass between the trees? The idea is to use the mallet to strike at the coloured balls and drive them through the hoops."

"To what purpose?"

"None other than any sport, dear Sister. Merely amusement."

"For my part it looks both frivolous and tedious."

"It is a leisurely game for gentlemen and ladies," said Henry, "but I prefer golf."

Now I could make out the tiltyards of Whitehall off to the right, the chalky spires of the palace in behind, and the winding Thames beyond. I thought it the most pleasing in appearance of all the palaces in London, and imagined for a moment what changes my brother might see fit to make should he chose to live there after his coronation.

Henry coughed with a little heave of his shoulders and chest.

"You still have that cough," I said.

"Only the last remnants, which shall soon pass."

We had just taken the curve in the road that signalled our arrival upon The Strand when a young man ran up beside the carriage and stuck his head in the window.

"Is this that same noble majesty whose father we call yet King?" the man rasped, his hair tousled and a wild look about him. "Mark well, good Prince." He ran alongside, gripping the window ledge of the carriage with a pair of pale hands. "It shall be you who rules soon enough, if we have aught to say about it." One of the footmen kicked at him until he released his grip and fell back. "Mark my words," the man shouted after us.

"There, you see?" I said. "Just as I've told you before, the people are for you."

"It is no more than one discontented pauper."

"This speaks of some intrigue afoot."

"You make too much of it. They are no more than the ramblings of a malcontent. There's nothing new in that."

"Those who would see you crowned seek to hasten circumstances to their favour."

Henry looked over at me. "You give credence to utterances better dismissed for idle threats."

"Would our father felt as much," I declared. "This young man's sentiments are the very reason he forbids you from travelling abroad."

"He will say it is for my own safety."

"More like to keep an eye on you."

"You really think he believes I would plot against him?" Henry seemed genuinely surprised at such a notion.

"Or he might fear that you should come under some foreign influence."

"The history books side with him on that. Reason enough to keep me close at hand."

"He has nothing to fear, as you have ever been a faithful son."

"All the more reason I should acquiesce in this matter of the masque."

The conversation ended there. We had arrived at Somerset and the carriage made its way through the gates into the courtyard. When it came to a stop, Henry hopped out before the footman could jump down and offered me his hand. "No need," he said to the attendant.

"I had not seen this latest," he said as I stepped down. We stood for a moment, looking up at the grand columns that lined the façade of the palace. "I see Mother has commissioned a new entrance. Florentine, by the look of it. I might have guessed her ambitions would lean to that architecture."

We made our way up the marble steps, lined on either side by enormous statues. "For myself I should have chosen Doric for the capitals on these columns," said Henry. "This Ionic is a bit ostentatious, don't you think?"

"If you think this is too much," I said, "wait until we get inside."

We made our way across the foyer to the east wing, where our mother would be waiting, and found her in the drawing room seated at a desk, with Alfonso Ferrabosco leaning over her, the two of them going over some sheet music laid out before them.

My mother rose from her chair when she saw us. Alfonso straightened and turned to us.

"Henry, at last you've come." She walked toward us with arms outstretched. "Elizabeth, I was not expecting you." She brushed past me and hurried to greet Henry.

"Good to see you, too, Mother," I said.

She reached out and clutched my brother by the arms, dragged him into the room. "Come, come. We have much to do. Over here. Take off that cloak."

Alfonso stepped forward. Though it might have been said of him that he was impeccably dressed, well groomed, and not without courtly manners, I found him shifty and seedy-looking.

Hair oiled, beard and moustache shiny to excess, he was small of nose and weak of chin, with sunken eyes under half-closed lids.

"Your Highness." He took up my hand and bent to kiss it, lingered over it too long as he was wont to do, his thin lips yet pressed against the back of my hand even as I pulled it away. "We are honoured to be in your elegant and delightful company. Here is the music I have composed for your mother's new masque." He picked up a few of the sheets from the desk and held them up. "It promises to be an excellent production."

He turned to the Queen. "Your Majesty, your daughter grows in beauty by the day, it would seem."

"Yes, yes," said the Queen, "let us dispense with needless flattery." She pointed to a table at the far end of the room where two tailors stood in attendance. "They have laid out your costume for you," she said to Henry. "Come and try it on." Her eyes sparkled with anticipation, as they always did when she was immersed in her preparations. "I am eager to see my Oberon in the flesh."

"Mother, you catch me unawares," said Henry. "I came merely to look upon it."

"The tailors would know how it sits upon your frame."

"I fail to see the need," Henry protested. "The measurements have all been taken."

"As a favour to me." Mother smiled ingratiatingly. "Is that so much to ask?"

"You shall see me in it soon enough," said Henry. "What need have I to wear it now?"

"Do my eyes deceive me, or are you somewhat thinner about the waist?" She looked him up and down.

"I admit I am a little off my appetite of late," said Henry. "Perhaps that may account for it."

"All the more reason we must see to a fitting," said Mother, "as these tailors may see the need for some alteration. We would be assured of an excellent fit." She pulled him over to the table while one of the tailors slid over an ornate dressing screen and unfolded it while the other guided Henry into position behind it.

When she began to undo the buttons on his doublet he took her hands away. "Leave off, Mother," he said irritably. "I shall manage this on my own."

"We have no need for undue modesty. There shall be little time for that when you are in the midst of all the other players about the stage."

"I shall expect a dressing room to myself."

"I shall you get an entire wing if it will quell this unseemly pleading."

"A pity." Alfonso Ferrabosco closed in on me. "We shall not get to see Your Highness take the stage in a fairy costume of her own." The way his eyes took in my body left no doubt as to his inclinations. "It should give me the greatest of pleasure."

"My daughter shall soon have means to her own ambitions in that regard," said my mother.

"Are there productions such as these in your future?" asked Ferrabosco.

"It is my fondest hope that there are not," I said.

"As you see," said my mother, "my daughter sits in unrepentant judgment as only a child can."

At this Henry emerged from behind the partition dressed in the Roman style, carrying a helmet with feathered plumes under one arm and wearing a scarlet cloak adorned with a set of Leonine shoulder pieces. A bold sash of bright blood-red cut across his golden thorax, and the leggings, their tops filigreed with lace, were embroidered with the face of a lion. On his feet he wore a pair of leather calcei lunati that came halfway up his calf.

"It flatters your physique," said my mother.

"I dare say I had not seen such a leg upon a prince," said Ferrabosco. "There's something of the gladiator in him."

"I will say it impresses," said the Queen.

"Well," Henry looked at me, "what did you think, Sister? I look the fairy, don't I?"

"I think the ladies shall find you quite fetching," said my mother.

"Not to mention some of the men, the King's favourites among them," I added.

My mother bristled at this remark but kept silent.

"If you are pleased then I am pleased, Mother, and so I retire." He made to return to the partition, but she took hold of him.

"No, wait." She spun him around by the shoulders until she had brought him full circle. "We like it well."

"Now may I go?" asked Henry.

"I had hoped you might walk about a little in it."

"You have seen me walk from there to here, and now you shall see me walk back."

Ferrabosco turned to me. "What think you, Your Highness?" he asked. "You have not said."

"It is a good fit."

"It speaks to your brother's physique." Ferrabosco lowered his gaze. "Or indeed such charms as yours, which flatter those garbs that conceal them."

I ignored him. "Mother, it would appear this promises to be the most extravagant of all your productions. How do you plan to pay for it? And what about all this new construction? Do you have any idea what all of this costs?"

"I do not concern myself with such matters."

"You think it wise? There are rumblings that the exchequer is all but bankrupt."

"A tedious business best seen to by Parliament."

"Which grows unwilling to finance more needless expense."

"Indeed they will have us grovel for what is rightfully ours."

"You stand to leave your son an inheritance of debt."

"I have no wish to discuss it further, least of all with you. Is that why you came, to needle me with these petty concerns?

And why are you traipsing about London when the foreign prince is eager for your company?"

"I thought you would rather I wed the new Swedish monarch."

"Your father would choose a prince over a king."

"I should prefer to choose neither."

Henry had finished changing back into his clothes and come over to join us. He was impatient to return to St. James's now that our mother's curiosity had been satisfied. She herself eagerly resumed her consultations with Ferrabosco, and so we took our leave.

The evening's performance at Whitehall saw me seated once again next to the Palatine, awaiting the raising of the curtain. The Queen had chosen to sit in one of the loges with the trio of Alfonso Ferrabosco, Inigo Jones, and Ben Jonson. The King occupied a separate balcony, accompanied by his bodyguards and his usual entourage of young male courtiers.

"There is yet one seat empty next to Lady Anne," noted Count Schomberg. He and Lady Anne were seated in behind us, engaged in a pitifully transparent flirtation.

"One more guest has yet to arrive," I explained. The two of them were a little too cozy for my liking, and I had arranged to bring a little disquiet to their excessive congeniality.

"I had thought we might see Mr. Shakespeare here this evening," said the Palatine.

"Busy with one of his own productions, no doubt," offered the Count.

"The man harbours a great fear of the plague," said Lady Anne.

"How does that speak to his absence here?"

"As he would have it, there are deadly sprites that flit about," I said, "and more easily find their mark within the confines of an enclosed room such as this, being bounded by four walls and a roof."

"To that end did he build the Globe Theatre open to the air?" the Count enquired.

"Indeed," Lady Anne answered. "So that those who pay a penny can stand in the pit without a roof over their heads, and in inclement weather suffer themselves to be rained upon, even as the actors shrink back from the stage."

"Or that upon a clear night the moon might play her part." The Palatine smiled over at me. "If it should suit the scene."

"Do you suppose he might think of a masque like this as competition?" asked the Count.

"That would better fall to the Beargarden I should think," offered Lady Anne, "but a stone's throw from the Globe."

"And what productions do they put on?"

"None but where the actors must play their part to the death."

"Ah, tragedy, then."

"More like to comedy."

"Some would call it comedy," I said. "I would call it barbarism."

"Bear-baiting and such," Lady Anne explained to the Count.

"Prince Henry told me," said the Palatine, "that upon the last occasion they set loose a pack of ravenous dogs that proceeded to tear the entrails out of a declawed bear."

"He's been, then," mused the Count.

"I suppose you should wish to go and see for yourself."

"Quite a sight, I imagine."

"Theatre of the worst kind," I said disdainfully, "with naught to recommend it but blood and gore."

"No doubt tonight shall offer spectacle of a more civilized fashion," said Lady Anne.

"Don't get your hopes up," I cautioned. "Whatever the case, we are sure to have more sizzle than steak."

I saw that my special guest had arrived at last, and beckoned him over. "Look who it is." I turned to Lady Anne, who fixed me with a contemptuous glare.

Tobias Hume strode toward us dressed in an ill-fitting knee-length coat, soiled and wrinkled, a pair of worn brocade breeches, and scuffed knee-length boots with spurs. It was apparent his beard and moustache had not been trimmed in some time, nor the hair upon his head combed, all of which pleased me greatly.

"You know him, then?" the Count asked.

"We have some mild acquaintance," Lady Anne admitted.

"He has upon occasion made overtures to your favour, has he not?" I teased.

"With all the subtlety and charm of a fishmonger."

"And yet I've heard you call him Toby."

"I've met the man," said Prince Frederick. "Henry introduced me to him only yesterday." He turned to Count Schomberg. "He has written a book of ayres the Prince is very fond of."

"If only we could separate the man from his music," Lady Anne said dryly.

"I admit he is rough around the edges," I acknowledged, "but we must seek to overlook such shortcomings. Even coarseness has its uses. There's something to be said for vulgarity if it should serve to subvert pretense."

"Your brother remarked that the other composers are eager to study his works, though only in secret."

In the course of the ensuing introductions and formalities, Captain Hume made a great show of going down on one knee before Lady Anne to take up her hand in his and kiss it with his lips puckered, after which he proceeded to seat himself next to her in a most boisterous and demonstrative fashion. Lady Anne, much to my delight, was clearly discomfited, and Count Schomberg hardly knew what to make of the situation.

"How is it this masque takes place at Whitehall Palace rather than Somerset," Prince Frederick enquired after some moments, "where the Queen resides?"

"It does so upon the King's insistence," I answered, "the better to let him take as much credit as he can, an option he never fails to exercise. See where he has taken pains to ensure that all in attendance know whereof he is ruler." I indicated the stage curtains, onto which an enormous, detailed map of the British Isles had been sown.

"What did you say is the title of this production?" asked the Count.

"*Oberon, the Faery Prince.*"

"And those corbies seated there with the Queen," Captain Hume scowled, "have pocketed the chinks for it. Therefore we can be assured of three things: a second-rate script from the priggish Mr. Jonson, lurid costumes and garish scenery by the profligate Inigo Jones, and most scandalous of all, an utterly unoriginal musical score thanks to the oily Alfonso Ferrabosco."

"Do I note some slight animosity?" the Palatine offered sarcastically.

The Captain ignored the comment. "We are sure to have some Italian slop offered up tonight."

"Look how the composer sits very near to the stage." I goaded him on.

"Did I but strut those boards, I should be sure and allow him some spit."

Prince Frederick leaned toward me. "How is it the Captain holds this gentleman in such contempt?"

"They have ever been rivals for one court appointment or other."

Captain Hume's open disdain for Alfonso Ferrabosco could hardly be faulted. The man could not be trusted. He had already made a sly pass at me on one occasion, and considered every woman vulnerable to his lubricious charm. I had urged Henry in the strongest possible terms not to consider him for his court, but my brother would only answer that the matter was a delicate one. Sir Raleigh should certainly have put him in his place soon enough.

Now the candles were snuffed out around the room and the crowd quieted. The curtains ruffled as they were drawn wide to reveal upon the stage an enormous boulder, jagged and ugly, and above it a thin moon that traced a barely noticeable path across the stage and whose light lent the set a pale, milky texture.

A muscular man wearing a robe draped loosely across his torso and holding a leafed staff took centre stage and began to recite.

Melt earth to sea, sea flow to
air, and air fly into fire,
Whilst we in tunes, to Arthur's
chair bear Oberon's desire;
Than which there's nothing can be higher,
Save James, to whom it flies

"Look there, how dutifully the King suffers his flattery." I glanced up at the balcony, where my father sat surrounded by fawning courtiers, and wondered how it must make Henry feel to see his father prefer the company of such young men to that of his own son.

"This player sports the ears of a horse," the Count remarked.

"He is Silenus," said Lady Anne, "god of dance."

"And drunkenness, no doubt," I added.

But he the wonder is of
tongues, of ears, of eyes.
Who hath not heard, who hath not seen,
Who hath not sung his name?

"What bodes this horse-eared fellow?" asked the Count.

"He comes as harbinger, I venture," said the Palatine, "to prophesy that Oberon shall bring good order and benevolent reign upon his subjects."

> *The soul that hath not, hath not been;*
> *But is the very same*
> *With buried sloth, and knows not fame,*
> *Which him doth best comprise:*
> *For he the wonder is of*
> *tongues, of ears, of eyes.*

"How likes the King these words, I wonder?" the Palatine ventured.

I looked up at my father and saw he had grown more attentive, listening now to the import of the words.

> *He is a god o'er kings; yet stoops he then*
> *Nearest a man, when he*
> *doth govern men;*
> *To teach them by the*
> *sweetness of his sway,*
> *And not by force.*

Now an array of outrageously attired satyrs in oversized codpieces who had been perched upon the crag rose and began to gyrate about the stage, suggestively playing their flutes, while nymphs with breasts exposed under diaphanous fabric, appeared and flitted about among them. From time to time unseen hands from off-stage deployed artfully decorated partitions onto the wings to change up the scenery.

"What do you make of this scenery construction?" said the Palatine. "See how the backdrop is made up of separate pieces they disassemble and configure in a new arrangement to yield a different effect. I had not seen this upon a stage heretofore."

"A ploy to squeeze additional remuneration out of coffers, no doubt," offered Captain Hume.

"And what say you for those backcloths?"

"I can only imagine what the stage at the Globe would look like with such clutter upon it. Let us hope these affectations of Inigo Jones do not become the fashion."

"The audience seem impressed by it," the Count put in.

"Their taste is bred out of privilege and entitlement, and ever has comfort tendered a false sense of refinement. They would make excellent guests at your Banquo's banquet."

Now there arose a general murmuring in the audience as the nymphs and satyrs formed into couples that writhed about the stage with lewd and salacious gestures. I thought how utterly misplaced my brother must feel to find himself part of such a garish production. The masquers continued to gyrate in anticipation, the audience in twitters and whispers, until the crag split open with a clap of rolling thunder that echoed from off-stage.

"Impressive, that sound effect," said the Palatine. "I dare say Mr. Shakespeare might have learned a thing or two here tonight."

"A cheap ploy to divert the attention of the audience," protested the Captain. "A bit of trickery to fool them into believing they are witnessing something worthy."

"Notable nevertheless," the Palatine held his ground, "from a technical point of view."

When the crag had finished splitting wide, there inside was revealed the interior of a palace hall, its throne illuminated by a host of lights in a variety of colours. From out of this fissure sprang a throng of yet more masquers, and from their midst, riding in a chariot drawn by two white bears, appeared the Prince of Wales himself.

"There he is!" said Lady Anne.

"His complexion is as pale as the creatures before him," I remarked.

"This is but make-up and lighting," Lady Anne offered, "that make it appear so."

"Those bruins look real enough," said the Count.

"No doubt their coats were dyed."

"Can they be men in costume?"

"There are such bears in the polar regions," said the Palatine. "I myself have met a man who hunted them there."

"Then we are sure to see them one day baited at the Beargarden."

Now a band of ten musicians walked out onto the stage, all of them playing lutes, followed by ten pages attired in costumes of green and silver that proceeded to dance to the music, then yet more masquers to frolic about the stage.

"What a fever of excess is here."

"Such are the follies of royalty."

"But look at my brother. He is in agony amidst all this nonsense."

When the chariot had made a full circle about the stage and come to a halt, one of the players walked up and beckoned Prince Henry to step off, in what was clearly an unscripted development, but he declined. The audience began to cheer loudly, and the applause grew thunderous. Still the Prince of Wales demurred, until another masquer appeared on the other side and together they managed to pull him from the chariot and bring him reluctantly to centre stage, at which the audience rose as one to their feet with chants of "Henry! Henry! Henry!"

I turned to gauge my father's reaction where he sat watching, and saw his countenance darken as he looked down at the audience, then up to the stage, then back down to the audience again.

"The English do love spectacle," said the Count.

"They love this prince." The Palatine looked at me.

When Henry turned his eyes up to my father, the audience followed his gaze up, at which the King forced a smile and waved unconvincingly.

"Look there how the King acknowledges his noble son," said the Count. "He should be much pleased at this."

"Such a smile would drown a cat," said Lady Anne.

"Your brother is popular with the people," the Count assured her. "It bodes well for his future."

"Though ill for his father's, perhaps," remarked Palatine, whose presentiment left me a little taken aback.

"A king cannot be too popular," Captain Hume insisted.

"How then for a prince if his father be yet king?" the Palatine ventured.

"Surely he can take comfort at the prospect of a son whose good graces sit so well among the people," Captain Hume replied. "A loyal son makes a father sleep well."

"Mine sleeps with armed chamberlains at his bed," I said dryly.

Henry turned one way and then another, beckoning all the players to come out and join him, which they did from the wings until the stage was filled, but even as the applause continued the King rose to his feet, took up his heavy cloak, and allowed himself to be led out by his sentries, entourage in tow.

When at last the curtain came down and the audience had begun to make their way out, a commotion was heard upon the stage. I knew instantly what it was and rushed to draw the curtains apart. There was my brother collapsed upon the stage in utter exhaustion, being attended to by some of the players, and this time I would not be assuaged by his assurances that it was nothing, allow no excuses that he should be fine after a few moments. I personally saw him back to St. James's and into his bed, where I stayed until he had fallen into restless sleep.

Chapter Four

Upon the following morning I arrived at St. James's Palace to a disturbing number of practitioners mulling about my brother's outer chambers — physicians and apothecaries, surgeons and chamberlains — all of them looking very serious and wearing the garb of their various callings. Many of them were familiar to me, including Dr. William Butler, the apothecary Ralph Clayton, and members of Henry's household, including Thomas Chaloner, his comptroller. There was an unmistakable air of gravity about their exchanges, a sense of urgency in their gestures that set my stomach to churning. There also, to my surprise, was Alfonso Ferrabosco, who had obviously found some means to insinuate himself into the situation.

I brushed aside the bows and greetings that my arrival affected as I crossed the room, eager to make my way to Henry's bedside, along the way catching snippets of conversations that spoke of remedies and ointments, clysters and cupping glasses. At the door to my brother's privy chamber I was halted most rudely by two Yeomen of the Guard, one on either side, who crossed their halberds with a metallic clang and barred my entry.

"Stand aside," I said. When they failed to do so I added, "Princess Elizabeth Stuart would gain admittance to the Prince of Wales." They were very tall and large of shoulder and chest, in the fashion of such beefeaters, and kept their eyes straight ahead, expressionless, without answer, as though I had not spoken.

"Do you not see it is the King's daughter that commands you?" I tried again: "I order you to let me pass." Still they refused and when I made to step forward and push through into the room closed ranks and stood shoulder to shoulder. "This is an outrage. Who orders you to bar my entry? I demand to know. Henry," I yelled past them, "are you in there? Henry? Can you hear me? It's Elizabeth, come to see you."

The door opened and the Yeomen stepped aside to allow a heavy-set man dressed in black to come and stand before me. I knew him to be a physician by his long dark robe, white cuffs, and collar beneath, but he was no one I recognized. His chubby fingers were curled around a jar of swollen and writhing leeches, and he stepped toward me with such menacing authority that in spite of myself I fell back a little.

"I must insist that you withdraw at once," he rasped, "as we have need of quiet hereabouts." His scraggly beard, parsed into two uneven white tufts, showed traces of red here and there and gave him a mildly oriental look. He was portly of frame and bloated about the face, hair thinning and eyes set close over a prominent nose. "We have matters of the utmost urgency to attend to in the care of this prince, and you, Madam, are making quite a scene."

"As I am well entitled to do, Sir." I felt a heat rising in my cheeks. "Inasmuch as this Prince you speak of is none but my own brother."

"Ah." His demeanour became at once deferential and yet condescending. "Then you would be Princess Elizabeth, if I'm not mistaken."

Those others about the room had quieted down, listening to the exchange. "And who might you be?" I asked.

Alfonso Ferrabosco had been hovering nearby, listening intently, and now he wheedled himself into to our exchange. "Doctor, if I may be allowed?"

"By all means."

"Your Highness, allow me present Sir Theodore Mayerne, physician. Doctor, allow me to introduce Her Royal Highness Princess Elizabeth Stuart."

"Your Highness." Dr. Mayerne nodded ever so slightly, never lowering his eyes. "We are honoured to make your acquaintance."

"Theodore Turquet de Mayerne?" I enquired.

"Indeed, Highness."

"Late of Paris?"

"You have heard of him, then?" Alfonso Ferrabosco smiled ingratiatingly at the Doctor.

"I have read some of his work."

"Have you indeed." The Doctor let slip a smirk.

"*Remedia Chemice Praeparata.* Do I remember the title correctly?"

"You do." The Doctor seemed a little unsettled, looked awkwardly at Ferrabosco, then at me. "We are flattered."

"It is not for blandishment I recall that volume."

At this the doctor's ruddy complexion paled somewhat and his eyes grew narrow under furrowed brows. I had for some time been engaged in the study of medical practice, reading such texts on the subject as I could manage to get my hands on. I had come across the volume in question in my brother's study, where he went out of his way to make such books available to me. He thought my studies worthy, and notwithstanding my father's disapproval, encouraged me to pursue them nevertheless. As it turned out, my father had nothing to fear, for beyond the rudimentary elements of basic anatomy I found in my readings precious little advancement in the field of medicine. It seemed to me the practice was founded upon little else but the tenuous ruminations of an ancient philosopher.

"If I'm not mistaken, it endorses the use of such chemical preparations as met with your expulsion from the College of

Physicians in Paris. You look brought up short, Doctor," I continued. "Is something amiss? Tell me, how is it you come to minister to my brother?"

"Your father, the King, has engaged my services, Highness, and I have offered them most humbly in hopes that, along with these other physicians and practitioners you see here, we may in all haste restore the Prince to his former good health."

"All well and good, but I would for the present dispense with further formality. Now if you will excuse me, I shall attend to my brother's bedside."

"As it is, Highness, I'm afraid the Prince may not have visitors but for those under my service and direction."

I looked beyond the doctors into the room, where I could make out a man in dark robes leaning over Henry's bed. "If you are in the midst of some treatment" — I indicated the jar of leeches he held yet in his hands — "I suppose I am content to wait out here until you have finished."

Alfonso Ferrabosco interceded once again. "Forgive me, your Highness, but I must ask that you wait in the antechamber, where after some short interval I may send one or more of these physicians to give account of your brother's condition."

"I will do no such thing. And who are you to order me about? And what exactly are you doing here?"

"Your father, the King," Alphonso gave me a penetrating stare, "has only this morning appointed me Groom-in-Extraordinary to the Prince of Wales's bedchamber."

"What?" I turned to Dr. Butler, who gave a barely discernible nod. "But this is preposterous." I felt my blood rising, unprepared for my irritation with these men. "You would be among the last my brother would choose for such a position."

"Nevertheless."

"Sir." I summoned Dr. Butler closer. "Surely this impertinence cannot be allowed to continue."

"You haven't spoken to your father, then?" he asked awkwardly.

"Can you not order these men to let me pass?"

"This is most unfortunate." Alfonso smiled condescendingly.

"They have no right keep me out," I said to Dr. Butler.

"Your father, the King, has ordered it so," he seemed embarrassed to admit.

"He suspects the plague. Is that what's going on here, Dr. Mayerne?"

"There may be a miasma in the room, Highness."

I turned to Dr. Butler. "Tell me, does my brother have swelling under the arms?"

"I have not seen any."

"Nor any sign of rash?"

"None to speak of, but where the leeches have been applied."

"Then he has not the plague." I stared at Dr. Mayerne. "You will agree, Doctor?"

"You would be about practice of medicine then, Highness?" Dr. Mayerne's lips curled derisively as he glanced at those others about the room.

"As well and better than you, it would seem, for though I am no physician I know he has not the signs for the plague."

"We must take all due precautions, Highness, as surely you can understand."

"If you are concerned for the plague, answer me this: Why are you then not attired in the appropriate garments? Where is your beak? Where are your goggles?" I was familiar with the practice of physicians who attended those infected with the plague to be clothed in an elaborate wardrobe for protection. A long overcoat and cane were requisite, as was a mask resembling the head of a bird, stuffed full with all manner of strong smelling ingredients.

"I wear none at my discretion, Highness."

"And what of these other doctors? What say you, gentlemen? I smell nothing upon your persons of suet or vinegar."

"We have been patient, Highness." Dr. Mayerne exchanged glances with Ferrabosco. "But now we must be about our business, and so I will say good day to you." He stepped around me and walked across the room.

"And I must see to my duties, as well, if you will excuse me." Ferrabosco passed between the Yeomen into my brother's room and closed the door behind him.

I turned to Dr. Butler. "How be if you command these Yeomen to let me pass?"

"They will not, Your Highness; but for Dr. Mayerne's permission or that of Monsieur Ferrabosco, none of us may enter."

"We shall see about this. I'll to the King and have it set right. Will you come with me and give account for my sake?"

"Your Highness." Dr. Butler's eyes pleaded with me. "I would gladly speak on your behalf but am bound to remain here, should the Doctor have need of my services."

"Are you powerless, then? Is there nothing to be done?"

Dr. Butler took me aside and spoke in little more than a whisper. "This physician would seem to have such endorsement from your father as none of us can mitigate. It were as though he had come down to us from Heaven itself and not across the channel from Paris."

"I have always thought of you as a kind and honest man, Doctor. Tell me, do you trust this physician?"

"It hardly matters whether I do or no. It is out of my hands."

"I would know what remedies he employs."

"Those very same, for the most part, as would I, such as bloodletting, dry cupping, enemas."

"Nothing more?" I saw him hesitate to answer. "Speak. I command you."

"I have witnessed the administration of calomel."

"I know of it. It is a compound of quicksilver and acts as a powerful purgative."

"I can attest to that. The Prince's body expels it some few moments after ingestion, with great violence."

"Like to a toxin which serves merely to weaken him the more. And you allow him to proceed with this so-called remedy?"

"Dr. Mayerne will not be moved in such matters."

"But tell me yet one more thing, Doctor." I placed a hand on his arm. "In all honesty, how is my brother?"

The Doctor hesitated.

"I would know the truth."

"He fights with all of his strength, Madam, but the affliction will not yield." He looked around the room, took a folded paper out of his breast pocket, and handed it to me.

"Your brother asked that I give this to you."

"From Henry?" I took it from him.

"My best wishes go with you, Madam. I pray you may yet make some headway where I have failed."

It was not until I was on my way to Whitehall, riding in the carriage through the streets of London, that I opened the note and read it.

Dearest Sister,

That your presence at my bedside should be a great comfort to me goes without saying, though I understand you are not absent by choice. I hardly know the need for all this secrecy, except to say that there is some concern for a miasma in the room, which they would not have you exposed to, and so I am content to exchange correspondence with you for the time being.

I am under the care of a new physician and suffered to ingest all manner of purgatives the better to discharge those noxious humours from my body as give rise to this infirmity, though I fear these violent expulsions serve only to make me weaker. More than anything I would vanquish this affliction and send these meddlesome physicians packing.

Until that time comes give me leave to make a request of you. Will you to allow Prince Frederick into your company? I would never presume to speak for your feelings nor question your keen insight, but I tell you the young man is entirely smitten with you, and if you cannot love him you must tell him so in all honesty and let that be an end of it. By all means follow your heart's instruction, but for my part I will venture he may yet prove himself honourable and worthy of your affection. Will you give him a chance?

I tire greatly of a sudden and will end here, that this note shall find its way to you with all haste.

My best wishes for you, dear sister, from your loving brother,
Henry

I looked out to Hyde Park and the Thames beyond, the people about their business, the day unfolding as though everything were the same. The world seemed cruelly indifferent to my plight. I was alone in this, as was my brother there upon his sickbed, suffering the custom of feeble physic to dictate that his skin be sliced open, his flesh burned, and not to have the hand to hold nor face to gaze upon that loved him more than any other in the world.

Upon reaching Whitehall I enquired immediately after my father's whereabouts, brushed aside any attempt at escort by the Master of the House, and made my way through the halls of the palace until I found him in the great room, bent over a large ornate table, a set of drawings laid out over the polished oak surface. Inigo Jones was there with him, and the two of them looked up when they saw me rush in. Mr. Jones was no doubt foisting some construction plan upon my father that would see him paid a handsome stipend and drain the exchequer even further.

My father straightened up from the table. "Daughter, I had no word you were coming."

"I sent none."

Inigo stepped away from the table and bowed. "Your Highness."

I ignored him and turned to my father. "I would speak to you on a matter of some urgency."

"Have you seen these?" My father used the magnifying glass he held to indicate the drawings on the table. "They are designs for the construction of an English wing at the castle in Heidelberg, where you shall reside after the wedding. Mr. Jones is setting his best skills to the task, and you shall not want for elegance or comfort. Come and see how generous are the dimensions he has set out."

My father in his arrogance sought to bring his plans into effect by proceeding as if everything had already been agreed to, all the decisions made, as though I had no say in the matter. Infuriating!

"It promises to be quite magnificent," offered Mr. Jones. "See here, where I have drawn up a spacious balcony off the banqueting hall that promises to allow for a spectacular view of the town below. Your Highness shall have the best vantage point in all of Heidelberg."

"Whatever the plans may be, they carry in them nothing from my part of either consent or consultation."

"Nothing like it has ever been seen in Heidelberg, I dare say." My father acted as though he had not heard a word of my protestations. "No expense shall be spared."

"Including such a handsome salary, no doubt" — I glared at Mr. Jones — "as shall be paid for services here rendered."

"Your father is a man of vision, and as such may not be ruled by matters of vulgar finance."

"Nor by such as a daughter who would have her inclinations acknowledged. I would wish a moment of my father's time, if you please, Sir?"

Mr. Jones looked at my father. "Will His Majesty see fit to excuse me?"

"Very well." My father waved him off. "Do but stand by, for we have more to discuss."

"By all means, I will remove myself only as far as the next room, where I shall be taking a pipe of tobacco."

My father wrinkled his nose. "If you must do so, then go rather out into the courtyard, where the smoke may not so much foul the air."

"Yes, your Majesty."

"It is a filthy habit." My father turned back to me. "And to think we have Sir Raleigh to thank for it."

Upon his return from one of his voyages the New World, to set up a colony in Virginia, Sir Raleigh brought back with him a group of colonists who had taken up smoking tobacco. They brought with them a generous supply, which they shared freely. It wasn't long before the habit caught on at court, much to my father's annoyance.

"I suppose you would have him kept in the Tower so much the longer for it."

"He shall remain there for exactly as long as I deem necessary. It is a simple matter of *rex regis per divinus vox*."

"Of course, the divine right of kings." I did not try to hide my sarcasm.

"And as I am that king, the rest is a simple matter."

"Even a king might find it fitting to cultivate some semblance of humility."

"Such a trait sits unseemly on one who rules."

"And yet how it sits upon your eldest son most admirably." I saw his features cloud over. "You have probably guessed it is Henry I have come about," I continued. "I went to see him this morning at St. James's and was rudely barred from entry to his bedchamber."

"I'm relieved to hear it."

"Relieved? I would be relieved of your high-handed officiousness, your unfeeling callousness. I do but wish to comfort my brother and should not be denied."

"The reason is simple. There may be a miasma in the room which, if you should enter, may afflict your person with the same malady."

"Then I'll wear a beak and goggles, though Dr. Mayerne does not. And what made you decide to appoint him to my brother's care? He is insufferable, not to mention incompetent."

"He has a reputation that precedes him."

"He does indeed, though not such a one as you make reference to. And Alfonso Ferrabosco is now appointed groom to my brother's bedchamber? What can you be thinking? He is worse than this . . . this worm who awaits yonder at your beck and call. They have all of them but one gambit, and that is to feed at the trough of courtly extravagance."

"*Condemnant quod non intellegunt.*"

"And I will answer, *quidquid Latine dictum sit altum videtur.* Whatever is said in Latin seems profound."

"These matters need not concern you."

"I want to see my brother." I took a step toward him. "I demand it."

"I'll not lose my only daughter." He stood facing me, hands on his hips.

"And yet you are eager enough to forfeit her to Bohemia."

"This impertinence tests our indulgence."

"Temper your impatience awhile." I raised a hand tentatively. "And I'll do the same with my disdain."

"These are the churlish reprimands of a child."

"And yet you would have me married off as a woman."

"Your mother married when she was two years your junior."

"And look how well she turned out. She has a child's mind in a woman's body. Indeed 'tis the body brings the bargain if I understand your logic. You would seek to vouchsafe my health and avoid any risk to the bartered goods."

"The Palatine will have you for his wife." My father pointed a finger at the floor.

"The Palatine can go hang." I turned away defeated, then back again to face him once more. "Why am I not permitted to see my brother?"

"Now then, we will have an end to this." There was an edge to his voice that was all too familiar, which meant anything I might say at this point would only strengthen his maddening resolve, fortify his obstinate and self-righteous intransigence.

"Yes, by all means, you must be allowed to get back to your precious drawings. Mr. Jones awaits. But be assured the matter is not put to rest."

"Good day to you, daughter."

The silence that fell between us in that moment was deeper and more troubling than any that had come before. It bore witness to those last remnants of my privileged naivety, now forever vanquished. I turned to hasten from the room.

"And good day to you, Sir." I shivered, turned to look back over my shoulder. "But shall I call you Father?"

And upon that uttering, I tell you, my father became a ghost to me, as he remained ever after.

Chapter Five

I despaired of being admitted to my brother's bedside that I might minister to him myself, provide some modicum of comfort if nothing else, for I had witnessed such remedy effect a cure where all else failed, but then something quite unexpected happened that gave me hope. It came about as a result of my father's insistence, his eldest son's illness notwithstanding, that the regaling of the visiting Palatine should carry on unabated. He had arranged for an evening of musical recitals at which Prince Frederick should be the guest of honour, and insisted upon my presence. I was in no mood, but being pressured on all sides, not the least by Lady Anne Dudley, and remembering the pleas of my brother's letter, gave consent to do so.

By my guess Lady Anne's urgings had less to do with an interest in music, or any desire to obey protocol, than with the prospect of Count Schomberg's company. Whenever she spoke of him an animation came over her that was unmistakable. To think that even my Maid of Honour's trusted advice should now be compromised by her own interests!

The evening passed uneventfully, and though I was seated next to Prince Frederick, we spoke little. I was content to let him devote his attentions to the various musicians until, thinking the proceedings ended and making ready to take his leave, he was as surprised as the audience when I held him back.

“I have arranged for one final performance,” I announced, “if you will indulge me.”

“By all means, Madam, let’s hear another.” The Palatine sat back down in his chair.

“It is not one chosen by the King” — I glanced up at my father, dared him to intervene — “but rather a favourite of his eldest son.”

“Would Prince Henry was here tonight with us and not confined to his sickbed,” said the Palatine. “I shall think of him when I listen to this music.”

At that I signalled to the attendant and Captain Hume made his way onto the stage, followed by a page carrying his beaten and tattered viola da gamba, which he leaned against a chair next to the fireplace. The Captain made his bows, sat down to take up his instrument, and set it firmly between his knees.

“It is that same fellow we encountered at the Queen’s masque the other night?” observed Count Schomberg.

“Indeed,” Lady Anne remarked. “And no less shoddy in appearance.”

“The same could be said for his instrument,” offered the Count.

“Sir?”

“His viola da gamba,” Count Schomberg explained. “It looks to be in dire need of some refurbishing.”

“Much like the man himself,” added Lady Anne.

The page now set the sheet music on the stand before Captain Hume, at which he took great pains to arrange it.

“You should like him well enough if it came time to defend your honour,” I said.

“Be assured I have no need of such.”

“I should be in a better position to defend it,” the Count boasted eagerly, “than that scruffy musician.”

“It may be of interest to you, Count,” I said, “that when the Captain is not composing music to play upon his viola da gamba, he serves upon the battlefield.”

"You mean as a player for the men."

"As a soldier in his own right." Lady Anne's firm response surprised me.

"One with a reputation," the Palatine added. "Apparently he can acquit himself with a sword as well as with a bow."

"Musician and soldier, you say?" The Count sounded sceptical. "It is rare to find in one personage two such ambitions."

"I dare say he has yet ambitions to more than that." I glanced at Lady Anne.

"That same viola da gamba you see there," said the Palatine, "Prince Henry tells me that his young page totes it along for the Captain wherever he goes, that he might compose music in the comfort of his tent after a day in armour upon the battlefield."

"It seems unsuited to a man," said the Count, "that he should seek to be both artist and warrior."

"How so?" asked the Palatine.

"The battlefield will make a different kind of man out of you," said the Count.

"You do not say if't be for better or for worse," I said. "Which would you venture, Lady Anne?"

"Neither. A man is still a man and nothing more."

Now the King spoke up. "What are we to hear?" He was surrounded by the usual entourage of popinjays, young men who strutted about in every manner of ridiculous, if fashionable, attire. They were, to a man, sycophants of the worst kind. The only one who despised them more than I did was my brother Henry.

"A new composition, Your Majesty," replied Captain Hume. "I trust it shall be to your liking."

"The King cares not for his compositions," Lady Anne whispered to Count Schomberg.

"And yet you shall hear such playing as never fails to give his son much enjoyment," I said.

Now Captain Hume took up the bow and adjusted the tension with great care and prepared to play.

"We would know the name of this piece, Sir," I said loudly. The Captain had a habit of bequeathing upon his compositions unlikely and often suggestive titles which lesser composers liked to ridicule.

"Beg pardon, Madam. We have entitled it, 'My Mistress Hath a Pretty Thing,'" he answered.

"There's a bawdy reference," huffed Count Schomberg.

Now the Captain began to play, and no sooner had he started than he fell into those eccentric mannerisms that always proved to be such a distraction to the audience. Not once during his playing did he bother to consult the tablature before him, but rather with eyes now cast down, now turned up at the ceiling, set his body to writhing in the worst kind of way, as an actor might, having been slain upon the rough boards of the Globe. His body seemed under torture, as though he were engaged in some great inner turmoil. And yet, such glorious and melancholy notes flowed from his instrument that the audience became entirely silent and attentive. When he had finished he sat for some time, shoulders stooped, head down, seemingly exhausted, before lifting his head to acknowledge the polite applause.

The Palatine eagerly beckoned the Captain over. "Tell me, Mr. Hume."

"Captain Hume, if't please Your Highness."

"By all means — Captain Hume, then. I'm curious, Sir, how is it you came to be not only a musician but a soldier as well?"

"By that same manner as do other men, namely by the taking up of arms and donning of a uniform."

"I see." The Palatine seemed not the least put off at this sardonic reply. "And have you campaigned of late?"

"I was most recently in Sweden, where I fought under King Gustavus Adolphus."

"Tell me, Captain," Count Schomberg enquired, "which do you prefer upon the battlefield, the sword or the bow?"

"I should think a worthy soldier would be master of both," allowed the Palatine.

"As an unworthy one should be of neither," the Count replied.

"I am content to be formidable at both," said Captain Hume.

"See how the man steeps himself as ever in deepest humility," Lady Anne scoffed.

"Well, I for one think it admirable you should have proficiency in both," said the Palatine, "and commend you for it."

"I pray Madam found the performance to her liking?" Captain Hume looked affectionately at Lady Anne.

"Measure for measure," she answered.

"And better in between." The Palatine seemed quite taken with Captain Hume. "For you, Sir, are a veritable master of division, if I am any judge."

"Division is all fine and good." I turned to Lady Anne. "But there must be passion as well."

"Just so," said the Palatine. "Passion and division, each in their portion."

"And you, Madam?" Captain Hume enquired further of Lady Anne. "Did you think I played with insufficient passion?"

"Just the opposite," she replied haughtily. "If I were your instrument, I should faint from excess of it."

"You would have me play you, then?" teased Captain Hume.

"Hmph. That's bold," muttered Count Schomberg.

"As one might play at cards, he perhaps means," said the Palatine.

"I think he meant the viola da gamba," said Lady Anne.

"Well, then that could be only one way," pronounced Captain Hume.

"And what way is that?" asked the Count.

"Why, between the legs, of course," the Captain answered. At this the Count drew back, eyes wide, then made to step toward the Captain, but the Palatine put a hand on his shoulder. For my part I could not disguise my amusement at seeing Lady Anne blush so deeply.

"I have hardly seen such a rising of his cheek," I offered.

"More than cheek such rising would arouse, it would appear," said the Palatine, and we each of us let out a little laugh.

"I had not thought the English court so ribald," said the Count, still fuming.

I felt a sudden pang of guilt, realized that in spite of my best intentions I had been at sport with this prince, the enjoyment of whose company I had sworn to disavow, and that I could not despise him altogether. Yet though he seemed a decent and amiable fellow I knew already I could never love him, that much was certain. And yet here I was, about the business of contenting myself with companionship and civility, ready to barter an uncertain future for one I might tolerate.

It only occurred to me later that I may have acted out of fear, that perhaps beneath my self-reproach lurked a deeper misgiving I hardly dared acknowledge. I knew full well what my father was capable of. Ominous and threatening possibilities hovered over me, gave birth to thoughts dark and foreboding, and subverted my conviction. And buried deep beneath all of that was something even worse. What if by some design the King had a hand in his son's infirmity, and what if he should see fit to set those same designs upon his only daughter?

My father now saw fit to call the Palatine over, at which Count Schomberg went to accompany him, and it was then Captain Hume took me aside and slipped a note into my hand.

Written this day of October 25, 1612

To be delivered into the hands of Princess Elizabeth Stuart

Your Highness,

The news has reached me that your brother is gravely ill. I thought to have heard from him myself by now but there has been no word, and any correspondence I send goes unanswered. I cannot help but wonder whether by some means my letters fail to reach him at all. My contacts are increasingly limited here in the Tower, and those clandestine visits such as you and your mother on rare occasion paid here are no longer advisable. I still remember those last few times you were permitted to accompany her. How thoroughly enchanting it was to see you becoming such a striking young lady right before my eyes. It hardly seems possible that upon the next occasion you should have grown yet more exquisite.

I have placed this correspondence into the hands of Captain Hume who, upon what authority I hardly know, saw fit to hump his viola da gamba up the stairs of the Tower and play for me yester night. I think he can be trusted as well as anyone to see that it reaches you, and that your reply finds me in return, and so let me come to the matter at hand.

Do you remember some years ago when your mother fell ill and the doctors could find no remedy for her? I prepared a cordial for her which, if you recall, brought about her complete and miraculous recovery! I would see some of this same confection administered to your brother. The good Captain has procured the ingredients for me and would see it brought to you. Will you allow me to do this for Henry?

With admiration for your charmed personage, I remain,
as ever, your faithful servant,
Sir Walter Raleigh

This correspondence sparked in me an idea that should not only restore my brother's health but offered a chance to be alone with Sir Raleigh in the bargain. I should make my way to the Tower of London, notwithstanding that commoners and royalty alike were forbidden entry, save for special permission granted by the King himself. Unbeknownst to my father, I knew of a means to gain access, and I had my mother to thank for it, though she would hardly have approved of me going alone. She had been for some time paying regular visits Sir Raleigh in secret and on some occasions even saw fit to let me accompany her. To what end I know not to this day. I remembered it as the most delicious kind of daring, and the only real secret the two of us ever shared. But then she stopped going, or at any rate insisted that she had, and now I was determined to carry out the venture on my own.

The very next night found me alighting from a carriage that had come to rest before All Hallows Barking, and walking up the steps into the church. I had come upon the pretext of late-evening prayer, though the gown I wore under my cloak testified to a less devout purpose. I made my entrance unannounced, walked alone, unseen and unheeded, between the pews and past the altar, along a series of dimly lit hallways and stairs that led down into the deepest nether regions of the old church, until I arrived at a scarred, blackened wooden door of an ancient Roman vault. Here I took from a cleft in the stone wall a key known only to myself and my mother, proceeded to turn it in the lock, and pushed the heavy door ajar. The door creaked and groaned open wide enough that I might slip through and lock it once again behind me. Torches sparsely placed along the damp and grimy walls of a long, dimly lit passage led me underground and at last into the very heart of the Bloody Tower itself.

It had been some time since I had accompanied my mother along these hallways, and now I had to admit it was considerably more daunting without her. I found myself wondering for what purpose she had seen fit to bring me along in the first place. What was it she had wanted me to see, to hear? I thought of turning back but carried on for my brother's sake. He did ever love Sir Raleigh as something akin to a father, which he was certainly old enough to be. I once heard Henry say of his imprisonment, "None but my father would keep such a bird in a cage."

From the very first I had never thought of him as old in the way I did my father, but rather as a handsome and dashing figure of some considerable maturity. I had sensed on those earlier visits that there was something going on between my mother and him, something both illicit and exciting, and which roused in me a troubling sense of anticipation. It was true that one of his medicinal confections had once cured my mother of a terrible illness that none of the doctors could vanquish, and that I wanted to procure the same medicine for my brother, but though I hardly dared to admit as much, I wanted more than that from Sir Walter.

I had made sure to bring sufficient coin that I might bribe the Yeoman Warders who, though mostly a soused and sorry lot, would have to be mollified, as they could hardly be counted upon to act nobly otherwise. It was my hope that I might be allowed not only to see Sir Raleigh but also to look in on my cousin Arabella, though I knew not where in the Tower she was being kept. It was my understanding the location was a strictly kept secret for fear that Lord Seymour, who was still at large, should make an attempt to rescue her. Still, I intended to enquire as to her whereabouts.

After ascending a flight of steep and narrow stairs I stood before a heavy wooden door where, after some hesitation, I steeled myself to take hold of the enormous iron ring hanging there and knock loudly. The percussion echoed back down the stairwell until it seemed the whole of the Tower must know I was there, alone, with nothing to protect me but my title. Finally a guard appeared at the door and pushed his bearded face up against the small barred window of the dank and blackened door.

"Who knocks here upon this door at such an inconvenient hour?" He eyed me up and down, still chewing on a beef bone, and wiped at his greasy mouth.

"As you see," I replied evenly. I had deliberately timed my arrival to coincide with the ceremony of the keys, the better to have as few Yeomen Warders as possible hanging about.

"I see naught but a woman cloaked and would know what lies beneath."

"To what end?"

"That such a garment may conceal that which I should have cause to appropriate."

"You have nothing to fear."

"I would have you remove it nevertheless."

"Very well," I took the cloak from my shoulders and draped it across my arm.

"Upon my word, save for that gown which naught but those born into royalty may hope to wear, your looks betray you for a saucy wench."

"Take care, Warder. It is the Princess Elizabeth, come to see Sir Walter Raleigh."

"But this cannot be that scrawny lass we call the King's daughter."

I held out a pouch of coins for him to see. "Here is some enticement that may speed my entry."

He put his hand through the bars to grab for it, but I pulled it away.

"I would have admittance first."

"An' I would 'ave that purse, Your Graciousness."

"I can as well offer it up to another Yeoman Warder and not yourself if you will persist in this insolence."

"You come alone." A sneer flashed across the Yeoman's lips. "Where is your mother?"

"I have business of my own to see to."

"It will cost you extra."

"On the contrary, it will be less, as there is but one to admit."

"A royal princess travelling alone requires careful handling, Your Eminence."

"I would have you open this door."

The key turned in the lock and the heavy door creaked on its iron hinges as the guard swung it wide. No sooner had I stepped through then the Warder held out his hand for the pouch, which I placed into it. He weighed it in his palm, fondled it with blackened fingers, all the while looking me up and down.

"And how be" — he leaned over me, his cheesy breath upon my neck — "if I should require yet some favour more than this?"

"Then you would be a fool" — I forced myself to speak in a steady voice, breathed evenly — "as your lechery should quickly see you beheaded."

"I grant the interval between pleasure and punishment might prove short." The Warder scratched at his beard. "But oh, what delights might lie 'tween the two."

"On second thought, before they hang you, I shall see your mutton dagger is cut off and burned before your eyes." My forced viewing of those atrocities visited upon the guilty Mr. Fawkes some years ago now served to conjure up these images for this drunken lout. "After which I shall have you gutted and disembowelled."

The Warder's expression changed and he drew back a little. "Upon reflection, Your Magnificence, this coin may yet suffice to bring about by other means less royal that which I now forsake. This way," he grumbled, and led me down a hallway bounded on both sides by gloomy stone walls until we reached Sir Raleigh's quarters, where he shouted through the barred window of the heavy wooden door: "Visitor. Will the prisoner be seen?"

"Who is it?" I heard a familiar voice say.

"None but she what was a scrawny freckled princess and is now burgeoned into shapely womanhood." He leered at me, coughed and spat. "I say this only that you should be better prepared to recognize her as at first I did not."

As much as this Yeoman's stare disgusted me, the prospect of Sir Raleigh's gaze sent a thrilling hum of expectancy through me. I had seen him look at my mother in a certain way, seen how his mannerism, even a simple gesture, effortlessly undid her composure and caused her to blush uncontrollably. What effect should he bring to bear upon me? I wondered.

"Make entry."

The Yeoman turned the key in the lock and swung the door open to reveal within a chamber of bare walls, but a single shuttered window set into the whitewashed stone at one end of the room, a tiny hearth at the other where a few embers smouldered, and not a single arras hung to keep out the damp. Sir Walter looked up from his writing desk, quill poised above some papers upon which he had no doubt been scribbling furiously. The chair and desk were of dark burled wood elaborately carved, and their baroque appearance seemed misplaced in such an austere setting, but the same could be said for Sir Raleigh himself. He lowered the quill slowly down into the inkwell, rose from his chair, and stepped out from behind the desk. As much as this Warder was the embodiment of filth and dishevelment, Sir Raleigh was a picture of fashion and grooming unmatched even in the highest circles beyond those walls. He was dressed impeccably in a tight-fitting leather jerkin closed at the waist and worn over an embroidered doublet that accentuated his narrow waist and broad shoulders. A crisply frilled Tudor ruff encircled his neck while a finely cut pair of trunk hose, quilted and paned, complemented the silken cannions upon his shapely legs and the polished leather pinsons upon his feet.

"What's this, then?" He looked at me with such open and piercing attraction that I was speechless. "Can it be?" He stepped toward me. "Do my eyes deceive me?"

"I had hoped to catch you at your leisure," I managed, "and not intrude upon your work."

"Your Highness." He bowed and brushed his lips lightly across the back of my outstretched hand. "We are humbled and honoured at your presence here." He straightened, reached for my cloak, "Here, let me take that," he said, lifted it from my shoulders and draped it across his arm, then stepped back a little to take in the length of me, starting at my feet and rising slowly until his blue eyes were looking into mine. I tried to act nonchalant, but in truth had gone to some lengths that the manner of my clothing and appearance should accentuate those charms that were new even to me.

Bad enough I had a brother — the very person I loved more than anyone in the world — who was gravely ill, and that I was about to reconcile myself to an arranged marriage, but to play at seduction with a married man twice my age? To be a wanton creature of flesh chasing what it desired? And yet my young blood could not lie. Such urges and yearnings as might have been conquered by scripture and prayer I had no inclination to stifle. I was enamoured, undaunted by the limits of age or station, certain that it was more than mere infatuation. There was something about the way he carried himself, the timbre of his masculine voice, the trim of his beard and moustache, I could not resist.

"By Heaven." Sir Raleigh took up a thread of my hair, which I had deliberately chosen to wear down, that it might fall freely across my shoulders and over the raised lace collar, "this Yeoman may be a drunken and insubordinate fool but he's right about one thing: you are indeed flowered into beauteous womanhood."

"And you," I replied evenly, "manage yet to maintain the height of fashion even under these trying conditions."

Sir Raleigh turned to address the guard. "Yeoman, we would have some privacy. Leave us."

"It is not for you to order me about." The Warder stood defiant, swaying slightly from side to side.

"I have given him no small recompense," I informed Sir Raleigh.

"You are well paid for your services, Yeoman." Sir Raleigh waved him off with the back of his hand.

"That's none of your doing."

"Take heed not to overstep your bounds" — Sir Raleigh glared at him — "for I have yet some means to compel your compliance if it should come to that."

"And so I'll take my leave, but it shall not be long until my return. Make it quick." The Yeoman turned to go.

"And remember" — Sir Raleigh pointed at the bag in his hand — "some of that's for the others. We would be assured of their complicity."

Sir Raleigh draped the cloak over the back of his chair and strode over to the stone hearth. He picked up two small pieces of wood and knelt down to lay them into the embers. "Come, sit here and warm yourself." He indicated the chair before the fire. "You must be chilled."

When I had seated myself he pulled up a small wooden stool and proceeded to poke up the fire. "I would put on more wood, but the daily ration I am provided with is hardly enough to keep my hands from freezing. So often I am tempted to build a roaring fire, but when it dies I am faced with prospect of a cold and empty hearth."

"To long for that which one may not have is cruel punishment indeed."

"I confess there have been times when I thought of burning these same papers to bring some much-needed warmth into the room, yet would I gladly endure the cold to have some means of recording my thoughts."

"You work upon some grand treatise, no doubt."

"I have undertaken to write a history of the world in three parts, the first of which is near completion."

"I could hardly imagine taking on such a task."

"It requires only sufficient knowledge and the necessary resolve, though I will say the latter is made easier when four walls enclose your entire life from sunrise to sunset, from one day to the next, year upon year. Even then I should make better progress if naught betimes I turned to scripting verse."

"And for whom do you write these verses?"

"For none but their own sake, so I should not go mad."

"And they are not written for a secret lover?"

"You shall have many a verse written for you, I don't doubt. I might deign to scribble one or two if I were a younger man."

"An older man may flavour his rhymes with a more seasoned affection," I offered.

Another wave of guilt washed over me. To think I should see fit to stoop so selfishly into indulgent flirtation, play at such intrigues even as my brother Henry suffered in his bedchamber. Shameful! And yet I wished Sir Raleigh would try to kiss me.

"I am well-seasoned, I grant," he had moved a little closer now, "and you are so very young."

"Not too young to marry, it would seem."

"I had heard something of this." He leaned back and turned to rub his hands together over the fire. "They say a Bohemian prince is come to woo you."

"By my father's arrangement."

"And you like him well enough?"

"What think you on this dress?" I asked.

"Madam?"

"I would know if it pleases you." The tawny orange gown I chose had a closefitting boned bodice cut low and trimmed at the neckline with lace. The sleeves and bodice were embroidered with black velvet brocade and edged with gold trim, the skirt adorned in blackwork and flared out sharply, supported by a boned satin kirtle beneath. Hung about my neck was a string of black pearls set into white ivory.

"I'm pleased the wearer lends it such a lovely shape."

"Do you flatter, Sir?"

"As I might flatter any garment if it be made to look so well."

"I would hear a verse or two of your poetry." I rose from the chair. "What have you written of late?"

"Shall I recite off the top of my head?"

"As you like."

"Very well, but I must walk. Let me see . . . 'Fain would I, but I dare not . . . I dare, and yet I may not.'" He was on his feet now pacing about the room. "'I may, although I care not . . . for pleasure when I play not.'"

"That's more like doggerel," I said disdainfully.

"'You pierce,'" he teased, still reciting, "'although you strike not.'"

"I hope for what I have not."

"This foreign Prince shall count himself lucky if you consent to marry him."

"Yours am I," I stepped toward him, "though I seem not. Yet bleed I where you see not."

We were close now, standing before the flickering fire. "These are visions that would tempt a man." Sir Raleigh looked into my eyes.

"But have I tempted you?"

"I forbear." He stepped away, strode across the room.

"Lest the King should hear of it and find his only daughter spoiled for marriage immaculate," I scorned.

"That would be such sweet sabotage to play upon your father. But I would know if you think him worthy."

"Who, my father?"

"I mean this Palatine. I have it that upon first meeting you fell to gazing into each other's eyes, followed thereupon by a kiss as two lovers might exchange."

"Much may turn upon a kiss."

"He has prospects for a kingship, this Palsgrave, as your mother is wont to call him?"

"She's been here, then?"

"I hear things."

"I take him for a pawn and myself for another," I said, and turned the conversation, at last, to the stated reason for my visit. "But I didn't come here to talk about that. I would see my brother freed of his affliction, and you say you have the means."

"I understand your father has engaged a French physician of some repute to take charge of his care."

"One whose remedies do more harm than good, I fear."

"And also that Alfonso Ferrabosco, of all people, is now appointed Groom-in-Extraordinary to your brother?"

"You seem to know quite as much as I about all of this."

"Would Henry were here for me to greet and give warm handshakes to. Your brother will make an excellent king one day, perhaps sooner than people think. I should take better measures to see to his good fortune and future if I were a free man."

"He has assured me more than once that as soon as he is king you shall be exactly that."

"When you see him next, tell him the first volume of this book I am completing shall be dedicated to him."

"I should be glad to do so, but I cannot. I am not allowed to see him."

"But what can be the reason? Say not they fear the plague."

"My father has seen to it I shall not be admitted to his

bedchamber, and goes to such lengths as to post guards at the door."

"This bodes ill. But how then shall this medicine reach him?"

"Leave that to me."

Sir Walter walked over to a corner of the room and reached up to open the door of a cupboard on the wall. Inside, the shelves were cluttered with jars, vials, and the general apparatus of alchemy. He brought out a vial, lifted it up to the light, removed the cork, and sniffed the contents before placing it on the small table beneath. Next he took another jar from the shelf and removed a few strands of dried plant material which he placed into a mortar and pestle that sat before him on the table.

"The ingredients are numerous and varied." He took up the pestle and began to grind up the leaves. "And some I have only just procured, as these leaves of scordium, which some call water germander or creeping plant of Malta." He pinched some of the ground-up material between his fingers, lifted up the vial, and sprinkled it in.

Some I grew myself in the small patch of garden they allow me, such as flowers of borage, sundew and rod elder, betony and cubebs of juniper berries. Others I obtained from Yeomen Warders in exchange for malted spirits I prepare and make available to them when their rum rations run out. For this batch I have also added shavings of hartshorn, and roots of angelica . . . oh, and valerian, and fraxinella and tormentil."

"It is a dizzying list of elements."

"There are yet others of more import, as viper's flesh, hearts and livers, juice of kermes, and dittany of Crete, also bastard ditanny and zedoary." He took down a small green bottle and removed the cork. "I'll just add this last."

"What is it?"

"Virginia snake root, which may serve to ease a fever."

"Brought back from the New World, no doubt."

"Indeed."

"They say you brought back many an unknown substance from that place."

"It was at the King's urging I sought them out. He took a great interest in them, in particular those of a toxic nature."

"There are those who say it is your knowledge of exotic potions my father would keep under wraps, and to that end locks you up in here."

"Your father has a great fear of foul play."

"As his overstuffed peasecod will attest to, that a dagger thrust should not inflict a mortal wound."

Sir Raleigh spooned up the contents of the mortar and fed them into the vial, then twirled the mixture for a moment before re-corking it. "There" — he looked up at me — "it's ready. I fear I shall soon have some need of this myself, if only to stave off the ill effects of this damp and godforsaken place."

"It is a shade of kermes I have never seen before, almost as red as blood. Do you think it will make him well again?"

"I have seen it work against all but poisoning."

A squawking at the window interrupted us and I turned to see a raven alight on the window ledge, feathers askew here and there on his black body, head misshapen. I had seen these birds on previous visits as they were always about the place, fighting amongst themselves for scraps, but never one that looked to be so rumpled as this.

"That's Arthur," said Sir Raleigh, "come to visit of an evening as he is wont to do after the Yeomen are drunk and staggered off to bed. He lost an eye to a Warder's halberd, which gave him also his crooked beak."

"They say if a raven alight upon your window you shall know it for a sign."

"Of what?"

"I do not think I should say."

I stepped over to peek through the bars of the door and realized it had been left slightly ajar. I pushed at it a little until

I could see out into the hall, where I discovered the guard asleep, chin on his chest, in a wooden chair propped against the wall at the end of the hall.

"The guard is asleep," I said. "We can do as we like."

"There are others who come by, though they should doubtless be no more sober."

"I had thought to see my cousin Arabella Stuart while I was here."

Sir Raleigh seemed a trifle unsettled at this remark. "She is under strictest confinement."

"I received a letter from her."

"You are fortunate. The lion's share of such correspondence seems destined to disappear around here."

"She mentioned you."

"How so?"

"That she was jealous of your fireplace." I walked to the mantle and stood before it. "How would she know about this?"

"I can't imagine. There are always rumours and whispers scuttling about the Tower."

"But you haven't seen her?"

Sir Raleigh ignored my question. "This letter you received, you're certain it's authentic?"

"It is in her hand."

Sir Raleigh placed a hand on either side of his small writing desk. "There's naught and no one to be trusted in this place."

"What can you tell me of her circumstances?"

"The King is greatly displeased with her."

"As he is with me."

"You are his daughter."

"That counts for little." I went to stand before him.

"I have yet such means to keep the guards quiet about your visit here, but I cannot say the same for Arabella. You don't know what your father is capable of."

"More and more, I think I do."

"Then heed me."

"I have brought this," I held out the letter I had written. "Can you see she gets it?"

"Leave it with me." He indicated that I should place it on the desk. "But I make no promises."

"Answer me this." I put down the letter and stepped closer to the window, where the raven shifted awkwardly from one foot to the other. "Why do you stay here, when you could just as easily escape? It isn't as though these buffoons can muster the means to stop you."

"They were not so shabby a lot when the Tower was in the care of Sir John Peyton. He demanded discipline of his Yeoman Warders and always treated me with kindness and respect. I vouchsafe your brother will restore this place to good order when he ascends the throne."

"You know you will be free the moment Henry wears the crown."

"Indeed. He has told me himself that when the day comes for him to stay here on the eve of his coronation, as is the custom, he shall personally instruct the chief Yeoman to listen upon the next morning for the cannon at Westminster Abbey that signals his crowning, at which," Sir Walter pointed at the door, "the key shall be turned in that lock, and I shall walk hence a free man. But for now the matter is a delicate one."

"You should take leave of this place."

"Your father would send his men after me and I should doubtless be recaptured."

"But what if you sailed once more for the New World? When your cordial has made Henry well again, he would jump at the chance to go with you."

"Indeed, I did once broach that very subject with your father, but he would not hear of it."

"And I would come, too, if you would have me. I have a great longing to see it."

"You would doubtless find it a wild and frightening place." He went to sit before the fire and bade me join him there. "The untamed land broods with a kind of savagery that lends a raw edge to each day's blazing sun, and pale nakedness to the primitive moon of night."

"You speak of it as a poet might."

"And always the wilderness just beyond the gate."

"I think I should love it." I sat down across from him.

"A man may live in such a place and make of himself a king in his own right, with no one to answer to, and a few such men can change the world."

"The same might be said for a woman." I straightened, fixed him with a steady gaze. "Where there are such kings, there can also be queens."

"Indeed, Virginia is named for just such a one, that being your godmother."

"I should prefer to settle farther north. They say the Newfoundland is a glorious place. I have heard it is an island as rich as any on this side of the Atlantic. In any case, the New World seems better suited to my nature than this old one that sighs and moans under the weight of royal robes and courtly manners."

"You really wish to endure such hardship and isolation?" He leaned forward a little.

"These same things exist here, only they are dressed up in the finery of stately decorum."

"Those traits a woman may consider an asset here are more like a liability there."

"So the place would make a new kind of woman out of me."

"Woman or man, to both it brings a kind of sleep at night, a kind of waking at break of day hitherto unknown. A certain disposition for work and industry, a willingness to forgo luxury, forsake comforts. There's little room for human frailty."

I rose from my chair. "I would be put to the test."

"Madam." He rose as I approached him. "It is hard, I tell you."

"Sir?"

"You take me wrongly."

"You take me not at all."

He put his hand upon my waist and drew me nearer. "And what of the Palatine? Would you have him take you?"

"Not wrongly."

"We play at words."

"And little else."

Footfalls sounded hollow upon the stone floor and stopped at the door. The Warder looked in through the bars. "Time, Your Sumptuousness," he said, and turned the key.

Sir Raleigh squeezed the vial into my waiting hands. I took it from him with great care, felt the warmth of the contents. He took up the cloak from the chair and draped it around my shoulders. I tucked the vial into one of the inner pockets.

"Best take your leave," Sir Raleigh said quietly, "though I say so with regret." He turned to the guard. "Yeoman Warder, be sure to see to her Highness's safe passage, or I shall find means to bring you to account."

"Very well, Sir, she will not come to harm. Come along, Your Grandness."

I followed the Yeoman down the hall, and when I was sure we were out of earshot from Sir Raleigh, hailed him to stop.

"What would you have of me?" asked the Yeoman. "The hour is late and we must get you to the door."

"A moment if you please."

He turned to face me, waited.

"I would enquire of Lady Arabella."

"You and some others. What of her?"

"She's here in the Tower?"

"I know not her whereabouts."

"But there are those who do."

"It matters little. Your visit is at an end."

"Is there any way I might be allowed to see her, just for a moment?"

"You have not paid for such a visit."

"I've given you plenty."

"It will take more than that to bring such about."

"If I come back with more, will you see to it?"

"It will not be me you deal with."

"Whom, then?"

"Those I must answer to."

"Tell me what I should do."

"You should put off this nattering and follow me. I'll say no more. You are past your time." He turned and walked ahead of me, checked to see that I followed. We made our way back down the stairs and along the darkened passageway, the Yeoman glancing now and then over his shoulder at me in a way that made me finger the vial concealed beneath my cloak, steel myself to employ it as weapon of barter if it should come to that. Then we were at the blackened door and he fumbled with the keys to unlock it. When I had gone through and the door had closed behind me, I turned to address him one last time through the bars of the small window.

"There's nothing more you can tell me?"

"None but this: it were better that your royal personage should visit here no more. There's mischief afoot in this place such as you were best to keep clear of."

With that his face disappeared and I heard his footfalls receding down the hallway. As I rode back to Richmond in the carriage, I thought what Arabella would think of me, if she learned that I had been so near and failed to visit her. I was disappointed that I had been defeated so easily and promised myself I would find a way to atone for it. But first I had to make my brother well again, and thereafter I should find the means to see to all the rest.

Chapter Six

Upon my arrival at St. James's the next morning it was clear that word of my brother's condition had spread, as I found the outer chambers occupied with courtiers mingling about, musicians and artists, politicians and clergymen, all of them eager to hear some news of the Prince's condition, trusting that by blandishment of their concern the chances for an appointment might increase when he had recovered. Some were doubtless convinced that it could not be long before my brother should accede to the throne and by that ascendance see their ambitions realized. Others, though already in the employ of the King or Queen, were ready to jump ship, fearful that they should see an end to their privilege and profligacy, as there was bound to be less in the way of extravagant masques and frivolous building projects should Henry become king.

As I made my way to the inner chambers I was forced to endure their fawnings and greetings, suffer myself to be bowed and curtsied to, acknowledge their entreaties of sympathy, until at last Lady Anne came to my rescue and I took refuge in a private antechamber, where to my surprise the Palatine and Count Schomberg were already seated, both of whom rose when I entered the room.

"Your Highness," Prince Frederick strode toward me. I studied the details of his apparel as he crossed the room. He took my hand and kissed it politely. "I wish it were under happier circumstances that we meet again," he said, "and yet I confess I am glad to see you. I hope this is not too much of an intrusion. How is your brother?"

"What is the meaning of this?" I looked over at Lady Anne. The Prince was wearing padded breeches with knee-length cannions and silk garters over laced leather shoes, and a fine embroidered doublet with ruff and flat lace collar, all of which I recognized at once.

"Your Highness?"

"Those clothes belong to Henry."

"I took the liberty of making some of Prince Henry's wardrobe available to Prince Frederick," said Lady Anne.

"On whose authority did you so?"

"We spoke at the play," Prince Frederick explained, "and it was then your brother offered me the use of his wardrobe."

"I see. Still, it were better I had been consulted in this matter."

"You were busy with more pressing matters, Madam," Lady Anne offered, "and I thought to spare you the details."

"Tell me, Sir, how is it you seek after the health of a man you hardly know, yet whose clothes you see fit to don? If you seek to curry favour by this means, you miss the mark."

"Madam, I make no affect," the Prince brushed aside a few strands of thick dark hair that had curled down over his forehead, "and grant I know your brother only from a few short interludes, but you must believe I am in earnest." I searched his face for something to betray his sincerity. "I will attest he and I have exchanged little more than a few words and handshakes, yet it were as though I had met the best companion of my life." His features seemed darker, more mature than I last remembered. "I know not how else to give account but to beg your indulgence that I might be allowed to accompany you when you go in to see him."

"Then you've come for naught."

"You do not wish me to see him?"

"It is not my indulgence you need pursue in the matter, as I am banished from his bedside, else I should be there now and not here talking to you."

"But why should it be so?"

"The King decrees it," said Lady Anne.

"On what grounds?" asked the Prince.

"No doubt he fears a miasma in the room," offered the Count, "and would not see Her Majesty exposed to it."

"He fears a great deal more than that," I said, "but all the same his arguments are equally feeble."

Now a buzz went through the adjoining chambers and Dr. Mayerne stepped in from the far door in black gown and white collar, cap upon his head. "Oh, excuse me," he offered, "I was just on my way through and this is the quickest route." He was toting a carton of small glass vials in a carrying case. "Your Highness, if you have come to enquire after your brother, Dr. Butler can convey the latest reports."

"I would hear them from you. How does my brother?"

"Neither better nor worse for the morning." The Doctor was clearly annoyed, the tone of his words dismissive. "Give else enquiry to Dr. Butler if you must."

"You are in the midst of a procedure, dry cupping from the look of it."

"I will take my leave, Highness."

"You suspect some blockage of humours, I take it."

"I see you would yet grace us with your medical expertise." Dr. Mayerne raised an eyebrow.

"Bile, I should hope, for it will not work as well on other humours."

"Excuse me, but —"

"I have a request." I softened my tone. "If you will not allow me in to see him, will you at least grant that a musician may be allowed to go in and play for him, that it should bring him some small comfort?"

"I concern myself not with such matters, Highness, but you may take it up with the groom of the chamber if you wish."

"And if he agrees, then it shall be permitted?" I persisted.

"Yes, fine, but only for a few minutes. He must have his rest."

"Thank you, Doctor."

"Now if you will excuse me."

I made my way to the anteroom, where as usual all were about, such as grooms and apothecaries, surgeons and attendants. I was alarmed to see the vicar there. It was clear the situation had worsened. I searched out Dr. Butler and pulled him aside.

"Tell me, how does my brother?"

"He is very ill."

"What remedies do they now apply? I saw a man just now making his way into the room with a pair of chickens. Do not say it has come to that."

"They have tried everything, Your Highness."

"Say not flayed pigeons to the feet."

Dr. Butler's expression told me the answer.

"So now they will shave his head."

Dr. Butler nodded.

The image in my mind of my brother with all of his glorious locks shorn away terrified me, brought with it the prospect of suffering to come, of trials yet to be endured, of possible finality beyond contemplation.

"What if I should give you something for Henry?"

"Your Highness?"

"Some medicine. And perhaps a letter."

"Dr. Mayerne will not allow it."

"You could administer it yourself."

"I am closely watched. As it is, the guards allow only Dr. Mayerne and his attendants to enter."

In the despair of that moment I hit upon a plan that might

yet allow me to bring aid to my brother. They say the best ideas are born of crisis, though I can hardly characterize what followed as admirable. I'm not proud of what I did. Still, it was a small price to pay if it would save my brother's life. Given all that was happening in my young life, I very much needed Henry to stay alive. If he was going to die he should have to wait for a more suitable time to do so. Even as the fog of my own misgivings closed in on me, I pushed it away and set about to make him well again.

"What of Alfonso Ferrabosco?" I asked.

"He comes and goes as he pleases."

"And is he allowed to be accompanied by an attendant or two?"

"If he should deem it necessary."

"Very well. Thank you, good Doctor, I must take my leave."

And so I determined to render myself alone in one of the outer chambers with a man who made my flesh creep, if doing so would gain Captain Hume entry to my brother's chambers. It was well known that Henry was fond of the Captain's compositions and not unusual for musicians to play for the sick and dying, that it should bring them comfort. No one would think much of it. I had only thereafter to place into the Captain's hands Sir Raleigh's cordial and give him instruction for administering it.

I arranged to meet Ferrabosco in one of the antechambers near to my brother's room, making sure to be within earshot of assistance if I should deem it necessary.

"Sir," I began as soon as we were alone, "I understand you are appointed Groom-in-Extraordinary to my brother, the Prince of Wales."

"Indeed, the King has seen fit to confer that honour upon me." A triumphant leer thinned his lips.

"Then you may see fit to allow me entrance to my brother's chamber."

"You know I cannot." He seemed almost gleeful to give me his answer. "And more than this, I am expressly commanded by your father to see such a visitation does not take place."

"And what of another visitor?"

"Madam?"

"How be it if someone other than myself were to pay my brother a visit?"

"And who might that be?"

"Captain Hume."

Ferrabosco curled his lips in distaste. "Out of the question, I'm afraid."

"You understand it would only be to play a piece or two for my brother upon the viola da gamba."

"I could as well undertake such a task if it came to that."

"Of course, but you have other duties that must be seen to, and the Captain is eager to be of service."

"I'm sorry, I can't permit it."

It was obvious that a somewhat more assertive approach would be needed.

"Tell me, how is your new young wife . . . Ellen, is it? I have only met her briefly on one or two occasions at court, but I should think it easy enough for the two of us to become better acquainted."

Ferrabosco eyed me suspiciously. "I hardly see why you should wish to do so. What could it hope to come to?"

"Why, friendship, of course, and intimacy. You favor intimacy, do you not, Sir?"

"I should think she has little to offer your acquaintance, Madam."

"Ah, but what of the other way round? Perhaps she might like to learn more about your childhood, and how it was that you came to live in the household of Gomer van Awsterwyke while your father chose to take up residence in Italy." Alfonso the Elder had abandoned his two illegitimate children and left them to the care of others. "That would surely be a subject of great interest, don't you think?"

All the blood drained from Ferrabosco's face. He remained silent until at length the words spat forth: "I had not thought so refined a royal princess capable of such vulgar treachery."

I made sure to stay calm and detached. "You will do me this favour and that will be an end of it. Are we agreed?"

Ferrabosco offered a scowling nod.

"Very well, I shall send the Captain presently. And you will receive him, thereafter to allow him some privacy with my brother. Good day to you, Sir."

Having set the wheels in motion for my plan to be carried out, I sat down at the desk in my brother's study to await the arrival of Captain Hume, whom I had sent for. I made use of the intervening time to compose a note for him take to my brother along with the vial of Sir Raleigh's cordial.

Dearest Henry,

That I must pen these words rather than letting you hear them from my lips tears at my heart. I hope you can forgive me for not being there to take your hand in mine, place a gentle kiss upon your brow, offer such words of love and encouragement as I know you are in need of, but our father forbids it. I have pleaded with him to no avail. He insists there may be a miasma in the room and seeks to protect me from it, though I have made enquiries of the physicians and determined you have not the plague, so you may rest easy on that score.

I have met with Dr. Mayerne and doubt he can be trusted. The treatments he offers are more like to make things worse as better. In particular you must refuse the doses of calomel he seeks to administer, as I have better medicine for you. I have procured some of Sir Raleigh's cordial! As soon as you finish this letter, Captain Hume shall see that you get some. Do you remember how it restored our mother even when the physicians could do nothing? It is guaranteed to work against all but poison. Take it and refuse all the rest!

I write this letter seated at the desk in your study, and it gives me comfort to do so. I have taken the trouble to place my seal upon this letter and urge you to do the same. If you have not the necessary means, I can send them with Captain Hume upon his next visit. I think it best we keep our correspondence private, as there may be those about who would be privy to it for less than noble purposes.

Are they giving you proper food to eat? I should be there now spooning up a bowl of hot soup for you to enjoy. I swear if I am not soon admitted to your bedchamber I shall find other means to gain entry. Be prepared! I dreamt last evening that you and I were walking down a brightly lit hallway in an enormous palace. For some reason I was much older than you, though you seemed to be the same age as you are now. We strolled hand in hand, and the entire time you smiled over at me in the most beatific way. There was more to the dream, but I can't seem to recall the rest of it. I think it was a good dream.

I shall write more the next time Captain Hume visits, but now it is time for you to take your medicine. Know you are not abandoned, and that I am doing everything I can to see your health restored. If you can manage a reply, however brief, it will give me great ease.

As ever I remain your loving and devoted sister,
Elizabeth

I folded the letter, picked up a stick of sealing wax and held a candle to it, watched the molten wax fall in thick ochre drops onto the seam of paper until a small, glossy puddle had formed. I had made a point of bringing with me a few threads of silk floss, green and gold, which I always liked to use for decoration on my letters, and now I laid them over the hot wax before pressing my signet ring down into it. After a moment I lifted my hand away to inspect the seal, pleased with the results, then took up the special quill and ink I'd brought to write Henry's name in gold lettering above the insignia before setting the letter aside.

I was impatient for Captain Hume to arrive and got up from the desk to busy myself with a stroll around the room, inspecting the multitude of paintings and sculpture, books and drawings, collections of antique coins, medals, gems, various scientific instruments, models of ships — all the things Henry took an interest in, their number and variety a testament to his many pursuits. Wandering ponderously about, I picked up an item here, examined another there, thinking to see about a book he may have been reading or some artefact I might have the Captain take to him if possible.

I stopped to run my fingers over the carved wood along the back of the familiar oak armchair where Henry liked to sit. How often I had found him here, reading some document or text, examining some apparatus. I imagined him seated here now, my hand on his shoulder, his face turned up to mine to greet me. I stepped around and allowed myself to settle down into the chair's smooth comfort, enjoy the warmth of the fire nearby, stare into the hypnotic glow of the shimmering embers. Drawings were spread across the table next to the chair, and on top of them I spotted the diminutive bronze horse that had been Henry's favourite since the day he acquired it. I reached out and ran the tip of one finger along the brocade mane of its elegantly curved neck and over the smooth metallic haunches. When I picked it up to examine it more closely, I was surprised how heavy it was for its small size. The sculptor had depicted the horse in mid-stride, one foreleg aloft, head perfectly poised. It had been gifted to him by the Medicis of Florence as part of a set. They were seeking an alliance at the time which would have seen Henry marry into the family. The wedding never materialized, and though my brother never said so, I suspect the little bronze horse represented those pleasures of the wider world he yearned to partake of. My father would not permit him to travel out of the country, saying always that he feared for his son's safety, but I suspected the reasons lay elsewhere.

I knew my brother would not allow himself to be controlled in that way for much longer and imagined the time should come soon enough when, free of his affliction, he would find his way to the continent. His friend John Harrington was always urging that the two of them should become travelling companions and would send Henry long letters from foreign lands, offering detailed accounts of his experiences. Once he even presented Henry with a diary of his adventures upon his return, and I had no doubt if I took the time to search I should find it upon one of the shelves in his study.

I fingered the vial of Sir Raleigh's potion in my pocket and made my way over to the window, held it up to the sunlight filtering in. The thick liquid shone a ruby-red, as of seasoned wine or fresh blood, and I closed my eyes, imagined its curative powers coursing through my brother's veins, making him well again.

I heard footfalls and turned to see Lady Anne enter. "Ah, here you are." She crossed the room. "They told me I'd find you here. I've been looking all over for you."

"I should have thought it was Count Schomberg's company you were seeking out."

Lady Anne ignored this remark and pointed at the vial in my hand. "What have you there?"

"Medicine for Henry. Sir Raleigh has made up a cordial for him."

"May I?" She put out her hand for the vial, and I gave it

over carefully. She took it from me, made herself comfortable in a Wainscot next the window, took the cork from the bottle, and sniffed lightly.

"Take pains not to spill any," I said. "It's not as though I can conjure up more."

"It has a pleasant bouquet that boasts a certain complexity, and not the bitter smell such medicines are prone to give off."

"It smells to me of health and restoration," I said, "and I had even thought to taste it myself but that, for one drop less, my brother should fail to rally."

"And what of the ingredients?"

"Too numerous to mention."

"And you say you got it from Sir Raleigh. You went to see him in the Tower? I don't suppose you want to tell me how you managed to bring that about. I would have gone with you."

"It was easier to go alone."

"And no doubt more convenient."

"It is the same medicine that cured my mother, but for one or two ingredients."

"It has the same fragrance as that elixir. I remember the King, after it had made the Queen well again, making some demand for the recipe of Sir Raleigh, who refused to divulge it, and when your father asked him why, he reasoned that in the wrong hands it might be altered and used to less noble purposes." She looked up at me, while I remained silent. "And now you have managed to procure some more of it."

I was thankful to hear more commotion in the hallway, and in a moment Count Schomberg walked into the room, followed by Captain Hume.

"At last," I said, "I thought you would never get here."

"I came as soon as I could," said the Captain, whose appearance, as usual, left a great deal to be desired. And yet I found even this to be somehow reassuring. There was an honesty about his dishevelled attire, his scraggly beard and hair, his ungainly gait, that banished all pretense. The Captain allowed himself to be directed to a chair, and paused to hang his hat upon a corner of the carved wooden back before he lowered himself onto the embroidered cushion. "How may I be of service, Madam?" he asked.

"I have a request to make of you that concerns my brother Henry."

"Now more than ever would I be of some use to him, and to you."

"Will you agree to attend his bedchamber, there to play for him upon the viola da gamba?"

"I should be honoured, only the Prince of Wales is closely guarded. None but a few are allowed in, and I am not among them. Even you yourself, I'm told, have been rudely turned away."

"It is for that very reason I am in need of your assistance. Will you take some items to him for me?"

"Madam, I am not permitted."

"You are now." I forced myself not to look over at Lady Anne. "I have arranged for your admittance."

"Then I will do it. But are you certain?"

"Alfonso Ferrabosco will personally see to it."

"But this is the very man who would as soon see me banished from the royal court altogether. How came this about?"

"You need only know," I could feel Lady Anne's gaze upon me, "that it has been seen to."

"I see." Captain Hume looked up at the others, then back at me. "We are fortunate, then."

"Take this to him." I took out the cordial. "And see that he gets it without letting anyone know. He must take a spoonful at morning, another at noon, and then again at bedtime." I handed him the vial. "And here is a note for him."

"I pray he is well enough to read it." Count Schomberg looked at Lady Anne.

"Why should you think otherwise?" I asked.

"I hardly know." Lady Anne coloured a little. "But if he is not, then you, Captain Hume, must read it to him."

"By all means, I promise to do so."

"See you keep everything secret," I added, "especially from Dr. Mayerne. The physicians, indeed no one, can be trusted."

Captain Hume made to rise but I held him back. "I would have you observe closely my brother, mark you his mood, wakefulness, whether he sits up or lies prone, his hands, whether he gesture with them or they lie still."

"I'll look to't, Your Majesty."

"Mark his colour, also his breathing, whether he exhibit any restlessness, if there be yet strength in his voice or if it tremble and falter."

"Madam," Lady Anne chided, "give the man leave, he is no physician."

"He can do as good or better than those that attend my brother now."

Captain Hume put up a hand. "Be assured I shall seek to gauge his fitness."

"Go, then. And upon your return seek me out here once again."

"I shall, Madam."

"One last thing."

"By Heaven," Lady Anne complained to the Count, "the Prince shall expire before she is through."

I took up the small bronze statue from the table next to the armchair and placed it in the Captain's hand. "Give him this also."

"I saw your brother with that in his hand at the play we attended," the Count mentioned. "He fondled it as though it were most precious to him."

"What do you think he sees in it?" asked Lady Anne.

"Who can say how the mind will linger over its subject? I look upon such as she," the Count indicated Lady Anne, "and beauty assaults me without warning."

"And what of others when they do gaze at her?" asked Captain Hume.

"I cannot speak for them."

"Do you mean to imply that others look and see not what you see?" the Captain teased.

"I have already said too much."

"Let beauty be in the eye of the beholder."

"I know a playwright who said as much."

"Here, look." I held up the small ornate box carved out of burled wood with a colour much the same as the horse. "I found the very box it came in."

"Prince Henry will be delighted, no doubt," said the Count.

I wrapped it up in a small cloth before placing it in the box. "His friend John Harington travelled there and wrote to him that in the Piazza della Signoria stood an enormous statue of the duke riding without helmet, a scroll in his hand, upon just such a horse."

"Yet this is little more than a bauble against such a work," said Lady Anne.

"The horse is fashioned after the equestrian statue of Cosimo de' Medici, Grand Duke of Tuscany. Would my brother should yet have the opportunity to go and see it for himself in Florence."

"In any case, it shall cheer him, no doubt," Lady Anne remarked, "to know that it came from you."

"Cheer?" I turned on her. "Where is such to be found in all of this?" A current of anger surged through me; I knew not why, only that I was powerless to hide it.

"I only meant . . ."

"No sweet charm of merriment shall cure Henry of his affliction nor quit me of my purpose."

I handed the statue to Captain Hume, who took it from me and turned to go. Having seen him to his task, I found myself in no mood to be waited upon, nor did I wish to make idle chatter, and allowed that Lady Anne and the Count might follow the Captain out and wait for him in one of the outer chambers, the better to escort him back when he had finished. I sat down in Henry's chair, hardly aware of my surroundings, as though I might be on the brink of sleep and yet unable to cross the threshold into that world of dreams. I had not had a good night's sleep for some time, imprisoned in a state of tiredness where I felt no more rested in the middle of the day than I did in the middle of the night. The two had become indistinguishable. I had forgotten what it felt like to fall into peaceful sleep, to wake up refreshed. I seemed something of a stranger to my own thoughts, to my body, neither of which felt entirely like mine.

A restless reverie overtook me, and I found myself in Stanwell Manor, a young girl of ten, seated at my sister Mary's bedside in the home of Elizabeth Hayward and her husband, Sir Thomas Knyvett. I was holding her outstretched hand in mine as she lay beneath the rumpled blankets, matted hair strewn across the pillows, her small body ravaged with fever, her breathing raspy and rapid. It was plain to me that she was trying very hard to stay alive. My father had granted me permission to come and visit her. Just as he had done with all of us, he had sent Mary away at infancy to be cared for by others. He harboured an intransigent mistrust borne of treachery, a prisoner to the many imagined plots and conspiracies he entertained incessantly.

I'd only ever been allowed brief visits from time to time, but I loved Mary from the first, cherished every moment she snuggled in my arms. She would look up at me with such bright innocence that it never failed to restore me, even as the first intuitions of that darkness I should soon struggle with hovered over me. She was not yet two years of age, but already upon our rare visits we had managed to engage in such intimate and delightful exchanges as only sisters can enjoy. She was especially fond of saying my name, and I marvelled how it filled my heart to hear her utter it, what holy comfort I took from such a little thing.

I was still living in Coombe Abbey at the time, but Henry had been sent off to Magdalen College at Oxford. It had been my fervent hope the Harringtons might see fit to allow Mary to come and live with me, and I had spoken to Lady Harrington about it, promising to help as much as needed with her care, but then word came that my little sister had taken ill with a fever. The attending physicians had determined she was suffering from pneumonia, which threw me into a deep dread, for there was then, as now, little remedy for that affliction. I had already lost an earlier sister, Margaret, and before that a younger brother, Robert, both in infancy. Only a few months prior, my mother had given birth to another sister, Sophia, who had died only two days later. I was only a young girl and already I'd seen too much of dying. The Harringtons pleaded with the King on my behalf, that I might be allowed to go and attend my sister's bedside, but my father refused. At that, Lord Harrington, to his eternal credit, took matters into his own hands and brought me to Stanwell Manor in secret.

"Mary," I said, "it's your sister Elizabeth, come to see you."

She opened her eyes, two blue and darkened lakes, and a weak smile crossed her swollen lips.

"Lizbeth," she uttered, her little fingers closing around one of mine.

"Mary," I said, "dear little Mary."

Her face flushed over with pain and she took in a deep breath. "I'm cold. Can I have another blanket?"

I reached down to pull a blanket over her. "There. Is that better?"

"Will you stay with me?"

"I promise." I laid a hand upon her tiny, heaving breast. She was on fire! "I'll be right here until you are well again."

"Shall I get better?"

"Of course you shall. You must be thirsty. Let me get you some water, and then you must rest."

"I don't want any water. And I don't want to go to sleep."

I leaned over and kissed her heated forehead, ran my fingers through her wispy red hair, listened to her laboured breathing. There followed a long period of silence between us, with only her deep inhalations to mark the passing of time, until her breathing changed abruptly, became shallow and faint.

"It's here," she said matter-of-factly.

"What's that?"

"Can you hear it?"

"I'm listening."

"I see it now." Mary turned her innocent child's face up to the ceiling, lifted her head from the pillow a little, stared intently at some private surprise of great wonder.

"I go," she uttered, and again, "I go."

She squeezed my finger harder, eyes wide, mouth open, her breathing suspended. Then she stiffened, stiffened, into a terrible utter stillness. Never question that a heart can be torn from a body, for in witness to that aching departure was mine ripped from my chest. Yet strangely, what has stayed with me ever after is the grace and beauty of her dying.

The Queen, our mother, during all of this chose to remain at Hampton Court. How often I lamented what an uncaring harridan she was, though soon enough the experience of losing my own children should soften my judgment of her. Her husband had, after all, literally torn her first-born son out of her arms when he was but a few days old and removed him to Stirling Castle to be raised in the household of the Earl of Mar. I came to learn in later years that she fought very hard to regain custody of him, but her efforts went unrewarded. At one point she had defiantly undertaken the perilous journey to Stirling Castle on her own to fetch her baby back. But so formidable was my father's tenure that she was not even granted a brief visitation, and was most rudely turned away at the doorstep. The episode upset her so deeply that her next two pregnancies resulted in miscarriages, and thereafter a change came over her that no one could fail to notice. Upon the birth of yet another child, she took pains to distance herself from the girl almost entirely, rightfully expecting that she should suffer the infant to be taken from her at any moment, just as young Henry had been. I was that girl.

A more benevolent daughter might have been quicker to pardon her behaviour, but it seemed to me she let her suffering hold her hostage, where a more courageous woman would see her heart find expression by an act of sheer will. As for me, I might better have succeeded at loving my own children if only I'd been more comfortable around them, but there was always something that stood between us. I had no desire to watch them lose their innocence, which by my reckoning begins with the first breath. It was easier after they had entered their adolescent years. By then the damage had been done and I could engage with them in a different way. There wasn't so much to lose. Yet even then a mild yet pervasive anxiety ruled our exchanges, dulled the trials and triumphs to which I was witness. Why should it be so difficult to be noble?

But now I forced myself once again to take in my immediate surroundings, to become aware of myself sitting in my brother's chair inside his study. Captain Hume might return at any moment and I wanted to be ready. I checked to see where the bronze statue had been sitting on the table next to me. My brother had developed the habit of placing the little horse on top of whatever reading material was currently of interest to him, and now I took up the papers that had lain beneath it. They were a set of illustrations of the inner structure and composition of the human body that had come into Henry's possession by way of a French ambassador. He had mentioned them to me, but I had not had a chance to examine them. I had never seen drawings of such intricate detail. It was as if the artist had peeled back the skin and removed the outer layers to reveal a complex network of tissue and sinew beneath, spiral tubes and oval vessels, all manner of delicate organic structures, shapes and forms most intriguing. If these were indeed accurate, I thought, and not imagined, then the hidden workings of the human creature were nothing like those depicted by earlier anatomists, for here were no spurious arrangements of wheels and cogs and gears, but a symmetry and design entirely remarkable.

The drawings had about them a sense of noble detachment, as if the artist had been intent to vanquish all sentiment for the sake of accuracy, but there was an unmistakable tenderness in their aspect, as of a deep reverence for the subject matter. Crammed and wedged into every available space were copious handwritten notes scrawled in an indecipherable hand, the lettering inverted in some way. It was not until I picked up a small mirror from the table and positioned it over the words that I discerned they were written in Italian, one of the languages my father had seen fit to let me be schooled in. I wondered what the physicians of the day, with their talk of humours and vapours, their murky terminology, would make of these drawings and their depiction of what had heretofore remained unseen.

At my urging Henry had recently brought over from Holland an instrument designed for the express purpose of magnification. The apparatus allowed me for the first time to witness with my own eyes those tiny beasties I christened "creatomies": dozens of minuscule bodies swimming about in but a single drop of water I had collected from a nearby pond. We took turns looking through the eyepiece, equally amazed at the wondrous miniature world depicted there. And now as I sat there, a troubling vision overtook me of some such creatures travelling about, unseen and undetected, within my brother's body, spreading throughout its entirety by way of the circulation of the blood, and by that means bringing about his disease. I sat there poring over the drawings, imagining armies of impossibly tiny beings doing battle in the small arenas and recesses depicted in these drawings, waging crusades of attack and defence entirely unseen by the naked eye, inflicting wounds nevertheless as real as those suffered on the battlefield.

And what of the inner workings of the mind? Might the struggles that took place there correlate to some unseen process in that organ we call the brain? Were its secrets also capable of being explored, mapped, vivisected? Surely within the human body, I thought, were countless hidden mechanisms at work of which we were entirely ignorant. A nagging uneasiness gnawed at me, to think Henry's affliction might have originated in such intricate constructions as I witnessed in those wonderful drawings, entirely unknown to the physicians who attended him.

I thought of all the monies my mother and father devoted to their frivolous undertakings, she with her extravagant masques and he with his unwarranted building projects. And all it succeeded in doing was to bring them both into disfavour with the people. No doubt when Henry was king he should see fit put such monies to better use. He and I had already discussed the possibility of founding an institute for scientific discovery, to which we would invite luminaries from every country: Galilei from Italy, Gassendi from France, and yes, Sir Raleigh from the Tower.

It seemed like an eternity before at last I heard footfalls in the corridor and Captain Hume strode into the study.

"Come, sit." I grabbed him by the arm the second he walked into the study, and threw him into the nearest Wainscot chair, leaned over him.

"How is my brother?"

He seemed taken aback at my intensity as I searched his face for answers. "Did you give him the letter? Does he send a reply? The medicine. He took it? It restored his spirit some?"

"Madam," the Captain pleaded, "by your leave I shall be glad to tell you all."

"Then do so, in the name of Heaven. I want to hear everything. How looks he? What did he say?"

"When first I entered he was in restless slumber."

"Why say you restless?"

"He was wont to toss his head from side to side upon the pillows and softly moan."

"I trust you sought to ease his discomfort."

"No more than to seat myself upon a stool at the foot of his bed and there take up my viola da gamba to play for him."

"But where's the comfort in that? Did you not see your way to his bedside, take his hand, find some means to lay a hand upon his forehead?"

"Madam, these things I did, though not at first."

"But why not?"

"Your Highness," the Captain implored, "I am trying to tell you, but you must give me leave to make answer. I was cautioned by Dr. Mayerne, who made a great show of his authority, that if I overstepped my bounds it should bring an end to my visitation. I was to refrain from speaking to the Prince, as he might be suffering from delusions and his words should not be taken at face value. Indeed the man's precincts were such I wondered how I should manage to get near your brother at all."

"I might have known. I tell you it shall come to a head between us. He afforded you no privacy, then?"

"He laid claim that upon your father's express wishes Ferrabosco, as Groom-in-Extraordinary to your brother, should be present in the chamber with me at all times. Then of a sudden your brother moans and thrusts out his hands, limbs stiffened, and cries out in such pitiful bursts that Ferrabosco rushes from the room to fetch that same Dr. Mayerne, who has given him in turn instruction that he shall be summoned at such a moment of crisis. Still he posts one of the Yeomen to stand guard inside the door, to whom he gives instruction and so takes his leave, whereupon I take up my instrument and begin to play, tortured at the agony of your brother's turmoil, though the music seems to take its effect and after a few moments he is somewhat becalmed.

"Now a peacefulness comes over him until he quietly raises his head from the pillow and utters, 'Who is here?' I rise from my chair to make answer, step toward the bed. The Yeoman looks to intercede and thrusts forth his halberd. I plead that he shall show some mercy, at which he looks upon me of a sudden with such close inspection, then at the Prince, then back at me, and thus he speaks: 'Can this be that same Captain Hume I fought under on the battlefields of Scotland?' I give over that I am indeed that man, at which he concedes I shall command him as one soldier to another, and he will stand down and dutifully obey."

"This is providence indeed."

"Such bonds are ever forged upon the battlefield as no man can unmake."

"All well and good, but to my brother. You went to him?"

"'Captain Hume,' the Prince utters, and reaches out a frail hand to take mine, 'it is good of you to come, but how is it that you visit me and my dear sister does not?'"

"This wounds like a dagger. I take it you explained the situation."

"Be assured I told him you had done everything you could."

"But tell me how he looks. I would know his appearance in every detail."

The Captain's eyes turned down and a pained look came over his face. "I fear I have not the skill to convey such to your satisfaction."

"Say," I said, "and let me be the judge. Tell me what you saw."

"Your Highness, they have shaved his head."

"That's for the chickens," I said, "which they flay open and lay upon the skull to draw out a fever. A last resort. Their so-called remedies are bankrupt. But Captain, what of the confection? Did you manage to give him some?"

"I withdraw from my pocket the items you sent, Your Highness, and as soon as your brother sees the statue of the little bronze horse, he raises his head from the pillow to take it from me, looks upon it as though it were a priceless treasure, runs his fingers over it, clutches it to his chest. 'My sister sent it,' he says as though to himself, at which he holds it again out before him to gaze upon it with great fondness, as though it were a living thing. Next he spies the letter you sent and takes it from me with trembling hands, plays his fingers over the fine gold threads, then tears open the paper. He goes to read but falls back with a sigh and confesses that his eyes fail him, entreats me rather to read it out to him, which I proceed to do after I have brought a candle to give me some much-needed light. I pause from time to time and note his expression, at one moment cheerful, the next solemn, and at the last there upon his cheek a tear streams down which he will not deign to wipe away, but caresses instead the little bronze statue, his eyes now seemingly fixed on some distant image known only to him."

"This tears at my heart. I'll hear no more."

"Madam, forbear I beg you, for I think he wept with joy to hear your words."

"Proceed."

"Now again I go to offer up the cordial, but he pushes it aside, clutches at my collar and pulls me close, bids me be quick, that the time is short, takes from beneath his pillow this paper and hands it to me.

"You mean to say you had this the whole time?" I tore it from the Captain. "Why have you kept it from me so long?"

I opened it to see there my brother's unmistakable penmanship, though scrawled and barely legible:

Dear Elizabeth,

Forgive me that I write with such an unsteady hand, but my heart is to blame, for it beats with great irregularity and will of a sudden speed with impossible haste, fill my head to bursting with pulsing blood and heat, then slow as though to cease altogether, leaving me gasping for air. Havoc reigns so within my body that I am feverish one moment and cold the next, one instant exhausted and another bursting with frantic energy, as though some unknown force had taken over the reins of my being. How else to explain my thirst though I dare not drink, my hunger though I shrink from the sight of food? I am a stranger to sleep, and have not the strength to rest.

My fondest hope is that I shall yet have reason to burn this letter and laugh to think I should have written these next words, but I confess to some misgivings at the cause of this affliction. I pray they are but the ramblings of a mind made sick by fever, but I wake nightly into a dreamlike state to find a man standing at my bedside in a Paris beau that rests crookedly upon his head. He stares down at me with eyes half-closed, the skin beneath them sagging to expose the pink flesh there. Now he doffs his hat oddly and leers at me with a crisp "Monsieur," brings his hand behind my head to lift it from the pillow, takes from beneath his robes a small vial, and brings it to my lips with the words "I dare not, and yet I must. I must not, and yet I dare."

When I go to speak he puts a finger to his lips, shakes his head from side to side in a manner so menacing I am paralyzed into silence. Though I try meekly to resist, he holds fast to my chin and pours the liquid in, waits for me to swallow. No sooner have I done so than he returns the vial to his pocket, executes a short bow, and is gone.

Surely this is a dream, I tell myself, even as the bitter taste yet lingers on my tongue. I should be glad to dismiss the entire episode as imaginary but for this: I'm certain I saw this same man in conversation with my father at Whitehall not more than a fortnight ago! I swear it. There was no mistaking the Paris beau, the sagging skin beneath his eyes. I would know, Elizabeth, whether you ever remember seeing such a man at court, or indeed anywhere else for that matter? It would be a relief to know I am not hallucinating, though such an assurance might portend worse.

A haunting weariness has overtaken me and I can write no more. I know you are doing everything you can to see me, and I ask in your absence that you do one thing: pray for me. But for you, dear sister, I truly never had a family.

Your loving brother,
Henry

What was I to make of this? My head reeled. I felt as though I should faint. I couldn't recall seeing such a man as my brother described, and yet I had the greatest misgiving that this was no dream.

"Your Majesty." Captain Hume saw my distress. "I had thought to bring you comfort with this letter but I fear it has had the opposite effect."

I resolved that I should keep the contents of this letter to myself for now, that the fewer people who saw it the safer my brother should be, and here a dread surged through me I had never felt before, as of a world where no one could be trusted, everyone a possible enemy.

"Perhaps I had best take my leave. I can come back at a more convenient time."

"What? No, I would hear the rest. What of the cordial?" I asked. "You managed to give him some?"

"Upon handing me the letter the Prince fell back upon his pillow, silent and with eyes distant, as though he had taken leave of my presence. I took up the vial to try and spoon some between his parched lips when he roused himself yet once more and pulled me close, looked at me as though he would speak some great and final truth, eyes wide, mouth open, and at that very moment Dr. Mayerne and Alfonso Ferrabosco come barging into the room and I was banished at once."

There were noises now, and calls without that could be heard beyond the walls. Lady Anne went to the door, stepped out for a moment before returning to the room. "There is a general restlessness about the halls of the palace," she said. "People scurrying about in whispers and cries."

"What do they say?"

"The Archbishop has been summoned."

"I am going to him this very instant," I said. "Naught but a dagger in my breast shall stop me. Captain Hume, will you come with me and bear arms that we might see our way in?"

"I shall, Your Highness."

"Let's go, then."

There was a knock upon the door, and Dr. Butler stepped into the room, followed by Lady Anne and Count Schomberg as well as the Palatine. I saw by the look on the Doctor's face that he had news, perhaps of some more drastic measure of treatment now to be taken.

"You have word of my brother?" I asked.

"Such as I would forfeit my life to keep from uttering."

"Then do not," I said, "and join us, for we go, all of us, to attend my brother's bedchamber and will not be turned away. It has come to a head and we shall bring him hope and remedy. Will you join us?"

"There is no need."

"That's good news, then." I turned to Captain Hume. "He must have taken some of the cordial. But can it be so sudden?" I turned back to Dr. Butler. "A moment ago I had grave misgivings, but you mean to say the worst is over?"

Lady Anne stepped toward me, took my hands in hers. "Your brother's suffering is ended, Your Highness."

"Forgive me." Dr. Butler turned to Lady Anne with such a pained expression I could hardly think what troubled him. "I know not how to tell it." He looked down at the floor.

"You've said enough," I offered, "and thanks for the good news."

"But I was with him no more than an hour ago," said Captain Hume, as though to himself.

"Sir." The Palatine addressed himself to Dr. Butler. "I beg you speak plainly, that she not be made to suffer one more moment's false promise."

"Sir, I do my best."

"Tell it."

"The Prince of Wales . . ."

"He has told it," I cut him off, "and that the worst is over. Nevertheless we will go."

"You need not."

Lady Anne stood before me, tears streaming down her cheeks. "He means, Madam, that your brother is now beyond such good or harm as earthly endeavours may bring about."

I looked at the Doctor.

"He has been taken from us."

"Say yet plainer," said Lady Anne, never once taking her eyes from mine.

"The Prince of Wales is dead."

In the darkness of that hour all my comfort vanished upon an instant. I resolved that though I lost parent or child, sibling or spouse, no blade of grief should ever again cut so deep nor wound so gravely. There in that moment I pulled in the reins of my heart, vowed to apportion any and all future affection into more bearable increments. My brother took some part of me with him that day, and the tomb where they laid him to rest should ever after be the keeper of it.

Chapter Seven

Upon my brother's death, the cloak of dread that had hovered over me descended with a vengeance to smother all my hopes. By day friends and family, courtiers and clergymen, appeared and disappeared like apparitions, shadowy players upon a darkened stage. I wandered through the world and yet I was not in it. I became a ghost, forced to bear the weight of each day's passing in solemn ceremony, my needs seen to by Lady Anne alone. As much as possible I kept myself in solitude at Richmond, but when I allowed that Count Schomberg might pay a visit to Lady Anne, the two of them pressed me to admit Prince Frederick, who was eager to offer his condolences.

"If the Palatine hopes to gain favour by such means," I told them, "it will condemn him for a certainty."

"He would but convey his sympathies."

"There's little to commend what serves merely as a means to an end."

"He is in earnest. Give him an audience, I pray."

"If I cannot take solace even from a close acquaintance, how then from a stranger?"

"Betimes a stranger may succeed where others fail." Lady Anne assumed a gentle aspect.

"He dare not seek to flatter my grief."

"How then if to impart his own?"

"He hardly knew my brother. They spent a mere few hours together, conversed but a little. And as for me, we shared little more than pomp and ceremony at the hands of my father, and now he would commiserate? I think not."

So went our conversation, but in the end he was admitted, and I allowed that he might approach and make his sentiments known. I rose when he entered the drawing room, and offered my hand, which he took most graciously and bowed. He looked older than I remembered, and I wondered if he thought the same of me.

"Forgive me, Madam, if I say that in all this mourning and sadness I am yet glad to see you."

"I know naught of gladness. I have become a stranger to such sentiments."

"And yet your company brings me warmth."

"Even as I shiver in grief. There's naught here but cold comfort."

"May I offer my deepest sympathies for the loss of your brother?"

"These are but words."

"Words fail, I grant, as surely they must in these matters. Mourning takes a course no vessel of language can follow. But believe me, that I do ache to see you in such pain and would offer remedy if I could."

"Believe this also: that my grief stands unaltered by your compassion."

"Then, Madam, I will offer naught but my silence, if you will receive it."

"But why should you offer that for which I have no use?"

"For selfish reasons, that I would employ it to my own ends. I confess my sorrow finds me unprepared, that I should grieve for someone I had only just met, and yet it is so. I offer myself in service to you, if you should have need of it, and would remain here in London that I might be allowed to attend the funeral."

"I seek not for any company save my own, but stay for the funeral if you like, and thanks for your concern."

We sat quietly for a few moments and I had to admit that his solemn and silent attention gave me a modicum of ease, served as a buttress against the posturing court which strutted and boasted its bereavement in shameless spectacle. Then again, perhaps this was merely a tactic designed to weaken my resolve.

My brother lay in state at St. James's Palace under a canopy of black velvet; day after day, thousands upon thousands of mourners filed past his coffin. You may wonder as I did why so many should have felt such sorrow for someone they had no acquaintance of. My brother would have insisted that he was no more entitled to their grief than to their worship, but it occurred to me they wept not so much for his passing as for their own yet to come. Whatever our age or circumstance we all of us, in death, forfeit some lost destiny. Surely such a fate calls for a very great deal of weeping indeed.

Each night I waited until they had closed off the room where Henry lay before venturing to pay my own visit by way of a private entrance, moving silently across the floor to his casket, the sound of every hushed footfall or whisk of fabric amplified by the marble and stone. I reached out to touch his robes of state, his sword, the cushion laid upon the casket for his cap and coronet. This set my fingers tingling, my body to humming with a kind of frantic and unwanted energy, a disturbing frenzy of remorse. Later, when troubled and restless sleep overcame me at last, I had the same dream of standing among a crowd of spectators along a cobblestone street, watching Henry ride past mounted upon a white steed. Dressed all in armour and lace, he sat his horse with regal posture, locks thick and wavy around his shoulders, a page at his side holding his plumed helmet. Onlookers remarked how nobly the young prince had come into manhood, the last vestiges of boyhood innocence departed from his countenance, when before my eyes his face began to wither, eyes and cheeks to hollow out until he resembled a skeleton. And always, just before the horror of it tore me out of my slumber, Henry leaned down to me where I stood among the people, pulled me close with teeth bared, eyes bloodshot, and rasped, "Sister, they have killed me."

On the day of the funeral, the sky was overcast as I walked along behind the casket, followed by an endless procession of mourners, some on foot, some in carriages and on horseback. Six horses, all of them draped in black and plumed with black feathers, pulled the open funeral carriage, the clop of their hooves hollow on the cobblestone, steam hissing from their nostrils. A likeness of the Prince of Wales had been fashioned out of wax and placed over his casket, clothed in robes of purple velvet hemmed with ermine, complete with cap and coronet, gold sceptre in one hand and shining sword in the other. It struck me with a sudden fierceness that such a likeness must by then bear little resemblance to the withered tissues and brittle bones lying in the casket. And yet I wondered whether those disembowelled remains might yet harbour some relic of my brother's soul not yet departed.

Those walking solemnly behind the funeral carriage included my brother Charles, now heir to the throne, holding on to his mother's hand. My father was not among them. I looked for him, in spite of myself, thought if I might see him and read in his countenance a genuine expression of grief it should bring me some small respite from those misgivings that tortured me endlessly. I discovered upon his return some days later that he had made sure to take himself out of the city entirely until all ceremony had been dispensed with. For this unforgivable transgression he made no apology, and offered way of explanation only that he detested funerals.

When the procession arrived at Westminster Abbey the coffin was taken down from the carriage to be carried into the cathedral. Mourners filled the pews, and elegies of praise and songs of mourning commenced, one following upon the other. I had pleaded that Sir Raleigh be allowed to attend, even under heavy guard, but my father had left strict orders to the contrary. Henry's death would have come as a terrible blow to Sir Raleigh, for it meant not only the loss of someone dear to him but also condemned him to languish in the Tower without hope of release.

I did manage to arrange for Captain Hume to play a piece upon his viola da gamba, as Henry would have wanted him to. The Captain's usual disregard for appearance, manners, and decorum brought me assurance somehow, and when he took up his place before the assembled mourners, leaned his body into his instrument to feather the bow across the strings, his playing brought forth notes of such lamentation I thought the grey and towering arches of the abbey itself must crumble into broken stone under the enormity of their grief. Nestled within that exquisite music were some few notes that spoke of my own salvation, a day in some distant future when I might find a way to redeem myself for suffering a brother to die alone.

Perhaps it was an unhealthy conceit to seek atonement for something that was really out of my hands. The cordial might not have saved him in any case, as Sir Raleigh had cautioned that it would not work against poison. I found myself searching among the pews of the Abbey for a man in a Paris beau with sagging eyes, all the while wondering whether those nightly visitations my brother had described might have been nothing more than the fevered hallucinations of a dying man.

When the ceremony ended at last they carried the casket into the Lady Chapel and prepared to lower it into the crypt. Just as the interment commenced a young man, entirely naked and pale as Dover, sprang from the crowd, ran up to the coffin, and threw himself upon it with such a wailing as sent shivers through me. Then quick as a cat he turned and lunged at me, seeming to mean me harm, but a number of bystanders intervened and sought to get hold of him. Still he struggled and fought to free himself, crawled on his hands and knees toward me, threw himself forward, and clutched at the hem of my skirts.

"Do you not recognize your own brother?" he pleaded, "For I am that same ghost."

A number of guards grabbed hold of him, dragged him up by his arms and pulled him away from me. Even as they did so his eyes, full of terrifying madness, stayed on me, froze me to his countenance so that try as I might I could not look away.

"Sister," he uttered, "they have killed me."

Presently the guards dragged him through the crush of shocked bystanders to a small door that led from the chapel into the adjacent courtyard. He clutched at the portal and, before they managed to pry his fingers off the stone to take him out, shouted, "Mark it for a sign, all you who witness here today, that Prince Henry's ghost spoke thus."

"Naught but woe can come of this," I heard someone near me say.

"It bodes ill indeed," said another.

"Why should a ghost appear but to alert those yet living to treachery and untimely death?"

The burial was allowed to continue, but it was this episode that threatened to undo me entirely.

I woke up next morning from a sleep unnatural into a kind of paralysis, a stillness I had never experienced before, out of which emerged the faint sound of something cracking, breaking, followed by a sudden and violent concussion, an explosive collapse inside my head. Some part of me fell in upon itself, shattered inside me. In the silence that followed I became aware of an intense ringing in my ears, growing louder and louder, an affliction that has never left me from that moment to this. I have learned to live under the tyranny of its insistent din over the years, and for short periods of time I can even push it out of my awareness entirely, but always it re-emerges out of the false silence.

I fell for a time into an existence in which each breath became a chore, each utterance a trial. Lady Anne looked in on me at regular intervals, did her best to see that I ate something, and one day brought me news regarding the fate of the young man claiming to be my brother's spirit. He had managed to break free of his captors and make his escape along the banks of the Thames. My father, having returned from the countryside and learned of the incident at the abbey, sent forth a party of his best spies to ascertain the fugitive's identity and apprehend him at all cost, but without success. The young man seemed to have vanished entirely from the face of the earth, and to my knowledge was never seen or heard from again.

I wondered whether things might have gone a little better for me if my father had managed to track him down and he had turned out to be nothing more than another discontented Puritan intent on wreaking havoc upon the profligate and debauched rulers of the kingdom, or perhaps a deranged individual driven by forces only he was privy to, but as it was, my imagination conjured up all manner of explanations that were a good deal more insidious.

Thereafter came a protracted period during which I managed little more than to carry on a dull shuffle through each day. Weighed down by demands I was powerless to refuse, not quite present to my own company, let alone that of others, I felt much as Mr. Shakespeare's Danish Prince, set about on all sides by "the thousand natural shocks that flesh is heir to." This was the very seed of my affliction. I wanted only to slink away, hunker down in some dark and gloomy corner for fear of yet another jolt to my senses. My dreams became all the more bizarre, my waking and sleeping hardly distinguishable one from the other, day and night blurred into a dull grey. Lady Anne pleaded that I should allow myself to be attended to by my physicians, but I knew they would only attribute my disposition to an imbalance of humours and offer the usual ineffectual treatments.

I would have been content to spend my days in solitude, to live as a recluse indefinitely, if not for my father's insistence that the period of mourning, though hardly begun, should now be brought to an abrupt halt and preparations made for a royal wedding. I did not fight him. I was broken. Else I should have chosen instead to devote my energies to carrying on, in Henry's memory, those various endeavours he had undertaken which would otherwise go unfinished, and see them brought to fruition.

Instead I allowed myself to be dragged about from one ceremony to the next, beginning with the betrothal, to be dressed and undressed, courted and feted, all while the lion's share of my inner nature cowered elsewhere, held captive in some netherworld of unseen torture and despair that gave me to feel as though an enormous black fist were looming over me, waiting to strike me into a stupor if I should weaken my resolve not to give in, not to let go of myself entirely.

My mother, never one to miss an opportunity for lavish spending, set aside her objections to the match and took it as an opportunity to ensure that the wedding celebrations should include a masque as elaborate as any she had ever staged. She set about commissioning various stage designs and costumes, musical compositions and theatrical scenes, while my father saw to ever more lavish enhancements of his palace at Whitehall, so that between the two of them the exchequer was soon emptied of what little funds remained, after which their methods of acquiring additional monies tested further the already tenuous good will of Parliament.

But then, in the midst of this near-madness, I awoke one morning to a new kind of frenzied vitality coursing through me, an edgy desperation I could control, and so put to good use. I realized that there was no going back, that nothing was ever going to be the same and that I, Elizabeth Stuart, was never again going to be the person I was before. It didn't matter that my brother might have been poisoned, that his ghost might have visited itself upon me, that I might never be restored. What mattered was not to give in, to put the lie to the urge I entertained in secret hours that I should follow my brother into oblivion. Better to infuse myself with a will, put this torturous change in me to better use, and live.

How profound a transformation followed! Passion, born of urgency, galvanized by my heightened sense of fragility, overtook me. Thereafter I spent all of my chaotic days and sleepless nights contriving feverish schemes, frantic plots, laid the groundwork for a frenzy of excess designed to play my father and mother at their own game. I devoted myself entirely to such duties and privileges as befell a bride-to-be, ordered a new wardrobe and returned at once to court, that engine of manipulation and subterfuge which I would harness to my own ends. The lords and ladies remarked, upon my return, that I seemed enraptured with a renewed zest for life.

In fact, I was in the throes of cobbling together a new Elizabeth for myself, different from the one I had imagined, she being now forever lost to me. Lady Anne, cautiously enthusiastic at my restored animation, sensed that I was not truly cured of my ailment, but allowed that it was better than moping about all day. Frederick, though somewhat unsettled, welcomed my seeming embrace of the wedding and his company in the bargain. As for my parents, they hardly took notice but for the fact that as lavishly as they were spending, I now seemed eager to spend even more, making all manner of outrageous demands.

It could be almost anything that came to mind. One moment I demanded that my wedding gown must be embroidered with silver thread, the next that I should be granted seventeen pairs of silk stockings as part of my trousseau, one for every year of my young life and another for good luck.

I insisted that a mock sea battle should be staged upon the Thames on the eve of my wedding, followed by a massive fireworks display. The Royal Chapel at Whitehall must be decked out in ever more elaborate arrangements of flowers and garland for the ceremony — oh, and silver medallions were to be struck in commemoration of the occasion. If my father objected to any of my stipulations, I would wait for the appropriate moment when he was at court and there, in front of everyone, make some remark such as, "I hope it shall not be whispered about that the Scottish King was too piddling to provide his only daughter a proper send-off."

As the preparations for the wedding continued, Frederick for his part showed himself steadfast in his patience for my sudden excesses, content that I should see fit to tolerate his presence rather than dismiss him outright. Lady Anne, meanwhile, did her best to impose some semblance of restraint.

"You think it well I marry this foreign prince," I said to her one afternoon, the two of us seated in Henry's study, where I took myself often at that time of day, content to browse through one item or another I found there. It was a way to keep him close, as though the room harboured yet some semblance of his presence.

"Is that a question?" she looked at me.

"Is that an answer?"

"Forgive my brusqueness," she offered, "but it could be worse, when you consider those others who might have laid claim to your marriage bed."

"I suppose you will say next I should count my blessings."

I had given strict orders that everything at St. James's be left exactly as it was, and in this my father acquiesced, only because he could not be bothered about it one way or the other, and the same was true for my mother. To judge by their demeanour, Henry might hardly have existed. My father spent almost all of his time at Whitehall, where the wedding would take place, and my mother busied herself at Somerset, and so it was of little concern to them that at St. James's Palace there remained yet those accoutrements of a son they hardly cared to keep a memory of. I took myself there for the final week before the wedding, glad to have a safe haven from all that swirled about me.

"Shall I go over the names?" said Lady Anne.

"I care not to hear them."

"I think you should, if only to judge against those other matches that might have befallen." Lady Anne took a paper out of her pocket. "I have them here."

"You've been keeping a list?"

She began to read: "Frederick Ulric, the Duke of Brunswick-Wolfenbüttel . . . Prince Maurice of Nassau . . . Henry Howard, the First Earl of Northampton . . ."

"I think that last has died since," I interjected, "of old age."

"Theophilus Howard, Lord of Walden . . ."

"He married Elizabeth Home, didn't he — the Earl of Dunbar's daughter? I think it was in March. Your list is out of date."

"Otto, Hereditary Prince of Hesse, Son of Maurice, Landgrave of Hesse-Kassel . . ."

"His title is long where he is short, so I've heard tell."

"Victor Amadeus, Prince of Piedmont . . ."

"As handsome as the devil and yet still a Catholic."

"Gustavus Adolphus of Sweden . . ."

"Enough. This reads like a fishmonger's cry."

"Not one of these can promise to treat you as well as Prince Frederick."

"I would rather my life did not rest upon such a promise."

"You will want for nothing."

"Save love."

"But I say to you without hesitation that Prince Frederick loves you."

"All fine and good, but what of the love that I should feel toward my husband?"

"You may find you grow to love him."

"A shaky premise upon which to marry."

"Mark if it shall not come to pass, for he will do his utmost to earn it."

"As Count Schomberg does to earn yours."

Lady Anne smiled down into her lap, then back up at me. "I find it pleasant to be in his company, and feel no small affection toward him, but little may come of it."

"Less if this wedding my father has planned for me should falter." I inspected her features. "Perhaps you counsel with your own interest in mind."

"I would give this same advice had I never met the Count."

"You will come to Heidelberg with me?"

"Of that you may be sure, if you will have me."

"And the Count, you will have him?"

"In good time may we speak of such, My Lady, but for now this marriage must be the sole purpose of our daily endeavours. There is so much to do!"

"And even more after the vows have been exchanged."

"How so?"

"For my part I intend to cross the channel with an entourage the like of which has not been seen here or in any other kingdom. I tell you the navy had better prepare an armada. If I must go to live in Bohemia, I intend to see to it that a good portion of England comes with me. Did I tell you, Frederick has promised to build me my own wing at Heidelberg Castle, which I will deign to christen the English Wing? Oh, and when I told Frederick that Henry had started the plans for an English garden at St. James's he immediately made arrangements that the designer, Salomon de Caus, should accompany us to Heidelberg and incorporate those very plans into a garden there. Hortus Palatinus will be the name, he says, and it shall be the eighth wonder of the world."

"This tactic you have undertaken, of profligacy, is so unlike you. Is it necessary?"

"Absolutely."

"Is it wise?"

"You would speak to a sixteen-year-old princess of wisdom?"

"Come," said Lady Anne, "we are expected in the dressing room to see about another fitting."

As the wedding drew nearer I became ever more mired in a sea of rehearsals, banquets, visitations, and entertainments. My father saw to it that Mr. Shakespeare's company should perform a number of his plays as a lead-up to the wedding. I was naturally expected to be in attendance, though I hardly paid attention, for the inner workings of my mind were yet abuzz with a dizzying mixture of anger and undiminished grief. I caught only the odd snippet, as on one evening when another production of *Hamlet* was staged, which gave me to recall that last evening Henry and I spent together. In particular I made sure to secure my father's attention and stare him down just as the Danish Prince uttered to Horatio, "*The funeral baked meats did coldly furnish forth the marriage tables.*"

Mr. Shakespeare had deigned to play his part in the production but was called away to Stratford when his brother Richard took seriously ill. The rest of the family had already gathered there, that he might spend his last hours in their company. Richard went to his heavenly rest soon after, and Mr. Shakespeare stayed back to make arrangements for the funeral, which brought about yet another example of my father's reprehensible character. The burial was set to take place on the same day as the royal wedding, which my father took vehement exception to, declaring it to be a bothersome annoyance that the Shakespeare family should see fit to saddle their king with such an inconvenience, and remarked upon it several times in the course of the days leading up to nuptials, complaining loudly that he failed to understand why they would forgo a royal wedding the like of which London had never seen to attend the graveside of a brother who, my father had it on good authority, was an illiterate with no friends.

Frederick and I, thrown together as guests of one ceremony or another, fell into a certain level of acquaintance in which he took pains to be mindful of my state over the course of an evening's revelry, and having divined that I had reached my limit, would see to it I was given leave to withdraw. In short, he looked after me, and I was grateful for it. He and Lady Anne, along with Count Schomberg, engaged in a kind of benevolent conspiracy to see me through to the end with as little discomfort as possible, made things at least palatable, even as I welcomed every opportunity to show my mother and father how much I despised them. Frederick talked about the construction that was already underway at Heidelberg Castle in accordance with my wishes for an English wing, as well as the plans for the elaborate grounds which would be home to all manner of exotic plants and trees. He would spare no expense, he promised, and had already seen to my request that there should be an entire grove of orange trees, Henry's favourite fruit.

In the midst of all this, another letter from Arabella Stuart managed to reach me, and in its content I found yet more reason to wonder at the unspoken concern she had wanted to see me about.

January 23, 1613

Dearest Elizabeth,

I was beginning to think I should never hear from you again. It is becoming more and more difficult to get any correspondence through. Your letter means so very much to me, considering that you were here within the walls of the Tower and I did not get to see you! I realize you did everything you could. As it is, they keep moving me around, so that I spend one fortnight in this cell, another in that. I have forgotten the meaning of luxury, and wake more often now into days when I grow weary of living endlessly in hope unfulfilled. I take consolation in the news that your father's forces have not managed to capture my husband, William, whose whereabouts remain unknown even to me.

Still, what if your father should relent and see fit to pardon me? After all, I have committed no crime. Or what if Lord Seymour should yet find a way to rescue me from this misery? I have not heard from him for some time, but that does not mean he is not trying. And yet I confess there are times of late when I have the most disturbing thought: that William has forsaken me and sought to regain favour with your father by renouncing me. He is still a young man, after all, with his whole future yet ahead of him. No, I will not believe it.

I grow cold and my writing is become unsteady. As it is I am provided with but little paper and less ink. And even at that, to obtain as much requires of me that which I shall not deign to disclose. As for those intrigues I made reference to in my last letter, put the matter to rest. It has all been seen to.

To think you are now to marry to the Elector Palatine of Bohemia and go to live in Heidelberg! Do not say the castle there shall feel like a prison to you, for it promises to afford such comforts as I can only dream of. I live in hope the day may yet come when we shall meet again in liberty and happiness and until such time I remain,

Yours in undying friendship and affection,
Arabella Stuart

I hardly knew what to make of my cousin's situation, considering that my own was far from ideal, but perhaps it was unfair to make such a comparison. I wondered if she would have traded places with me, or I with her. What if it were I confined now in the Tower? How long should I manage to remain defiant, resolute? Who can claim to be truly free of doubt that none shall be the master of her fate but she alone? Is such a thing possible? Perhaps we all live in captivity, unknowingly shackled to the very thing we fancy ourselves liberated from. Where is true freedom of spirit, of courage, of honour, when we have not dominion over our own weakness? I grant these things became forfeit even as I acquiesced to my father's wishes, but perhaps they were never mine to begin with. Would my father really have me thrown into prison? For certain it should have been otherwise if my brother Henry were still alive.

On the eve of the wedding a massive and violent maritime battle was staged upon the river. An English fleet flying the Red Cross attacked a Turkish one, accompanied by a cacophony of cannon fire, which succeeded in maiming and seriously injuring a goodly number of participants and bystanders. The spectators took it as yet another example of my father's utter disregard for the safety and welfare of his subjects, but it aroused a crippling pang of guilt in me, to think I had brought about such needless suffering for the sake of my churlishness. At the end of the battle the Turkish admiral surrendered and was brought up the stairs that led down to the river, where he was made to prostrate himself before the King. It was all ridiculous and childish, and though my father clearly delighted in it, I felt sick to my stomach.

Now a massive display of fireworks shot up from barges along the river, just beyond the walls of the palace. Again and again brilliant plumes of showering sparks shot up into the sky, illuminating various intricate and complex scenes set out on the river, among them a castle surrounded by rock and forest, beyond which strange sea monsters and other creatures swam about in the midst of an artificial ocean. On one island, St. George was depicted slaying the dragon. A spectacular shower of light depicted a pack of hounds chasing a deer across the blackened night sky. I could only imagine what it must have cost. Count Schomberg for one was enthralled, remarking that nothing like it had ever been seen in Heidelberg.

I awoke upon my wedding day to the ringing of church bells, so that from the very moment of its beginning there could be no doubt what the day held in store. This was soon followed by the report of gunfire, which was repeated throughout the day. It also happened to be Valentine's Day. I was whisked about from one room to another, fussed over and fitted. I insisted that I should wear my hair down, long and flowing to my waist, which only served to make the preparations more taxing, and even at that, one of the attendants began to weave pearls and diamonds into my curls and tresses, which I condemned loudly to be in poor taste and put a stop to. At last the dressing had all been seen to and I was ready for the ceremony. A robe of white and silver, studded with diamonds, was draped around me, and a crown of gold placed upon my head.

I made my way to the chapel, my lengthy train carried by thirteen bridesmaids all dressed in white with flowing tresses of their own as I walked between my brother Charles and the Earl of Nottingham. Specially prepared tapestries adorned the floors and walls all along the way, where the guests were already seated, and three pieces of magnificent tapestry had been draped over the altar. Frederick, dressed in a Spanish hat and mantle, stood waiting for me there. I thought him passing handsome, wondered what Sir Raleigh would think of him if he were present at the ceremony. Frederick turned to me with eyes alight in amazed gratitude. I deserved none of it.

The Bishop of Wells now launched into an interminable sermon, during which the audience fell into a fitful boredom, until the bishop, himself exhausted and about to buckle under the burden of his own pretense, at last gave over and withdrew from the pulpit. I should witness this same phenomenon at my own daughters' weddings, and many others. Why must these clergymen always use such occasions to peddle their piety? I suppose it is a testament to the temerity of the church that even royalty may be held hostage to its petty excesses. I will say it did serve to forge a certain bond between Frederick and myself, in that we were obliged to suffer through it together. How often it is the wedding day that serves up the first test of a couple's endurance.

Now came prayers and hymns in great quantity, followed by a recitation of vows, after which we exchanged a pledge of love and honour. I had seen to it that for my part an avowal of obedience was conspicuous in its absence. Next the Archbishop saw to the benediction, and when that had been completed we turned to the audience and the herald-at-arms announced us by title, after which I was granted a brief interval to change out of my dress into a more comfortable garment, then join my new husband to accept round upon round of congratulations from various nobility while wine and wafers were served, at which there was much toasting. John Donne recited a poem to celebrate the occasion in which he likened the bride and groom to a pair of birds, two phoenixes coupled at the breast.

At this I deigned to partake of some wine, and then a little more, which mitigated to some extent my lack of enthusiasm for the entire affair. What shall I say of my wedding night? There was a coupling, little more than perfunctory and less than vigorous, after which my new husband promptly if politely took himself to sleep, and I made ready to spend another restless night, something I had by then grown used to. Was I disappointed in the consummation? I had neither the experience nor the inclination to pass judgment on the matter. Did I feel I had been violated? That's too strong a word. Frederick was thoughtful if somewhat awkward. I was compliant if less than enthusiastic. Yet amid all the discomfort and awkwardness, I had to admit to a certain satisfaction at having a man fill me up.

Soon enough the act became a more bearable experience for me, one I might even look forward to from time to time, but in all the years, all the countless couplings that produced so many children, never once did I reach the height of ecstasy. As it was, I had always been able to manage things well enough on my own. The deepest pools of my arousal did ever spring from the well of imagination. I had only to conjure up an image of Sir Raleigh, for an instance, to achieve some such, and so its absence with Frederick did not become the progenitor of further difficulties.

As we settled into our marriage, Frederick was ever ready to engage in the act of love at a moment's notice and took immense pleasure in my body. A single kiss or touch from my hand would bring him to urgent readiness, and if I so desired, to a quick finish with but little effort. His emissions, intense and prodigious, could be repeated almost upon an instant if I gave him opportunity. He was always more eager than I, but never forced himself upon me, content to partake of me only as much as I deigned to offer. I would seldom find occasion to turn him down, as he was always prompt and tidy, after which I could get on with more important things. The babies would come early and often, so that quite a lot of the time my young woman's body was busy with the manufacture of lineage.

But even as I prepared to leave England and see my way across the channel, settle into a new life elsewhere, the question remained as to what course I should chart for myself. It was no longer a matter of asking what my heart yearned after. That had been rendered forfeit. Still, there had to be a way to put all this frenetic energy coursing through me to good use. It was only a matter of finding something worthy of my aspirations. In the end I settled for something less noble than I care to admit, but you must understand there wasn't much to choose from. It came down to this: What should a princess seek to obtain? Why, to be a queen, of course. Frederick had told me from the start he had reason to hope for the throne of Bohemia. He would see to the means, and I should supply the resolve. I would be the *sine qua non*, the linchpin to his ascension, and in the process obtain a degree of sovereignty. There could be but one way to salvage some part of myself, one cause to rule my heart.

Part Two

Chapter Eight

In the days that followed, the popular accounts of the trip Frederick and I made from London to Heidelberg gave the impression that the excursion amounted to little else but revelling and merriment. Granted, we made many stops along the way and were feted and fussed over by all manner of well-wisher, but the journey was arduous, and any number of irritants rendered it far from pleasant, considering that my state of mind was yet eager to shrink from conviviality.

We crossed the English Channel in seven ships laden with cargo and passengers, put in at Amsterdam, and thereafter traversed over land, up rivers and down, by ship and boat and carriage, from one town to another, one castle to the next, one feast and festivity to another in such an endless orgy of excess that to have endured so many strange beds, dining rooms, halls, so much unwelcome food and favour, dance and drink, beggared belief. It was rendered all the more wretched by my utter disinterest at being entertained, yet it was forced upon me day in and day out. I suffered yet greatly from that affliction I have told you about, which left me wanting little else but solitude and silence.

I wanted to rest, longed for the time when I should feel well enough again to get a proper night's sleep. Every palace and manor we lodged in seemed to me a nightmarish labyrinth of theatres, ballrooms, and banquet halls. Here they had arranged an outdoor pleasure party, there a feast with every sort of exotic food and drink imaginable. And I was not the least bit hungry! The unfamiliar dishes laid out before me, rather than tweak my appetite, were as like to turn my stomach just by their smell and appearance, let alone taste.

In The Hague the local guests praised a dish particularly dear to their hearts which they referred to as *bitterballen*. The ladies and gentlemen among whom I was seated at the banquet table simply would not accept my polite refusals. I was instructed to first dip what looked to be a small fried or baked croquette into a dish of mustard before taking a bite. I did so, chewed, tried to swallow, but it simply would not go down. I gagged before the mortified dinner guests, much to the embarrassment of the lord and lady of the manor. They should have been thankful I did not bring it all back up.

We journeyed on, stepped from boat to carriage, ship to barge, ascended platform and stage, made our entrance into specially decorated banquet halls, courtyards adorned just for the occasion of our arrival, were escorted to our quarters every night, there to sleep in a strange bed. Lady Anne did her best to see I was not taxed too greatly, diverting attention away from me when needed, making apologies for my early departures.

"I hardly know how to account for it," I said to her one morning. It had been another restless night followed by repeated bouts of heaving that left me depleted. "Why should the little bit I ate last evening give me to suffer this heaving and retching only now?"

Lady Anne listened, made no reply, her expression somewhere between sympathy and blame.

"Perhaps it comes from lack of rest," I went on. "I would give anything for a night in my own bed, not that it should give me to sleep much better."

Lady Anne continued to examine me closely, as though she were waiting for me to make some confession.

"Why are you looking at me that way?" I asked. "If you are going to chide me for partaking of too much wine, I tell you I have of a sudden entirely lost my taste for it, I know not why, and have hardly touched a drop these last few days."

"And yet this sickness persists," she said, as much to herself as to me. "Your bosoms," she continued.

"Excuse me?"

"Tell me, are they changed in any way?"

"I hardly think such a matter need concern you."

"They appear to me to be more fulsome."

"You really do exceed your bounds, Madam, but if you must know, they do seem of late somewhat tender."

"I thought as much."

"You know something of this? I take it to be part and parcel of the passage from maid to wife."

Lady Anne smiled wryly.

"I think it a little cruel of you to make light of my situation."

"Forgive me, but I forget how young you are."

"I can hardly blame Frederick for it. The journey wears on him as well. We do little more than fall into bed each night exhausted, and yet these symptoms persist."

"Your naivety is endearing."

"Why do you mock me?"

"There remains yet something of the child in you, even as you are in the first stages of begetting your own."

"What are you saying?"

"This is something more than just a queasy stomach."

"Speak plainly."

"Madam, you are gravid."

"Gravid? What manner of expression is that? Do you speak of some malady?"

"My dear, you are pregnant."

"Nonsense. It cannot be. It's too soon."

"More than long enough, by my reckoning."

"You mean these discomforts I suffer have come about because I am with child?"

I knew little of something any young woman should have received in good counsel well in advance of her marriage, for my mother had never spoken of such things to me, nor much of anything else for that matter, and it was not something I had come across in medical journals I'd studied, which could hardly be bothered to acknowledge maladies associated with the fairer sex. As it turned out, I would suffer the same fate in each and every one of my thirteen pregnancies. No sooner would my monthly cycle cease and my breasts begin to swell than I would commence to retching and puking.

Had I allowed the physicians to attend me, they should doubtless have plied me with all manner of elixirs and cordials to abate my nausea, but the anatomical drawings I had pored over with such interest in my brother's study gave me pause, for I remembered one in particular which depicted a child growing inside its mother's womb. It seemed to indicate that substances ingested by the mother might readily pass from her to the child by means of the blood, reason enough to forgo such treatment.

I was determined upon that first night at the castle to sleep in my own bed, a great four-poster behemoth of a thing which I had gone to great lengths to see carefully dismantled in London and transported along with some other furniture to the castle. It had been taken on ahead as instructed, but I was informed upon our arrival that it had not yet been reassembled. I refused all entreaties to take my rest elsewhere for the time being, and insisted Frederick summon workmen to assemble it then and there in the bedchamber. It was the same bed I should take with me to Prague Castle some years later, and thereafter on to The Hague. I would see to it that it travelled with me wherever I went, no matter the cost, no matter the inconvenience. There was going to be one thing in my life that I could count on, one thing that was permanent. It would be the only bed I slept on all my life, my children would be born on it, the lion's share of my carnal acts would take place there, and I intended to die in its welcome and comforting bosom.

And so, in the middle of the night, with the rest of the sprawling castle's inhabitants already asleep, I sat and waited for them to put the heavy oak bed together. Frederick might have taken himself to bed in another part of the castle but instead, though none too happy about it, took up a hammer and threw himself in with the workmen. Together, accompanied by much groaning and heaving, for it was a monster of a thing, they assembled tenon and mortise, board and post, wrestled to lift the headboard into place, until finally the job had been completed. Then it was just a matter of the maids, who were standing by and should else long have been asleep in their own beds, arranging the sheets and blankets until all was ready. I threw myself upon the mattress with a final sigh and was not heard from again for the rest of that night and better part of the next day, at which I finally arose toward evening, thinking it should have done me a great bit of good, and yet even then I did not feel rested.

One day fell into the next, one week into another. To be sure, I was not prepared for all the changes my body went through. I grew fat! Though I lost my taste for certain foods, I became ravenous for others. Soon enough I was hungry all the time, but there were only a few things I wanted to eat, in particular oranges, which I would eat three or four times a day often to the exclusion of all else, though Lady Anne was always there to harass me into eating helpings of other dishes as well.

On the worst days the discomfort became such that I swore. To couch the experience of carrying a child as noble was naught but an affectation, a myth fashioned to depict us as beatific incubators, gregarious gestators, when in fact it is a squalid and bothersome business. New life requires a fissure, a gash. Something must be split. Even a small seed will rend and tear the earth to find the sun. What then of a baby writhing out of the womb, seeking to gain its first breath? There's a ferocity about it. And to think I should suffer to undergo the ordeal thirteen times.

If I were to add up all the months I spent waddling about in discomfort from one delivery to the next, it should stretch to the better part of a decade. What if instead I had devoted as much time to scientific study, searched for the cause of so many deaths in childbirth and the means to prevent them? I imagined a day when a woman might free herself of such an inconvenience, make use of a proxy, and thereafter have the baby dropped into her arms nine months hence. I never wanted much to do with them until they reached the age where they could carry on a decent conversation. Bringing children into the world was a dangerous enterprise for any woman, and I was lucky to survive it so many times. Far too often a young mother lived to enjoy her babe for but a few delirious hours, only to be been taken from this world by that same affliction so many suffer at the time of birth. I was convinced those tiny creatomies were to blame, invisible organisms allowed to invade the body at that moment. It was a simple matter of contagion. For my part I always insisted the midwives scrupulously scrub their hands, and no matter the pain or discomfort I was in, would not let them touch me until they had done so.

As I went through the trials of that first birth, suffered the apparatus of my body to become distended, distorted, and when the time came at last, be made to endure such excruciating pain, it seemed to me only a cruel God would see fit to reproduce the human creature by turning a woman's body into a meat works for nine months. By such means was my first child, a son, born on New Year's Day, January 1, 1614. We named him Henry Frederick, and he would grow with each passing year to remind me more and more of my deceased brother.

—

No sooner had I sufficiently recovered my strength than I left the baby's care to others and turned my attention to more important matters. I had sworn to devote myself to Fredrick's ascension to the throne. Childbirth did nothing to change that. If I could not live the life I had hoped for, I should see to one of my own making nevertheless, by such means as I had at my disposal. Soon enough Lady Anne took notice and called me to account for it.

"Forgive me, Madam, if I say you seem less than eager to attend to the needs of your young son."

"I am content to employ those who toil at motherhood as well as and better than I am able."

"Your husband no doubt wonders too at your seeming lack of interest."

"The child is well cared for and wants for naught."

"Save his mother. It troubles me that you should be so unengaged."

"I have more pressing needs to see to."

"I fail to see what could be more urgent." Lady Anne drew closer, looked at me intently. "Is this seeming indifference of your own making?"

"Whose but mine should it be?"

"Your mother was most cruelly forbidden from caring for her first-born. Your brother Henry was taken from her."

"What is that to me?" I turned and stepped away a little.

"You have no such precincts placed upon you."

"Though I am suffered to endure plenty of others."

"By my reckoning you are free to devote yourself entirely to young Henry if you so desire."

"Yet I desire it not."

"I think you do." Lady Anne pointed in the direction of the nursery. "I know your heart, and I know you love him."

"You must think me cold and unfeeling."

"If there is some other reason, I would hear it."

"You make too much of this. I will see him often enough."

"What is it you fear?"

The question gave me pause, and I determined to answer as honestly as I could. "My own survival."

"Whatever can you mean?"

"The need to nurture will not stand me in good stead where advancement is the measure. And I have made it my aim to advance."

"Yes, so you have said. I had thought motherhood might dull the edge of that ambition, but it seems only to have sharpened it. Tell me, what is it you seek to gain?"

"All that stands within my grasp. Where is the accomplishment in raising a baby? Any dim-witted wife can do as much."

Lady Anne took me by the hand, turned me to face her. "This is not the Elizabeth I know. You are changed."

"They say treachery will have that effect on some."

"But here is a beautiful new life for you to cherish."

"Then let it be cherished. There are attendants and wet nurses for that. I would not see my breasts employed as dugs for a suckling."

Lady Anne took me by the shoulders. "You cannot be so callous."

"I must." I tore myself away.

"You are yet ill. This speaks to as much. Soon enough the old Elizabeth shall reappear. And I for one will welcome her."

As for Frederick, in all of this he never took issue with me, gave me full autonomy and remained steadfast in his devotion, so that I could hardly be otherwise but entirely civil to him. The days turned into weeks and months, and soon it was plain the fulcrum of our marriage lay nearer his end of the plank than mine, that I could tip him up or down as I saw fit. Did I take advantage? Was I dishonest? Before I answer, let me relate to you what he did for me on my nineteenth birthday. The day had hardly begun when he insisted on leading me out of the English Wing to the Thick Tower, where I was made to put on a blindfold, after which we proceeded along the West Wall through the artillery garden toward the bridge house and the entrance to the gardens behind the castle, where the Hortus Palatinus should be built in my brother's memory. Its construction was not yet begun, but I often had occasion to take myself there to meander amongst the trees and flowers, Henry's spirit hovering over me, thinking to see how the plan should be made to work.

Now Frederick stopped me and bade me remove the blindfold. There before me stood a magnificent gate of rose-coloured stone in the form of a triumphal arch. It was lavishly garlanded with scrolled masonry, its four pillars carved out to look like trees, with ivy winding up in a spiral along each one, and birds and animals nestled in among the leaves. Above the pillars sat two lions facing each other, also a pair of nymphs holding cornucopias, seated amid an orchard of fruits and flowers. An inscription had been chiselled along the top in Latin, dedicating the arch to me.

The lords and ladies of the court were assembled, eagerly gauging my reaction to this effusive gift my husband had fashioned for me. I had brought with me from London an entourage as inflated as I could manage, the better to give my father pause that he should have sent his daughter off with such cavalier indifference. The sprawling castle was filled to bursting with every manner of artist and musician and playwright. Even at that, many more had made their own way to Heidelberg from England in hopes of an appointment, having arranged their own lodgings down in the town, from which they made regular forays up the mountain to request an audience.

The patience of the townsfolk was growing thin, as hardly a day went by without reports of some disturbance or other in a tavern or an inn, usually precipitated by some allegation of slander and collusion against one party or another. There had been a number of outright brawls, a couple of duels, and several incidents of vandalism and robbery, all of them perched upon some point of contention regarding the royal court: sabotaged appointments, undeserved preferential treatment, proclamations of rightful entitlements, and the like. Up at the castle, the atmosphere between the English and Bohemians was tepid at best, as the two factions constantly vied for positions of power and influence, each side seeking to gain advantage over the other. The English courtiers were considered invaders of a sort, each appointment considered to have come at the cost of a Bohemian one. The division was in clear evidence out on the grounds of the castle that morning, as the spectators had separated themselves into two distinct groups, one on either side of the triumphal arch.

One of those present was the Countess Louise Juliana of Nassau, Frederick's mother. I took note that while everyone else had chosen to stand, she was seated in a chair which two attendants had carried out for her. I knew her to be in good health and recognized it as a gesture of her general displeasure with the entire arrangement. She was always eager to sabotage any occasion at which her daughter-in-law stood to receive more attention than she. By then I had become accustomed to her obdurate demonstrations and took them in stride. At present she was making a great show of not bothering to look up at the triumphal arch even once, instead staring straight ahead with a dour expression.

Countess Juliana had held the title of Electress Palatine following the death of her husband, Frederick's father, and had ruled in the name of her son, but now that Frederick had married, that designation had fallen to me. From the moment of my arrival at the castle it had been a source of tension between us. She considered herself better suited to make decisions on matters of state and made no secret about it, though soon enough it became obvious Frederick was more like to acquiesce to my wishes than hers, in particular where his eventual bid for the crown came under discussion. I was naturally eager for the day when his coronation, and so mine, should become a real possibility. The Countess, on the other hand, felt it would be best if her son were not so hasty in assuming the throne.

"Well, dear Elizabeth." Frederick stood before the gate, looking eagerly at me. "What do you think of it?"

"You've gone to a lot of trouble," I said. "There was no need."

"Of course there was, but you haven't said whether you admire it or no?"

"It is decorative in design."

"There's a ringing endorsement if ever I heard one," I heard the Countess mutter to those assembled nearby.

"What I want to know is how it got here," said someone in the crowd.

"Indeed," Count Schomberg spoke up, "I had occasion to walk here yester evening and will attest there was naught here but lawn and shrubbery."

"I, too," Captain Hume offered, "came this way last night and encountered nothing of this imposing edifice." He was dressed shabbily as usual, poorly groomed, and looked generally to be out of place among the rest of the bystanders. I had seen to it that he accompany us to Heidelberg, if for no other reason than that he had been the last one to see my brother Henry alive. I had secured a special appointment for him as musician and soldier, though it came as no surprise that his welcome was less than enthusiastic at court, where they nattered and mocked his unpolished manner. For his part the Captain remained steadfast in his coarse yet candid demeanour, and for this I prized him. He had placed himself next to the Countess Juliana, who was doing her best to ignore him.

"What think you on't, Madam?" Captain Hume enquired of her. "Is it not a fitting tribute from a loving prince to his charming wife?"

"And not his possessing mother," Lady Anne whispered in my ear.

"It lists a little to one side," the Countess pronounced.

"I had the workmen up all night," Frederick ignored her and turned to me. "Look there," he pointed up to the top of the arch. "I have had the dedication inscribed in Latin. *Fridericus.V, Elisabetae, Conjugi cariss,*" he read out loud. "And here it shall stand day upon day for all to see," he spoke louder now for all to hear, "a testament to our marriage, that all those lords and ladies upon a visit to the Hortus Palatinus cannot fail to pass through its portals."

"One can get there as readily by way of the drawbridge," I heard the Countess mutter.

If Frederick heard this last remark, he did not acknowledge it, and I was relieved when at last the party began to disperse that the occasion should come to a close. Would that it might have been otherwise, but the edifice, as imposing as it was, had left me unmoved. Whatever gift Frederick might have presented me with, however rich or elegant, the effect should have been the same. Another bride might have thrilled at such an offering from her husband, but such should have been her sentiment, if she loved him truly, even for a paltry bauble.

It was only that love will not be bribed into existence, but must arise of its own accord, and no amount of gift-giving could conjure it up in me, save in some disfigured form. Do you see what a monolith the heart is? It stands alone and will not be moved — until it is moved. In that regard it is much like that impressive and heavy gate. I wonder, does it stand there yet at the entrance to the garden? When shut, it will not be penetrated, yet once penetrated, it will not be shut! The failure was not Frederick's but neither was it mine. For my part I should live all the years of our marriage in appreciation of his affection, but how could that hope to be enough?

As it was, I found him an adequate lover, in the sense that if he did not thrill me with his touch, neither did I shrink from it. He had a playful phrase for the entire proceeding, which he liked to refer to as "shaking the sheets." Whenever he said those words, he did so as though it were something terribly sinful and naughty. He was always very anxious to begin, giggled and moaned as a child might at some illicit play, and finished in a hurry. He took a great deal of enjoyment from the act to be sure, but as for any indulgence in the flesh, that was another matter. I sometimes imagined what it must be like to have a lover linger over my naked body, explore it, caress it, but there was precious little of that to be had from my husband. But do not mistake me. He was considerate and kind and gentle. He neither commanded the proceedings nor suffered to be commanded. The act as decreed by God would take care of itself, and all we needed to do was that which our nature led us to. There was no mystery in it. No magic.

There were times when I questioned whether I was capable of love at all, or whether that door had somehow been closed to me. As for adoration, worship, devotion, and the like, these were the very sentiments I disdained. I was happy to forgo them as they stood only to weaken my resolve, make me more vulnerable to deceit, disappointment, betrayal. Did I not want to love Frederick? Did I not try? And as for Sir Raleigh, was it mere infatuation? He could have made me do anything, go anywhere with him. I would have given up everything. But what is the true nature of love if not passion which divides a woman from herself? It's much the same for a man, I venture. Sir Raleigh had no reason to love me. I was hardly more than a girl. In years to come there would be men who openly expressed their love to me, who fell upon their knees before me to declare as much. And yet I should never hear it from those I cared for most.

"The Countess knows full well that you are not a good match for her son," Lady Anne told me one morning.

"I suppose she cannot be blind to the fact that I am not in love with her son."

"Such a matter should be of little concern to her but for

the fact that Frederick is so clearly in love with you. It is that which gives her cause for worry."

"I'm afraid I don't understand."

"Every man who takes a wife is faced with a choice, and by that choosing he sets in motion the wheels upon which much else will turn."

"Between wife and mother, you mean."

"Because her son's affection for you runs so deep, by that very fact is your indifference put to advantage. His devotion to you, his eagerness to please you, robs Countess Juliana of that territory which had hitherto been her domain. If Prince Frederick sees fit to defer to your judgment before hers, her position becomes tenuous. Take this matter of accepting the Bohemian crown. If she should counsel too much against it, her influence shall be all the more diminished when he takes the throne. You see how delicate it is."

Now here stood poor Frederick with me on one side and his mother on the other, the gate before us, everyone watching, and I thought he seemed in need of some reassurance. I went to embrace him, kissed him gently upon the cheek, and when he smiled at me with deep appreciation it was both comforting and unsettling to think I had so much power to make him happy or no. I hardly knew what was demanded of me. Still, I thought him not undeserving of love, even if it could not be mine, and it should cost me little to offer such affection as served to content him. And so there upon the palace grounds that day, I made a silent and simple pledge by which to steer the course of our marriage henceforth.

Chapter Nine

Hardly more than a fortnight had passed before the court was abuzz with new rumours regarding matters of the heart, this time concerning the budding romance between Lady Anne Dudley and Count Schomberg, who of late were hardly be seen out of each other's company.

"I vouchsafe the gossip is as thick as nectar," said Frederick to me one morning. We had decided to take our breakfast out on the terrace of the English Wing.

"More like molasses if you ask me," I said. It was a beautiful spring day and we sat at the wrought iron table, looking down at the river Neckar flowing between the houses of the town below.

"You don't think the courtiers are happy for them?" Frederick asked.

"So long as they find themselves neither increased nor diminished by the matter, I doubt they have a preference either way."

"That fact that one is English and the other Bohemian makes for added intrigue."

"What is the latest rumour?"

"That the Count has asked Lady Anne to marry him."

"Of course there's nothing to it, I take."

"Just the opposite, I'm afraid." Fredrick put down his cutlery and pushed back his chair. "The Count has asked for an audience with both of us, and I have granted it. They wait even now to be admitted here, as soon as we have finished our breakfast."

"I must say this is rather sudden."

"Oh, come now, don't tell me you haven't seen it coming." Frederick waved to an attendant that the guests should be shown in.

"I hadn't thought Lady Anne to be seriously considering marriage."

"Who said anything about marriage?"

"Why else should they seek to meet with us?"

"Your Majesties." Count Schomberg, Lady Anne at his side, appeared on the terrace.

Frederick indicated a set of benches along the wall that sat across from each other, and I rose from my chair to join them. When we had seated ourselves the Count took up Lady Anne's hand in his before addressing us with great formality: "Your Majesties, we come before you with great hopes to humbly enquire whether I might be allowed to ask Lady Anne for her hand in marriage."

"Well. This comes as a bit of a shock." I feigned surprise.

"I hardly think it can be so." Lady Anne seemed a little ruffled.

"What has my Maid of Honour to say?" I asked matter-of-factly.

"Indeed the Count has made certain overtures." Lady Anne was blushing like a school girl.

"And you find them agreeable, no doubt." Frederick smiled over at me. "Or I mistake the sparkle in your eye."

"Well, it seems the matter has already been settled." I made to rise from the bench.

"We have agreed," Lady Anne put out her hand to stop me, "that the matter may not be decided until we have your sanction."

"Just so." The Count collected himself. "And to that end, we pray you will deign to offer it."

"What have you to say, Elizabeth?" Frederick turned to me. "Do we accept his proposal?"

I couldn't help prolonging the suspense. "They are in our service and their first duty is to us."

"For my part," said Frederick, "I put no chattels on my chamberlain in this. He may do as he pleases."

"Madam, what say you?" Lady Anne looked at me with such apprehension I could torture her no more.

"I say . . . there shall be a wedding."

"Then we have your blessing." The Count rose.

"Without reservation." Frederick stood to shake his hand.

"This is happy news indeed." Lady Anne was visibly relieved.

"I would caution," I teased, "that the Count is a great deal older than you are."

"I seem to remember a young princess completely infatuated with a man twice her age."

"Indeed I warned of just such a one in my first letter to your mistress," said Frederick.

"I dare say there were many rivals for her Highness's affection," said Count Schomberg.

"But she would have none of them," said Lady Anne.

"And so was she forced to settle for me." Frederick looked at me playfully, but around the edges of his smile a tightness crept in, and my heart ached a little to think I could not love him. What he longed for was neither mine to give nor to withhold. It seemed unfair to both of us. He deserved better. But then, so did I.

Count Schomberg became very serious. "We would be most grateful to remain in your service."

"Though perhaps not with the same degree of devotion," offered Frederick wryly.

"No doubt their duties would be curtailed," I played along.

"Somewhat," the Count admitted.

"In this there is nothing to fear," Fredrick reassured them, "for your value to us has ever been less of duty and more of good counsel and companionship."

"And I will say as much for my part," I conceded, and took Lady Anne's hands in mine. I felt suddenly quite sentimental and thought to embrace her, but held back.

"You may be sure these shall continue," said the Count.

"Then let the wedding preparations begin," said Frederick. "You shall have use of the chapel here, or if need be, down in the town at the cathedral."

"We had thought," the Count seemed a little unsure of himself as he glanced over at Lady Anne, "to travel to England, that the ceremony might be held there."

"My family has asked that we take our vows in the Abbey," said Lady Anne, "but I have made no promises."

"Of course you shall go to London," I said.

"And you shall travel with us?"

"I'm afraid not." I spoke without looking at Frederick. "I am even now not yet recovered from my last journey," I lied, "but I will see to it there shall be a grand celebration upon your return."

"Very well." Lady Anne eyed me closely, the relief obvious on her face. "We shall look forward to it."

It was but one of the many ironies that royalty were not free to partake of just any occasion they might desire to attend. My presence at Lady Anne's wedding would have turned it into an unwieldy spectacle, not to mention saddling her family with unnecessary and burdensome expenses. That I might have harboured selfish reasons for not wanting to return to London and the very people who had forsaken me was another matter entirely.

It seemed no time at all before the happy couple had taken their leave to sail for England, and finding myself unprepared for how much I missed Lady Anne, I busied myself with the matter of the Hortus Palatinus, the gardens I had promised to build in honour of my brother's memory. Salomon de Caus, in consultation with my brother, had drawn them up for the grounds at St. James's Palace, but now I was determined to see them brought to completion in Heidelberg. The greatest challenge rested with the landscape. The castle lay nestled too close to the side of the mountain which rose up behind, and left little room for such an ambitious project. The dimensions of the garden called for a great tract of level ground many hundreds of feet in length and breadth.

"I fail to see," Monsieur de Caus had already cautioned me, "how these plans can be made to work. We will have to make extensive modifications, and the whole project will have to be scaled down immensely."

"There will be no scaling down," I told him. We were out on the grounds behind the castle, the plans he had brought from England laid out on a table before us. "We shall build it precisely as large as these plans call for."

"But look you there, Your Highness" — Monsieur de Caus pointed — "where a mountain rests in the place you would see your brother's garden created."

"My brother would not have allowed himself to be so easily defeated. Look." I took him by the arm. "You say you see nothing but rocks and trees, but I see orchards and lawns, fountains and shrubbery to rival any found in Italy or Spain. Picture there a great black marble fountain in the very centre, just as the plans call for, with four walkways leading away in different directions, and alongside each of them hedges, and in behind pavilions with trellises and arches, arbours and bowers. Now look over there. It shall be the place where we build a great grotto within which Henry's portrait shall be mounted. I tell you, it will happen because we will make it so."

"Forgive me, Your Highness, I do not see how it can be accomplished."

"If the mountain will not see fit to allow for this garden, then we must insist that it withdraw."

"Your Highness . . ."

"It will have to be removed, some portion of it at any rate."

"But such an undertaking is hardly possible. The task is too great."

"Monsieur de Caus, it was my brother's dream to travel the world," I said. "More than any other place, he wished to visit Italy, for there he had heard how the families of the Medici and Borghese saw fit to cultivate a great flourishing of art and culture, architecture and music. He was determined that if my father should not allow him to see it for himself, some semblance of it be brought to England. These plans are the embodiment of that intent. You will see to it."

"But how?"

"A portion of the mountain will have to be taken away, but only as much as is needed to allow for the construction."

"But Highness, a great dense forest covers the mountainside."

"It will have to be cleared."

"And then what? Beneath lies naught but a great mass of granite rock."

"Then smash it up and cart it away."

"That will take an army of quarrymen, and even then it would mean cutting out a rock face a hundred feet high. Impossible."

"Very well, how be it we carve out a series of flat surfaces, one set above the other, with stone steps leading from one level to the next?"

"A set of terraces." Salomon de Caus put a hand to his chin as though we were working something out in his head. "Laid one against the other, up the side of the mountain."

"Just so."

He gave me a long look. "It will be a daunting challenge, but by such method might the Hortus Palatinus yet be accomplished."

"Then you had better get busy."

And so it was that a corps of men set to work cutting down trees to clear away the forest, slicing into the rock, and hewing off great slabs to haul away, along with endless carts of rubble and stone. Hour after hour they laboured, day after day, until they had created a set of five terraces, each one several hundreds of feet in length and breadth. When the day came at last that Monsieur de Caus took me to see the result, there before me was a huge tract of land where only the side of a mountain had been, a series of terraces each as smooth and flat as an enormous table. I took him about, pointing here and there, telling him in intricate and enthusiastic detail where everything was going to go and how it was going to look.

"And this," I pointed, "is where a grove of full-grown orange tress shall be planted. I have already seen to their procurement as well as to the construction of wooden walls and roof so that each year they are protected from the weather in the cold months. And that is only the beginning. We shall have a water works such as no garden, even in the southern countries, has ever boasted of. My brother had plans for a water organ to be built from a design he discovered in an early Roman text. The water, he told me, would flow out of one fountain and into another, from one terrace down to the next, each one adorned with statues of nymphs, satyrs, gods, and all the noble creatures of the earth that move about, nearer and farther to the viewer, all while spouting streams of water. Can you do it?"

Before Monsieur de Caus could answer I carried on.

"And there," I indicated, "a set of double convex stairways shall lead from one terrace to the next. There we will have beds of flowers in endless variety, such as he has specified were to his taste and liking, and in the midst of it all a labyrinth cut out of hedges at the centre of which shall be an arrangement of fountains. Oh, and there beyond the orange grove, set into the side of the mountain, an elaborate grotto adorned with Venus fountains where fish move about the water and mechanical birds flutter their wings and sing while the water bubbles and frolics and plays about them. And within the grotto, a special alcove where a portrait of Henry shall hang."

Salomon de Caus weighed every idea, and rather than pronounce judgment upon them, nodded politely at each one. So it was that by degrees the Hortus Palatinus blossomed into fruition, until the day came that Frederick and I led Lady Anne and the Count, newly returned from England, through the elaborate gate he had erected for me, and into the gardens.

"They are far from completed," I cautioned, "but I couldn't wait any longer. I had to show someone."

"It's going to be magnificent," said Lady Anne.

"It already is," added Count Schomberg.

We walked along one of the many paths, past flowers and fountains, until we reached the orange grove, where the setting sun had turned the blossoms a shimmering golden yellow. Lady Anne and Count Schomberg walked ahead of us, arm in arm.

Upon their arrival back in Heidelberg they had been greeted with celebration and good wishes, and it was not until they had taken a few days to settle into their new living quarters in the English Wing that Lady Anne and I found ourselves at last alone in my privy chamber of an evening. I wanted to ask her about the wedding, and to hear details of the journey, which she gave over freely, but it seemed to me there was something of an edge in her recollections and I wondered what it was.

"I can hardly imagine what it should have been like to travel back to London and see the place for myself again. Tell me, do the lords and ladies still play Pall Mall along St. James's Square?"

"I never thought you cared for the game."

"I don't, but Henry loved to play at it for hours on end. And when it wasn't that, there was tennis and golf and tilting.

I suppose it is not so much London I miss as my brother. But what news is there? Surely you can catch me up on some spicy scandal or other."

"Madam, that has ever been the very thing you profess to disdain. You cannot be so changed in the short time I have been away."

"But there is some news. I see it in your eyes. Does it concern my mother and father?"

"They write to you, do they not?"

"My mother only wants to brag after some masque she has plans to mount, my father to make enquiries after matters of state. Other than that, their letters could hardly be more perfunctory. There's little in them of any import. They will not even deign to ask me so much as a single question about my life here. The lion's share of our correspondence is a paltry façade of empty pleasantries. The truth is, I really have nothing to say to them. But enough about that, what's the latest news from the Tower? Surely you must have heard something. Sir Raleigh languishes there yet, no doubt. And Lady Arabella?"

I saw immediately in Lady Anne's expression that I had at last hit upon the cause of her reticence. She looked down into her hands, then back up at me. "I heard something of her, though I put it down to no more than rumours, which are always in generous supply."

"I would know it."

"I cannot attest to the truth of it."

"You can't mean she is freed. Lord Seymour managed to rescue her! Oh, that would be such sweetness. Perhaps they may see fit to make their way here. It may be that very subject she would have broached with me had I but given her private audience. She could not write it in a letter. It would give me great satisfaction to harbour them here. I'm sure Frederick would have seen his way to allow it."

"It is not that which I have heard," Lady Anne cautioned, "nor any such."

"Then what? Tell me."

"That she gave birth to a child."

My thoughts fell back at once to the last letter Arabella had written to me.

September 2, 1615

Dear Elizabeth,

I have never been one to give up, but these days a vermin gnaws at my spirit, and I despair. Already the chilling breezes have begun to blow in through my cell here at the Tower. Winter is coming for me and I dare not be here when it arrives!

My appetite has left me. Who can hunger for food such as this? I have chosen to forego my meals of late, which having been brought to me, I dutifully accept, but after the Yeoman has gone throw out through the bars of my small window and down into the courtyard below. There the waiting ravens enter into conspiracy with me and immediately swoop down to gobble up the evidence as quickly as I throw it down to them. The last upon the scene is always Arthur, that same bird with one eye and crooked beak that is soon chased off by the others. But we have made an arrangement that sees him sneak back later to perch on my sill, where I have held back a small portion just for him.

A growing weariness runs deep through my body. Thankfully such hunger and cold as I may experience are mitigated by sleep, which I do a great deal of. I am writing because I want you to know, Elizabeth, and I hope you can understand, that I have come to the point where there is simply nothing more to be done. My only comfort is that I shall take everlasting consolation in knowing of a place where a young life waxes even as mine wanes.

If you should hear aught of me, know it was not by bloody dagger, nor poison, nor any such as these by which I took my leave, but rather those peaceful means you are now privy to.

Yours with undying affection and regret that we may not be reunited,
Arabella Stuart

"'A young life waxes even as mine wanes . . .'" I recited.

"Madam?"

"It was something Arabella said. Now I understand."

"The baby was born in good health they say," Lady Anne assured me, "a miracle, considering the conditions, but no sooner had it managed a lungful of air than it was torn from her and brought away to be taken by ship across the channel."

"And Arabella?"

"They say she has since fallen into a state of deep distress and melancholy, at which she refuses all food and drink, but lies upon her cold bed day and night without word or sound."

"If this be so, it can hardly be sadder. If I were yet in London I should go and see for myself no matter the risk."

"It may only be hearsay."

"I must find a way to reach her."

"There are always stories coming out of the Tower, many wildly inaccurate."

"I grant it is hard to believe, but just the same I would know for certain. We will celebrate your nuptials for the present, and thereafter I must see to a means of learning the truth."

"I hope you would not go to much trouble for my part. The Count and I have had our fill of revelry."

"There shall be some festivities just the same. I won't hear otherwise."

Why, I wondered, did I so often have need to engage in

feigned merriment even as my heart lay elsewhere, far from such frivolous pursuits?

I held a reception for them in the Hortus Palatinus, next to the fountain of Father Rhine near Henry's Grotto. So blissful was the couple's demeanour that it could not help but rub off on the guests, who drank in their pure happiness with their wine, swallowed it down with their food, English and Bohemian alike willing to set aside their petty differences for one evening and join in the merriment. Lady Anne fairly glowed. I had never seen her so happy. How many brides had I witnessed, exhausted by the day's effort, receiving guests, their inner misgivings thinly veiled by their outward ebullience, and yet here was Lady Anne utterly devoid of such pretense, bubbling over with pure joy.

The way her eyes fell upon her new husband, the way I had never looked at Frederick and never could, brought me up short against a harsh reality. My own wedding had taken place while I was still numb with grief, sick with disquiet, and hardly in a position to care that I was marrying a man I did not love. But what could I say of myself now?

"Quite rare, don't you think?" The Countess Juliana had come to stand next to me and I was a little taken aback.

"Madam?"

"That two people can make each other so happy." I had not expected her to attend the reception and her sudden appearance surprised me.

"Indeed," I replied. "They make a charming couple."

Lady Anne and Count Schomberg were making their way among the guests, exchanging kisses and handshakes with one party after another.

"If only every wedding couple were so blissful," I said.

"Too often one party must supply the passion for both. But when you see it like this . . ."

"And yours?" I asked.

"Mine?" The Countess stared back at me wide-eyed, clearly unsettled by my question.

"Your wedding, how did it fare against this?" From time to time, attendant to my affliction, I would descend into a state of raw emotion that gave me to feel my centre compromised, at which my reaction would be that of unexpected boldness.

"I didn't marry for love, if that's what you mean. But then, I think you know something of that."

"And so you saw fit to content yourself with civility and other niceties of matrimonial affection."

"There were certain benefits to be had from a position of neutrality," said the Countess.

"You would couch the matter in the language of nation states."

"The matter? And just what is the matter you speak of?"

"There are always elements of sovereignty in any marriage," I offered.

"A husband's unrequited love for his wife puts him at a disadvantage if he seeks but to please her and never succeeds."

"And sees fit to keep on trying nevertheless," I added.

"By such means may a wife enjoy the stronger position, even in matters of considerable import."

"Indeed love is blind, so I've heard it said."

"Some will say as much of ambition. My son is going to need someone with a level head to see him through this business of the Bohemian crown."

"You fear he is not up to it."

"Of more importance may be whether you are."

"How so?"

"He has little to benefit from your ambition, but much from your faith."

"He is more able than you deem," I said sternly.

"The Holy Roman Emperor shall have something to say about it, you can be sure."

"There are many who would stand to defend your son's reign."

"And what if those allies prove insufficient, or worse yet, unwilling? Then what fate awaits us? You have a son of your own to think of now. Or perhaps the prospect that he should one day be king is what drives you on."

"King Henry. It has a nice ring to it."

"I say it is wise to temper ambition with humility."

We fell into a silence thereafter, stood and watched together as Lady Anne and Count Schomberg moved through the crowd, smiling as they accepted congratulations, making sure always to stay within arm's reach of each other. That familiar gloom which had been my acquaintance for too long lifted a little, for here before me shone irrefutable proof that happiness could well and truly exist in the world. It was only a matter of finding it. Perhaps it was wrong of me to deride my life so eagerly in the face of such a testament to how good it could be. What had my derision accomplished? For just a moment I allowed myself to believe things would get better.

Lady Anne had hardly been married more than a few months when she announced to me one morning that she was with child. By then my own son Henry was almost a year old, and in that time his grandmother the Countess Juliana had come to dote on him and all but given herself over to his care and keeping, a task for which she seemed in my estimation to be entirely well-suited. In as much as young Henry clearly loved his grandmother, and that Frederick seemed reconciled to the arrangement, I was content to let it be so. But it simply had not occurred to me that Lady Anne might soon be looking to the needs of her own child. No doubt she would make a devoted and loving mother, but I was still adjusting to her diminished attention to my needs, and found the idea that she should soon be rearing a child of her own an unwelcome prospect.

The pregnancy was uneventful, as was the birth of an

infant son, whom they christened Frederick. But no sooner had baby and mother been pronounced healthy and whole than Lady Anne complained of a severe headache, followed by stomach pains and nausea. Not long after, she began to exhibit periods of delirium, and the baby was taken from her. Thereafter Count Schomberg sat constantly at her bedside, holding her hand, speaking to her, stroking her cheek, even as her features changed before him, face turned puffy, olive skin become blotchy red, unseeing eyes swollen to twice their size. He could hardly be convinced to leave her side, and when he deigned to do so for a moment, became utterly inconsolable once out of the room, his heart breaking right before our eyes. Frederick and I shared his torment, much as we had my brother Henry's, and though it gave rise to a certain tenderness of feeling between us, there was an aspect of cruelty to it. Why did it have to be tragedy which brought such a thing into being?

When it was clear that the worst was indeed imminent, Frederick sent for the preacher Abraham Scultetus, who had seen to the baptism and now arrived to perform the last rites. He appeared in his usual garb of clerical robes, cap pulled tightly down upon his head, cropped beard and moustache accentuating his dour expression and severity of manner. My husband placed a great deal of trust in him where clerical matters were concerned, and though his office did not call for counsel in matters of state, Scultetus seemed eager to offer it. The few exchanges between us had already made it clear that we should hardly be allies when it came to my ambitions for Prague, but at the moment I was eager to set all that aside, content to let him perform his spiritual duties. When he had finished, Count Schomberg returned at once to the bedside.

"Hans, is that you?" asked Lady Anne. It was the first and only time I heard her address her husband by that name. "I'm so glad you came by. I thought we might go to the countryside. London is so hot this time of year."

The Count turned to look up at us helplessly, then back to Lady Anne.

"My head." Lady Anne put up her hands. "My head is become a cathedral and within it such a ringing of bells as I have never heard . . . I had a baby once, a boy . . . when the bells have finished I shall take my rest. Will you stay until then?"

"I shall."

"Light. I feel so light."

Now she gripped the Count's hand tightly in hers and pulled herself forward with great effort, clutched his shoulder, and as he leaned back a little, straightened herself almost to a sitting position, every muscle of her body strained with some invisible force. "Is it time? I hardly thought the hour was so late. But who will see to My Lady?"

Her eyes fell shut and her body went limp. Before the Count could lower her back onto the pillow she had passed into a sudden sleep. There was nothing to be done, and so for a time I withdrew into an antechamber, but after a moment Count Schomberg appeared and beckoned me to the door.

"Your Highness, she has awakened of a sudden, and wishes to speak to you."

"Of course, let's go in."

"She asked to see you alone."

"Very well."

"I shall be right outside the door."

I went to the bedside, just the two of us now in the dimly lit room, for even though Lady Anne was by then completely blind, the light bothered her, and as I leaned over to inspect her features it was clear she was in tremendous discomfort.

"Elizabeth?" asked Lady Anne. "Is that you?"

"Yes. Yes, I'm here."

"They will not bring me my son."

"No. The physicians fear a miasma in the room."

"But you can see to it."

"What has the Count to say?"

"He defers to the physicians and thinks it best not to."

"Then perhaps we were best to leave it by."

"My baby," she whispered. "I want to hold my boy just once more."

I thought of Henry calling out for me from his deathbed, what it must have been like for him, and decided I was not going to stand by and let it happen again.

"Then I will bring him to you."

I stopped at the door, where Count Schomberg was waiting, and stood before him. "She would hold her son one last time."

"But the physicians have said . . ."

"Hang the physicians. Will you allow me to bring him to her?"

"They will forbid it."

"Let them try and stop me."

"Do it, then."

I made straight for the nursery and returned after no more than a few moments with a nursemaid carrying little Frederick wrapped in swaddling.

Before I could enter the room, one of the physicians stepped before me and put up his hand. "Your Highness, what do you think you're doing?" He was one of several who had been treating Lady Anne, all of whom practised much the same way as those in London, that is, with rigid adherence to useless learning and so methodology of pitiable effect. Though none were so abusive of authority as Dr. Mayerne had been, it was pointless to speak to them, for they uttered only the same tired platitudes.

"I'm bringing this child to its mother," I said, "and you will not stop me."

"I'm afraid I can't allow it."

I looked beyond the physician to where Count Schomberg was kneeling at Lady Anne's bedside. "The father has given his permission."

"There may be a miasma in the room."

"I don't care if there are bats flying around the bed, this baby will go to its mother, and you will not interfere."

"I'm afraid it's out of the question."

I felt I was reliving much the same scenario I had been forced to endure during my brother's illness, save that there were no guards posted at the door, and thought to call out to Count Schomberg for assistance. But just then who should appear but the unshaven and shoddy Captain Hume, sword hung at his side as usual, looking as though he had not slept in days and carrying a sorry bouquet of wilting wildflowers in his hand. I was never so glad to see the man in my life.

"Good day to you, Your Highness. I came to see whether I might have a moment to place these flowers at the feet of the Lady Anne Dudley, if you will allow it, but now I see that you would bring this baby to its mother and will defer until a more suitable occasion."

"This is outrageous," said the physician. "There shall be no babies and certainly no visitors the like of this beggar allowed in the room. I simply won't have it. Your Highness, this man is filthy."

"When did that become a concern for your profession? I have never seen one of you yet that washed his hands before sticking his fat fingers into a mother giving birth."

"I will not be lectured to, even by you, Your Highness."

"Then stand aside and leave us to it."

"And who might you be?" said Captain Hume.

"He is one of the physicians," I said. "A great bother, as they are wont to be."

"Stand aside, Sir," said Captain Hume, "that we may enter."

"I will not."

The Captain put one hand on his sword, "You will give passage."

"I shall summon the guards."

"Then do so. You will find them in the courtyard. They offered me a salute as I went by. But when you return, I suggest you have a weapon of your own at the ready."

"Go in," the Captain turned to me. "I shall wait here and see you are not disturbed, that you should have all the time you need."

Lady Anne raised her head as soon as I entered. "Who's there?"

"Elizabeth," I said, and the nursemaid followed me to the bed. "I have brought you your son. Here." I motioned, and the nursemaid lowered the baby gently down into Lady Anne's outstretched arms. She took him tenderly, her eyes straight ahead that could no longer see, and brought her cheek down to rub it along the top of the boy's downy head. "My boy," she uttered softly, "my sweet boy. Perhaps one day you shall hear how it came about that the first time your mother held you fell so nigh to upon the last, but know that you shall feel this cheek brush against your own when as a man you stand before the wind, and this kiss upon your brow when the sun warms your upturned face. Remember me in this way. Remember me."

They lay in quiet rest for some silent moments, baby and mother, until Lady Anne grew agitated, her eyes wider, as though perhaps some unsettling vision appeared before her, and I motioned for the nursemaid to take the baby from her.

"Deliver him," said Lady Anne, her fingertips still outstretched, "into the care of his strong and loving father. I go to my rest."

A curtain fell across her eyes, their light muted, while the maidservant carried the baby out of the room, and as Count Schomberg knelt at her side and wept, I motioned for Captain Hume to step into the room. He stopped at the foot of the bed, still clutching the flowers he had picked, their stems crushed in his great fist, and placed them gently upon the sheets without a sound, tears streaming down his cheeks.

Now a long, languid stiffening ran through the length of Lady Anne's body, began at her feet and made its way slowly along the sinews of her body until it reached her outstretched neck, at which she turned her head up to the ceiling in the strangest way. A loud exhalation followed, punctuated by a tiny rattle, as slowly her body came to rest again upon the bed, though not seeming to lie on it, her head upon the pillow and yet making no indentation there. She became inanimate before our eyes.

We wept each of us together and by turns, now this one upon that shoulder and then another, and cried out our anguish, but mine was tinged with wonder to think I had been witness to something so mysterious that left me profoundly saddened and yet, somehow, with a deeper reverence for life than I had ever known. It seemed to me I had been transformed in some small way by her dying, that the floor beneath me shifted ever so slightly, the room a little tilted now, the light somehow altered. I left the room not quite the same Elizabeth as the one that had entered. In a short span of time I had lost the two people closest to me, who each in their way had served as a touchstone for me, a compass of sorts. But now I was truly on my own.

It occurred to me that Lady Anne's passing marked the terminus of a great chain, forged from all who had come before her. The spark of her life had originated from another life, and that from another before her, and so on back even to the first, to the start of creation. We were each of us the last link in a chain of life that traced its origin back to the very beginning. Though we might pass that same spark on to a son or a daughter, ours was destined to be snuffed out. In that way, death was final. Let the body struggle to the last to stay, to live, to say it is not the end, still it must come to a finish. Leave it to the mystics to riddle the rest, though they have little invested until it comes their turn. Lady Anne was gone, but perhaps some part of her had not disappeared altogether.

Life by its leaving created the unknown, and it was precisely that which awaited us all. For certain, what was left behind to bury amounted to no more than meat, but what of some other? What became of our ethereal and inconvenient souls?

That evening I made my way through the gate Frederick had erected for me and into the Hortus Palatinus, where I wandered along its paths in solitude, until I had reached the highest terrace of the garden above the fountain of Father Rhine, where a small, unguarded gate opened into the forest beyond. It had never struck me to walk through that gate, but now for some reason it seemed the very thing I should do. Perhaps it would lead me to the meadow where Captain Hume had picked his wildflowers for Lady Anne.

When I had pushed open the gate and stepped beyond it, there seemed only to be unbroken forest, but after a moment I came upon a little-used path and decided to follow it. Soon enough it led to one more well-worn and I took that. The trail wound its way along the mountainside, where from time to time it intersected others leading in different directions. The sun had descended low in the sky, and I walked mostly in shadow. This was an entirely different experience from my wanderings amid the manicured lawns and pruned shrubbery of the garden. Now I took a trail that led me higher up the mountainside until I reached a small clearing that offered a glimpse of the castle below, its turrets of thick and impenetrable stone aglow in the evening light.

I had the mountain to myself. Birds sang their late evening songs in the darkening wood, thrushes and finches and warblers; a raven's caw echoed from an outcropping of granite rock. I listened to the sounds of the forest: a small rodent scurrying about among the leaves and twigs, the dying breeze sighing high up in the pines, and then something else, something moving behind me. I imagined some gentle creature and turned to see. A lone wolf, large and grey, shoulders high, stopped in mid-stride, one paw lifted into the air, and posed there, furry head turned toward me, blue eyes piercing and cold. Neither menacing nor friendly, he stood in perfect stillness, let me feel his power, even as he seemed to be trying to make up his mind about something. He took a silent step, stopped again, a different paw raised in the air. Something in his eyes of calculation. I was being judged. Was I to be feared or hunted? I felt myself as a creature in a way I never had before, all my artifice come to naught. I wanted to run, couldn't, waited. At last he resumed his gait, eyes never relinquishing their grip on me, until he had loped far enough to disappear among the trees.

It was then I realized I had been holding my breath, and now exhaled, then took in a great gulp of fresh air. My breath restored to me, I next became aware of my heart beating with great force and urgency, my limbs tightened in rigid readiness. Even as my body slowly returned to a more relaxed state, I felt its waning readiness to run farther and faster than ever I had in my life. Was this what it meant to be in a state of nature? My vision was as sharp and clear as I could ever remember it, my sense of smell aroused, every sound intensified. Were those yet the sounds of his distant, furtive footfalls upon the forest floor? And was that yet his scent still in the air, or my own? And was it relief I felt that he had chosen to move on, or regret? I couldn't recall a time in my life when I had felt so alive.

I followed the trails, one leading into another, and by the time I had wound my way back down the mountain and entered through the gate into the garden, it was almost entirely dark. Lights had come on in the castle and as I walked across the manicured lawns toward its hulking presence, it felt more familiar to me than it ever had. I would go for many more such twilight walks after that day, always half-hoping, half-dreading that I might run into the wolf again, but I never did. I sometimes fancied it might have been the ghost of my brother, or perhaps even Lady Anne, come in that form to visit itself upon me, shake me out of my melancholy and despair. I don't know where I should have ended up that day, or indeed if I should ever have come back, but for that encounter. I was glad for the lights of the castle, warm and inviting, though it promised to hold fewer comforts for me now. It might be better to starve my heart for the sake of preserving it, and for a time go hungry.

Chapter Ten

After Lady Anne died I took myself daily to the mountainside behind the castle to wander the trails aimlessly for hours on end. Frederick worried that I was inconsolable, but the truth was that I had no wish to be consoled. I suggested he direct his concern to Count Schomberg, whose grief had crippled him entirely, to the point where he lost all capacity to see to his own needs, let alone those of his infant son. For my part I took little interest in my own Henry, suffered intensely the same affliction in which that black-fisted darkness threatened to smother me, and which I was powerless to defend against. I only wanted to be alone. Then came news that Count Schomberg had taken ill and been confined to his bed, and soon after that he succumbed to a raging fever and was lost as well, until it seemed to me that tragedy had become my most reliable companion and sorrow my natural state.

I had the need to acquire the services of another lady-in-waiting, for which there were any number of young women eager to apply. I granted a small number an informal audience that they might demonstrate to me their suitability for the position, but there was not one among them I was eager to employ. It was more of a necessary evil than anything. If I thought I could have managed on my own I should have been glad to do so, but there was simply too much I could not accomplish by myself. I couldn't even dress myself on some occasions. A French Farthingale, for example, required an entire orchestration of manoeuvres to get into. There's as much of chattel as privilege in the accoutrements of royalty, and so I was resigned to be fussed over daily, to the point where patience lost its battle with decorum.

In the case of my lady-in-waiting, the secretarial tasks alone were formidable, from sifting through correspondence to composing replies on my behalf, for I made it always a point to keep very much abreast of any developments that might prove advantageous to my ambitions. I already knew that whomever I chose, the two of us should never enjoy that degree of intimacy Lady Anne and I had indulged in. In the end I chose Amalia von Solms, a woman of little means some six years younger than I, not because she was ambitious, self-important, and scheming, which all of the candidates were, but because in addition to all these traits she promised to be the most efficient, and this turned out to be the case.

Things returned somewhat to normalcy for a time, and I began once again to take interest in matters of state, though none too soon. My husband had always been easily swayed by those nearest to him, and now I saw plainly that he took counsel from the assembled clerics with great reverence, Abraham Scultetus among them. They were not in favour of Frederick bidding for the crown, and it soon became apparent that I should have to summon my resolve and take action if I wanted to see my way to Prague.

My task was made somewhat easier when Countess Juliana announced one evening at dinner that she intended to take up residence at her private estate in the country.

"I think it is best for all of us" — Juliana offered a brief glance in my direction — "that I see my way out of Heidelberg altogether, at least for a while."

Frederick looked up from his plate. "It has always been your favourite retreat, but do you mean to say you want to go and live there? No doubt you shall miss your entertainments."

"Perhaps, but I grow ever more weary of court life and welcome the chance to retire from it."

"There are other considerations. Surely you don't mean to abandon your interest in affairs of state for the sake of country life."

"I am content hereafter to leave such matters to others" — she regarded me with a condescending smile — "who can give you counsel as well as I. Besides, it isn't as though I'm going abroad. It is only a little more than a day's travel. I shall not be far if you should find the need to summon me."

"And what of your grandson?" I asked.

"Yes," Frederick put in, "it is plain Henry adores you."

"I can attest to as much," I said, then added: "No doubt he shall miss his grandmother terribly," a comment which seemed to catch Frederick off guard.

Juliana put down her cutlery. "I was wondering whether I might take young Henry with me."

"I suppose the country air might do him good," said Frederick, "and we could come to fetch him in a week or two."

Juliana and I exchanged a quick glance.

"I had in mind rather a longer period of time." She played with her napkin.

Frederick put down the cup of wine and looked at his mother, then at me, then back at Juliana.

"You mean to say you want to keep him there?"

"There's a lot to be said for an upbringing in the country. And you could come to visit him as often as you like."

"You would take upon yourself the raising of our son." Frederick was looking at me.

"It would do him good to be away from all this fuss and bother, don't you think?"

"Elizabeth" — Frederick had not turned his eyes from me — "what have you to say on this?"

"I myself was raised away from the royal court," I offered, "in a peaceful country home. There is a lot to be said for it."

"But . . . he is your son."

"As it is, the boy is seen to in large measure by attendants and nurses," Juliana said evenly.

"I always thought a child should be with its mother." Frederick looked down at his plate, then up at me. "You have no objections?" he pleaded.

"We can visit as often as we like," I said weakly.

"Then you find this proposal agreeable."

I nodded.

"I feel as though I am being conspired against," said Frederick.

"I think it stands to be quite an agreeable arrangement, don't you?" Juliana waited while I pretended to consider my answer.

"After all," she added, "you are Electress Palatine now, and must see to all the responsibilities that go with the title."

The bargain would be made all the more palatable by the fact that she truly doted on the boy and he delighted in her constant attentions to him. Juliana would leave her son's affairs to me and I would leave the raising of Henry to her.

"You must admit it will make things easier," I said to Frederick. "There's a great deal to do, and our son would be in the care of someone who loves him."

"Someone who loves him," Frederick mumbled to himself.

If my husband thought it cold of me to turn down such a path, it was only that Lady Anne's passing had stirred me into an unsettling jumble of emotion. I had been both freed and abandoned, felt at once daunted as well as intoxicated. Notions of mother and wife seemed suited for little more than employment as tools to stifle my ambitions. For the first time in my life I had no one to answer to. There was nothing to stop me now.

On the morning Juliana took her leave with young Henry, I retired to my chambers and remained there for the rest of the day, but that evening I sought out the privacy of my balcony in the English Wing, which I was often wont to do at that time of day. I leaned over the stone wall that ran the length of the terrace and regarded the town below, already under a cloak of darkness though the castle was still lit by the last rays of the setting sun. The houses below sent lazy spirals of smoke up from their brick chimneys, lights glowing out of the windows as I watched the street lamps being lit. I thought of all the mothers toiling within the walls of those modest homes, tending even now to the endless needs of their children, and after seeing them all to bed at last, the day's chores completed, left with naught to look forward to but to fall into exhausted sleep before another day dawned. I felt an uncertain mixture of guilt and gladness that I was free not only of my mother-in-law's meddling but also of child-rearing duties.

I would set myself to redoubling my efforts to counsel my husband upon a course of action that should see us to Prague. I had little doubt he would see fit to carry out my ministrations, and that little stood in the way of success. But as in nature, where the exit of one force predicates the arrival of another, an equally formidable adversary promptly made his appearance in the form of Abraham Scultetus. Having presided over the funeral of Count Schomberg, he had hardly uttered the last prayer than he began to insinuate himself into that same role the Count had played so well. I suppose I might have seen it coming, as Frederick had ever been inclined to such influences, eager to heed the judgments of those in authority. In no time at all Scultetus had managed to become his closest advisor. While Frederick gave me my due, made sure to pay my suggestions and opinions full value, he would make a habit of adding, after I had finished putting my case, that he should thereafter take the matter up with Abraham Scultetus.

My efforts to move things along became increasingly thwarted and I determined to settle the matter with Scultetus himself. I arranged one evening to intercept him on his stroll through the grounds of the Hortus Palatinus, where he daily made a great show of walking in solitude, stopping now and then at a bench or grotto or fountain to engage in the most ostentatious contemplation, at one time with hands clasped in prayer, at another with his eyes cast heavenward, so that anyone watching should see how devout he was and with what gravitas he considered all matters pertinent to his counsel.

Perhaps another woman might have determined that she should see to the matter in the privacy of her bedchamber, where she might apply her charms and by such means get her husband to do her bidding, but that was never going to work with Frederick. Though I was content to grant his conjugal visits, he never stayed long and discussion regarding matters of state was entirely out of the question. The blame fell as much to shyness as inconsideration. He was timid to the point where, even after years of marriage, he would not let me see him naked. I think on it now and I cannot say for certain that I ever saw him entirely in his God-given flesh. For his part he was always eager to look upon mine at his leisure, lift off the covers that he might feast upon my nakedness. Having done so he would douse the lights, take off the rest of his clothes, and jump under the covers, making sure to pull them up around me as well, before he launched into the business of shaking the sheets without further ado.

I should have welcomed the chance for some small variation in the routine but there was little to be had. Though I hinted at a more vigorous engagement now and then, not once did Frederick take it upon himself to ravage me. How could I explain to him there might be times when I wanted to be taken with the full force of a man's need, considering that in such imaginings it was Sir Raleigh who enraptured me in the frenzy of his passion? On the whole, Frederick being that most considerate of lovers made things easy for me, but it was far from enough.

I tried on occasion to inject a little mischief into the affair, perhaps only to reach under the covers and say, "What now that this member should rise to full address . . ."

"Madam?"

". . . and seek to gain admittance to the inner chamber?"

"You jest."

"There to penetrate the lusty loins."

"I am ready, if that's what you mean."

For Frederick's part he did not lack enthusiasm. My body excited him tremendously and when he was about to penetrate me, hovering over me with arms planted on either side, his breath would come in short bursts, his body shivering with anticipation. Having spent himself, he would withdraw almost immediately, but not before holding me very tight and whispering in my ear, "You are so precious to me." Then he was up out of bed, pulling his robes about him to make his way back to his own bedchamber.

"You are always so quick to leave," I said one evening after a particularly short coupling, "but no matter, I am eager to see myself through to completion."

"Beg pardon, Madam, but what can be left to accomplish?"

"Naught but that same ecstasy you just now enjoyed."

"What God gave a man to do with his wife I have done, have I not?"

"Yes, and I shall see to the remainder in my own way."

Frederick looked at me with an expression of stony disapproval. "It falls to needless indulgence."

"You think my pleasure gratuitous. Surely you satisfy yourself from time to time when you are in solitude."

"I am determined to exercise the utmost restraint in that arena."

"But why should you have need to do so?"

"To indulge in pleasure for its own sake is sinful in the eyes of God. Abraham Scultetus would attest to as much."

"Do you mean to say you've never taken matters, as it were, into your own hands?"

"Those times I have indulged myself have always been followed with prayer and penance."

"Then I shall be sure to do the same when I have finished."

By such means did I inadvertently make matters worse when it came to the amount of time my husband spent in my bed. After that he seemed even more anxious to remove himself, lest he might have to witness me writhing about under the sheets and moaning.

If I was going to make any headway in my ambitions to Prague, I would be better off devoting my energies to seeing what influence I might exert over Abraham Scultetus. If I could get him to endorse my plan, it should go a long way to bringing my husband down the same path.

One evening I made my way through Elizabethentor, the gate Frederick had so lovingly erected for me, and headed into the Hortus Palatinus, hoping to come upon Abraham Scultetus and intercept him. I walked straightway to the retaining wall and ascended the first set of stone stairs leading up to the second terrace, from which vantage point I hoped to spot him more easily. The evening was peaceful and the sun low, its last rays still lighting up the side of the mountain above the castle. I had not walked for long when I saw him emerge from the grotto next to the fountain of Father Rhine, where he proceeded to seat himself upon a stone bench and enter into a state of deep contemplation. I made my way straight there, and as he saw me draw near he rose from the bench and bowed.

"Your Highness, I bid you a good even."

"And I you, Sir."

"I hadn't thought to see you walk about here at this late hour. It will soon be dark."

"I have little to fear from the dark. It is those who sometimes linger about in't that we must needs be wary of." I gestured along one of the paths that led away from the fountain. "Will you walk with me?

"By all means, Highness. It will be my privilege."

We made our way over the stones, walking side by side. In the past our exchanges had invariably turned into each taking the measure of the other, a wary game of words to determine whether we might become formidable opponents or conspiring allies.

"This is the best time of the day, I often think," I said.

"Perhaps, like me," Scultetus answered, "you rather enjoy the fading of the light."

"Light will have its uses," I replied, "for that which would remain hidden under cloak of night cannot fail to find itself exposed in the broad light of day."

"I come to take advantage of the solitude and quiet."

"The Bible says it is not good for a man to be alone."

"Forgive me, Highness, but you apply the passage improperly. Those words of scripture were meant to convey a different meaning."

"That a man may benefit from the companionship of a woman. I am well aware of such."

"That would constitute only a portion of the teaching."

"Another might be that it allows for a wife to offer advice to her husband."

"He would be wise to take counsel as well from those others who have his trust in such matters."

"Just as you, for example, might counsel my husband in the matter of his ambitions to the Bohemian crown."

Scultetus folded his hands solemnly across the front of his dark robes. "Those opinions I might offer come only after careful consideration, and always accompanied by prayer."

"My husband values your counsel greatly. Tell me, how is it you advise him where this matter of the crown is concerned, now that he has seen it offered to him?"

"I take neither one position nor the other, only caution him that it must be a matter of prudent judgment, one in which haste should play no part."

"But what if hesitation be the very thing to bring about trouble?"

We had come to stand before a low stone wall overlooking the town below, the lights coming on here and there, the river a ribbon of darkness. The Pastor turned to look up over his shoulder. "Look there how the woods high up on the mountain capture yet the last rays of the sun, even as that which lies below has already fallen into darkness."

"Then it would be better to seek the mountain top."

"Not if all there is to look down upon lies in the gloom."

"Light will come again."

"Just so. It only needs patience to wait for morning."

"Yet sometimes waiting allows for those who would act under the cloak of darkness to do their worst. My husband has every right to ascend the throne, and there are many who would see him do it sooner rather than later."

"And who stand to gain a great deal, a fact like as not to cloud their judgment."

"Yet you yourself would be among those who benefit much."

"And so with you."

"Then how is it we are not of the same mind?"

"Where there is much to gain there is much to lose. If your husband takes the throne, it shall be seen as an affront, indeed a threat, to the sanctity and security of the Holy Roman Empire, a provocation impossible to ignore and full of danger. You must agree in this."

"But surely we can prepare ourselves for what will come of it."

"War. That is the only outcome."

"Then it means war."

"I hadn't thought Your Highness to be so fierce."

"I would not shy away from battle."

"But it is your husband who will have to fight."

"Then he will fight."

"And if he should lose?"

"You will enlist the help of our Lord, to whom you pray daily with such devotion and piety, and in this you can be a powerful ally to help him win."

"The Catholics will do as much for their side."

"Then God will have to choose."

"Prayer notwithstanding, it is soldiers that are needed. It will take a very great many of them to see it through. War is simple mathematics, and if the Hapsburgs should wish it so, they can produce numbers from Spain that do not bode well for us."

"But what if by this gesture to take the crown for the region we spark courage in those of our side? Would you not have it so?"

"He will make as many enemies as allies, I fear."

"He has both now."

"I beg pardon, Highness, but it is time for vespers, and so I take my leave. Perhaps we may talk of this again at some future time."

"I mean not to intrude upon your duties, but can we meet here again tomorrow evening, that I might to seek further counsel from you?"

"Highness, I am at your service, and would see you satisfied."

"Until tomorrow, then." I put my hand out and he bent to kiss it, hovered over it at length, then with lips pursed, kissed it with an unbecoming delicacy that made me withdraw my hand rather abruptly and wish him a good evening.

I decided next day to consult with Captain Hume, all that was left to me now in the way of counsel I could trust. I thought him capable of some sway in the matter and hoped he might offer some insight into the man Scultetus. The Captain, though unbound by the lesser protocols of courtly propriety, disdainful of its gossip and backbiting, nevertheless did not shrink from sticking his nose into affairs when he felt the need to. He was the best kind of pariah, one who disdained pretense and piety yet seemed to have a talent for exposing it in others. I found him one afternoon upon the grounds of the artillery garden, where he engaged almost daily in physical contests of one sort or another with the young men of the castle eager to take instruction from him. His reputation as a formidable adversary in hand-to-hand combat was by that time well known, and when I approached on this day he had before him a group of men in armour wielding sword and shield. When the Captain saw me he put up a hand to stop the proceedings immediately, but I insisted he carry on, that I might play the part of spectator for a while. My presence seemed to bring the young men into a state of increased energy as they puffed out their chests, redoubled their efforts, and made a great show of grunting and shouting as they engaged the adversary.

The exercise consisted of the following: The young men stood in a line to one side facing Captain Hume, and when ready he would call upon one of them to step forward with sword and shield to engage in an exchange of blows with him. In between bouts the Captain's page would hold out a cloth that he might wipe the sweat from his eyes, and perhaps offer some drink from a chalice. The young men would discuss amongst each other the strategies he had instructed them to employ, while the Captain pointed out the weaknesses he'd spotted that invariably gave him the advantage over his adversary.

He signalled now that he was ready and a young man stepped forward, curly of hair, wearing only a breastplate and greaves, who circled the Captain warily, transferring his weight nimbly from one foot to another, eyes fixed upon his opponent, that stood before him with neither malice nor concern in his bearing. Now the young man brought his sword to an overhead position, at which the Captain adjusted his stance, turned a little to one side, and set one foot slightly behind the other. The challenger attacked, bringing his sword down with a slashing motion, but even as he did so the Captain, rather than retreating or raising his shield to fend off the blow, stepped toward his opponent with startling quickness and with the hilt of his sword struck the young man across the back as he went by and sent him stumbling to the ground. He lay on his back looking up at the Captain, who stood over him, one foot resting on the vanquished opponent's chest, sword ready to deal the death blow.

The Captain looked at the assembled hopefuls. "And what may we gain from observing the particular method of combat I have just demonstrated?"

They looked at each other, uncertain, not daring to speak for fear they should be mistaken.

"May I?" I stepped forward, and they all turned to look at me.

"Your Highness." The Captain gave his sheepish attacker a hand up. "We are heartened by your interest in these crude manoeuvres, and would by all means hear your judgment."

"I am no soldier, but could it be that sometimes the best strategy in combat is to step forward rather than fall back?"

He turned back to the men. "There you have your answer in finer words than I might have mustered. The technique is meant to put a man down fast. In this case my attacker thought to strike a blow for show, and I made him pay for his mistake. His objective was to damage but his approach was clumsy. Remember, waste no time nor any unneeded effort." He turned to me. "Your Highness, would you see some more of this?"

"Perhaps another time, thank you. I wondered if I might have a word with you when you have finished."

"Gentlemen, let's have no more today. We shall resume tomorrow."

With that the men disbanded into smaller groups and went on their way while the Captain composed himself, took a drink from the chalice held out to him, then dismissed the page as well.

"Your Highness, I am at your service."

"Tell me about this weapon you carry." I indicated the sword still in the Captain's hand.

He held it up before him and I took a closer look.

"I see that you keep only the tip of the blade sharpened," I said.

"For easy entry." He made a short thrusting motion. "The rest I leave with a dull edge to keep it sturdy and better able to withstand a blow when I use it to block a strike."

"Some will say there is hardly the need for skill with such a weapon when the battles now are fought with more advanced instruments of war."

"It is all very impressive to blast away at each other from a safe distance and make a lot of noise, but the contest that begins with the musket and pistol still ends with the sword and dagger."

"And failing that, hand-to-hand combat, I suppose."

"It is one thing to shoot a man with an harquebus, but to kill him with your bare hands is something altogether different."

"And which do you prefer?"

"I prefer not to kill a man at all if I don't have to or even to fight him, but the battlefield insists I must, and I prefer to do it with a sword. I think it is the most civilized. When two men are aiming pistols at each other where is the parry, the block, the thrust?"

"And which of these manoeuvres would you recommend for someone like Preacher Scultetus?"

The Captain glanced over at me with a quizzical expression, then broke into a knowing smile before he answered, "Well, I should think the most likely way to bring a man like that to ground would be none of those, rather one I have not yet mentioned."

"And would you see fit to instruct me upon it?"

"It would be my privilege, but not before offering up an old adage."

"I would hear it."

"Those who choose to live by the sword are as apt to die by it."

"I mean not to bring harm to the man, only to bring him around to my way of thinking. What do you know of him?"

"Enough to forgo his company, though your husband is eager enough for it, as you well know, and receives counsel from him daily."

"Even at that it should not concern me but that Frederick sees fit to heed it at the expense of my own. He has convinced Frederick that only one chosen by God can accept the crown of Bohemia, and waits for a sign. He believes divine providence is dictated by the stars."

"I have seen him oft at study," said the Captain, "book in hand, there in the garden, looking to the heavens that its machinations inform his piety and self-proclaimed authority. He considers the stars and the alignment of the planets to be integrated into the writings of the Bible, which together serve to augur the events of our present life, speaks of the disciples in relation to the symbols of the zodiac, of the Saviour's birth within the winter's solstice and such."

"My husband will hardly deign to question a single word from his mouth."

"You say he waits for a sign. What say we give him one? Since much of his theology is founded upon study of celestial bodies and the heavens generally, he should take it as most prescient if something unexpected were to occur there that you, Your Highness, had preordained."

"He would not take me for a witch?"

"So long as he fears you. Your Highness, I have made the acquaintance of a woman who lives up the mountain upon a promontory where very few venture. Though she dwells there in solitude, she is neither hermit nor pauper."

"And she is not a madwoman?"

"Far from it, though I will say I have never met anyone like her. There's a hard line runs through her few men can lay claim to. She resists where a man will yield, triumphs where a man will fail, and yet she can muster charms to render him clay should the need arise. Her courage is of another sort, her cunning more ruthless. She can defeat you in ways you never imagined, wield triumph without mercy and yet relinquish her victory of an instant if it suit not her purpose. She is not afraid of sacrifice. Where a man allows himself to be counselled, she shuts out all considerations but total victory. Beware when she has made up her mind. I fear no man on the battlefield, and he may kill me if he can, only save me from a war of wills if she should want my blood, for she should be sure to draw it from a place no sword or shield can defend. The place where she lives is no shack, but well-appointed, and holds within it objects of art and science most astonishing. She has in her possession an instrument to observe the heavens, the existence of which is known to but a few."

"I know of such an apparatus," I said. "My brother Henry acquired one shortly before his death. It came to him by way of a Florentine who called it a telescope. I remember the first time he bade me look through it at the heavens. What a marvel I saw! There in the blackened sky a sea of stars such as I had never imagined, the heavens full to bursting with twinkles and pricks of light."

"Indeed. Upon my last visit she gave me to do as much."

"I should like to meet this woman," I said. "What did you say her name was?"

"Sophia. It is an arduous journey."

"I am no stranger to the trails along the mountainside."

"But to my point. Upon fixing the instrument to a particular region of the sky by means of a chart she had before her, she gave me to spy through the eyepiece such a celestial body as is rarely seen to visit itself upon the earth — a comet, Your Highness, growing brighter even as I gazed upon it."

"I remember one from my childhood. I was no more than eleven or twelve when Lord Harrington took us out to the lawn one summer evening, and there in the heavens a comet with a great glowing tail streaked across the sky."

Captain Hume stood listening, a most peculiar smile upon his face. "No doubt the talk thereafter was of celestial harbingers, and what its appearance might augur."

"So it has ever been upon their arrival."

"A man's imagination will make a formidable adversary," said the Captain.

"My father saw it as a sign that he should soon be king," I said. It was then the full import of Captain Hume's comment struck me. "By Heaven," I turned to him, "Scultetus will lap it up like a dog."

I hope you seek not to look upon me with judgment. We all of us engage in calculation, learn to scheme and connive almost from our first mewling. It is in our nature to grasp. There's hardly a woman born who would not choose, had she the means, to bend the world to her will, nor a man who would not bring all of nature to its knees if he had the power to make it so. Day in and day out we seek to discover the lengths to which we can go.

Chapter Eleven

Captain Hume had agreed to take me up the mountain that I might meet the solitary Sophia and see for myself the comet he had spoken of. The opportunity presented itself when one morning Frederick announced that he had arranged for us to travel to Juliana's estate in the countryside to see little Henry. I insisted it would better if he went alone this first time, to judge for himself how things were getting along. It was a transparent ruse, and needless to say he could not disguise his disappointment, but I assured him I should be eager to accompany him upon the next visit and insisted he should make his travel plans without me. It was a significant moment for both of us, one that would inform much of what was yet to come, but if I thought I saw an accusatory look come into his eyes it was only for a moment before he seemed to resign himself to the implications of my decision.

And so it was that only a few days hence I found myself following Captain Hume along a trail that led up the side of the mountain. We had started out in the late afternoon and should, he assured me, arrive before sundown, thereafter to stay until well after dark and make our way back by lantern light. Failing that, we should be prepared to stay the night. I was adamant that we should not, and didn't relish the thought of sleeping in such a strange place, but had prepared myself for the possibility by packing a light sack of clothing and other articles. Amalia had been instructed that upon my failure to return she should raise no alarm but rather keep it in strictest confidence. I had also taken the trouble to strap a small dagger to my leg, something I had never done before, and which I found surprisingly invigorating. To feel it there upon my inner thigh brought a small quiver of arousal, a tingling of being alive. Merely to have such a weapon secretly within my grasp amounted to an illicit pleasure. What must it be like then, I thought, to gird oneself for combat in full armour, with sword and dagger, shield and spear?

For his part the Captain, who walked before me, had as always a sword hanging at his side, which seemed a lot of weight to lug up the mountain. I felt the dagger rub against my leg with every step and this reassured me somehow. I had ambled along those familiar trails many times and never encountered anyone I felt fearful of, but his talk of this strange and powerful woman gave me to feel as though I might want to be wary of her, or that I could not trust the situation completely.

At first the trails were known to me but soon grew narrower and the undergrowth thicker, after which we encountered an outcropping of rock unfamiliar to me, then a stand of birch I did not remember, with holly and ivy thick along their trunks. The forest had darkened against the setting sun when before me the Captain turned of a sudden to one side, lifted away some leafy branches, and took us along a hidden trail where I should surely have continued straight on. I stayed close behind as we followed a path seldom trodden upon, ascending sharply then doubling back along the side of a steep rise. Still the woods grew thicker, and it was impossible to tell where upon the mountain we might be. Then we were standing in a clearing, surrounded on all sides by thick growth and tall trees, and there, in its midst, a dwelling rose up that sat on wooden stilts skirted on all sides by a terrace running along its length and breadth. The construction was crude, of rough-hewn planks and timbers. I could discern no visible means to ascend to the living quarters above, and we had only taken a few steps out into the clearing when a voice called out.

"Who walks there below?"

I looked up but saw no one.

"Captain Hume, Madam, and I have brought a visitor."

"Say who it is."

"That same personage I spoke of who resides in the castle below."

"Very well, come up," said the voice. "I've been expecting you."

At this a wooden ladder descended from the deck above, which the Captain proceeded to climb and I followed. When I had made the ascent and got my feet under me again, there before me stood a woman of perhaps forty or fifty, who eyed me with an expression neither welcoming nor suspicious. She raised the lantern in her hand higher and I saw there a face whose features were not those I had envisioned. Here was no gaunt and wrinkled visage but the slender and handsome face of a woman who might just as well have dwelt in the town below and gone quite unnoticed as she walked along its streets, save for the fact that she was dressed in pantaloons and shirt.

Captain Hume took a step forward and gestured in my direction. "Sophia, may I present Elizabeth." He had warned me beforehand that he would not introduce me by my title, as Sophia neither recognized nor acknowledged such forms of address. I had told him it should be a relief to be freed from that formality for a change, and now hearing my name so simply spoken, I welcomed the brief liberation from the tyranny of my entitlement but also felt a little vulnerable, knowing that I had entered an arena where I should be forced to assert my identity in a fashion almost entirely unfamiliar to me.

"Sophia." I put out my hand. "I am honoured to make your acquaintance."

"Honour is for fools. I possess none, neither do I seek any. The Captain here says he has fought for it upon the battlefield, though I suspect he did so more for the reward of those who paid him than his own. In either case it amounts to little more than self-importance. Why fight to preserve a chimera? You, for instance, are a sovereign I am told, raised from infancy to consider your worth above that of all but a few. Yet of what value is such in the absence of those accoutrements that lend it credence?"

"I welcome the chance to be free of them, if only for a short while."

"I am glad to hear it. And yet, I doubt you can say in all honesty that you consider me your equal."

"You are almost certainly my better in some respects."

"The Captain warned me that you would try to be humble, but I tell you there is no need for it. I am not in the habit of welcoming strangers into my home, and friends have I few, though this Captain may think of himself as such. I prefer to be as much as possible in my own company, as I find most anyone else's either tedious or annoying. Still, in your case I'm willing make an exception. Come, you must be tired after your journey. We will sit and you will take some refreshment, and then we shall carry on with that which has brought you here."

Sophia led us through the doorway into the interior of the dwelling, which was all of one room, with a high ceiling of timbers and beams, the walls of plain wooden planks and covered almost entirely over with drawings, charts, diagrams, sketches, and such. The furniture, though sparse, had also upon it wherever space was available books and papers, instruments and curiosities, and in some ways it reminded me of Henry's study back in London, though this had more clutter and disarray than his. It had that same air about it, the certainty that all of the various material at hand had not been strewn about casually, but that each article had arrived at the place where it now resided for a particular and important reason, held a place there to provide access to one exploration or another, and in its totality represented a great deal of knowledge and learning.

"I see you inspect the place, but consider it not an idle conglomeration of gratuitous artefacts, rather an elaborate and careful arrangement of necessities. You come from a world where keeping up appearances is paramount, a world I have renounced. Propriety and decorum are of little value when their underpinnings have been removed. Here things appear to be in chaos when they are in fact orderly."

"I would hear more about these underpinnings you speak of."

"Haven't you ever wondered why it is your subjects give themselves over to your rule?"

"They deem that entitlement and authority make it so."

"But why should the few rule the many?"

I allowed myself a closer examination of her features for a moment. She was of substantive build and stature, and as I stood before her I realized that she was a good six inches taller than I, but this did not seem to have an effect on the way our eyes met. Her hair was long and grey, and fell well below her shoulders, which were sloped and wide. If the received requisites of beauty were left wanting, if there was little in her appearance and manner that might be called delicate, she had nevertheless a bearing of graceful strength and feminine power.

"I will tell you." Her eyes met mine with a deep and penetrating intelligence. "It is because subject and monarch serve the same master. We are all afraid of the same thing."

"I would venture," Captain Hume put in, "that would be our own impending mortality."

"I grant as much," Sophia said, "but I am thinking of something else, that rather than dread, we profess to strive for above all else."

"Now you have my attention." Captain Hume smiled over at me. "And I would hear tell of this double-edged sword."

"We are not willing to live in a state of total freedom, and choose rather to let ourselves be ruled over by one thing or another, be it monarch or deity or even a single compelling idea, whether it be loyalty or privilege, duty or ambition."

"Don't forget honour," Captain Hume added.

"I suppose some would say love." I looked at Sophia.

"More like to fear," she answered.

"But at what cost," I asked, "are we ruled by none of these, if we must live in solitude and isolation?"

"It is the only way I have been able to manage it. Perhaps there are other ways to accomplish as much."

"A monarch, perhaps," Captain Hume offered, "might manage it better than most."

"In truth it is just the opposite," I answered.

"We all serve the master of our own making, I suppose," the Captain said.

Sophia turned away a little. "For my part I am beholden to my loneliness."

"But why should we fear the very thing we profess to treasure above all else?"

"The payment for freedom demands a formidable currency."

"I have often thought to free myself of my entitlements."

"You desire an ordinary life, then?"

"A royal life can be ordinary."

"But surely you don't consider yourself so."

"And yet I suppose there would be a certain freedom in it," said the Captain.

"It seems to me you, Sophia, live here as a kind of queen, only that you have not a gaggle of unruly and petulant subjects to rule."

"And so I am a ruler of nothing and no one."

"How be of your own desires?"

"What woman can say she is master of these?"

"Or man, for that matter," the Captain put in. "Some say the heavens rule our lives and augur our fortunes."

"Which brings us to the reason you have come." Sophia led us toward a doorway that opened onto the veranda.

"The Captain tells me you have a looking glass that will reveal what the unaided eye cannot yet apprehend," I said.

"Now that darkness has fallen you shall witness as much." She eyed me coolly. "Though I understand it has more to do with ambition than discovery."

I looked at Captain Hume. "You've told her, then."

"There's no need for recrimination." Sophia stopped at the threshold and put up her hand. "We're all guilty of duplicity in this matter." She picked up a lantern from the table and led us out onto to the back terrace. There, a telescope mounted on a trivet pointed up into the darkening heavens, where already the brightest stars pricked their light down to us. She walked over to a nearby table and placed the lantern on it, shedding light on a map of sorts laid out there. She studied it for a long time, then set about arranging the glass to point at a particular spot in the heavens.

"Look there." She pointed. "Take the two bright stars you see before you, draw an imaginary line between them, and then bisect it. From that point let your eye wander a little higher into the heavens until you see what appears to be a hazy smudge of light best observed by looking in the vicinity rather than directly at it."

"The technique is known as averted vision," Captain Hume informed me.

"It's nothing I invented," Sophia was quick to add. "It has been known since ancient times. We see better in the dark by this method. We look away from the object of our interest, but only just a little, and so it comes into better view."

I did as she instructed, and there indeed was a small patch of hazy light. "I see it."

"Good. Now I am going to bring it into view with this." She looked into the eyepiece and turned a small knob along the side, made some adjustments in the position of the glass, looked up with her naked eye, looked into the glass again. "I have it," she said. "Now come and look, but take care not to move the glass inadvertently."

I looked through the eyepiece and there before me was a spectacular sweep of scattered light emanating from a small point, as though some celestial fireworks had been set off far out in the darkened heavens.

"Remarkable," I said. "Captain, have you see this?"

"I have, but welcome the chance to look again."

"By all means, do." I stepped aside.

He bent over the telescope. "It's grown brighter. And more beautiful."

"It will get brighter each night," said Sophia, "but not enough for people to notice until it has swept around the sun and come out the other side. Then it will be visible for all to see in the heavens, and stream across the sky with a brightness that dwarfs anything we witness now."

"And you can calculate the day upon which this will occur?" I asked.

"That is what you came for, isn't it?"

"If you can divine it."

"You would use the information" — Sophia fixed me with a stare — "to gain advantage."

"I grant as much."

"It is not a certainty, understand. It may be that this comet travels too close to the sun, is drawn into it, and so consumed in that roiling fire. But I think not."

"How do you know all this?"

"I have been at study long enough to understand that even in those vast uncharted places the heavenly bodies that travel there do not do so freely, but are ruled by forces which determine their path with great accuracy."

"You are ahead of your time," said Captain Hume.

"Soon enough there will be more of these glasses, and more powerful, so that it will become common practice to observe such goings on up in the heavens as the naked eye cannot hope to espy."

"But you are one of the very first," I said. "You deserve recognition."

"Why?"

"Other men will surely seek to have such achievements acknowledged."

"They seek advancement — or some such reward."

"And you do not."

"I have not the need. I hope this knowledge brings you what you want." Sophia's mood seemed to change abruptly. "Will you stay the night?"

"If you will be so gracious as to have me," I was surprised to hear myself reply.

"It will be my pleasure. I find you good company, and the Captain has already proven himself in that respect."

This brought a somewhat embarrassed smile from Captain Hume. "And so, knowing my way about, I will take my night's leave and see you in the morning. Good night."

He took himself out of our company, and as he did so I felt a tinge of apprehension at being left alone with so formidable an interlocutor, but it was only for a moment, as it was almost immediately replaced with feeling that I could set aside my reservations, that if I feared this woman's intellect I need not fear her judgment, that if she thought me in need of humility or insight, she had no desire to impose her will upon me.

"Now I shall make us both a cup of cocoa," said Sophia, and took a small urn down out of the cupboard. "Do you know it?"

"I have only just become familiar with its use a restorative, and find it quite bitter and not to my taste."

"I make it with milk and sugar, and so you shall enjoy quite a more pleasant experience of it."

The drink Sophia offered me some minutes later was truly marvellous, and I immediately thought to have it made available to me at the castle. It tasted of sweet indulgence, but with a side effect of soothing comfort, and it soon made me quite sleepy.

"I can hardly imagine what it must be like," I said idly, "to spend day upon day in the company of only my own thoughts and the natural world around me."

"It is an acquired taste."

"I seem ever to live in want of something more."

"It is the nature of youth, as it was of mine when I was your age."

"But now you are satisfied?"

"It's still difficult."

"Is it our fate to be ever in a state of discontent?"

"The construction of the world would seem to make it so."

"But how did it come to be built this way?"

"You think it could have been otherwise."

"It seems to me we are not where we should be and live in a state other than the one natural to us. What keeps us from it, do you think?"

"This man you seek to dupe will say the answer lies in sin."

"He knows of little else but his received teachings, and looks not beyond them."

"But you say he looks to the heavens."

"Not as you do. Not with a clear eye."

"In truth I know not what I look for, only that I must look." She set down her cup. "Tell me, what is the natural state of a woman?"

"It seems to me that left to my own devices as you have been, free from the limitations imposed by the larger world, you should by now have found the answer."

"I seek it still."

"Better not to search, perhaps."

"And yet your search continues."

"What has Captain Hume told you of this man Scultetus?"

"Little, but that he is vainglorious in the usual manner

and so vulnerable to his own self-importance. For that reason you shall get the better of him with this artifice, and yet the question remains whether the plot is worthy of its author."

"My lady-in-waiting always said that I should refrain from judging myself, as there were so many others already eager to do so."

"Come, we'll to sleep now."

Sophia led me to a small room where I found a bed made up for me. It was as modest as any I had ever thought to make use of, a far cry what I was accustomed to, but no sooner had I laid myself down upon it than it welcomed me with surprising comfort. A pleasant drowsiness overcame me and I slept quite soundly through a night as quiet as any I'd ever experienced, although once or twice I heard the Captain snore from the other room.

In the morning we had breakfast, at which I eagerly indulged in some more of Sophia's delicious chocolate, and then it was time to make our way back down the mountain. I had what I came for, and the date of the comet's appearance was firmly etched in my memory. It should happen only a few weeks hence, and so I was anxious to get back and prepare Scultetus. Our journey back to the castle was uneventful, and I tried to take note of any landmarks which might be of help if I ever decided to venture back to the place and visit Sophia again, but I didn't think that was likely if I should soon find myself in Prague.

Over the course of the next several days I arranged to meet up with Scultetus in the garden and so began in a subtle manner to make him aware of my daily prayers for guidance in the matter of Frederick's ascension to the throne. Thereafter I began to allude to a vivid and recurring dream that had begun to visit itself upon my nightly slumber. When I thought he was ready I at last revealed to him, with feigned reluctance, that in these nightly reveries the vision of a fiery comet appeared, which interested him greatly and gave him to question me at length for details. At this I gave over that a particular day of the year flashed before my eyes, followed by an apparition of Frederick seated upon the throne. And so by degrees I gave him to divine the precise date upon which the comet was to appear in the heavens as a sign.

The weaving and deployment of this deception threw me into an annoying state of ambivalence. It was a less than favourable pronouncement on my character, and yet I felt a tingling anticipation to see it brought to fruition. Would my brother Henry be proud or ashamed of me? If the latter, I should counter that my deceit was for good cause, my reasons for wanting to be queen perfectly understandable. I had been left on my own, after all, and so I had all the more need to accrue as much power and influence as a coronation could muster. Perhaps I might yet aspire to that which Sophia spoke of, and find the means to stand in unfettered freedom.

I took great pains to feed Scultetus bits of information that should allow him to think he had figured it all out on his own. My methods were many and varied, as by revealing, for example, that in one of my nightly slumberings a symbol had appeared before me, as of something shaped like a horseshoe but with a stem in the manner of a cross. This was of course the astrological symbol for the day of the week the comet should appear, which was a Saturday. I will say that he made an excellent dupe and eagerly gave himself over to my forgeries, so that I increased my embellishments until at last he had determined the comet should arrive on September 6, 1618. In the meantime I was also at work on Frederick, now returned from visiting his mother, and in short, everything was in place that he should soon be counselled to take the appointment and see us off to Prague, if only the comet would appear as Sophia's reckoning foretold it.

On the night in question I had arranged for Frederick, Scultetus, and myself to be upon the balcony of the English Wing at the appointed time. My information decreed that the comet should appear approximately an hour after sunset to the north and east, so that we might be seen to stand overlooking the town and the blackened river below at that time. I could hardly contain my exuberance when it happened exactly that way! No sooner had the sky turned a darker shade of night, than the comet appeared in glorious brightness as though falling out of the sky. There was great excitement about the castle, and soon others came out to the balcony to observe with us. So great was the stir that we witnessed the townspeople pouring out into the streets below us, muttering and exclaiming at every turn as they took in the wondrous sight.

And what of Abraham Scultetus himself? Even in the darkened light I could see his face go pale. "The prophecy is come to pass." He kept his eyes to the heavens, his jaw set.

"We are witness here to a great revelation," said Frederick.

"What do you think it can mean?" I asked innocently.

Scultetus turned after a long while to stare down at me. His expression told me everything I needed to know. It left no doubt he was taking my measure in a whole new way, convinced now that I was a force to be reckoned with. I was content to let him indulge all of his worst fears for the moment, and let the wheels of his own cogitations do my work for me. I had learned by then that in times of great import it was often best to say nothing and let the event speak for itself.

By and by Scultetus and I found ourselves alone on the balcony.

"Your Highness, what have you to say in this matter?"

"There is nothing needs saying," I assured him, "save that I am not the instrument of this celestial harbinger, only its preordained messenger. All glory goes to God."

"Your husband shall be king. Of this there is no denying."

"It would seem so."

"Nay, more than seems. The heavens have spoken. I'll forthwith to your husband and tell him of my decision."

"I think it wise, though, not to speak of my premonition.

Best we keep that between us. There are some at court who will incline to sorcery."

I found it an intoxicating elixir to think someone like Scultetus had reason to be wary of me. From that day forward he revered me, and I was happy to let it be so and use it to my advantage. I found myself luxuriating in the role of merciful prophet, made a great show of offering him assurances that he should not be left behind when the time came to reap the rewards of life as advisor to the king, but in doing so I was always careful to intimate that it would be prudent to side with me on matters concerning the path that should lead us to Prague.

If I was content for the moment to be thought of as a harbinger of God's munificence, soon enough I should garner my fair share of his wrath. How could I ever have imagined what was to come? To think my bit of chicanery would set in motion a series of events that tumbled the better part of Europe into a devastating and protracted war that was going to cost thousands upon thousands of lives. All for the sake of advancement. Countless men would be killed in battle, women raped and murdered, children slaughtered. It would start out as a series of skirmishes between Catholic and Protestant interests, but soon escalate into an all-out war for political dominance. The Thirty Years' War would pit many of the great rulers of Europe against each other, and in the process condemn me to a life of exile and poverty.

Had I known that goading my husband into pursuing something he never wanted would unleash so much destruction and chaos, I should have acted otherwise. But who among us can divine the full import of our actions? Did Romeo foresee that in trying to keep the peace between the Capulets and the Montagues he would inadvertently cause his cousin Mercutio to be slain, and by that action unleash forces that destroyed both him and his Juliet in the bargain? We miscalculate because we wield not the degree of control we imagine ourselves to possess. The outcome should have been quite different if the Elector of Saxony had but offered his support, or if a few more members of the Protestant Union had elected to favour my husband's acceptance of the crown. But fate will have its way with us.

Scultetus had warned Frederick again and again that if he chose to accept the crown of Bohemia, the Protestant Union would not unanimously endorse him. Without the weight of that considerable influence, the Hapsburgs would use it as justification to bring the full force of their might against my husband. There were many who wanted a Protestant monarch to stand against the increasingly pervasive abuses of the Holy Roman Empire, but if the Elector did not back Frederick, the Hapsburgs would have all the reason they needed to characterize his coronation as an illicit uprising.

In the midst of all this turmoil I would be obliged to carry two more children to term and find myself pregnant with yet another even before we reached Prague. I would give birth first to a second son, Charles Louis, who thanks to my relentless efforts on his behalf would many years hence reign from Heidelberg, and who would show his ingratitude by banning me from the familiar comforts of the English Wing and the Hortus Palatinus.

Thereafter I would give birth to a daughter, Elisabeth, who more than any other is the child I should wish to make amends to . . . but leave that for later. Suffice it to say the better part of the next two decades would find me almost without exception engaged in the process of incubating progeny, pushing one squalling infant after another out of my robust womb, hardly recovered from the ravages of one gravidity before I was obliged to suffer the next, a pattern that continued unabated until very nearly my fortieth year. From shortly after my wedding to some twenty years thereafter, whether I was in Heidelberg or Prague or The Hague, my body would be obliged to withstand these repeated assaults. Thankfully I was blessed with a constitution that saw me through with surprising resilience, but it was surely the great absurdity of my life that so much effort should issue forth naught but ungrateful children. Even upon the day of my coronation I would be forced to dress in a gown that accommodated my grossly swollen belly, and close upon the celebrations would follow the grunts and indignities of yet another inconvenient childbirth.

In the lead-up to our departure for Prague there were any number of state balls and receptions, and it was at one such that a most unwelcome visitor appeared among the guests. Alfonso Ferrabosco claimed to have been invited to come to Heidelberg by a member of the court, but no one seemed eager to acknowledge as much. He managed to insinuate himself into the occasion, and after dinner announced before the assembled lords and ladies that he had news of Sir Walter Raleigh.

"I myself hardly knew the man," he let his eyes travel in my direction, "though there are no doubt those among you who were very fond of him."

Rumours had reached the castle from time to time, but it was hard to distinguish truth from gossip. People came from London and scurried about, whispering all manner of intrigues, but I held little stock in any of it. I was preparing to excuse myself from the evening's chatter when Ferrabosco spoke up loudly that he could vouchsafe the events he was about to relate, as he had been there to witness them in person.

"On the day before All Hallows' Eve," he began, "I was among those in the gallery at the Palace of Westminster when he was brought from the Tower to answer to the charge of treason."

There was a general murmuring among the crowd, which thereafter fell into attentive silence.

"I can tell you that he dressed for the part, as always, and this occasion found him decked out in his best doublet and hose. A number of the ladies remarked upon his finery as he was led past them and set before the King's Bench Bar, at which it was demanded by the Master Attorney General why the sentence should not be carried out. Thereafter the Lord Chief Justice commanded the Sheriff of Middlesex to take the prisoner into his custody for that purpose.

"Sir Raleigh was removed to the Gatehouse and I took myself back to Whitehall, there to enjoy a good night's sleep and rise on the morrow to return for the execution. I made my way to the Palace Yard at Westminster next morning, and there to my astonishment stood a large scaffolding where none had been the night before. It stood in the very place where some years before those gruesome punishments had been carried out upon Guy Fawkes and his co-conspirators. Your Highness may remember," he turned to me, "for your father the King gave you to bear witness, did he not?"

I made to answer, speak to his offence and dismiss him from my presence, but a stubborn paralysis overtook me that rendered me unable to react, and I could only sit in stupefied silence as he went on with his story. I was nine years old again, thrown instantly back to the horror of that scene, watching as a man wide-eyed with terror grimaced and writhed while being gutted like a fish. But it was not only this that froze me. The man Ferrabosco seemed to employ some unknown force that held me in submission. I have suffered, from time to time, that a man should wield power over me for no good reason I can fathom. It makes me out to be a willing victim, when in truth I would fight.

"Now they brought Sir Raleigh forth," Ferrabosco continued, "looking even more resplendent than before, having undertaken a complete change of wardrobe, which included a very fine pair of shoes indeed." He paused to muse for a moment. "I wonder what happened to them? It was a pleasant sunny morning and a very large crowd had gathered to witness the proceedings. It seems we in London have developed rather a taste for these occasions of late, as they are happening with more and more frequency. Sir Raleigh saluted the lords and ladies present in a most amiable fashion, after which the crowd fell strangely silent as he was made to remove his ruffed collar for the sake of better exposing his neck to the axe. Beg pardon, ladies, but these are the facts. Now he made to address the assembled crowd, but I shall not bore you with the details, as there was little in it of merit beyond the usual sort of thing: 'I would beseech those present . . .' and 'I am thankful for . . .'; something about God to be sure; though at the last his voice trailed off and some drew nearer to the scaffolding the better to hear his muted utterances. For my part I kept a safe distance" — and here Ferrabosco allowed a hideous grin — "as I knew from experience there should be blood spattering about when the axe fell, and I had chosen to wear a new doublet that morning."

I wanted to leap from my seat and slap him across the face as hard as I could, take his dagger from its scabbard and sink it into his chest, but I sat motionless.

"When he had finished he was obliged to remove his hat, which he did in a most regal fashion and offered to a bystander, who eagerly accepted it; next such monies as he had in's pocket; thereafter his doublet and gown; and at this point exercised a most unusual privilege and beckoned the axe man nearer. The executioner hardly knew how to proceed, never having suffered such a request before, but Raleigh urged him again to come forth, at which he did so, and here the prisoner reached out that he would examine the instrument that was to do the deed. The dumbfounded executioner obeyed and held the axe out for inspection while Sir Raleigh ran his thumb along the length of the edge as if to gauge the sharpness of the blade!"

Some of the ladies had by now taken to leaning on their gentlemen as though to keep from fainting, but Ferrabosco carried on nevertheless.

"Having concluded that the axe was up to the task, Sir Raleigh made some clever remark as to its usefulness as a cure for all diseases. Then somewhat of a prayer, I think, after which the executioner knelt before him to ask his forgiveness, which Sir Raleigh, with a hand upon the axe-man's shoulder, granted. Next he was offered a blindfold, which he refused, before being made to kneel and place his head upon the blackened block, stained with the dried blood of its last victim. Deathly quiet it was now and the executioner, axe raised above his head, seemed to have become as a statue, unable to bring it down until Sir Raleigh was heard to shout, 'Strike, man, strike!' and even at that the executioner faltered before he made to do the deed with a distinctive lack of vigour. He had been better to give it the full force of his considerable strength, as the first blow from the axe did not succeed in severing the head completely. The executioner pulled the axe out of Sir Raleigh's neck, which had now a frightful gash more than halfway through, and it must be said that to the prisoner's credit he kept his position as he waited for the second strike and moved no more than an inch or two in the interim. Do you not think it admirable?"

I had no doubt Ferrabosco must be addressing me as he posed this question, but I kept my head turned away and would not look at him.

"What if he had thought to stand up after the first and there should have been his head, flopped over to one side so that perhaps he had to prop it up?"

A few of the gentlemen made to laugh at this jest but there was no bravery in it.

"In any case he stayed exactly where he was as the axe was raised once again and a second blow struck into the very same wound created by the first, at which the severed head fell with a thud to the wooden scaffolding and rolled off to one side. The executioner, axe dripping blood, stooped down to pick it up and held it up for the crowd to inspect as he was required to do before carrying it down the crudely constructed stairs, where Sir Raleigh's dutiful wife — I believe her name is the same as yours, Highness — stood stoically waiting. She held open a red leather bag for the axe man to drop the head into and made her way through the crowd to a waiting carriage."

"Now what do you think she was going to do with it?" asked one of the gentlemen.

"I have learned since she intends to have it embalmed and carry it with her always."

"I cannot think for what purpose."

"Perhaps as a reminder to all who pass."

I threw myself up from the chair and made straight for Ferrabosco, eager to spit in his face, but even as I approached he proffered a derisive smile and reached into his breast pocket.

"Your Highness." He held a letter out to me. "This letter is from Sir Raleigh. He insisted I deliver it to you in person, and I am bound to do so. Will you have it?"

I snatched it from him, looked down to see the handwriting was plainly Sir Raleigh's.

"Get out."

"Beg pardon, Highness, but is this the thanks I get?"

"I should have you clapped in irons."

"How is it I offend?"

"That you stand yet before me. Show me your back and never seek to come again into my presence."

I took myself at once to my privy chamber and tore open the letter.

October 18, 1618

To the fair Elizabeth,

I trust this final correspondence shall find its way to you. I have used the last of my money to see to it, though your father may yet find the means to waylay it as he has so many others. As you may know, he released me from the Tower after you left for Heidelberg, but freedom was not truly mine to enjoy. Whatever stories you may have heard, you shall now learn the true account.

Your father freed me on the condition that I set sail once again for the New World, which I agreed to do, but alas we suffered an encounter with the Spanish that cost my dear son Walter his life, and I was left with no choice but to return to England empty-handed. Upon my arrival in London the Spanish ambassador accused me of attempted piracy and demanded satisfaction, at which your father capitulated and ordered my arrest. I made hasty arrangements to escape to France, but even as the oarsmen rowed me out to the ship anchored nearby, a conviction overtook me and I insisted against their urgings that we return to shore. For some reason I was convinced that if only I might be allowed to explain things to the King, he should vouchsafe my honour. As it turned out I could not have been more wrong, for not only did your father elect instead to send me back to the Tower, but now he has agreed to set the date for my execution.

Needless to say the time is short and so to the crux of the matter. I would confess something to you. Do you remember the last occasion you had to come to the Tower and visit me? I think about it still. The restraint we showed honoured us both, and yet, how often I have tortured myself wondering whether the greater sin might have been that we failed to act. It should have been a fiercely righteous act of love we made, and I hardly see now how it could have been wrong. It was that same conviction which prevented me boarding the ship to safety which kept me from sweeping you into my arms that day: that I have ever sought to do the honourable thing. And look what it has cost me! First my heart and now my head, I fear.

There's something else I've wanted to tell you. You may be interested to learn your father's true purpose for sending me to the New World in the first place, which has ever been shrouded in secrecy but shall now be revealed. After all, what more do I have to lose? The goal as stated publicly was that I should go in search of gold, but in fact the ends were far more sinister. Your father expressly instructed me to procure by any and all means those potent and hitherto unknown poisons rumoured to be found there, and bring them to him. As to his reasons for wanting to acquire such, I was forbidden from enquiry, but I thought it was something you should know.

The hour of my execution approaches and I must prepare. My wife has spoken for my head and vows to carry it with all her life in a velvet sack she has already purchased for that purpose, but know this: you shall carry my heart. Do you know that just by looking into my eyes you could set my loins to shivering? It is true! Indeed naught but a soft cascade of words upon your tongue could accomplish as much. How often I have imagined you whispering close in my ear, telling me what you want me to do. Though they separate my head from my body, it shall not divide me from my passion, which belongs to you and always shall. Farewell.

Yours ever in sweetest desire,
Raleigh

And so was lost to me yet another of those who had never truly been mine. What had I done to deserve such punishment? Was there no brother or sister, cousin or friend, lover or confidant I might be allowed to keep? It seemed all such belonged not to me but to death. If I suspected things might turn out much the same in Prague, I was undaunted, and eager as ever to plunge ahead. The prospect of rushing headlong into a ruin of my own making didn't dishearten me. Much as Sir Raleigh had expressed in his letter, what was there left to lose? Whatever lay ahead could be no worse than what had already come to pass. If I was fated to fail then best proceed.

Part Three

Chapter Twelve

The journey to Prague was uneventful and we had managed to settle into our opulent apartments within the walls of the palace quite comfortably as the day of Frederick's investiture approached. The castle sat high upon a hill overlooking the town below, much as in Heidelberg, but here it was the Vltava River that flowed past and not the Neckar. The place seemed a formidable fortress and I found it reassuring that we should find ourselves in a place so well defended. The assembly of my bed had been accomplished, and I had taken pains to see to the installation of several Johns, just as I had in Heidelberg. Those were the two things I simply would not do without.

I'd become accustomed during my time at Coombe Abbey to a convenience not even the royal palaces of London could lay claim to. While the rest of my royal family was condemned to make use of a close stool attended by a groom, in the Harrington household I had no need for such. I had at my disposal a privy the like of which could be found in only a handful of chambers anywhere, an invention of Lord Harrington's cousin John, who referred to it as "the Ajax." I never cared for that name and took to calling it "the John" instead, after the Christian name of its inventor. He had installed a number of them in the house, including one for my exclusive use. Here is what made it so delightful: no sooner had you finished with your rather nasty business than you pulled upon a velvet cord, and what do you think happened? A torrent of water stored up in a tank affixed to the wall flooded into the basin with sufficient force to flush it all away and send it down a set of pipes to a cistern far below. Magic!

I was certain the invention should make John Harrington a rich man, and was as baffled as he when it failed to catch on. People seemed intent to go right on using a chamber pot or closet stool as they always had. I suggested he write a book about his device to generate more interest, which he did, but that proved to be disastrous as well. As consolation I arranged for him to become tutor to me, as well as to my brother Henry. It was also my intention that after my marriage to Frederick he would accompany us to Heidelberg and oversee the installation of several privies in the English Wing there. But how tragedy ever nipped and barked at my feet even from the very day of my brother's passing! Only a few days after Henry's funeral, John fell ill and died within the week. Lord Harrington made the journey in his son's stead and saw to the work. Upon its completion I granted him leave to return to England, but no sooner did he depart than he too fell ill, and died on the journey home.

But now we were making a new beginning in Prague, where I was obliged to a meet a host of lords and ladies, most of whom spoke hardly a word of English, and with whom I could exchange little more than awkward greetings. I had been through as much before on many occasions in Heidelberg, but always with Lady Anne Dudley by my side, and now I missed her terribly. Amalia, the lady-in-waiting employed in her stead, was efficient enough in her duties but in these situations offered little in the way of counsel or comfort. For my part it should have been insincere to solicit these things from her, for we were not kindred spirits in that way and never would be. As much as Lady Anne had served as something of a mother to me, so Amalia might have done for a sister, but as it was we were quite formal with each other and both of us content to let it be so. There never had been more than a handful of people in my life that I admitted into private confidence, and if I wanted to continue keeping people at a distance then Amalia was the perfect fit.

The preparations for my coronation were soon underway and I allowed myself to be dragged about from one venue to another, notwithstanding that I was less than a month away from giving birth to another child. When the day arrived at last, the audience that filled in the pews of St. Vitus Cathedral was still fresh from celebrating Frederick's coronation, which had taken place three days earlier. I had been there as well to witness the vestments of royalty placed upon him, the sceptre and orb, robe and crown, all of it accompanied by tedious ritual and much preaching, though not of the kind which had been practised within the holy confines of that cathedral in centuries past. By order of Abraham Scultetus the interior of the church had been stripped of all its ornamentation, that those in attendance should be left with no doubt as to the denomination of the services taking place within. St. Vitus would henceforth be a place not of Catholic worship but of the strictest Calvinism.

Such lengths had Scultetus gone to that even the sanctified vaults beneath the stones of the church floor had been caved in and the remains removed. Though such adornments as altars and crucifixes might have been removed and carted off to some other location, they were instead torn most rudely from the walls, dashed to the ground, and smashed to pieces. All this with such conviction it gave me second thought that I was the author of such zeal, fuelled as it were by the theatre I had arranged, and which now set him so firmly upon his path of destruction.

Only Wenceslas Chapel, where that ancient King's relics lay entombed, had been left intact, and it was within this chamber I now stood with Amalia dutifully at my side, awaiting the arrival of the coronation vestments. Ornate Gothic frescoes, magnificent in artistry and detail, decorated the upper regions of the walls, while hundreds, nay thousands, of precious jewels adorned the lower portions. Emerald and sapphire, jasper and amethyst had been fixed into the walls, each one bordered with gold inlay. In the centre of the room sat the sarcophagus of the revered Saint himself, entombed in stunning decoration, and next to it the altar whereupon I should soon be required to kneel and receive such holy blessings as were appropriate to the occasion.

I was instructed to pray while I waited for the crown of St. Isabella and other vestments to be fetched down from the upper chamber where they were kept for such occasions. This required an elaborate ceremony in which seven prominent citizens of the city each turned a key on one of the locks that sealed the door to the chamber, after which they had to repeat the procedure upon another inner door before making their way up a spiral stone staircase to the chamber high above to retrieve the necessary items.

The proceedings would on any other occasion have been overseen by the Archbishop of Prague but he was conspicuous in his absence, which might have accounted for the somewhat muted tone of the whisperings and mumblings amongst the parishioners. Even as the spoon and vial were brought forth and my temples anointed with oil, I had my first misgivings about this moment I had plotted and schemed for. At last the crown of St. Isabella was placed upon my head, and I was taken out into the cathedral and up to the altar to be seated upon the throne. I was glad for the chance to sit, as I was in my eighth month of pregnancy and finding it a little taxing to be so long on my feet.

Rupert would be my fourth child after Charles, Henry, and Elisabeth. There would be five more sons and four more daughters before it was over, and it seemed the reward for my prowess at making babies was to be employed much like a breeding mare. Every pregnancy was an invasion, my body subjected to occupancy by an organism growing ever larger until the cramped quarters set it to squirming and poking about inside me. Each gestation brought home the brutal reality that I was an organism whose function was the propagation of the human creature. The process was an inconvenient one that suffered my spine to be curved out of all symmetry, my internal organs to be rearranged, and for me to walked about bloated, nauseous, now gorged, now famished, my body to give off rude noises and disgusting odours. I groaned, I moaned, I ached.

And what was required of my husband on each occasion? Naught but a simple act of penetration and insemination to initiate the process. What an accomplishment. If there was little in it of intention, there was less of design. I had no say as to the nature and appearance of the child that was to be born nine months later. I had no control over any of it. Each torturous confinement seemed endless. Even as the next issue swelled toward its arrival inside my belly, my gloom became such that I saw my future as one of little hope. I had thought to become another kind of woman than one that brought forth children the way a sow brings forth piglets.

Frederick had been crowned three days earlier, so that attendance at this day's tiresome proceedings amounted to little more than courtesy. The crown they brought forth was much like that of any monarch, fashioned out of refined gold and inset with gemstones, pearls and diamonds, sapphires and amethysts. Even as it was set upon my head with great ceremony, it seemed to me a silly contrivance. The whole idea seemed childish, as a little boy and girl at play might decree themselves to be king and queen by placing a cooking pot each upon the other's head.

To be sure, I had not imagined how uncomfortable the thing would be. It dug here and there into my skull so painfully it was all I could do not to yank the thing from my head and dash it to the marble floor. It seemed a most unnatural accessory, one that no sane person would wear by choice. As I sat there in awkward discomfort, I wondered once more how it ever came about that people should suffer themselves to be ruled over by others. If not violence then perhaps some more cunning art played upon their fears. Perhaps our Heavenly Father had ordained it that one creature should seek to gain dominion over another, but here were all these men and women crowded into the cathedral to see me crowned in a ceremony that had no substance at its heart. To think the masses should so easily be appeased by the equivalent of props in a play. Was I to be more regal now than before?

Perhaps Mr. Shakespeare had been better to say in agony lies the head that wears the crown, for I seemed at that moment no better off than some beggar with a scrap of metal from an ironmonger's shop stuck to the top of his head. If that was not bad enough, Rupert, my unborn child, chose that moment to effect a sharp kick at my guts which caused me to let out an audible yelp and gave the administrator pause to interrupt his litany. I forced a smile and bade him over the murmurs of the crowd to proceed with the ceremony.

The festivities which followed my husband's coronation having only just concluded, now a second round of celebration began. The palace lay yet in decoration, and the feasting and dancing essentially took up where they had only just left off. I should have been glad to dispense with all of it, but instead was forced to endure three more days of revelry. Had it not been for Captain Hume I should never have managed it. Frederick had agreed that the Captain should accompany us to Prague, and I was glad for his company amidst so many courtiers eager to offer congratulations and begin at once their efforts to gain favour. His unkempt appearance and gruff manner served as something of a buffer to so much unwanted attention. The more the lords and ladies of the court failed to disguise their distaste, the more content I was to let it be so, and to enjoy their discomfiture and revel in their offended sensibilities.

"Madam, how soberly sit the royal garments upon your person," the Captain remarked. He was dressed on this occasion in clothes poorly tailored, among them a white shirt badly in need of a washing under a loose-fitting black gown. "I should have thought this would be a happier occasion, one you worked very hard to achieve."

"I should have donned the robes of England with greater enthusiasm."

"I grant they might have allowed for more comfort."

"There's naught of comfort to be had in anything I wear of late." I put a hand on my rounded belly. "I am swollen to bursting with pregnancy."

"No doubt your new title shall soon afford more than mere suffering at the hands of pomp and ceremony."

"Though my prospects amount to more than privilege, true effect falls within the purview of my husband."

"You will be there to give him good counsel," the Captain assured me.

"I am content to let that fall to Abraham Scultetus."

"He is no doubt eager to offer it."

"I grow weary of resorting to tiresome persuasion."

The Captain seemed surprised at this, as I might have been, save that in the very moment of Frederick's coronation a serpent of doubt slunk into my soul and coiled itself around my ambition. Perhaps I sensed already that the tenure of his rule should last little more than the winter, for we had hardly settled into our apartments at Prague Castle before things began to fall apart. Scultetus continued after the coronation to affect such actions as enraged the Holy Roman Emperor. He had the Great Crucifix which had been for centuries a mainstay upon the Old Bridge not only taken down but demolished. At this rumours began to swirl that it was on my behalf he had acted so, and that I had decreed not to cross the bridge so long as it stood. At every turn were committed atrocities and insults, injustices and transgressions against the authority of the Hapsburgs. He had the Jesuit churches converted to evangelical sanctuaries. It was almost as though he were baiting them.

I was content to let him carry on in this way, though in hindsight any fool could have foreseen that the reaction to such blatant provocations was bound to be swift and forceful. For the moment I had not the strength to fight him. Other forces were at work on me that came not from without but from within. After Rupert was born I fell into a terrible melancholy from which I seemed powerless to free myself. That same affliction which so often struck me after the birth of a child visited itself upon me with a greater vengeance than I had known hitherto.

The protocols of my new office were now squarely set before me and I was confronted with a shocking array of uninviting prospects, among them those of seeing to the establishment of a new court, at which I was obliged to accommodate endless entreaties for employment and requests for special consideration from merchants and tailors, musicians and artists, ambassadors and noblemen. I set Amalia to see to some of these matters, the better to spare myself the annoyance, and if I suspected her of making decisions based on little more than her own self-interest I was too beset with duties of my own to bother about it. There were any number of appointments to be made, from the sergeant-at-arms to the keeper of the seals, from the lord chancellor to the master of the horse.

The duties of Queen Consort proved for the most part to be as tedious as they were numerous. Meanwhile, the kinds of decisions I should more eagerly have had a hand in making fell to Frederick, or more accurately to his advisors, who were considerable in number and led by Abraham Scultetus. Frederick seemed content to do little more than listen attentively and sign whatever document was placed before him.

A good many of these had to do with Scultetus's continued efforts to make as many inroads for his Calvinist doctrines as he could manage, and in the process alienate what little good will remained in those who took offence at his bullying ways.

I had also noticed that there was an unmistakable change in Scultetus's demeanour toward me. From the moment of my husband's coronation he had adopted a dismissive attitude that took me by surprise. Perhaps he sensed that I was in a compromised state, neither as able nor as willing to summon the resources required to stand up to him. In any case he took full advantage of the situation and seemed eager to flaunt his newly inherited powers. I suppose it might be said that I got what I had hoped for, but I quickly came to the realization that the title of Queen Consort brought little in the way of substantive reward. The same could not be said for Scultetus. In the capacity as newly appointed religious leader of Prague, his authority to purge the city of Catholicism and replace it with his own brand of strict Calvinism seemed unbounded.

With my melancholy at last somewhat abated I found myself one morning unwilling to remain content with trivial household duties while important matters of state were left to others. I made my way to the Hall of the Imperial Court Council and arrived at the entrance to the chamber just in time to see my husband seating himself at the head of the table, where a number of advisors, Scultetus among them, hovered over him with papers in hand, while others sat or stood in small groups about the room. When Frederick looked up from the table and saw me about to enter he pushed back his chair to greet me, but Scultetus put a firm hand on his shoulder and gently coaxed him back into his seat. Frederick looked up at him, then over at me, then leaned back in his chair while Scultetus made his way to where I was standing, took me rather forcefully by the arm, and directed me back out into the hall. He pulled me a little off to one side and spoke at close quarters in an urgent tone.

"Highness, it is good of you to grace us with your presence. May I be of some assistance? Nothing's amiss, I trust."

"No." I wrenched my arm away from his grasp.

"Nothing urgent?"

"No."

"May I enquire, then, as to the matter of your presence here?"

"I will attend this assembly."

"Beg pardon, Highness, but I'm afraid the occasion does not call for it."

"And what occasion it that?" I rubbed my arm.

"You need not concern yourself with these affairs of state. We have the matter well in hand."

"Then it should be of no consequence either way if my husband, the King, should choose to let me sit in on the proceedings."

I glanced over at Frederick, now on the very edge of his chair, looking as though he might jump up at any minute and come out to me.

"I'm afraid it isn't that simple."

"And why is that?"

"It lies outside the protocol . . ." He hesitated for a moment. ". . . of a queen consort." Scultetus subtly manoeuvred himself to stand before me in such a manner that I had to lean around him if I wanted to catch sight of my poor husband. It was clear to me Frederick was torn, that there was in his manner more of the school boy than the master.

"You no doubt have many duties to perform" — Scultetus adopted a condescending tone now — "that are of greater import for your husband's comfort and good cheer than these tedious deliberations." I could see in his eyes that he was no longer afraid of me.

"I am happy to leave off those obligations for the moment." I looked again into the chamber and saw Frederick staring out at me, his features contorted.

"It is in your realm to see to them." Scultetus was firmer now. "Just as it is in your husband's to see to others."

"But these proclamations do daily bring us farther into disfavour with those who stand to do us harm. I can hardly think my husband should grant these undertakings willingly if he knew the extent and scope of their repercussions."

"Surely you were better to concern yourself with matters more immediate to your present condition." Scultetus lowered his eyes to stare at my swollen belly.

"Tell me, Reverend, whether these sentiments be yours or those of the King? In any case my 'condition,' as you put it, has nothing to do with my admission to these deliberations."

"I only meant that you have more pressing concerns as to matters domestic."

"Much as the livestock, you mean — horses and sheep and such?"

"You know I meant not that, Highness, but we all have our place."

"And I must be kept in mine."

"Now if you will excuse me, we have urgent matters to attend to."

"I would learn for myself the manner by which my husband assents to these provocations upon the Holy Roman Emperor, which amount to the repeated poking of a nasty beast."

"I hardly think that is an accurate characterization."

"I will speak with him."

"We are pressed for time."

"Nevertheless."

At this Scultetus turned and walked back into the room, made his way over to Frederick, still seated at the head of the table, and leaned over to talk closely into his ear. My husband listened, then turned to look at me for a moment before he nodded at Scultetus. It was unquestionably a gesture of resignation, and though my instinct was to charge into the room and make a scene, some part of me would not allow it. While

Frederick conferred with those around him, now addressing Scultetus, now others nearby, I felt a chasm open up between us wider than any that had been there before. And last he turned to me and the expression written upon his features gave me to understand that I might take my leave. Scultetus made as though to come over and speak to me a final time, but before he could add to my humiliation I turned abruptly and hurried away.

Scultetus was allowed to continue his brash and insulting behaviour toward all things Catholic, and it was not long before word reached the castle that an army deployed by the Hapsburgs was marching toward the city. The invasion of Prague was imminent, and as Bohemia had managed to alienate those allies who might have seen fit to offer aid in the conflict, there was precious little in the way of resistance. Even so I held out some hope that help might be on the way. My father had after all married me off to a Calvinist prince the better to consolidate the interests of British and Bohemian Protestants. Frederick himself had made reference to as much in his very first letter to me, but his words would soon come back to haunt me. By my reckoning the King of England would feel obliged to come to the aid of his Bohemian counterpart, if not for political reasons then for his daughter's sake. Surely he would send an army across the channel to fight at her husband's side against the Catholic forces.

But once again I failed to appreciate the scope of my father's treachery. Instead of sending troops he used the crisis as an opportunity to foist one final act of betrayal upon his only daughter. Notwithstanding the entreaties of all parties concerned, and in complete dismissal of my letters to him personally, he not only chose to abstain from any involvement in the conflict but made the offence even greater by electing instead to seek an alliance with the hated Spanish. Even as the crisis worsened, word came that the King of England was deeply involved in negotiations that would see his son Charles, heir to the throne, take for his wife the Catholic daughter of Phillip III. Rat!

In no time at all, the situation degenerated into chaos. How cruelly the fates descended upon me! I became enveloped in a fog of disbelief and despair, even as I bore witness to our brutal and swift overthrow. In Prague and elsewhere the meagre armies Frederick managed to summon in defence of his crown were soon falling back, and it was only a matter of hours before the city lay under siege. We were left with no choice but to throw a few precious belongings together and hurry out of the palace or risk losing our heads. I will venture that an army of well-trained British soldiers should not so easily have allowed themselves to be overrun as those who were sent to defend the city. Much like Frederick himself, they didn't put up much of a fight. Had Henry still been alive, no doubt things would have gone differently, and he should have been there with an army of his own. Even at that, Captain Hume, who was still very good with a sword, wanted to go down and fight alongside the men, but I insisted he remain behind to see to my personal safety.

How can I make you appreciate the humiliation and degradation of that hurried departure from Prague Castle? It didn't help that it all came crashing down just as I was beginning to turn the corner and dig myself out of all that melancholy and disappointment. I had been busy arranging a room for myself much like the study Henry liked to spend so much time in back in London. There were book shelves to organize, artefacts to unpack, paintings and hangings to arrange, and I was moving a lamp into place next to the chair I intended use for reading, when Frederick burst into the room. He stopped abruptly, as a boy might who had stumbled upon the very person he wanted least to throw into distemper.

"Elizabeth, we have . . . you have to . . . the children . . ."

"Frederick, what is it?" I stepped toward him. "You look ghastly."

"The children. Where are they?" He looked around the room. "See to them at once." He turned to go, hesitated, then stepped closer and took me by the hand. "We have to go," he pleaded gently. "All of us. Now."

"Go where? Whatever is the matter?"

"It's not safe here. The castle shall soon be under siege, and we may not linger."

"But how can this be?" I ran to the window. "What of the soldiers who stand always at the ready to defend these walls?"

"We have been granted safe passage, but only for one night."

"Passage?" I turned back to face him. "Passage to where?"

"We must be out of Prague by noon tomorrow, else our lives may be forfeit."

"Who issues these caveats? Have they the force of effect behind them? Surely we can negotiate some other arrangement."

"There is no barter to be had save that which I have already stated. We must be gone from here at once."

Just then Captain Hume came into the room. "Your Highness," he said, "I have received word that the Duke of Bavaria approaches the gates of the city."

"Then it is just as I feared," said Frederick. "His forces are no doubt formidable."

"It cannot be long now."

"I have arranged for us to make our way into the Old Town, there to accept such humble lodgings as may be available to us. We set off on the morrow for Breslau."

"And after that?" I said.

"Heidelberg."

"Back where we came from. With all we brought from the place hardly uncrated."

"Pack up whatever you can. We leave within the hour."

"A little more time, surely. It cannot be so soon. This is a rude turnabout." I turned to Captain Hume. "Sir, is the situation really as dire as that?"

"I fear it is. I cannot vouchsafe our safety if we remain. I'm sorry."

"It is not for you to apologize," Frederick intervened. "None of this is your doing."

The Captain and I gave each other a quick glance.

"We depart from the square beyond St. Vitus Cathedral," said Frederick. "I have seen to as many coaches and carriages as I could muster to be loaded and assembled there. Beyond the gate is a private road, little used, that wends its way down to the river, and by such means shall we make our way across the Old Bridge into the town. Now I have some other urgent matters of my own to see to."

Frederick left the room and the Captain turned to me. "Your Highness, I am at your disposal. What would you have me do?"

Before I could make answer, Amalia hurried in through the door. "Your Highness." She looked at Captain Hume.

"She has been apprised of the situation," he told her.

"Very well." She turned to me. "Then you understand we must make haste."

"Yes, yes, so I am told. Hounded out of the castle like a plague of rats."

"We must see to the children," Amalia continued.

"And there is the matter of my jewellery and wardrobe."

"Shall I send for Master of the House?" the Captain enquired.

"I'm afraid he has already fled," said Amalia.

"The Lord Chamberlain, then."

"Also departed, I fear."

"And I suppose the Lord Steward is nowhere to be found. Damn them all, the cowards."

"There's also the matter of my bed," I said.

"Madam?"

"I will have to be dismantled and loaded. As many wagons as it takes. Then see to other furniture if there's time." I looked intently at him. "Can you do it?"

"Come," said Amalia, "there's much to do," and hurried me off before I could hear the Captain's answer.

The palace was a madhouse of bustle and confusion as people scattered here and there, some taking whatever they could carry. Even as disorder and chaos swirled about me I saw my possible future. If Frederick should be captured or killed, what would become of us? For certain I should have to see to my own financial resources. To that end I busied myself with the gathering of as many valuables as I could manage. I dared not set those few servants still remaining to the task, as they might be tempted to run off with it themselves. I started with my personal jewellery, rummaged for every diamond and sapphire, every necklace and earring. The entire collection of Medici pearls had to be found, as their worth should be greater if all the pieces remained intact. Those of my gowns studded with diamonds and other precious stones I also packed up. When the trunks were ready I summoned only as many attendants as absolutely necessary, paid them handsomely on the spot out of a chest I kept for personal expenses, and had the trunks toted out before me through the doors and across the square to the waiting carriage and wagons.

"These cannot be out of my sight," I said to one of the footmen, indicating the trunks. "They must come with us in this carriage."

He looked off to one side, unsure of himself, and there I saw Frederick come around the carriage to stand before me.

"These," Frederick told the footman, "will have to go elsewhere. The children will be coming with us in the carriage."

I turned again to the footman. "None of this can be left behind. You will see to it?"

"Where are they?" Frederick persisted.

I heard some commotion behind me and was greatly relieved when I turned to see Amalia herding the children across the square toward us.

"I have done what was necessary," I said.

Henry, almost seven now and dressed in his day clothes, went to stand beside his father. Charles Louis, almost three, followed, holding his younger sister Elisabeth's hand in his. They were in their nightclothes, looking unsettled and roused from sleep.

"Alright," said Frederick, "let's get you loaded up." He picked up little Elisabeth to lift her into the carriage, after which the rest of the children boarded, followed by myself and Frederick, and we were just about to depart when Captain Hume came striding awkwardly across the courtyard with a baby, swaddled in a blanket and cradled in his arms.

"Rupert." Frederick brushed past me and alighted from the carriage to take him from the Captain.

"Governess, nursemaid — all fled in the confusion," the Captain said breathlessly, "and so it fell to me."

My husband stepped back into the carriage, and after Captain Hume had closed the door behind him I reached out to take Rupert, but without a word Frederick leaned past me and handed him over to Amalia. I sat back stiffly and we drove off in silence.

It seemed a harsh indictment that the welfare of those trunks should have come at the expense of a child, but I was caught up, preoccupied. Perhaps it was only that he was still so new. It could have happened to anyone. I had seen enough by then to understand that motherhood was not a foolproof business, nor was I the first to overlook an offspring. What of those mothers who saw fit to offer their children everything save what they were most in need of? In any case it should only have been a moment or two before one of us realized he was missing. Why did it seem so unforgivable?

The horses set off at a trot and soon the other wagons and carriages followed. The lane leading from the palace was lined on either side by high stone walls and tall trees in behind them that leaned over the roadway. It was one I had already come to know, having walked its curved meanderings down the hillside and along the river. It was so little used I could often traverse its entire length in quiet solitude and encounter not a single soul. Now in the awkward silence, save for the horse's hooves clopping hollow on the cobblestones and the intermittent squeak of leather or rattle of a wheel, the journey took on a sombre tone. I was reminded of the funeral dirge a few years earlier that had brought my dear bother Henry to his resting place at Westminster Abbey.

We followed the river, black and glistening outside the carriage window, until we came to the Old Stone Bridge and made our way under the towers to cross to the other side into the Old Town. I would learn later that its stone ramparts should soon be adorned with the heads of those who had seen fit to bring Frederick to power, and that mine should certainly have been among them if we had not fled. As we travelled along, the lampposts on either side lit our way through a fine mist that wafted up from the river, and we passed the small crucifix that marked the site where John of Nepomuk had been thrown from the bridge and drowned. His tomb had been among those destroyed in Scultetus's vehement excoriation of the cathedral. I had heard his story and become fascinated with it. He had been the confessor to an earlier queen of Bohemia and remained faithful to his covenant of secrecy even under threat of death. He refused to divulge the adultery her husband the King suspected her of, remained steadfast even as he was taken out to the middle of the bridge and unceremoniously tossed over the side into the Vltava River. I wondered what Captain Hume should have done under such circumstances, to preserve the secret pact which had brought us to this place of rude and sudden ruin.

Should it be said of someone who commits an act of unselfish loyalty that it was his finest hour, or is it misplaced? I should have confessed, I think, having granted myself permission to do so on the grounds that no one should be expected to keep such a compact no matter the consequences. Would my children grow up to think I might have abandoned them? It was said that the ghost of John of Nepomuk walked the bridge. Did I see him there now? Shaking his finger at me?

We passed beneath the tower at the far end of bridge and made our way between the dark houses along the narrow cobblestone streets into the Old Town, where at length we found ourselves herded into the humble quarters of a residence afforded us there. It was very dark, the streets narrow, and we were put up in an inn that was very near the old church of Our Lady Before Tyne. I had never stayed in such a modest room, but it was thought we best not take refuge in a place too well known to the authorities or we should be found and slaughtered in our beds. We woke up very early the next morning and proceeded down to a barge, where we boarded for Breslau. Bribes were offered once again, just as they had been on the night before, and as they would continue to be all along the entire length of our journey.

We endured many days of arduous travel, slept in countless uncomfortable beds, in cramped rooms, with hardly enough servants to see to the needs of the children let alone ours, and what was provided in the way of food hardly passed for such at times. Dreadful!

If in the course of all that hardship I learned humility, it was not of a kind that did me much good. Perhaps if it hadn't seemed largely self-inflicted, I might have garnered more from the experience. The fact of the matter was that things were going to get much worse, though I didn't know it at the time. I thought we should return to the castle at Heidelberg, back to the English Wing waiting for us there, to the Hortus Palatinus with its groves of orange trees, its ornate sculpture and flowers.

I even thought that it might be a way for me to start over again, forget the silly ambitions I had become swept up in, and live out my life there, content to learn a modesty more becoming to my nature, where I might once again leave the machinations of the court to those with a penchant for it and see myself up the mountain to walk about the trails, perhaps to visit Sophia, who would teach me to covet less and appreciate more. I would make an effort to spend more time in the company of my children, teach them and mentor them into a more promising adulthood than mine had turned out to be.

But none of that would come to pass. We had taken temporary refuge at some lodgings in Breslau thanks to my cousin Maurice of Nassau and expected to depart at any time for Heidelberg when word came that the armies of the Catholic League under the command of Count Tilly had overrun the town, laid siege to the castle, and laid waste to a good portion of it. Soon after, we were hounded out of Breslau and so, by degrees measured daily in strife and hardship, crossed Bohemia. In some places we were only grudgingly permitted to stay for a night or two before we had to move on. In others the welcome was a little warmer but invariably followed close upon by a poorly disguised ruse designed to hasten our departure and see us move on. And so it went from day to day, place to place, until the day approached when I should have to suffer another child to be born. We managed to reach Brandenburg in the snow, where accommodation at the Castle of Custrin had been afforded us. It was Christmas Eve, and along the streets, lamps had been lighted which illuminated the decorations mounted upon the houses along both sides. The castle now came into view and looked inviting in all of its adornment and brightness. I was thankful to consider I should be allowed to birth my fifth child in what looked at first glance to be a comfortable and well-appointed castle.

By then there had been somewhat of a thaw between Frederick and I after our departure from Prague and we were looking forward to some means, however modest, of celebrating Christmas with the children. Frederick had gone to the trouble of arranging a small gift for each of the children to open upon the morrow, and these along with our other necessaries were carried into the castle by the few attendants still in our employ. You might be surprised to hear that the yuletide was one of the few times in the year when I managed to engage in the spirit of family life, if only for the sake of the children, and as we were led along I was glad to see the hallways brightly lit with enormous Christmas candles and adorned with decorous leaves of holly and ivy, bay and laurel.

We passed a chamber where an atmosphere of good cheer reigned within, a fire of uncommon brightness burned in the hearth and all looked festive and gay. A great long table had been set with all manner of succulent dishes, and one of the children remarked upon the peacock pie at the centre which boasted a great fanned tail. A man stood at the head of the table, dipped his cup into the bowl of wassail set before him, and held it high to offer a toast to the seated guests for a merry Christmas and a happy new year. The children cheered at these sights as they chattered amongst themselves, and it occurred to me how so many things I had always been wont to take for granted suddenly seemed quite wonderful.

Three burly men carried upon their shoulders an enormous yule log, and one of the children remarked that perhaps they might have been sent to set us a jolly fire in our apartments. The men turned off into a room up ahead, but we were led on farther down the hall until the sounds of cheer had all but died out behind us and the walls stood devoid of candles and decoration. An unwelcome silence settled about us as we were led into a remote corner of the castle.

"I suppose it is for our own safety," said Frederick, "that the lord of the manor wants us as far away from the main living quarters as possible. All the better to remain incognito."

At last we arrived and made entry to the rooms provided for us. They were all but barren! The echoing starkness of those quarters rings yet in my memory. No more in the way of furnishings from one chamber to the next than a table here and a mattress there, all of them equally uninviting, walls bare of so much as an arras to mitigate the cold and damp. No fire in the hearth nor any stick of wood to light one. I should have insisted on having some of the furniture we'd taken out of Prague brought up, but those wagons no longer accompanied us. Most of them, including the ones that transported the great bed I had taken pains to see dismantled and loaded, had been sent on ahead. Indeed a great many of our original party had been scattered here and there and might never be seen or heard from again.

Amalia helped me into a chair, and as I laboured through intermittent bouts of birthing pains, the sheer bleakness of it all threatened to overwhelm me. Was ever a place so foreign and unwelcoming? Now the intensity of my birthing pains increased greatly and I was taken into the next room and made to lie down upon the cold mattress there. Amalia shouted out orders to the attendants and gave forth great resourcefulness. By means I hardly recall she managed to get a fire lit in the hearth and to see to a kettle of boiling water and such. I had yet enough wits about me to insist that if she was going to act as midwife she must wash her hands thoroughly with soap and hot water. In all of this she was compliant and made not once to question my wishes as the physicians surely would have, and insist on poking their filthy hands about my insides without a second thought for cleanliness. And so I was suffered to give birth to a son, Maurice, there within the confines of those all-but-empty and unwelcoming quarters. The delivery was uneventful and Amalia heroic.

Christmas Day came and went and I was glad for it to be over. I thought of the story told with such sentiment in the Bible verses of the humble stable where Mary gave birth to Jesus, and how the story had hitherto evoked feelings of tenderness in me. I realized that it altogether dismissed what an ordeal it must have been for poor Mary, and ever after abandoned any romantic notions I might have had about the unfolding of that first day of Christendom.

When I was feeling up to it we continued on our way and eventually arrived at The Hague where, thanks to the Prince of Orange, some modest lodgings had been set aside for us in Binnenhof. The apartments there were situated within an entirely unremarkable red brick building that sat next to a wide boulevard. Square white-trimmed windows ran along the side in an even line, and the overall design of the place boasted an almost complete lack of imagination. The place was hardly a palace, but then I'd had no illusions about what we might find when we got there. The small grounds in behind were surrounded by a hornbeam hedge that afforded some much-needed privacy, and there were even a few flowerbeds and a fountain to enjoy. It wasn't exactly the Hortus Palatinus, but for now it would have to do.

I was somewhat unprepared for the gloominess of the interior, which featured walls of dark wainscoting under a high ceiling. Oak cupboards and shelves cluttered with all manner of pottery ran along the walls, and the fireplace appeared to be covered in a bawdy arrangement of coloured tiles. The place was far from well-appointed, the furniture inadequate for our purposes, but we settled in with what meagre possessions remained to us to set up a modest household. At the very least my bed had made it through all the turmoil, and I was grateful for its familiar comforts, but we were forced to make do with such a paltry allowance provided by the Prince that I was far from content, and struggled to keep from complaining too bitterly about the poverty and privation we were being subjected to.

One evening, emboldened by more than a little wine, those unseemly aspects of my nature which drink was wont to engender got the better of me, and so bitterly did I berate my poor husband that I was hardly surprised when next morning I discovered he had disappeared, and Captain Hume along with him. Neither of them was anywhere to be found.

Chapter Thirteen

I thought I might have driven Frederick away, and that perhaps he and the Captain had gone off to raise a glass or two at the nearest inn, if only to seek some relief from my displeasure. But the better part of a week went by and still there was no sign of them, until one afternoon they were back as mysteriously as they had vanished. The two had about them the air of an adolescent conspiracy. Frederick in particular seemed very pleased with himself and could hardly contain his excitement.

"Alright," I said at supper that evening, "you have waited all day to offer me your explanations, and now I will have them."

The table was set with a feast unlike any we had enjoyed in a long time. Frederick had ordered an extravagance of food and drink, and when I sought to chide him for spending money we did not have he looked and me and said, "Dearest Elizabeth, be assured that I bring us not to hardship but rather to celebration, the need for which you shall soon hear of, only leave off until we have dined and then all shall be revealed."

When at last we were done eating and drinking, I said, "Very well, I have kept my end of the bargain, and now you must keep yours. The two of you have been acting like schoolboys newly returned from some secret adventure and seem quite satisfied with yourselves." I turned to Captain Hume. "You have not turned into a pair of highwaymen, I hope. Where were you all this time?"

"Here." Frederick passed me a handbill. "Captain Hume himself tore that from the door of the great cathedral in Heidelberg."

"Heidelberg? You mean to say you travelled all that way?"

"The Hapsburgs seek not only to withhold that which is rightfully ours," Frederick continued, "they are determined to make an example of us. I had not fathomed the lengths to which the Holy Roman Emperor would go to humiliate us."

I held up the poster and read aloud: *"A king run away some days since,"* it said, *"of adolescent age, sanguine colour, middle height, a cast on one of his eyes, no moustache, only down on his lip, not badly disposed when a stolen kingdom did not lie in his way — his name is Frederick."*

"I can hardly imagine what he might have had to say about me," I offered. "But you say you got this in Heidelberg?"

"There is much encouragement that the people should see fit to disparage your part as well," said Frederick.

"And you have heard something of this?"

"Naught but insult and provocation," said Captain Hume. "Not worth repeating."

"I will hear it."

"Not from me," said Frederick.

In all this Captain Hume continued eating with great relish, washing down the generous portions of roasted meats with great gulps of wine, but now he paused, swallowed.

"Captain Hume, what do they say about me?" I demanded.

The Captain looked over at Frederick, who shook his head no.

"I command you," I said.

"Madam, I disdain."

"We are all in this."

"Why should you wish me to repeat such talk as is not worthy even of your contempt?"

"I'm waiting." I stared him down.

"They say that the English king's daughter is fled from Prague . . . like . . ."

"Say!"

". . . an Irish beggar-woman with her babes at her back."

"And what else?"

"That's enough." Frederick brought the flat of his hand down upon the table. "We will have no more of this."

"I suppose it's not altogether inaccurate to characterize the situation as such," I said.

Captain Hume took up his goblet. "I say such filthy slurs make the venture your husband and I undertook all the more satisfying."

"Am I going to hear what it was?"

"Your husband merely saw fit," said Captain Hume, "to take back what was rightfully his."

"You don't mean to say you set about to steal your crown back?"

"Nothing so ambitious or foolhardy, I'm afraid."

"And yet the spoils have made this fine feast possible." The Captain replenished his chalice from a large bottle.

"You say you went to Heidelberg. I understood it lay in ruins."

"Your Highness, this thrift of detail," said Captain Hume, "is borne of modesty, and so" — he turned to Frederick — "with your permission, I shall tell the Queen what we have been at."

"Very well." Frederick sat back in his chair.

"Your husband, prior to your leaving for Prague, had made provision to store a considerable sum of money and treasure for safekeeping in Heidelberg Castle. It was one of the reasons he was so eager to return, and so disappointed when that option was denied him. He determined that if he could not take back the castle, he could at least try to procure what was rightfully his, and to this end we set out."

"Do you remember the replica of Mr. Shakespeare's Globe Theatre you had constructed as part of the English Wing?" asked Captain Hume. Without waiting for an answer, he added, "Well, then you may also recall that for the presentation of *Hamlet* a secret trap door was built into the floor of the stage, the better to allow that the ghost of Hamlet's father should make a spectacular and frightening entrance, as suited your fancy. There beneath that stage, in a secret compartment beneath the dirt floor, your husband saw fit to bury money and gold, as well as some jewels and such."

"So it was only a matter of sneaking into the castle to retrieve it." Frederick thought to take over the story, but Captain Hume would have none of it.

"But what a sight greeted us there," the Captain carried on, "when we first laid eyes on that once-noble fortress."

"Better not to have seen such ruin," Frederick tried again, "not to mention the grounds of the Hortus Palatinus. It would have made your heart ache, Elizabeth, to see how the place had nearly been destroyed!"

"Much as the patrons of St. Vitus must have felt, I suppose," I offered, "when they saw what Scultetus had done to their precious relics."

"We made our way through the woods in behind the castle, which you know well." The Captain slipped a furtive glance in my direction. "And there did we bide our time until nightfall, then lowered ourselves down into the drained moat where once you kept your menagerie of animals but where now all was in ruins, and so by degrees through the chapel and along the hallway to the theatre. There was hardly anyone about, and we thought to have the place to ourselves, when a guard stationed in a recess of the wall stepped forth to demand who goes there. At this I ascertained at once that he was one of those same combatants I had trained during my time there, at which he allowed us to pass.

"And so at length we gained the theatre, still pristine, as the troops of General Tilly had not bothered with it, though the same could not be said for much of the castle. In particular the General seemed to have taken great relish in destroying utterly the terrace from which you, Your Highness, so oft deigned to gaze down upon the town below."

"Speak no more of it," pleaded Frederick, "but finish now the story."

"In any case, we managed to garner the treasure and carry it off. With no small effort we made the long journey back here, all the while taking extra care to go by the roads less travelled, else we be captured." The Captain took a final drink from his chalice and pushed back his chair. "And here we are." He rose from the table, a little unsteady on his feet. "It would appear I have over-indulged a trifle, and to that end I take myself away to bed at once, lest I fall face-down into snoring sleep here in my chair. And so, I say good night to both of you."

When he had seen himself out of the room I turned to Frederick. "You should have told me."

"I hardly know why I failed to do so, but that it should have caused you greater distress to know it was there and unavailable to you than to remain ignorant of such a provision."

"It gives me cause to wonder what else you may have squirrelled away that I know naught of."

"It was Mother's idea."

"Juliana?"

"That we should only seek to make use of it in the most dire of circumstances."

"No doubt she swore you to secrecy."

Frederick looked at me for a moment, then lowered his gaze, shrugged his shoulders and shifted awkwardly in his chair.

"You will not say so, but she did so for want of trust in me. And you were content to go along with it."

Frederick looked as though he was about to speak but at the last moment held back, retreated, as he was too often wont to do, to the safety of silence.

"I had a right to know."

"You know it now."

"If you had failed, or worse yet perished, I never should have."

"I did neither."

"But why did you leave it there?" I didn't wait for an answer. "You didn't bother to take it with you to Prague because you were resigned to losing your crown even before you had obtained it. You knew you were coming back to Heidelberg. That's it, isn't it?"

"I will grant I considered as much."

"And how if by that very act you condemned yourself to failure?"

I stopped, reproached myself for inflicting such needless recrimination on poor Frederick.

"How much is there?" I asked.

"Enough to do us for a while, provided we show restraint."

But the reprieve from penury that Frederick's adventure provided was short-lived. We were soon in debt again. I grant much of the fault was mine. But which was worse: to torture myself with penny-pinching and self-inflicted suffering, to live unsatisfied, or to fly in the face of austerity and spend as I pleased, be it but briefly, thereafter to endure the hardship that was coming in any event? Those who live poor and have yet riches, who forsake indulgence in the name of moderation, what do they profit? Better to live a pauper than a miser, for what is more wretched than a cheapskate? To hoard, to covet, was not in my nature. I was no magpie, no squirrel!

Soon enough our apartments fell into disrepair and neglect, my wardrobe into shameful redundancy; the children were not properly fed, the servants left unpaid. Nevertheless I was required to bring more babies into the world and gave birth to Louise, then Edward, thereafter Henriette and also Louis, who lived only a little more than four months. I was time and again occupied, ballooned out of all proportion into unattractive bulkiness. Had I been a commoner I should not have had to marry so soon. A cottage girl might not have to wed until she was twenty-five. By that age I had borne six children. Nothing I wore pleased me. I looked drab and dowdy in everything, my breasts enormous and blue-veined, spilling out of every dress. I refused to wear my husband's waistcoats, as some women preferred to do, which they let out in the back as the baby grew; I opted instead to walk around all day in an Adrianne dress, unattractive as it was.

And yet, I suppose I should have been thankful not to have lost my looks as so many women did. There were those among the ladies at court so desperate not to conceive again they turned to remedies, some untried and unproven, others dirty and dangerous. One might wear an amulet containing the testicles of a weasel, the dried liver of a black cat, the anus of a hare, only to find the effort spectacularly ineffective. Another might rub herself with salves — oil of rue, oil of savin, oil of mint — all equally so. Of course the husbands had no knowledge of their meddling. The women only talked about it amongst themselves, and never in the company of their men. They had reason enough to be so secretive. Any talk of intervention in the natural process of propagation was strictly forbidden, let alone the practice of it. Catholic or Protestant, there was an ever-present threat that we might be accused of practising witchcraft. To broach the idea that certain measures might be taken after conception was even worse. The men at court found nothing so frightening as the thought of a secret society of women, and I had no interest in being burned at the stake. No pessaries for me, nor beeswax or small stones.

One morning I was seated at the table in the antechamber, writing a letter to my brother Charles.

September, 1627
Binnenhof, The Hague

Dear Charles,

Let this be the last in the long list of correspondences I have composed, all of which remain unanswered. I grant you may have little interest in receiving my letters and even less in answering them when time and again they concern matters of money, but I had hoped these entreaties would appeal to your sense of obligation if not your generosity. Along with the throne, you have inherited the responsibility to live up to that recommendation decreed by Parliament, which entitles me to a pension. If the funds have been made available to you why will you not see fit to release them to me? I cannot think you would stoop so low as to appropriate them for yourself, to squander colossal sums of money on your own estates and lavish court while I am forced to live in penury.

I am determined to make a clean break of it and instead of asking for my money yet again I have but one final request to make of you. Will you give me an honest explanation for your treatment of me? At the very least you owe me that much. I confess I am less than eager to hear the answer, but will you grant me this much? Perhaps there is some long-festering resentment that yet gives you cause to deny me. If so I would know what lies at the heart of it. For certain there were times I acted unkindly toward you, but who should bear the greater guilt: I for having treated you poorly, or you for holding it against me all these years? If I was selfish and petty as a child, the same was true for you. How could it hope to be otherwise for those raised in royalty? I say neither of us need seek forgiveness. I ask only to know the reason for your inexcusable neglect. If your purpose is to exact a kind of revenge, be assured you have succeeded.

Your sister in good faith,
Elizabeth

The room was silent and empty, and as I read over what I had written I became aware of a faint sound as though of muted nibbling or chewing. When I turned to see what it was, there at the foot of the damp wall a rat sat up on its spindly hind legs, gnawing at the arras. I ran from the room and right into Amalia, who had been on her way to see me. When I told her what I had seen she sent immediately for the chamberlain to see to the matter, but something about that harrowing experience brought the same black fist I have told you about to hover over me. For a time I fell into a kind of madness amidst all the humiliation and hardship, became convinced that Frederick must be hiding more treasure from me, berated him for not disclosing it to me lest he should meet an untimely death and I be made to suffer needlessly.

Amalia remained steadfast through it all, saw to my needs as best she could, served as midwife and chambermaid, seamstress and confidante. It seemed a mystery to me that she should choose to do so.

"There's something I've been wanting to ask you," I began one evening. We were alone in my bedchamber, and Amalia was busy seeing to my bed and toiletries.

"Madam?"

"Why do you stay with me?"

"I am bound. It is my duty."

"You are no more bound than those who have already seen fit to depart, and I must concede I hardly blame them for doing so."

"I suppose they must see to their own needs."

"And what of your needs?"

"They shall be seen to in good time."

There had been many difficult days and I had begun to feel like myself again, thanks in no small measure to Amalia's efforts. She had laboured herself into a state of near exhaustion to see me through, but I could hardly think why.

"By now you could have made your way back to England, I have no doubt of it, yet you suffer yourself to endure these privations, not to mention my thankless abuses."

"You are too harsh. I grant the conditions are less than favourable but I am determined to remain."

"The future holds little promise these days," I said.

"Things are sure to get better."

"Your assurance is admirable, though perhaps ill founded. Our plight grows daily more difficult and hopeless. I want you to know you are entirely free to look to your own ends should you choose to do so."

"Your Highness, mine was a very modest upbringing, as you are aware. Austerity and deprivation were my daily companions. But you, Madam, have from the moment you were born known only luxury and opulence."

"If you say this to impeach me, I have no defence."

"Where I might hope for a new dress once every year or two, you would think twenty or thirty barely adequate."

Though Amalia had little in the way of resources for a decent wardrobe, she nevertheless managed to attire herself tastefully, and bore herself with a refinement that belied her station.

"This sounds a harsh judgment."

"It is not intended to be so. The fault is no more yours than mine. Naught but circumstance made it so. You were a princess, and then a queen." Amalia was dressed plainly enough, but wore an elegant lace wrap about her shoulders that provided a decorous touch.

"A queen no more."

"A queen still, to be addressed as such whether in exile or no. I'm afraid I must insist on that. The future may yet bring fortune's favour upon you. We are not easily defeated, you and I."

"By my reckoning the odds are not in our favour. I had thought that at the very worst I might find myself once again ensconced in the English Wing at Heidelberg Castle, but now it is hard for me to believe things will ever get better."

My pessimism might well have turned out to be warranted had it not been for Lord Craven. His arrival from England brought about an unexpected and welcome change in prospects. I had been told of an English nobleman coming to The Hague, intent on mounting an attack against the Hapsburgs which would see Frederick restored to the throne of the Palatinate. He had apparently been born into a poor family in North Yorkshire but thereafter his father had moved the family to London and become a man of considerable means. Upon inheriting that vast fortune Lord Craven had managed to amass additional wealth, to the point that his worth was said to be greater even than that of the king himself. He had bought and paid for his own army and crossed the channel with it, determined to throw himself into a campaign alongside my husband.

Upon Lord Craven's arrival, Frederick arranged for a dinner to be held in his honour, and I did what I could to see to a proper gown and a decent spread of dishes upon the table. I had for some time, unbeknownst to Frederick, been selling off my jewellery, some of those same items I'd managed to escape from Prague with, and now I pawned the last of it, save for the Medici collection, to bring about the necessary purchases. The evening was hardly an elaborate affair, and rather informal at that, as there was little in the way of amenities at Binnenhof and not much of a court. The modest apartments we had been granted use of, thanks to Frederick's cousin the Prince of Orange, were hardly sufficient to allow for much more than a miniature court-in-exile, but I had managed to cobble together something of a guest list for the occasion.

Sitting at dinner and observing Lord Craven's youthful manner, I was reminded in some ways of that first time Frederick was introduced to me at Whitehall. It seemed so long ago now, and I felt so very much older. Lord Craven, though considerably younger than I, had about him an air of maturity and wit, and he made conversation in a calm and courtly manner. The ladies found him altogether agreeable, with the slight cleft in his chin, his long hair curly and dark, and his somewhat sculpted nose.

"Lord Craven, we should be pleased to learn, if only for the sake of this company," Captain Hume enquired, "how it is you have come into our midst."

"I understand you have been appointed commander of the English forces," said Frederick, "levied by the Marquis of Hamilton to ally with those of Gustavus Adolphus of Sweden."

I had asked Captain Hume to join us for the evening, intent that he should exercise the same unfailing judgement of character he had ever been possessed of. He had as usual dressed for the occasion in less than stellar fashion, having arrived looking as though he might have come straight from a public brawl. Lord Craven nevertheless met him with equanimity, and if he took exception to the Captain's appearance gave no expression to it.

"And that you intend to march with us against Ferdinand II?" Frederick added.

"If I may be allowed," Lord Craven replied. His narrow moustache and thin goatee were trimmed with a neat flourish around a generous mouth, and his dark eyes wrestled with a restrained intensity. He had about him the kind of enthusiasm only a young and naive gentleman could evince. As he talked of the campaign to come, Frederick and Captain Hume exchanged knowing glances, suspecting they had in their company a soldier who should soon discover the harsh realities of the battlefield.

"I can't imagine why you should want to bother," the Captain declared, to which Lord Craven took immediate exception.

"Sir, why would you say such a thing?"

Captain Hume stroked first one side and then the other of his ragged moustache. "I have it on good authority that you are a man of considerable chinks, Sir — exceedingly wealthy, in fact."

"What of it?"

I addressed myself to Lord Craven. "I think Captain Hume means that you could just as easily have taken up some other, perhaps less perilous, pursuit."

Over the course of our dinner conversation I had not failed to notice Lord Craven looking at me more than once the way young men were wont to do. I thought it nothing more than the usual sort of infatuation. In those days it happened quite often that a young soldier or musician, perhaps artist or nobleman, would come into my company and be stricken thus. It happened with surprising frequency and I considered Lord Craven, though many years my junior, but another of these. I was not a great beauty nor possessed of those attributes associated with voluptuousness or carnality, but whether aught appealed of voice or mannerism, charm or personality, I had no need to contrive it.

"I'm told you campaigned here once before." Captain Hume exchanged a knowing glance with Frederick. "Isn't that so?" It was clear the two of them doubted this young man's sincerity and intended to press the matter of his intentions. "And that you served under Maurice and his successor, Frederick Henry, that same Prince of Orange whose roof we dine under even now?"

"And for which you were knighted upon your return," Frederick chimed in, "by that same brother of my wife's who now sits upon the throne of England."

"Ah." The Captain leaned back a little in his chair. "We speak now of that same monarch who sees fit to finance endless and elaborate constructions to his palaces, yet fails to send his sister so much as a farthing" — he poked up a slab of beef from the plate before him — "that she should be reduced to serving her guests only three kinds of meat at table."

"Knighted, you say." My deference was poorly feigned. "Perhaps we were better to address you as Sir Craven."

Lord Craven turned to address me. "I should very much prefer if you would call me William."

"And so let us be frank, young man" — Captain Hume lowered his gaze directly at Lord Craven — "and insist that you tell us in all honesty why you seek to join our cause. It is not unusual that a nobleman such as yourself should seek to undertake such a venture for the sake of enhancing his reputation, making sure all the while not to put himself in any real danger."

Lord Craven had not taken his eyes from me. "I come because a queen most fair has been torn from her rightful place, and I would see her restored to it."

"And how for her husband, the king?" asked Frederick.

"That goes without saying." Lord Craven's gaze remained fixed upon me.

"A brash young man boldly declares himself to my wife's service," Frederick said to no one in particular, "and this would seem to be another of those. They are invariably enamoured of the Queen's affection." He held up his chalice for the attendant to refill. "And being full of callow youth and vigour, wear their passion like a second garment easily shed."

"Doubtless not in this case, though." Captain Hume allowed a sideways glance at Frederick. I grant my husband had witnessed his share of such fervour — extravagant compliments, not to mention bold remarks and selfless gestures — and I could hardly blame him for his behaviour, but if he let slip his jealousy he had no cause to be so! I had never indulged these harmless overtures. I was not unfaithful. And yet on this occasion I had to admit I felt my guard slip a little. There was an innocent charm about Lord Craven I found disarming.

"I suppose next you will be hoping to wear a glove of Her Majesty's into battle." Captain Hume leaned forward in his chair.

"She shall take it as an affront if you don't." Frederick raised his cup again to drink.

"Madam, I would be honoured to receive such," said Lord Craven.

"Then I must grant it," I said defiantly.

"You see?" Frederick fashioned a crooked smile. "My wife would not withhold from a gallant soldier her favours for such a worthy cause."

"And what of me?" Captain Hume made a great show of holding his folded hands up to his heart.

"You, Sir, shall have a scarf," I said.

When the day arrived that they had made their preparations and were set to depart, the three of them came to stand before me. They were all of them dressed in full armour and quite dashing, although the Captain somehow managed to look dishevelled even in such attire, his greaves unpolished, his breastplate poorly fastened.

"I see you intend to play for your evening's rest, as always," I said to Captain Hume, noting that one of the pages stood waiting next to a horse with a viola da gamba encased and firmly fastened upon its back.

"I shall compose something for you, Madam," said the Captain, "to hear upon our return." With his beard and moustache in disarray as always, greying locks sticking out at odds and ends from under his helmet, nose red and bulbous, he carried a glint of merriment in his eyes.

Lord Craven, dressed all in black armour and with his plumed helmet under his arm, his long black locks curling over the shoulders of his shiny doublet, stepped forward and knelt before me.

"Madam." He looked up at me. "I am in your service and declare to you my loyalty with all my heart."

"Then take this." I offered my glove, which he took from me, brought to his lips, and gently kissed before rising to his feet.

"And this" — I turned to the Captain and produced a scarf — "is for you." He bowed and took it from me.

"And to you, my husband, I offer this kiss, for all good fortune and a swift return."

Frederick, though smartly attired in a well-fitting suit of armour, seemed to me to have aged overnight, his features pinched, eyes sunken, cheeks collapsed into hollow pockets of care. I thought it might just be that the previous night's drinking had taken its toll, but I did not recall his hair so wispy, his ears so wrinkled. I kissed him on the cheek and he returned it dutifully. "Farewell, dear wife. I pray when we meet again I shall have good news to tell." He turned to the others. "Gentlemen, the King of Sweden awaits."

"Madam," announced Lord Craven, "I shall wear this upon my helmet for all to see."

"And if you should lose it?"

"Then I should prefer to lose my head with it."

"As for his heart," the Captain rolled his eyes at me, "'tis already lost, I fear."

They mounted and rode off, leaving me, by Frederick's reckoning at any rate, to do little more than stitch the standard and pray for their safe return. But I had other ideas. If my children had been relegated to an impassive mother disinclined to expressions of love and affection, such would not be the case when it came to their education. To that end I set myself the task of procuring placement for them in the best schools, the services of the most accomplished tutors, that they should develop into adults possessed of self-reliance and resourcefulness, exhibit neither expectation nor desire for privilege or entitlement, for these were the very seeds of disappointment and folly. I would turn such favours as I might, muster assistance where I could get it, persuade and cajole and bribe, do whatever was necessary to see them properly schooled. Some of it would be unpleasant and perhaps even demeaning, but it would be that much easier to accomplish with Frederick out of the way.

Chapter Fourteen

Months passed with little news of the campaign save for reports of advances and setbacks, and the occasional letter from Frederick in which he poured out affection and longing, misgivings and promises, all in equal measure and in which I took little interest. If I judged myself cold-hearted that correspondence from my husband, engaged in battle almost daily, should meet with such an appalling lack of enthusiasm, it was only that if I had read one such letter I had read them all. They were of far greater benefit to him to write them than for me to read, and thus it has ever been and will ever be with letters from the battlefield. My interest lay in the upshot of their efforts. I wanted results.

The outcome remained uncertain and I had not heard any news for some time when they returned at last without Lord Craven in their company. The three of them had fought side by side in the siege of Creuznach and on February 22, 1632, had emerged victorious. Captain Hume reported that Lord Craven had fought bravely and suffered quite a bad wound to his leg in battle, after which he had seen fit to cart himself back to England. But then came the truly disappointing news. Although the campaign had been successful, the same could not be said of the negotiations that followed. Gustavus, having led the greater forces into battle and emerged triumphant, gave over that he should be allowed to keep control of the lands thus acquired for the Swedish interest, rather than cede them to the Palatinate.

I could not hide my disappointment at this news and understood at once why I had not heard from Frederick for some time. More than anything he should have liked to return with the news that we should soon be on our way back to Prague, and now to bring word instead that it was not to be made the occasion an awkward one for both of us. I grant I might have seen fit to show more understanding of his feelings in the matter, but in his absence the circumstances of my day-to-day life in The Hague had only grown worse, and now to be told that I must continue in penury indefinitely put me in a less than charitable mood. Even so, it was obvious from Frederick's demeanour what a terrible blow it was to him, one he would never fully recover from.

Not long after his return he began to suffer intermittent bouts of infirmity that debilitated him for days on end, sent him to his bed, where he would lie in the gloom, beyond the help of any remedy from the physicians who attended him. These repeated afflictions took their toll, and by the autumn of the year he showed signs of more serious illness. It occurred to me that I might be guilty of exacerbating the situation with my obvious dissatisfaction, and I went to his bedside one evening after he had suffered a particularly difficult day. He turned to look at me when I entered the room, lifted his head from the pillow.

"I came to see how you're feeling," I said. "A little better, I hope."

"How do you do it?" he asked.

"Beg pardon?"

"Even after all this time, the mere sight of you never fails to cheer me. It has ever been so, even from the first time I saw your likeness painted upon that miniature portrait. Do you remember? I wrote to you about it in my first letter."

"I made sure to send up some supper. Did you eat it? You have to keep up your strength."

"My affliction is one of sunken spirits, I fear." He reached for my hand, and I let him take it. "But now you have raised them a little with this unexpected and welcome visit."

"I wanted to talk to you." I sat down on the bed.

"I'm afraid I have little to offer in the way of conversation, nor much else but that which I seem best able to fashion in generous measure, namely hardship and disappointment."

"You place too great a burden upon yourself. You did what you could. Captain Hume himself reports that you fought bravely and proved a pillar of strength to your men upon the battlefield."

"And look where my gallantry has gotten us."

I took him gently by the shoulders, as I had all those years ago when I first brought his lips to mine for the assembled banquet guests, and bent down to kiss him on the forehead. "I have something I want to say to you. Perhaps I should have said it sooner, but I say it to you now. You have been too eager to shoulder the blame in all of this, and I have been too eager to allow it. It was my ambition brought us here. Better to have left Prague to the Hapsburgs."

"This does not sound like you."

"I see what all this is doing to you. It is hard for me to watch."

"I suppose I have always been a figure more worthy of your pity than your love."

"If I admit to neither, will you allow that I am in earnest?"

"Perhaps I can mount another campaign."

"The cost is too great."

"And what is the cost that I have lost my crown and failed to regain it? That my wife and children live in want and ridicule."

"We shall find a way to get through." I placed a hand on his chest. "Things will get better."

"You misuse me with these unconvincing assurances."

"I am content, I tell you."

"You gave me thirteen children. And what did I give you?"

"I would not have those same children in danger of losing their father, if he will not leave off this self-recrimination."

"Well deserved though it is."

"Listen to me. If I have not loved you as you might have hoped, it is only because it was never in my power to do so. But you must not think I am disappointed in you. You have been a good husband, a good father, and now you must get better that you may continue to be so."

"Your honesty, as ever, shakes me from my complacency. You're right. This despondence accomplishes nothing. I must find a way to free myself of it and see to my family."

It was soon after this Frederick began to recover his strength, day by day, until at length he was able to resume his daily activities. He seemed to regain his enjoyment of life and things might have been alright after all, just as I had assured him, but for that cursed hound of tragedy which ever nipped and bit at my heels even to the very last.

The day came when Frederick was feeling well enough to embark on a trip to the Zuydersee with our eldest son, Henry. They would take in the sights, in particular the spectacle of the many captured Spanish galleons moored upon the Sea of Haarlem. Watching them make their plans, I was glad to see the two of them engaged so amiably in each other's company. I had little interest in spending time fussing over my children, and preferred their company after they had matured into young men and women, but if there was some vague spark of resentment on Henry's part that his mother had not taken a greater interest in him as a youngster, he rose above it and was as loving toward me as I could have expected under the circumstances. And what a fine young man he was turning into! He was intelligent beyond his years, keenly insightful and curious, and like my own brother Henry, had about him an intensity of emotion, as that he might love and hate with equal fervour some aspect of the world or another, and thirst for knowledge of anything he could get his hands on.

Henry had just celebrated his fifteenth birthday and the trip was meant to be something of a present to him. The departure was unremarkable and I expected to see them back in a week or so. I busied myself with the usual pursuits that took up my days, most often concerning those interactions and overtures that might serve to bring much-needed money into the household and allow me to maintain a decent standard of living. I didn't want to burden Frederick now that he was feeling better, but I was far from resigned to a life in exile and continued to explore every possible avenue that might lead to some progress in getting us back to Prague. I spent my days in letter writing, in planning and consultation, my evenings entertaining and making overtures and solicitations to those who might take an interest in our predicament or have some means to help us. Of course they always wanted something in return.

I was busy one morning with correspondence, a chore that required my attention almost daily and which I found tedious but necessary. The letters had by nature to be couched in language loquacious yet utterly bereft of genuine feeling, to contain scarcely anything of real interest save the one overriding request at last given expression to, though even then it should not seem so. The forthcoming replies promised to be of equal verbosity, their contents stuffed to bursting with florid prose but little information, the entire exercise an elaborate web spun of power and need, entreaty and privilege, best navigated with cautious equanimity. Noblemen and lords, landowners and statesmen, scholars and clergy all played their part. The fact of the matter was that we were being kept, and that those who kept us had needs be assuaged. The trick was to hint at the possibility of an alliance, to solicit funds, request a favour, without ever actually saying so. It was really a very sophisticated form of begging. But how else could I hope to see to my children's education, not to mention some semblance of opulence that I might live in the manner to which I was accustomed?

I was absorbed one morning in the duties of this disagreeable correspondence when I looked up from my desk to see Frederick standing in the doorway with a look on his face that sent me into terrible dread. I had no idea how long he'd been there or why he had not bothered to announce himself. He appeared to be fighting some unseen force that kept him from entering the room.

I put down my quill and turned to him. "Frederick, what are you doing standing there?"

He stayed in the doorway, unable to make himself move.

"Come in, come in. Is everything alright? You're as pale as a ghost. Have you taken ill again? Is that what brought you back so soon?"

He took a few tentative steps into the room and stopped. I rose from my chair and went to him. "What is it?" He was clearly in great anguish. "What's the matter? Where's Henry?"

"There's been an accident."

"He's been hurt. Not badly, I trust? Take me to him. Where is he?"

"Gone."

"What do you mean?"

"Lost."

"But how?"

"Drowned."

Frederick steadied himself against the back of a nearby chair, sagged down into it, head down while I stood before him in disbelief, and seeing the pitiable state of ruin my husband was in, went over to place a hand gently on his shoulder. He brought his own hand up to cover mine, and we stayed that way for a long time, as parents will who have lost a child. There was nothing more to say just then. What use to fling a few pitiable and empty words at such tortured grief? It would not be conquered by a mountain of them. No recourse but to suffer. Frederick couldn't tell me what happened, couldn't seem to get another word out, only sat with his head down, shoulders shaking as silent tears fell upon his lap. The scale of that loss could hardly be measured, stretched far beyond mourning.

For my part I fought the temptation to turn inward, to wonder how it was that time and again those within my circle of affection seemed destined to die. Better to leave off conjecture as to what manner of curse, conceived by whom, and for what purpose, made me the common element in all of these tragedies. I told myself I no more deserved to be thought of as such than they deserved to die. And yet I had a nagging sense I might have done something to bring them about. Perhaps it might be better to pursue a life such as that of Sophia, up on the mountain above Heidelberg, live alone and put an end to so much suffering.

Perhaps I was meant to consider myself the beneficiary of all this loss and take some lesson from it. But it was surely the height of selfishness to think that way! Would the Heavenly Father deem it just that one among us should be punished with death merely to teach another? Our son Henry had no more deserved to die than to live. Neither was warranted but the fates made it so. Better, I thought, to become inured to grief, grow derisive and scornful of life if it be naught but a celebration of death.

It was only later that I learned what had transpired to take my eldest son's life. Frederick would not talk about it, though I could see that it was eating him up inside. I sought out Captain Hume soon after and demanded whether he knew of the circumstances, and if so that he relate them to me, reminded him that he had done as much years earlier at my brother Henry's passing, and that he must offer them up in every detail.

"Husband and son made their way to Haarlem," the Captain began. "There they boarded a yacht, the better to be allowed a closer look, and had just made their way out of the harbour when they were struck by another, much larger vessel. Their craft being capsized, the situation soon became one of every man for himself. A number of ships came immediately to the aid of those stranded in the water but the rescue was made more difficult by the weather, as it is so often in January, when the seas are rough. Your husband was fortunate to be pulled from the water by some nearby sailors, but no sooner had he been hauled up into the rescue boat than your son called out to him, and he turned to see him struggling that he might remain afloat amid the waves. Your husband shouted for the men to row toward him as quickly as possible, but even as they did so your son uttered one last plea for help before he slipped beneath the surface of the waves, and did not reappear."

"Did Frederick relate all of this to you?"

"Not a single word or utterance from him of these particulars, but I learned them from those who had witnessed the disaster first-hand."

"I have heard some too, though I know not hearsay from fact. They say he made a last utterance."

"Your husband? I'm afraid I know naught of such."

"You know I meant my son, Captain."

"He was a fine young man, as good a one as any mother could have hoped for, admirable for those same qualities as were so generous in your dear lost brother, of whom he reminded me daily."

"You know something of these last words."

"I grant as much."

"I would hear them."

"He called out as any man would who lived yet in hope of being rescued."

"Say them."

"Madam, I would not."

"Say the words."

"He was heard to call out 'Save me, Father,' and again, 'Save me.'"

What father could have hoped to escape the greedy clutches of guilt brought about by such an utterance, to feel it grip him even in the paralysis of his grief? If the unspoken canon decree that every mother nurture her son with love, the corollary must insist that every father rescue him from danger. Captain Hume revealed to me more than once how oft he had heard a young man upon the battlefield, at the moment of his dying, call out for his mother. And yet to think how my own dear brother Henry called out for me to no avail, condemned at the last to receive no help.

Though he never said so, Frederick thought it better if he had drowned instead of his son, and I might have done more to banish the thought from his troubled mind, but it was impossible to talk about any of it. Whatever words one of us might utter, no matter how carefully chosen, they brought only more pain. My lame attempts at comfort might just as well have condemned, and so by degrees I watched him lose what remained of his spirits, forced to live when death was surely more favourable. An ever louder silence echoed through the halls and rooms of our waking and in our sleeping thundered above us through the night.

Frederick kept mulling over various scenarios, posing hypothetical questions, subjecting himself to repeated anguish. Why hadn't he hired a bigger boat? Why hadn't they waited until the seas were calmer? Why hadn't he tried harder to wrestle himself free of the men who held him back when he tried to jump in and save his drowning son? The list was endless. For my part I threw myself even harder into the work at hand, seeking out such benefactors as would make available the best possible education for my remaining children, exploring every avenue of entreaty that might bring some money into the household. But the gloom of recrimination hung over Frederick like a poisonous stinking fog, and he was never the same again.

By November of that year he had fallen gravely ill. The official diagnosis was pestilential fever, known as the sweating sickness, and of course they had to send for an eminent physician of the time, in this instance a Dutchman man by the name of Peter Spina, who was brought in to administer a bout of remedies. I myself sought out one or two of the medical texts I had once taken such a keen interest in, but which of late held little interest for me and had been relegated to the more obscure corners of my library shelves. As it was a great many of them had been lost over the years, having failed to make the journey to Heidelberg, fewer still to Prague and on to The Hague, so that what remained was hardly a proper collection. Nevertheless, and much to my surprise, I managed to dig up a volume in which the disease Frederick was diagnosed with had been written about by a Dr. Thomas Forestier in 1485, penned in language decorous and utterly bereft of meaningful information:

"*The exterior is calm in this fever, the interior excited . . . the heat in the pestilent fever many times does not appear excessive to the doctor, nor the heat of the sweat itself particularly high . . . But it is on account of the ill-natured, fetid, corrupt, putrid, and loathsome vapors close to the region of the heart and of the lungs whereby the panting of the breath magnifies and increases and restricts of itself . . .*" And so on. Rubbish!

It was clear to me that though my husband did indeed exhibit the symptoms of a fever his affliction stemmed from more than this. His weakness and lethargy were due to nothing so much as being consumed from the inside out. Guilt was the affliction, remorse the disease. It was only a matter of days before the fever would take him and death announce itself uninvited and unwelcome yet again upon my doorstep.

I came to stand at his bedside one evening, pleased to find him animated and eager for my company, a marked improvement from my last visit.

"Elizabeth." He sat up and leaned forward. "I'm so glad you came." Though he had a renewed vigour about him, there was something in his eyes that gave me pause.

"I'm glad to see you feeling so much better," I said. "I looked in on you earlier and you seemed less than eager to see me."

"There's something I need to ask you."

"Of course, what is it?"

"You must answer honestly."

"As ever I have done."

"I have no reason to doubt you. And yet I fear to hear the answer." He looked at me intently, searched my eyes with his. "Have I been a good husband to you?"

"As good as a wife might hope for — nay, better."

"Truly?"

"You have been kind and generous, and made little in the way of demands."

"If only I could have made you happy. I know it was too much to expect, but I very much wanted to."

"It was neither in your power nor mine to grant as much."

"You must have felt cheated."

"It was none of your doing."

"I have brought us misfortune and grief."

"I tell you in all honesty it was my ambition led us here. And as for the other, that was an accident, nothing more."

"This is not how I wanted to leave you."

He fell into a calm silence then, eyes closed, his breathing even and relaxed, as though he were falling into peaceful slumber.

"Sleep now," I said, "and recover your strength."

I sat a while longer, thinking him to be gaining valuable and restorative rest, until I noticed his breathing become shallower, then more so by degrees, as though he were indeed taking his leave at a slow and easy pace, until at length he slipped into utter stillness. I had by then seen all manner of dying, but that furtive departure left me breathless and weeping, my tears borne of mystery and sorrow.

I mourned him as best I could. If I seemed disaffected it was only that I desired to be truthful. I did not fall into frailty and misgiving as I had seen other wives do, wringing their hands and wondering whatever should become of them. I had to a large extent been steering the course of my life for some time by then, and the loss of my husband tended less to collapse than to disruption and inconvenience. How else to describe what is required of a wife after the burial of her husband? I did not begrudge my duties, but as with any funeral it was of greatest benefit to those farthest removed from its darker implications.

I had learned to carry with me through my life a quick dismissal of the dead. Some might have argued I was guilty of as much in my dealings with the living, but in any case I mourned briefly, intensely, and then I moved on. It seemed to me that to do otherwise was to hold death in too high a standing. There were those who brought to their mourning an ostentatious manner I found unbecoming. Better sorrow should hardly warrant notice.

We have each of us the experience of some particular mourning unlike any other. It may be the very first of such or perhaps only the most recent, and little to do with the manner of departure or the intensity of loss. Some aspect of enlightenment attends our grief, allows us a glimpse into the best and the worst of living and dying. With its passing we feel ourselves changed, departed from a place we can never come back to. So it was with me after my brother Henry died. I knew I should never grieve that way again, let death do its worst. Where once a great river had traced its source to the wellspring of my grief, in future but a meagre trickle should be allowed to flow.

I had the sense, too, that I was grieving for myself, caught up in an indulgent and unseemly sorrow. Life is a matter of degree, and some of us are more alive than others. But dead is dead. Though the manner of our departure may be noble and steeped in courage, the state we arrive at amounts to a banal singularity. If death serves any purpose at all surely it must be to reveal to those who remain some small aspect of their life.

My husband's death at age thirty-six ushered a watershed moment into mine, and into the life of my family, for it threw everything into a new and unforgiving light. My son Charles Louis immediately took it upon himself that he should now see his way to the throne his father once occupied, but made it clear that he thought little of my methods in hastening such an eventuality. He had seen enough of my ineffectual ways, he told me, and if he wanted to make progress he would have to do it himself. Hardly a week had passed since the funeral when he sailed for England, intent on positioning himself as the spearhead for reformation on the continent, hopeful that certain Protestant parties would declare themselves to his cause. He intended to ingratiate himself to my brother the King, that he might be allowed to present himself at court to further those ends. If his uncle agreed it would be for his own reasons, as he had married Henrietta Maria of France, a Catholic, and such a gesture might mitigate those that accused him of straying too far from the Protestant path.

For the same reason, I felt sure, my brother let it be known soon after Frederick's passing that I might be allowed to return to England and live under his roof if I so desired, but the offer came with only vague intimations of how the children and I should be provided for, and I had by then grown weary of his repeated equivocations. No doubt he himself was short of money, locked as he was in a power struggle with Parliament, having refused to convene that body and thereby unable to raise revenues through the usual channels.

"I see no reason to go back there and live in virtual servitude," I told Captain Hume, who enquired of me why I was so set against returning to London. "You can be sure I should be reduced soon enough to begging for any crumbs my brother might see fit to throw my way, and I can just as easily do that here. But how for yourself? What arrangements have you made?"

"I am accepted into Charterhouse," said the Captain, who had just informed me that he himself was returning to London. "Do you know it?"

"Did not my father stay there upon his first arrival in London after he came down from Scotland?"

"Indeed. It was there he prepared for his coronation, just as your godmother did before him."

"I seem to recall it was Elizabeth's father . . ."

"That would have been Henry VIII," the Captain put in.

". . . who drove the Carthusian monks from the place."

"And had a good number of them executed most brutally," added Captain Hume, "for refusing to acknowledge him as the head of the church."

"Why must all these monarchs have so much blood on their hands? Even to my own father and now my brother Charles. I wonder if my Henry had lived and was now seated upon the throne, whether he would have chosen to follow such a family tradition of wanton carnage."

"Alas, we can only speculate, but I have no doubt he should have been a just and gentle ruler."

"And what think you if it were me that now reigned as Queen?"

"I think the country should not now be teetering on the edge of civil war."

"My brother Charles has no idea a storm is coming. All the better I remain here in The Hague when it arrives."

"At any rate those very cells at Charterhouse in which the monks did once reside now house men such as myself."

"And what manner of men are these?"

"Soldiers, musicians, scholars. Those who have been of notable service to their country and now find themselves of limited means."

"You would be one of these?"

"I shall be provided for in perpetuity."

"Surely you don't mean to live the life of a monk?"

"I shall become a Brother, but I am not required to take any vows, only to forfeit my worldly goods."

"You cannot mean to surrender your viola da gamba."

"I am allowed to keep a few personal items in my possessions, that instrument among them."

"And a sword or two, I will venture."

"I think it shall be permitted."

"Do you think you will be happy there?"

"Happy?" The Captain raised a disparaging eyebrow.

"Alright, you have caught me out. I grant it is not a fitting idea for either of us to indulge in. Very well, perhaps something a little less romantic: Do you think you shall be content there?"

"I shall have my daily needs seen to."

"I can do as much for you here, and it would be a great comfort to me if you stayed."

"I don't want to be a burden."

I placed a hand on his shoulder and set my eyes to his, shook my head a little from side to side. "You have never been such nor ever will, but rather a true and loyal companion."

"I will say the very same for you, Madam."

His eyes moistened before he pulled himself together, cleared his throat, and replied gruffly, "Nevertheless it is time for me to retire, and I long for the familiar comforts of England."

"Will you write?"

"As much as I am able."

I found myself thereafter feeling more alone than ever. My husband had left me with a household full of servants and children and very little money. I was granted a small pension, bequeathed to me upon Frederick's death, but it didn't last long, and soon enough I was forced to employ once again those same unseemly measures I had been practising all along, though now that Frederick was gone certain parties seemed less sympathetic to my predicament, and so I had to redouble my efforts to stave off financial ruin. In this way I managed from one day to the next, though not without considerable personal sacrifice. Having pawned the lion's share of my valuables, I had now to begin selling off some of the furniture to make ends meet.

In all of this I nevertheless refused to part with my great bed and swore I would starve to death before I resorted to such a desperate measure. It was the one place of true sanctuary left to me, and I took pains to see that no one, including the children, should disturb me there. Amalia, much as Lady Anne had done before her, stood as a vanguard against all that lay beyond the comforts of those sheets, though her loyalty remained a mystery to me.

One month bled into another, one year into the next. I saw to my children's education, sent Maurice, Edward, and Philip to be schooled in Paris, which I managed by a combination of uncompromising diplomacy and delicate coercion. My brother had married Henrietta Maria of France, who would later suffer the same fate as myself in that she would also lose her husband (though in Charles's case it would be the axe that saw him dispatched) and thereafter find herself impoverished. At present she was marooned in London just as I was in The Hague, and though we had never met we were soon corresponding regularly and by this means it came about that she saw fit to make arrangements for my three boys to come to Paris.

As for my daughters Louisa, Henrietta, and Sophia, I took pains to bring them into society so that suitable husbands might be found for them, but it was Elisabeth who presented the greatest challenge for me. She wasn't like my other daughters, did not conform to the interests and ambitions they shared so amiably, and conducted herself in a manner intriguing on one occasion and troubling the next. She displayed a singular disdain for courtly manipulations and feminine devices, and carried herself with a deep seriousness that was difficult to penetrate. She showed little interest in competing with her sisters for the attention of the young men at court, let alone with her mother. There were still times when it was I, rather than one of my daughters, who became the object of a handsome young suitor's interest, and this sometimes caused friction between us, especially when Elisabeth would accuse me openly of fostering the situation, something I did not appreciate.

My son Rupert had some time ago gone to England at request of his brother Charles Louis, and even as I considered to what degree the two of them were falling under the influence of my brother the King, I was in receipt of a letter from none other than Lord Craven.

March 12, 1637
Drury Lane, London

Madam,

Please accept my deepest condolences on the passing of your dear husband, Frederick. I should very much have liked to be there in person to offer you what small comfort I could, but circumstance would not permit it. There is considerable turmoil of late here in England, and I fear it shall lead to no small conflict between the two factions opposed to each other. It has been some considerable time since I came to The Hague and first enjoyed the pleasure of your beauteous company. As you know we emerged victorious in that campaign against the forces of the Hapsburgs but I sustained a wound which took me back to England, whereupon I learned the Swedish emperor, notwithstanding Frederick's contribution, declined to restore him the Palatinate as would have been right and proper. He deserved better, and so did you.

I wanted to write and let you know I am now in a position to once again be of use to you, and to that end seek your approval that I might make my resources available to your son, Charles Louis, in that same spirit they were first offered to your late husband. I pray you will not refuse me, for I have within my power the means to effect that same restoration you have so long sought after, only now it would see your son Charles Louis ascend to the throne of the Palatinate. I have amassed a considerable army which upon your word I shall convey across the channel and march into Bohemia. It would give me the greatest satisfaction to help you achieve that which you toil yet to bring about. Will you let me do this for you?

I still have the glove you gave me and I carry it with me always. I thought you should doubtless have remarried by now, as there must be many young men who aspire to your excellent company and seek to gain your favour. I tell you not one among them shall prove to be as loyal and true as I, if only you see fit to let me prove myself to you. I look forward to the day when I find myself once again in your fair company and remain, as I have and ever will be . . .

Yours in filial obedience and fond affection,
Lord William of Craven

Here was a chance to free myself from the scheming and subterfuge I was constantly forced to engage in for the sake of income. Lord Craven's considerable wealth would provide for my own needs. If he was eager to serve me I would take him at his word. We both stood to gain from such an arrangement, and it would all be quite respectable.

What good would it do to accept the advances of those young men that possessed gallantry and devotion in abundance, and had not the chinks? It was money I needed more than anything. My daughters required each of them an ever more extensive and costly wardrobe, that they might dress the part befitting their station, not to mention the expense of elaborate balls and banquets that would have to be arranged in order for them to mingle with the right people. As for my sons, they were bound to undertake further ventures that required financing, not the least of which was Charles Louis's campaign to make his way to the throne my husband had once occupied. It was the least I could do for my children.

I replied as follows:

April 1, 1637
Binnenhof, The Hague

To the Valiant and Noble Lord Craven,

Sir, you are most gracious to offer your services to my son's cause, and while I should be most grateful for any assistance you might offer, your declaration of loyalty to my person leaves me at a disadvantage. I hardly know how to respond to your entreaty except to say that I would not have you go into battle for my sake. I am flattered at your expression of regard for me, but as for my assent, it is mine neither to give nor withhold. As much as I welcome the prospect of seeing the Palatinate restored to its rightful heir, the matter must rest in the hands of my son Charles Louis, who is old enough to make the decision for himself, though I have no doubt he would go ahead with the plan with or without my approval.

Should the course of events lead you here to The Hague, I should be eager for the chance to welcome you into my company, that we might make better acquaintance of each other. Your expressions of loyalty and favour give me reason to believe I might find in you a champion such as I am at present in need of. In hope we may find ourselves face to face soon and . . .

With regard for your kindness and affection,
Elizabeth

Henceforth I began receive regular correspondence from him as to the progress of the campaign, in the course of which he never failed to pledge his high regard for me, not to mention his dedication to the safety and well-being of my sons Rupert and Charles. The three of them crossed the channel with a convoy of ships and arrived in Holland in the summer of the year. From there they marched up the Lower Rhine and by the time they reached Wesel had seen other men enlist in the cause until they had amassed an army of four thousand men. They emerged victorious in one battle after another while Lord Craven eagerly reported to me how bravely Rupert fought alongside him, on one such occasion ready to sacrifice his life if Lord Craven had not ordered his men to hold my son back from advancing. It seemed certain the campaign should soon be won, but when they reached

Limgea, Lord Craven suffered a terrible wound and their forces were overrun. He and Rupert were taken prisoner but Charles Louis somehow managed to escape.

Thereafter Lord Craven continued to write to me from prison, where he insisted on remaining even though he could have bought his freedom any time he wished by the simple payment of a generous ransom. He was adamant that Rupert should not be left to fend for himself, and to that end elected to stay and see to my son's safekeeping. I thought it was an exceptional sacrifice for someone in his position to undertake. If he was acting in the fashion of a courageous and noble gentleman there wasn't anything for me to do but admire him for it, but I also wondered to what extent he was doing it to try and impress me. I pleaded in my correspondence that he not resign himself to a life behind bars for my son's sake alone, and certainly not for mine, and further that I would not hold it against him if he bought his freedom and found his way to The Hague. What I did not articulate was the fact that he was no good to me there. Better he should find his way into my presence if he was going to be of any use to me as a benefactor. Lord Craven maintained that he would not be able to face me knowing he had left my son behind. Rupert having fought so bravely and being yet so very young, it was the only honourable thing to do under the circumstances, and I should not think he had any motive but that of duty to his fellow man. And so we were at an impasse.

I thought it could not be long before the situation was resolved, but days became weeks and then months, during which time I grew less and less indulgent of Charles Louis who, having made good his escape, had in the interim managed to make his way back to The Hague, where he seemed quite content to remain while the other two languished in captivity. The longer the situation carried on the deeper my resentment grew at being forced to witness his seeming complacency, until a wedge had been driven between us that would prove impossible to dislodge.

When at last the day came for the prisoners to be released I invited Lord Craven to come to The Hague that I might thank him in person for everything he had done. I was certain he would accept my invitation, and if he should go so far as to openly pledge his love for me, I had determined to insist that ours be a courtly love, at least for the time being. I still entertained the notion that I might one day return to Prague, if not as queen consort then as queen mother, and for that reason such passions as we might wish to act upon must necessarily be couched in gestures designed to maintain the proper protocol and decorum. Soon enough we would find ourselves adrift on a sea of unspoken intention, our motives as like to be noble as base, vulgar as poetic, and there we would linger day after day and year after year, and I confess I find myself even now swimming in the waters of that duplicity.

Chapter Fifteen

When at last the day came for my son Rupert to be released from prison he had already determined to return to England rather than The Hague, but I insisted he and Lord Craven stop in at Binnenhof, where a reunion of sorts might be allowed to take place. Upon their arrival my son presented himself to me with such a noble and confident air I hardly thought it was the same man! He had gone into battle as little more than a boy and now he towered above me, a good six inches taller than Lord Craven, so that I had to look up into his handsome face. For Lord Craven's part his features had taken on a slight ruggedness, and he had grown perhaps a little thinner, but his noble and dignified manner remained undiminished. The two of them seemed to have become good friends, and though Charles Louis professed to be happy at his brother's safe return, a subtle awkwardness nevertheless crept into their exchanges.

Rupert had no trouble convincing Lord Craven that they should stay a few days before travelling on to London, and so I arranged for a modest banquet to be held in their honour. Lord Craven soon became acquainted with some of those at court, humble as it was, and seemed at ease in such surroundings. He welcomed every opportunity to be in my presence, talked passionately to me about any subject I cared to listen to, and generally left no doubt whatsoever of his unabashed affection for me. In no time at all the rumours were rife, and among those who took the strongest exception to the situation was my son Charles Louis. To that end I redoubled my efforts to keep Lord Craven at a safe yet accessible distance, lest anyone think I had intentions to marry. I did not want to fall out of favour with the heir to the throne if it should hurt my chances of returning to Prague when the day finally came that saw the Palatinate restored.

I was sometimes quite cold to Lord Craven, even dismissive, particularly in my son's presence, and though this was deeply hurtful to William, as I now deigned to call him in private, he continued to take an active part in the daily life of the court, content to worship me from afar, as it were, and I was content to allow as much, for it was nothing unusual that there should be a number of men at court inclined to such behaviour on any given occasion. I took care to note which of the ladies at court might be eager for his attentions as well, and was not a little unsettled to find that one of them appeared to be my own daughter Elisabeth. For his part Lord Craven never wavered from his attentions to me, and in the privacy of our exchanges pleaded that he be allowed to help me with my financial situation, to which I agreed with feigned reluctance. This he did even as the situation continued to deteriorate in England and in spite of the fact that he was in danger of losing his lands.

"I want to thank you, William, for everything you're doing," I told him one evening. We were in my study, where we were allowed to enjoy each other's company in private under the guise of a mutual interest in such dispassionate pursuits as literature and astronomy. "I know it cannot be easy for you."

"It is the easiest thing I have ever done, Madam." We were seated across from each other before a small fire in the hearth. My chair had a table set by piled with books and artefacts, where I liked to retire of an evening to study and be about my own private pastimes. I treasured quiet and solitude to a degree others found confounding and at times even insulting, but it was in my nature to be so and I saw no reason to run counter to it.

"You stay when you might just as well go back and see to your holdings," I said, my hands folded over my lap, "and all the while insist on furnishing me with these generous gifts, but it shall not be forever. Soon enough my wealth shall be restored when I assume the life of Queen Mother to the reinstated Elector in Prague. Then you shall be free of this burden."

"It is one I would bear eagerly for as long as I might be allowed, the better to see first-hand to your comfort and happiness."

The air of guarded reservation that tended to pervade our conversations seemed to suit both of us, but on this occasion I was determined to cast aside formality and get to the heart of the matter.

I rose to stand before the fire. "You speak of happiness even as I withhold from you that which you most desire."

"Madam." He got up from his chair and stood to face me. "You have made it clear that decorum must be preserved."

"And what if each of us was free to do entirely as he wished?"

"Then I should seek this instant to take you in my arms and kiss you."

"Very well, I give you leave to do so."

"Madam?"

"If it will give you satisfaction."

"It can do no less and a great deal more."

"Proceed, if you will."

He stepped forward, grasped me by the shoulders and kissed me stiffly upon the lips. It was neither as long nor as warm as I might have expected.

He stepped back a little. "Madam, you have made me the happiest man on Earth." He made this last statement with an unexpected air of finality.

"You would you have nothing more of me?"

"More?"

"Surely a kiss is but a prelude to favours of the flesh that come after."

"I seek no such favour."

"But how can you say so? Did this kiss not stir something in you? Another man might seek to undo these stays" — I pulled gently at one of the laces on my bodice — "and help himself to more."

"You mock me."

"I do not mean to. Will you put your hands on me?"

"Madam, I will not."

"But why?"

"Pray, what would you have of me?"

"To see you satisfied. Or shall I use other means?" I brought my hand down to his breeches.

He swept it away and stepped back. "Madam, this is unseemly."

"But surely you want me for a lover?"

"It were better to refrain."

"Then why not seek out a younger woman who can give you children and not one that has already borne thirteen?"

"You think me peculiar."

"I find it peculiar that those few times in my life when I have practically thrown myself at a man I have been rebuffed."

"I have made my peace that ours must be a courtly love."

"Do you think we shall be the better for it?"

"For my part I am ever improved in your company."

"Then I am happy to provide it."

Lord Craven seemed relieved at this exchange. He raised my hand to his lips, as he would on a more formal occasion, and took his leave. We had come to an agreement that should hardly have satisfied another couple. But such is the nature of circumstance when two people find a way to serve each other that only they understand.

—

And so the years went by and those considerations I have already named multiplied as the children saw their education take them to various colleges, universities, and lecture palaces so that there was always something that needed to be paid for. I took pains to see my girls turned into elegant young ladies, armed them with all the weapons they would need to survive the subterfuge and duplicity of courtly life, and made sure they were ready before I allowed them to enter that treacherous arena. I introduced them to admirers both suitable and unworthy, that under my supervision they might by degrees learn to judge between the two, and so marry with the promise of means and surety. If they thought me overbearing and calculating, I maintained the unspoken conviction that they would thank me later. Naive!

When I commissioned painters to fashion their portraits, I chose those artists who promised neither to flatter nor offend. If my daughters had not the features of classic beauty, I did not want them made to look that way. They had each of them a certain poise, a vivacity not easily rendered on canvas. I suppose it is only natural they should have wished to be envisaged in the best possible light, but in such matters care must be taken lest the meaning be lost. Suppose it should come to pass in some distant future that we should be granted the capability to render endless likenesses of ourselves, and then be allowed choose from among them only the most flattering public for display? Better to leave off such embellishments in matters of appearance, for true beauty will ever seek its own way out. I suppose it is easy enough for me to utter such sentiments, because my daughters are not unattractive. Their portraits hang even now in halls and rooms where mine are doubtless no longer to be found.

Did my daughters marry for love? Lady Anne would have insisted it is a romantic notion best left to the fancy of playwrights and poets. Perhaps, but in any case I had no such ambitions for them. Do I believe such a thing really exists? I do, but as is the case with everything else in this world, it suffers at the hands of impermanence. Nothing lasts. My daughter Henrietta married in May and died unexpectedly in September. Her husband died a few months later. So much for love.

Rather than dote on my daughters I sought to discover in them any special aptitude or talent they might possess and thereafter urge them as much as possible to pursue it. I saw to it that all my children were educated and trained in the fine arts, and from a young age took note of their talent. My daughter Louise, for an instance, turned out to be to a very fine painter and artist. I managed to obtain the services of none other than Gerard van Honthorst, fresh from the house of Medici in Italy, as her teacher. I was not surprised when he later saw fit to attribute her finer works to himself, after trying to bed her as well as myself, not to mention any other woman in court who might have him. In this regard he was just like any other artist. My daughter was soon sought after for her paintings and became known as Louise Hollandine of the Palatinate. She never married but took herself instead to Paris, where she entered a convent.

As for the boys, they were as handsome in their own way as the girls were in theirs. Besides Rupert and Charles there was also Edward, who married a French princess who turned out to be Italian, and Philip Frederick, who was the only one of my sons to fight a duel over me, though it wasn't the first time a young man had deigned to do so. In this case I'd seen fit to accept an exiled young French Lieutenant Colonel at court for a time, who had a habit of drinking to excess. One night he made a loud boast to everyone at the dinner table that he had bedded my daughter Louise. That was bad enough, but thereafter he insisted he had accomplished as much with me as well. He should have been roundly dismissed as a drunken fool by those about the table and the matter should have ended there, but my hot-tempered son took exception to his remarks and would not be assuaged. He challenged the drunken Colonel to a duel, which Lord Craven managed to quell at least for a time. But the two young men met up again a few nights later and agreed to fight a duel outside the grounds of the palace. Philip suffered a slight wound in the ensuing contest, but thereafter fatally stabbed the young Frenchman with his sword. He was called to answer for it by the authorities and had to leave the country, after which he hired himself out as a mercenary, not unlike Captain Hume, whom he had always idolized. The whole thing was a terrible mess, and for what? As it turned out the Frenchman's scandalous assertions were only half-right.

And then there was my daughter Elisabeth, who was altogether different from her siblings in the way she talked to me. Rather than outright defiance or provocation, her utterances offered a disconcerting mixture of subtle dismissal and flagrant truthfulness. Our attempts at meaningful conversation inevitably lapsed into mutual aggravation, if not outright paroxysms of temper. Just like my other daughters, she had spent her formative years elsewhere, in education and refinement, so that I did not see a great deal of her until the time came for her to return to The Hague and be introduced to the court. It was she, more than any other, whose future I wanted a hand in shaping, notwithstanding that she was loath to be persuaded of anything merely for the sake of contenting her mother. Her will was as strong as mine, not to mention that she could outthink me, outlast me, and by the age of fifteen was already better educated than I could ever hope to be. She thought her sisters vain and shallow and hardly worthy of her time, though she humoured them to a greater degree than she did me, for whom she invariably saved her harshest reproach.

She had been going to school in Leyden, where I had

attended a number of times to see to matters of placement. It had served as the former residence of those ardent Calvinists who had set sail for the New World and who continued yet to do so. When I discovered that they sometimes allowed those of lesser religious conviction to take passage on those same ships, I was tempted to cast aside everything and sail away from all my troubles, start over again in the place I had always longed to travel to, but of course I never acted upon these impulses and no one knew they existed in me.

Perhaps I might have cobbled together an entirely different life for myself there. It was ever little more than a fantasy, but I left instructions with Lord Craven that any monies forthcoming from my estate, such as it was, should go toward the financing of an expedition to the New World. My son Rupert had been contemplating such an undertaking for some time, the better to explore the possibility of establishing trade with the natives at Hudson Bay. I sent him word about a ship that had come to my attention which might suffice for the voyage. It was called the *Nonsuch* and I thought it would do nicely.

For a time I entertained the notion that Elisabeth might be the one to do what I never had, and sail for the New World. I should certainly have encouraged her to do it, but she was too interested in education to take herself to such a primitive place. It seemed wherever I sent her it was never long before she became unruly and disobedient. I even resorted for a time to having her stay with her grandmother Juliana at her country home not far from Heidelberg, where she was sure to receive proper discipline, but the more I thought about her there the more it rankled me, and so I sent for her to return to me in The Hague. One evening I had her brought to me in my presence chamber, which was where I generally took an audience with those of my children I wanted to advise or inspect on one matter or another. They were not allowed inside of my privy chamber, let alone my bedchamber. These I reserved for myself alone and those servants who had by necessity to carry out tasks for me, though I was very self-sufficient and didn't like to be handled.

Elisabeth came in and stood before me dressed in a modest gown, her hair in ringlets and a simple string of pearls about her neck. While perhaps not as accomplished in appearance as her sisters, she was by far the most intelligent and her demeanour had about it an air of proud forbearance. She could seldom be bothered to go to the trouble her sisters did to make themselves look remarkable, and this occasion was no exception.

"Good evening, Madam." She sat down across from me, neither too far into her chair nor out of it, and straightened down the front of her dress.

"Good even, Elisabeth. I'm glad to have you back home at last."

"Home." She looked down at her hands, then back up at me. "I had hardly thought of it that way."

"It has ever been something other than home to me as well." I felt myself off balance already.

"Well, then." My daughter's composure seemed unassailable, her words expressionless. "In that arena we are of one mind."

"How was your stay in Silesia with your grandmother? Did she treat you well? She tells me you have a particular aptitude for languages."

"I am in constant study, and so by necessity must learn those tongues in which the important books have been written."

"And do you have a favourite?"

"Book?"

"I meant language."

"I have a great fondness for Latin."

"Your grandfather, King James, forbad me to learn it. He said it made a woman more cunning."

"I wonder what he meant by that."

"You can be sure it leaned toward intolerance."

"I never knew him."

"Nor I."

"And yet he was a king."

She offered a wry smile and I wanted to fill the silence with something so I carried on: "They tell me you had a nickname at school. They called you 'La Grecque.' Was it a term of endearment or did they mean to taunt you?"

"I suppose it must have been a little of both. They were adolescent young women after all, fatuous and easily harried by their peers."

"Nevertheless you were known for your studies."

"If I must be known for something, then all the better I earn my reputation."

"Tell me, what do you study these days?"

"History, geography, and mathematics for the pragmatic disciplines, then there are painting and dance, though I should be happy to spend that time on the study of philosophy. And of late I have been pursuing a detailed examination of poetry with Lady Vere. It was she who schooled me in the social graces that I might at last be fit to come into your regal presence."

I determined to disregard the provocation obvious in that last remark. "I am happy to have you back here at last."

"Are you?" She looked at me with a steady and unwavering gaze.

"I have been eager to sit in conversation with you, but not about such small details as we are bound to annoy each other with, for this will always be the way of a mother and daughter — that each should seek to slay the other with a thousand pinpricks."

"I should prefer a nice juicy stab wound myself."

"Then here is your chance." My blood was up. "I give you leave to unsheathe your dagger and have at me."

"You will parry, no doubt."

"I stand at ease. Wound me how you will."

Elisabeth held her body rigid, back very straight, shoulders forward and legs tensed, as though she might spring up at any second from her chair. She fixed her eyes intently on mine, stared beyond them as though into my very core. I watched her expression change several times, one thought grappling with the next, fighting for control of her tongue.

"You are my mother, and there are certain things you shall not hear me utter. I will say this much. I hope you have not brought me back here on the pretext that I will entertain the niggling intrigues of those courtiers without."

"I am no less fond of it than you," I countered, "but I am forced to engage if I want to keep a roof over our heads and food on the table."

"As for me, what need have I to feign interest in such matters when I know for a fact you are under negotiations even now with the House of Poland, where a certain prince has expressed interest in my hand."

"Where have you heard this?"

"I even know his name, Wladislaw. He's a Catholic. You would see me follow the same path as you did, and your mother before you."

"I have no such intention. It is only that these are delicate negotiations and I must take care not to offend anyone."

"How perfectly awful it must be to spend your days in such a manner." Elisabeth fixed me with a cold stare.

"There is much I do not by choice but by necessity."

"You should give it up. It doesn't suit you."

"I do what I have to and I don't apologize for it."

"Many a mother has hidden behind that justification for the small and petty treatment of her offspring."

"If it qualifies as an excuse it also serves as the truth. And let me present another. If you consider it your bad luck to be born into this family of misfortune, think how many would yet trade places with you."

"Best I keep my mouth shut, then."

Even as I held myself back from lashing out at her I thought of myself at that age, mature beyond my years and yet so childish.

"I am tired," she said at last, "and would take to my bed, if you will allow it, Madam."

Was it relief I felt as she rose from her chair, or disappointment?

"Good night," she said, and took herself out of the room.

"Good night," I called after her, but she had already gone.

So it was that the days flowed into one another and the two of us floundered about, looking for a way to co-exist within the same confines of that sorry estate, money dwindling slowly down to a trickle, Lord Craven able to procure what he could out of an increasingly unstable situation in England. He could not be sure of his lands, and even his funds were here and there being confiscated. But he always managed to come through, and in the midst of it all I set aside every penny I could to further Elisabeth's education. I had determined that in spite of all our differences, in spite of the fact that she thought so little of me, it was more important than ever to provide her with every opportunity to succeed on her own terms.

It was for this purpose that I managed to obtain the services of the renowned French scholar René Descartes, who had been making a name for himself in the field of philosophy. I myself had always considered the study of that discipline impractical and should have preferred Elisabeth to take up medicine, where I was sure she could make great strides, but such an endeavour would be considered beneath her station and so out of the question even for the child of a monarch in exile. As it turned out, the arrival of Monsieur Descartes would cause a rift between us greater than any that already existed.

When he first arrived at The Hague two things were clear from the outset: that my daughter was at once romantically taken with him, and further that he was quite taken with me. For my part, as I have already told you, I had grown used to such attentions and passed it off as yet another in a long series of infatuations which were as like to burst into flame as to extinguish themselves. At any rate Elisabeth began her lessons and it was not long before Monsieur Descartes had become familiar to the court, though it was also plain he moved about in those circles with the same kind of reticence both I and my daughter were all too familiar with. Nevertheless decorum need be served and various protocols adhered to, so that court life took up more of our time than any of us cared to surrender.

"What think you on this Monsieur Descartes?" Elisabeth asked me one evening.

"He seems an able teacher."

"And what of the man?"

"How do you mean?"

"I think you know."

I knew at once what was coming and prepared myself as best I could.

"I have seen the way he looks at you," Elisabeth went on.

"I hadn't noticed."

"You can hardly fail to do otherwise. Why, whenever the two of you are in the same room he will hardly deign to turn his gaze upon anyone else for casting it in your direction."

"You exaggerate. He merely looks to see that I approve of him as a suitable companion for your scholarship. After all, it is I who holds the purse that pays him."

"And what of his appearance?"

"What of it?"

"Tell me, do you find him handsome?"

"It hardly matters that I do or no, but if you must know, I hadn't really given it much thought."

"You have not answered."

"I find his features rather more clumsy than refined, and his visage to contain more of toil than romance."

"There's little in it of elegance I grant, but I for one should not seek to find that quality in a man such as he."

"Perhaps we have different tastes."

"And yet I have seen him acquire very quickly a taste for your company."

"He seems equally fond of yours."

"He is my teacher. He has no choice."

"And you would like him to be something more." As soon as I had let slip this last I regretted it. When Elisabeth didn't answer I quickly added, "One thing is certain. It isn't every woman who can conduct a conversation with him at the level you are able to sustain."

"I hardly know of another woman at court who cares to. Men are not attracted to such, and I suppose in this regard Monsieur Descartes is no different than any other. They go first to appearance, even when they are philosophers."

"You would think he knew better."

"I confess I have pondered to what extent you trigger these bouts of enchantment in him."

"Excuse me?"

"Why should it be that he is so sorely smitten with you?"

"You know it is not my nature to strut and flutter. I have always disdained to do so."

"Perhaps by that very fact he takes notice of you. Perhaps you are unaware of your own schemings."

"What are you saying?"

"That you do it even as you deny it."

"Have I made suggestive remarks?" I felt the rush of blood in my chest. "Do I flirt? Why should I be derided for making conversation?"

"Heaven forbid any man should find your utterances less than stellar."

"I have always been at my best in close conversation." I forced myself to remain calm. "I am not much for idle chatter. Is there something wrong with that? Would you prefer I hobble myself for the sake of avoiding reproach from a jealous wife?"

"Or daughter."

The exchange ended there, but the undercurrent of discomfort between us persisted. It had a way of cropping up even in the most unlikely of conversations, as happened one evening when I had allowed that Elisabeth might throw a small dinner party in honour of her brothers Maurice and Edward, as well as her sister Louise, all of whom were at present returned from various endeavours for a brief stay in The Hague. I was surprised to see Monsieur Descartes also in attendance and took Elisabeth aside to enquire about it.

"I saw no reason not to invite him," she said casually. "He wanted very much to come. I'm sure you don't mind."

"I had hoped it would be just the family."

"That notion seems somewhat misplaced, don't you think?" She looked at me coolly.

Her veiled reproach left me somewhat unsteady, and though I allowed that Monsieur Descartes should join us, I took pains to spread my focus evenly around the table, making sundry enquiries after the pursuits of my children, and each time he turned his attentions to me, as he inevitably did, I made a point of directing the conversation elsewhere, most often to Elisabeth, but it seemed the harder I tried the more awkward the situation became.

"Elisabeth, tell us about your studies with Monsieur Descartes," said Louise at one point, which brought a sigh of relief from me, at first anyway, as I was glad to be left out of the conversation.

"Monsieur Descartes and I have been discussing the relationship between the body and the soul," she answered. "We are of two minds on the subject."

"They seem both of them self-evident to me," said Louise. "Wherein lies the argument?"

"I don't see why we have to spoil a perfectly good dinner by discussing such a serious subject," said Maurice.

"My brother has no appetite for philosophy," Edward said, thinking himself quite clever.

"Monsieur Descartes would put forth they are two separate and distinct entities," Elisabeth continued, "where I take the part that they are not so easily separated."

"I had always thought that one resides within the other," said Edward.

"Just so." Maurice nodded in agreement. "Now can we talk about hunting? I understand the game is quite plentiful in these parts this year."

Elisabeth turned to me. "What think you on this, Madam?"

"I say we have not yet heard from Monsieur Descartes himself. Sir, we would hear your interpretation of the matter."

"Your daughter has couched the dilemma quite accurately, Madam. Monsieur Descartes became intensely serious. We can all agree that we possess both of these, yet to say one can be found within the other leaves us open to a troubling challenge."

"How so?"

"Where, dear Madam, within the body should we say the soul resides? Is there any place we can point to?"

"Some will say the heart," said Louise.

"Ah, the heart." Elisabeth looked at me. "Now we are on shaky ground, for who among us can account for that organ's vagaries?"

"And yet it can be torn from the body if need be," declared Monsieur Descartes. "Not so the soul."

"How then when death arrives and it departs the body of its own free will?" asked Edward. "Do you mean to imply that the heart has no will of its own?"

"Who can say what it wants or why? Only that it does."

"And how for yours, Monsieur Descartes?" Elisabeth enquired.

"Madam?"

"Can you speak for it?"

"To what end?"

"What does your heart desire?" A slight awkwardness fell over the proceedings.

"I'm afraid the question is hardly relevant to the topic we are discussing," Monsieur Descartes replied stiffly.

"And yet I think it is," Elisabeth persisted.

"You see," said Maurice, "this is the problem with philosophy: that it seeks to ride above the waves which toss us daily into turmoil and disarray. I have no use for it."

"I think I can vouchsafe as much for myself," I added.

"Madam," Monsieur Descartes looked at me pleadingly, "I hope you do not mean to tar the practitioner with the same brush as the practice. In that case I shall renounce all claim to philosophy and take up hunting." He looked at Maurice. "I am an excellent shot."

"Or why not try mathematics. I for one can see how things are beginning to add up," said Elisabeth.

"And how is that?"

"Two make a nice even number, but three is odd."

I was desperate to steer the conversation elsewhere. "I think it is very odd indeed that we have strayed so far from our original discourse."

"The discourse of the heart and soul and body: these are all one and the same to me," said Maurice. "Their hunger is continual, so that none of them can ever be entirely satisfied. They all of them seek nourishment. The body for food and drink . . ."

"And for embrace, I would add," Monsieur Descartes looked in my direction.

"The heart for love . . ." Maurice went on.

"It also possesses a keen appetite for conquest." My daughter fixed a cold stare at me.

"And the soul," Louise enquired after no one in particular, "what manner of sustenance does it crave?"

"I venture more than anything it craves harmony," I offered, "that the other two not be at odds with one another."

"And to that end," offered Maurice, "I would see to it my body gets its proper rest, so if you will excuse me I have yet some study to pursue, and take myself to bed with a book."

"Whom do you read at present?" asked Louise.

"Tonight it shall be Mr. Donne. And so I'll say good night."

"How for yourself, Madam?" Elisabeth looked at me. "Whom would you take to your bed?"

"There is bound to be a dog or two upon the sheets, if I know my mother," said Edward.

"I had thought to take a walk, perhaps," I said.

Monsieur Descartes leaned forward eagerly. "Would you care for some company?"

"I'm afraid I prefer to take my evening sojourn in solitude, as has always been my habit."

"You could follow her, if you like." Elisabeth made no attempt to hide her disdain. "Her dogs are like to do as much. You could fall in with them."

I had managed to alienate the affections of yet another of my children, just as I had already done with some of the others and would surely accomplish, sooner or later, with the rest. I should find myself again and again put on the defensive for no good reason I could think of. I couldn't account for it. What was I missing again and again? Better not to know, perhaps. I wondered if the day should ever come when I might get up the nerve ask one of them, and whether they would be able to give me an answer.

I thought it best to make myself as unavailable as possible to Monsieur Descartes even as Elisabeth's lessons continued, but when the time came that his contract expired, no sooner had he departed from The Hague to take up residence elsewhere than my daughter chose to shamelessly follow him and take up her studies nearby, in hopes for a better outcome with her mother out of the picture. I could not help but think back to Sir Raleigh, in that he had been so much older than I, and here was my daughter, chasing after a man old enough to be her father. Then came word one day that Monsieur Descartes, as he was wont to from time to time, had abruptly forfeited all opportunity for social interaction and shut himself off from the world that he might better devote himself to the completion of a new philosophical treatise without distraction.

He insisted that he and my daughter correspond forthwith only through letters, and this they did, though the contents were mostly of a dispassionate and academic nature, amounting to little more than philosophical discourse. I suppose in this way the two of them managed to attain a measure of spiritual companionship, which some say is the only kind that lasts. I have always felt that the deepest of bonds were cultivated by matters beyond the flesh. My daughter showed remarkable insight in the field of analytical philosophy, but I feared her contributions to Monsieur Descartes's work should go unheeded unless the letters between them found their way into the hands of the right scholars. I intended to find some means to see that they did, but my task was made more difficult when I lost track of her thereafter and had to make do with various rumours that reached me of her whereabouts, including one that she had gone to Amsterdam to join a Mennonite sect for a time.

For my part I harboured yet the rather naive notion that somebody would come along, someone different from the others, who would take an interest in me unlike any before, a person for whom I might feel something akin to that which my brother Henry claimed he felt for my husband, Frederick, upon their first encounter. I never forgot how he insisted that it seemed he had made the reacquaintance of a long-lost friend, or that he had found the best companion of his life. I have felt this way only fleetingly, in brief moments when I thought it might be so, but in a matter of days or weeks the realization always came that I had been misled yet again. And I confess I thought my daughter Elisabeth might have turned out to be that person.

Through all of this Lord Craven remained true to his word and as good a benefactor as I might have hoped for under the circumstances. My children, hardly blind to the relationship we had, saw that he occupied a place of special privilege within the hierarchy of the court. They had not forgotten the devotion their father always showed to me, though some were quite young when he died, but I gave little thought to their sentiments. I had long ago decided there should be no more marriages in my future, save those vows I took to see myself wedded to the quest of freedom and independence. The talk at court was all about the fact that Lord Craven was not of equal station, notwithstanding that he was twelve years my junior, but I could not be bothered with any of it so long as it did not impede my means of obtaining supplementary income from those I needed to keep in my good graces. But by then I was a master of such techniques, and those lords and ladies of the court hardly knew how I spun them like so many whirling tops to do my business and see to my needs.

I stayed the course even as rumours became increasingly difficult to ignore that Lord Craven had taken a lover. In spite of my better judgment, the thought crossed my mind that it might be one of my daughters, and even as I enjoyed a degree of relief when I learned that it was not, I found myself sabotaged by unquenchable bouts of jealousy. I hardly knew what to make of them, and approached Lord Craven one evening to confront him.

"I suppose I can hardly blame you taking your affections elsewhere."

"You found out, then." He sat down with his back to me and let his shoulders slump forward.

"Did you think I wouldn't?"

"I suppose not." He shook his head slowly.

"Perhaps the opposite is true. That you wanted me to find out, the better to evoke some jealousy in me. Well, if that's why you're doing this, you're wasting your time," I lied.

I came to stand next to him and he turned to look up at me. "I would never want to upset you."

"But surely you knew that it would."

"But why should it be so?" He grew a little bolder. "You have made it clear you are not in love with me and never can be."

"I suppose next you will lecture me and say a man has his needs."

"And how be for a woman?" He looked up at me with a hint of accusation, rose from his chair, walked over to the window and leaned to look out of it.

"You are free to do as you wish," I said evenly.

"Neither of us has ever been free to do exactly as he wished."

"Tell me, who is she?"

"A lady of the court." He turned to face me. "You can dismiss her if you wish."

"Better if I did, perhaps."

When he made no answer I added, "No doubt you will find another."

Still he spoke not a word.

"Did you seek to make me jealous?" I said. "Or perhaps it was something else. You want to punish me."

"I have no defence but to plead that it was none of these."

"And yet I gave you leave to take some favour of me, and you would not."

"You gave me leave but little else. I could take what I desired, but by that very taking would my desire have been forfeit, for it should have been mine alone and none of yours."

"Many a man would have been eager to help himself nonetheless."

"I was never such a one of those. Surely you must know that by now."

"Where do you accomplish the deed? Was she eager?"

"You can't really seek to know these things."

"I would know what you'd have from me."

"Naught but what you cannot give, and so I am content."

"But where is your reward?"

"I reap it even now."

"By wanting what you can't have. In this, I suppose, we are the same. Fated to be together by some means neither of us understands or even wants, each evoking in the other that which we fail to arouse in ourselves."

"But there is something worth preserving."

"I have been sometime cruel to you."

"You have been kind when it mattered most."

We were face to face now, staring intently into each other's eyes.

"I think it better we should see to some long period of silence between us," I suggested. "Let something grow there, and perhaps we may reap the fruits of it."

And so things were allowed to go on much as before. I continued to pursue every course of action available to see my family restored to the Palatinate and my son Charles Louis instated as Emperor. At long last the day came when the squabbling and quarrelling between the various factions of the Holy Roman Empire and the Protestant League grew tiresome. After all, it had been thirty years by then. Isn't that long enough for a war? A treaty was signed at Westphalia that would see the Lower Palatinate restored to its rightful heirs, though the upper regions should remain in the hands of Duke Maximilian of Bavaria, and so were lost to us. Heidelberg and not Prague should be the seat of power for my eldest son, and in that same castle where he had his earliest childhood memories should he ascend the throne.

For his part Charles Louis had been languishing about my brother's court in England, where each had succeeded in bringing out the worst in the other. Charles Louis had managed to talk my brother into an ill-advised course of action, one sure to meet with stiff opposition from Parliament. By that means did my brother succeed in alienating him entirely from that body, as well as from a healthy portion of the general populace, to the point where civil war broke out in the country. The conflict came to a head with the appointment of Oliver Cromwell as Lord Protector of the Realm, and my brother's head in a bucket. Having never been paid the pension I was owed, I thought with Charles's removal from office that perhaps some monies might now be forthcoming, but instead the indenture itself was rescinded by Parliament and I never got a penny. My son, rather than make straight for Heidelberg to be invested there, managed to stay in London long enough to witness my brother's execution, and even went so far as to try and get an audience with him on the night before the axe came down, but Charles refused.

I suddenly found it highly appealing that I might be allowed to go and live in Heidelberg again. Charles Louis should be crowned there and rule the Lower Palatinate from that same fair and peaceful castle where I had spent my days as a young bride. How pleasant it would be to wander once more beneath the blossoms of the orange grove in the Hortus Palatinus, to sit again in that most favoured of places where the birds of the fountain sang my brother Henry's memory. And what of Elizabethentor? Did that gate still adorn the entrance to the castle? Perhaps the place had fallen into neglect and ruin. All the more reason to go and restore it to its former glory.

I thought, having come through so many disappointments and tragedies, to see myself slipping into contented old age there. Gone should be the need to shake cockroaches from my tattered arrases, to grovel incessantly for favour, to tend to each fragile strand of Lord Craven's unrequited affection. What thoughts flooded my mind! I might live a life of relative ease there compared to my present circumstances. I envisioned the castle nestled into the mountainside, the town below, the river, the trees and hills of Heidelberg.

Chapter Sixteen

I confess I was just as glad to be elsewhere and not in England after the news reached me of my brother's fate. It gave me reason to harken back to my own narrow escape from Prague and brought home the realization that I might have been fortunate to come away with my head. If I had made my way back to London, who knows what might have become of me? Perhaps I should have been sentenced to a life of imprisonment in the Tower. I might have been left to languish in the very cell where Sir Raleigh and I once suppressed our passions so admirably. Or Lord Cromwell may well have seen fit to have me beheaded as well.

I imagined myself in my brother's place, my own head brought down over a blackened and bloodied block of wood, the excruciating wait for the executioner's blow to strike, the axe slicing through the muscles and veins and bones of my neck. Might I expect, even for the briefest instant of time, to have yet some conscious awareness of my head separating from my body, my eyes open and still able to see even as it fell into the sticky bottom of the waiting bucket? Where exactly would I, Elizabeth Stuart, be at that last moment? Still in my body or departed from it? Was there any part of my brother Charles left in his body, or did it all come away when his head came off? Surely such an experience would speak to those very arguments my daughter Elisabeth and Monsieur Descartes had so often engaged in. It seemed to me the question would be answered there and then.

Did I mourn for my brother? Suffice it to say any grief on my part was tempered by the sense that he had been the author of his own undoing. He was arrogant and self-serving, and his utter disregard for the sentiments of the people could no longer sustain his crown. I learned from subsequent accounts, which were numerous and detailed, that the execution had indeed amounted to rather a gory business. There had been a huge crowd on hand to witness the beheading, and a great deal of blood was said to have spewed forth from my brother's neck even as the executioner's assistant held up his head for all to see, while people jostled each other to get to the scaffolding that they might soak some of the blood up with their handkerchiefs.

What can my brother's state of mind have been? What thoughts running through his consciousness but that he was moments away from the end of the world, for it might as well cease when he did? What is the world to us if we cannot be in it? Why should it be allowed to go on? How many among us, had we the power, should see fit at the moment of our departure to take the entirety of creation with us? Who could resist the temptation of such a final act? Can any living creature ever truly think of its own death as anything but wrongful? Who can hope to rise above that finality to some higher level, a brief moment of grace when we accept our fate and give ourselves over to something nobler? Even our Lord and Saviour failed to manage it entirely. Perhaps my brother saw, at the very last, the petty and spiteful nature of his menial life, welcomed the chance to have his soul transported elsewhere, to some higher plane of existence. It may turn out to be the same for me, but how can I hope to believe as much when even Jesus had his doubts? Who can go to his death willingly unless he suffer from some manner of delusion, whether self-inflicted or otherwise? The great allure of faith is the chance to put the lie to death, but life everlasting is not such a compelling idea. Be it Heaven or Hell, who can say which is more worthy of the human spirit?

Did not Jesus himself on the cross yet hope to be spared? Why is life so precious? Why are we so loath to give it up? We think even to the final minute that it belongs to us, but having glimpsed the abyss we are confronted by the truth that it was never ours to begin with. I wonder did my poor brother come to understand as much? What does it mean to believe something, to have faith, when we come to stand upon that final threshold and stare into black and eternal emptiness? There it lies before us, and in the next moment we must fall in. Perhaps my brother is falling yet.

Who is to say what comes after? Perhaps the moon and stars are fated to vanish when I do. The very heavens themselves may only have come into being when I did, and so are fated to depart along with me. It may be that my life is much more than merely a precious thing. It may be the only thing.

Sweet was my indulgence at the prospect of being back in Heidelberg once again, and my disappointment all the more bitter when I discovered I was not welcome there! I suppose I might have seen it coming. Having settled in Heidelberg, my son insisted on marrying Charlotte of Hesse even though he knew full well I did not approve of the match. As fetching a creature as she was in appearance she was equally wretched in disposition. Charles Louis had always been a terrible judge of character, easily swayed by looks, and Charlotte possessed the kind other women despised her for: tall and slender, shapely of limb, with lustrous flaxen hair and strikingly large breasts — all conspired to make them loathe the very sight of her. I might have seen fit to let it pass had she had been a better sort of person, but she was manipulative and devious, and used her voluptuousness to take advantage. My son Charles never stood a chance. He even tried to convince me that the decision to shun me was his, but I have no doubt Charlotte made sure that under no circumstances should her husband's meddling mother be allowed to take up residence in the castle.

When I intimated as much to Charles Louis he insisted that it was because I had turned to Lord Craven for finance and consolation. "If he is so eager to take care of you then let him do it now." Those were his exact words. He had seen all the concessions I made year after year, and claimed I had not remained true to the principles his father would have had me uphold in such matters, and so in effect was choosing to disown me.

And so life for me went on much as it had before, albeit with the financial burden somewhat eased after a number of the older children saw fit to leave the relative austerity extant under my roof and go to live in Heidelberg instead, where they were welcomed by their brother Charles Louis. Good riddance! Even Elisabeth went to live there for a time, though much to my delight I learned that she had soon found the conditions there unbearable and left. This gave me no end of satisfaction. There were stories of my son's wife, Charlotte, flying into rages of one sort and another, of violent arguments, gambling debts, and turmoil throughout the castle.

At one point news reached me that Charles Louis had taken up with a young woman of the court named Marie Luise von Degenfeld, who began immediately to bear him one child after another though he was still married to Charlotte. He even managed to estrange himself from my son Rupert after he became convinced that Rupert was making advances at Marie, and so by degrees the others of his siblings found reason to have a falling out with him, so that they were soon scattered far and wide.

In all of this Lord Craven's devotion to me continued unabated, notwithstanding that I continued to entertain young men of the court as I had always done. At one point

I was told there were certain factions in England favourable to my return from Bohemia. Apparently there was a movement afoot that I be crowned queen in order to take my late brother's place in the restored monarchy. I found it a tempting prospect, but I knew it should never amount to anything, which was just as well, for it brought me to mind of how eager I had been to see my husband, Frederick, take the throne when so many opposed it.

But there was something else going on. I had reached the limits of continually getting my hopes up only to see them dashed, longed for a life less fraught with disappointment. I must stop up the passion that left me always wanting more. Why should it be so hard to find contentment? How many of us are condemned to live out our days never gaining the thing we most long for? I heard of a woman once who wanted to be a poet. More than anything in the world she wanted to write a poem that would move the reader to tears of joy and sadness all in the same moment. Alas she was a bad poet, though she was careful to keep herself blissfully unaware of it. People began to avoid her lest she inflict upon them one of her dreadful verses. Whenever she managed to ambush someone they were made to suffer the worst kind of lyric. But to her, every word was precious! So, I thought, it is with my dreams. Better to keep them to myself and not inflict them on others. Perhaps the object of our desire continually eludes us precisely because we fail to grasp the true nature of that which we strive for.

All these elaborate fabrications we cobble together over the course of our meagre existence. Do they serve us in good stead, or only blind us to what we really need to discover? From the very first we all of us make up stories to tell ourselves. The little girl busy at seemingly innocent and unfettered play with her dolls is in fact about the very serious business of manufacturing a meticulous fiction for herself, that she may dwell within. And so we conjure ourselves up.

By such means are we from our earliest imaginings the author of our own becoming. But that we grow up under the influence of adults who care for us, who expected us to think and act in particular ways and to believe certain things, we should surely become another sort of person. And yet that which makes us truly who we are originates from deep within our own singular and separate being. Of all that is best and worst in us we are the agent. So have I done, so do we all, imagine ourselves into existence even to the last breath.

I have these last few days been entertaining a fanciful notion, I know not wherefore, that long after I am gone someone not of this time shall write of me, that my departed spirit shall visit itself upon some distant shore and there cause the ebb and flow of a future heart to seek out the inner workings of my own. What shall I make of such a ghostly experience? I suppose they shall think themselves seduced by forces beyond their understanding, but is it really so strange? How often, over the course of this long life, do we deny ourselves to ourselves?

"Tell me, which do you think is worse," I asked Lord Craven one evening, "to love someone though they be unworthy, or to love them not, though they be worthy?" We were having a quiet dinner, just the two of us, as we liked to do more and more after the last of my children had taken their leave. By then neither of us cared to bother much with the puerile antics of the court, having little need for it.

"I dare not answer, as I find myself in neither predicament."

"I'm relieved to hear it. But for the sake of argument, if you had to choose."

Lord Craven sat back in his chair. "I should have to give the matter some thought, though I don't know that I care to."

"Indulge me."

He had just returned from Prague, where he had visited the Cathedral of St. Vitus at my urging, to see an enormous wooden relief I had heard about, a telling recreation rendered in exquisite detail and mounted near the altar, of Frederick's and my humiliating retreat from Prague.

"It suppose it depends which side you find yourself on."

"Then choose a side."

The Archbishop had commissioned the work to hang there for all to see, the better to ensure that our disgrace should not be forgotten.

"I shouldn't like to think of myself as unworthy of love."

I put down my cutlery and dabbed at the corner of my mouth with my napkin. "I confess I have of late been given to such thoughts."

"You think me unworthy?"

"No. I mean myself."

"You must not. You know that I love you."

The artist had been instructed to carve out the procession of our hastily loaded carriages making their way down from the castle and over the bridge into the Old Town.

"But what can be said for my children?"

"It isn't as though they have been given a choice in the matter. There can be no discussion of blame."

"And yet the thought persists."

"You are worthy to be loved by each and every one of them."

"I doubt they should say they have received as much from me. They say those unable to give love are not worthy to receive it."

Lord Craven took up his goblet. "In any case I am of the conviction that the entire business is out of our hands, though some will say," he turned to me wistfully, "it is possible a person may grow into love for another." He brought the cup to his lips. "Do you think it may be so?"

I felt incapable of answering, thought it better to remain silent.

"I suppose the caveat," he went on, "may be that true passion cannot be arrived at by such means. Do you think that's too cynical?" He grew animated. "What is your dispassionate view on the subject? Will you say true love can only be fuelled by desire?"

"Some will argue just the opposite." I stared back at him. "Either way it must fade in time, no matter how intense to begin with. Some things simply cannot be sustained."

"How then of duty?" Lord Craven asked.

"How does that follow?"

"Passion brings duty with it."

"To what end?"

Lord Craven seemed surprised at my question. "Why, to be steadfast out of love for that person and so remain faithful."

"And that would bring happiness?" I looked at him.

"I would see to your happiness."

"What of your own?"

"One brings about the other."

"And yet cruelty can be borne out of too much kindness."

Lord Craven pushed himself back from the table and stood. "I think that I shall be going back to England." He walked to the window. "My lands have been restored to me and I must go and see to my finances." He turned back to look at me over his shoulder. "Will you come with me?"

"What, to London?"

"I should think you would welcome the chance to quit this place. I know you had thought to return to Heidelberg, and if your son had allowed it you would be there now, and no longer have need of me."

"That sounds a harsh indictment."

"I have some lands at Ashdown. Do you know it?"

"If I remember from my childhood, it is in Oxfordshire, is it not?"

"What if I told you I could build a place for you there, a manor nestled among the green and rolling wooded hills?"

"With little more to occupy my time than ambling along

a wooded path, I suppose, or sitting by a warm fire in the evening."

"It will make you happy, I think."

"That is certain to prove elusive, as ever it has been. This place . . . it would be for both of us to live in?"

"For you, I should of course hope to come and stay as you saw fit, but the place would be yours."

"Mine."

"I should sign the title over to you."

"Why would you want to do a thing like that?" I asked.

"Must you still ask such a question?"

"What in return?"

"There's another." He raised an eyebrow.

"You know by now my company is best taken in small doses."

"And yet I would seek after that good medicine and have need of it often."

"But . . . I am too old for such romantic notions."

"Your looks say otherwise."

"I grow into wrinkled age."

"You are as beautiful a woman to me as ever you were."

"You see what you want to see." I got up and strode to a far window. "This place you want to build. It will take time. Where will I live in the meantime?"

"We can take up residence at Drury Lane, where I have some apartments you could make use of. And Leicester House, though not so well appointed, is comfortable enough should you wish to make use of it. I grant they are not royal accommodations, but it would only be until Ashdown is finished."

"And what will people say when they learn that the Winter Queen has come back to England and taken up residence under the Earl of Craven's roof?"

"They can say what they like."

"You have a reputation."

"It will all be different once we get out to Ashdown."

"But even so, if someone should ask about our . . . arrangement, how would you characterize it, exactly?"

"No more than that we have always been kind to each other."

"Your memory betrays you, for I have not always been so to you."

"I cannot complain."

"I treat you poorly, or ignore you, or shunt you aside when it suits me, yet you insist on forgiving me, and look where it has led us."

"You think less of me for it, I know. But you have a need of care, and I have a need to provide it. What is so wrong about that?"

"It is entirely one-sided and makes both parties wretched."

"Even wretchedness has had its uses."

"But who should suffer the greater punishment: you at the hands of my stubborn discontent, or I under the tyranny of your obstinate forgiveness? Must we now insist on enduring yet longer?"

"I am satisfied."

"I warned you from the very first that you should not seek to cherish me."

"How often have you chided me for it." His tone spoke more of warmth than recrimination.

"And yet you persist." I hardly knew where my anger welled up from, and yet it would not be denied. "Do you not see how destructive it is? It runs first to pity, then to disdain."

"Not for my part." He came to kneel next to me where I sat stiffly in my chair. "Elizabeth, will you let me build this house for you in Ashdown? It will be the greatest happiness of my life."

"And how if I accept your proposal with no promise to be less ungracious than I have always been?"

"Then you shall soon find yourself in the sweet country air."

"There are bound to be those who will say I took advantage." I rose and made my way to the window.

"Let them think what they like." He waited for me to turn to him. "We know the truth."

"Indeed." I peered once more into the darkness beyond the window. "But will that be enough?"

Chapter Seventeen

We made the journey to England on a pleasant spring day in May, and though the channel crossing was uneventful I was not prepared for the storm of emotion that arose within me when first I set eyes upon my fair and long-lost homeland. Hearing that the ship was nearing land, and the weather being so agreeable, I took myself out on deck to enjoy the landing. I came to stand at the railing, and there before me lay the familiar shores of England, the chalk cliffs of Margate with its inns and cottages lining the pier, the tall ships and fishing boats anchored in the harbour. This was the very place Frederick and I had departed from fifty years ago! My heart made a great leap as a wave of bittersweet joy swept over me and tears welled up to blur my vision. Not for a moment, in all the years of living in Heidelberg and Prague and The Hague, had I thought myself truly in a place of my own, but now it seemed to me I had come home. For a moment I was young again, with all my hopes and dreams yet before me.

Lord Craven arranged for us to stay at his newly restored estate in Drury Lane, and as I was all but forgotten in England we managed, at least for a time, to settle quietly into the bosom of London. I was granted the use of one wing and lived much as I had before, save without the need to entertain even a small court. The transport of my bed had thankfully been seen to, but it was not until its assembly had been properly accomplished and I had spent a few nights in restful sleep upon it that I began to feel a little more comfortable.

For a time the days passed in modest and unassuming quietude, but news of my return eventually made its way to the royal court, and thereafter rumblings began in Parliament of an unwelcome drain on the exchequer should the King see fit to provide his aunt with a royal living allowance. As it is, Charles has failed to extend even the most perfunctory hospitality upon my return. He has little need of my good graces and no doubt deems the crown upon his head yet precariously perched there, inasmuch as the newly restored monarchy is still quite fragile. Not a farthing will he lift from the exchequer for my sake, and so eager is he to appease his benefactors that only last week he had Lord Cromwell's corpse dug up from the Abbey, beheaded, and hung up in chains for public display. For Lord Craven's part, he has seen to my needs well enough, but then quite unexpectedly my residence at Drury Lane became a matter of concern. It came to light that our situation, considering the fact that we were not married, had fallen into some disfavour. Accordingly the matter became a delicate one, if only because the remainder of Lord Craven's properties have yet to be restored to him. And so, rather than jeopardize their transfer, we agreed it would be better that I no longer remain under his roof.

So it is that I find myself here at Leicester House. The living quarters are hardly sumptuous, but I am comfortable enough, attended to by these few servants assigned to see to my needs. My bed has been seen to. I have use of a private bedchamber, albeit with naught but a water closet, as well as an antechamber, and this small study where my meals are brought in to me, though I hardly eat of them. It is the dead of winter and a stubborn melancholy has besieged me that began shortly after my arrival here. I thought at first I should manage to defeat it as I always have, but try as I may I cannot seem to shake it, so that waking and sleeping a troubling exhaustion is my constant companion. I can hardly think what afflicts me, but I grow weaker by the day. Lord Craven insists that I be tended to by a physician, but I refuse to spend my last days being poked and prodded by some practitioner who struts about in cap and robe, speaking of little else but the four humours and offering remedies dictated by the feeble teachings of antiquity. I shall not insult my failing body with purgatives and bloodletting.

But how if upon my return it was my dear brother Henry seated upon the throne of England and not this ungrateful nephew of mine? What a homecoming celebration there should have been! It would have been a different England I returned to, not this hobbled beggar of a country that is only now recovering from the ravages of civil war. Henry should be basking in the fullness of a long and happy reign, no doubt, and it should never have come about that Parliament abolished the monarchy, or bequeathed the title of Lord Protector of the Commonwealth upon a man like Oliver Cromwell. My brother would be Henry IX, and it would be his progeny that inherited the crown, perhaps even a daughter, for I don't wonder that during his reign he should have seen fit to amend the laws of ascension.

I went to see the place where he is laid to rest in the Abbey yesterday, a venture that cost me the last of my strength, I fear, and found him resting in the Lady Chapel, where his remains are encased under a grey and utterly unremarkable slab wedged between my grandmother's monument and that of the Countess of Richmond. The shallow inscription chiselled upon the vault is equally uninspired, hardly a fitting testament to the memory of a future king. Entombed there with him are various others, including some nephews and nieces born to my brother Charles and his wife, Henrietta. Two of these were no more than infants when they died, and as I knelt there upon the cold stone I thought how the wings of those tiny angels must surely have borne my sweet brother up from such a pitiable grave to glorious Heaven, where he belongs. Imagine my surprise when I read that my dear cousin Arabella Stuart had also been laid to rest in the very same vault! I shall write to my nephew to ask if I might be entombed with them as well. I think he may allow it, as it will entail little more in the way of expense than to pull back the stone and inter my remains with the others.

Lord Craven has been trying to see me these last days but I will not allow it, nor have I been receiving any visitors. He keeps sending people to the house with letters for me but I hardly bother to read them. He insists on telling me about his plans for the country house at Ashdown, and is adamant that I shall be allowed to come and live there when it is finished.

February 10, 1662
Craven House, Drury Lane

Dearest Elizabeth,

Why do you see fit to punish me so mercilessly? Though your servants assure me you are not suffering unduly and that your needs are being seen to, I cannot rest. Another man might find a way to be content, but I cannot! Will you at least see fit to take up pen and paper and write some few lines of reply as a courtesy? I don't expect forgiveness. Admonish me for my cowardice, upbraid me as harshly as you would, but to punish me further with your silence is beyond endurance.

Can I convey some news that should be of interest to you? Since your departure from Leicester House, my lands in Oxfordshire have been officially restored to me by your nephew, the King, just as he promised. Do you know what he said to me? "The matter is a delicate one" (I am quoting from memory) "as the chastened royal phoenix cannot be seen to ruffle a single feather of those peacocks that strut yet about the corridors of power."

This news must surely please you, for it means that work can begin at once on the country home I promised to build for you. The site where it shall stand lies near Aysshen Wood, beyond the pale where a valley slopes gently away to overlook the rolling countryside of woodland and pasture. The view from the upper floors shall include the grounds and gardens just as we spoke of, and beyond them Berkshire Downs where lie the sarsen stones that built the pagan temples. There the plentiful deer run free from the hunter's bow, and you shall see fit to tame as many of them as you wish! And just as you requested, it shall be christened Ashdown House.

But if only I could tell you all of this in person! I doubt not your ability to stand up to adversity, as you have ever been my better in that regard, but I fear your stubbornness fails to serve your best interest of late. For both our sakes I beg you to let me send a doctor. In the meantime I shall see to Ashdown House, and when it is ready everything will be different. We can live as we choose there, free from the probing eyes of king and court. I give you my solemn promise that by summer, or early fall at the latest, we shall be comfortably ensconced in the bounteous nature of Oxfordshire.

What do you say? Will you write to me? Please?

In hopes that I may be allowed to remain your humble servant and greatest admirer,
William

I grant Lord Craven has ever been attentive to my needs and I can hardly calculate what I owe him. He would see to letting me live out my days in the peace and privacy of the countryside, as I have always longed to, but soon he shall have leave to forgo such noble sentiments. I did ask him, as I was leaving Drury Lane, why he had been so kind to me over the years and he answered, "Madam, I have always enjoyed the company of a beautiful woman." I saw that he was in earnest, for though my looks have all but vanished, in his eyes beauty alights upon me still. And so I forgive him for sending me away. He has his reputation to uphold.

I suppose it only fitting that I should spend my last hour in this dimly lit room with none but myself for company. I've grown resigned to my solitude and do not wish a companion. If there were another here, one of us should almost certainly have something to forgive the other for, and that ritual has grown tiresome. Or else they should be eager to offer me counsel, which would only engender more unease. Better to be free of such considerations. In any case, whom should I seek to pardon at this late hour: my nephew the King for ignoring me, my children for their absence, Lord Craven for sending me away? As to those from whom I might wish to seek absolution, the best would surely answer that there is nothing to forgive.

I find this quietude an excellent tonic. Words can soothe but silence is a better balm. If only I had more time to think, to remember. What is it I should seek to hold in my memory? Days of childhood innocence? I can hardly recall such. Besides, who can claim to be in possession of a memory so pure that time and conscience have not altered it to some degree? What has my life been but that same practice common to us all: the calculation and conjuring up of endless schemes to bring about some coveted notion of victory? In truth ours is a base existence and a baser end. We are creatures at the core, and primal needs define our fundamental nature. We are no different than the beasts of the earth in this: that we ingest on a daily basis its fruits and turn them by means of the body's digestion into a foul and stinking putrefaction, which must then be expelled from the body in an act most vulgar. And just before we free ourselves forever from this enslavement, our last act shall be the release of one foul and final breath into the world.

I had hoped to bring a modicum of wisdom to these late hours if only to lend them some quiet dignity, but perhaps I deceive myself. Why should I seek to cobble all of this together now, so near the end of my life? I doubt it shall serve to bring about a more peaceful death. Dying itself has become tiresome. Even in death we cannot entirely escape the banality of life. Had I been allowed to live my life entirely as I pleased, as most assuredly I was not, neither shall I have that luxury in death. None of us owns the life we lived after we are gone. In death it is given over to others who remember it as they will. It may be changed, altered, even transformed. Who can say where the greater truth lies? Shall I in the end cast myself falsely? Having fallen prey to all the ambitions and calculations of a niggling life, shall I be forgiven for making of myself something of a fiction? It was only that I sought to fashion my life into art, and by such means render it purified.

Last night when I was all alone in my bed a thumping sound came to my ears, as of someone seeking admittance at a distant door, or perhaps the rumble of far-off thunder. My inhalations grew shallow until of a sudden I took in a great gulp of air, and it was then I realized what I had been hearing. It was the sound of my own heart beating! There was a strange urgency to it I couldn't recall ever being aware of before. And soon after there came indeed a knocking at the door, but it was only one of Lord Craven's messengers with yet another note for me. He has always been persistent; I grant him that. It has proved to be one of his most enduring qualities. It is hardly a romantic notion, yet how often by sheer staying power does a man succeed in winning the woman he loves! By such means he breaks down her will and little by little erodes her resistance. So it was with Lord Craven, although his relentless advances were more like entreaties, and my eventual surrender more like an armistice.

I can't think that anything good can be accomplished by letting him visit me. Shall I be suffered to hear him beg forgiveness for his actions? The time for that is past. No doubt he would speak to me of Ashdown Manor and his plans for a country home there. Why should I sit and listen to him tell me all about a place I shall never see? And even if by some miracle my health should be restored to me, it would only be for a little while at best. I know my time is near. I have no doubt of it. What should it benefit me to let him drag me out into the countryside that I might see the place, only to have it lost to me, as so much else has been? I shall spare myself that final torture.

Yet what if by some unforeseen good fortune my health should return to me, and I should live long enough to see the place finished? To view out of every window naught but the sights of glorious nature, take in the fresh country air with every breath. I have to admit it would be a good place to die. Ah, but I would make of my passing a romance, put the lie to that stale odour of death which stalks me, my vision darkening slowly into blackened circles, ears able to hear naught but the last beatings of a failed heart. That I might have been allowed to spend my last days in pastoral pleasantry is wishful thinking. Better not to imagine myself seated upon the front porch of such a place, looking out across an immense lawn, or ambling along a country path that wends its way through wood and meadow. It's too late for that.

What if Lord Craven should find his way in here when the time is come, to bear witness to my last few breaths? Would he still think of me as beautiful? Perhaps death brings another way to look upon the living. Ah, but when I imagine myself with jaws hanging open, spittle dripping from pallid lips, skin turned the colour of wax, hair thinned to that of a ragged marionette, then where is beauty? Suffice it to say that death paints upon the flesh such final strokes as no portrait would seek to match.

Better Lord Craven should not have to witness these indignities my failing body subjects me to. My nose will not stop running and I hack with a cough and wheeze as one ridden with the plague, though I know it is not that. A surfeit of humours congests my organs and my swollen ankles have turned the colour of burgundy. I confess that even as I have seated myself here in this chair, I am not altogether certain I shall have the strength to rise up from it once more.

I sometimes think it better I died early like my brother Henry. For his part he shall remain forever young, as he does even now in my mind's eye. I cannot imagine him as an old man. To be sure there are no unflattering portraits of him as there are of me, painted after age had done its mordant work. A hundred years from now, in every likeness that hangs upon a wall in one palace or another, the Prince of Wales shall look upon the viewer with youthful vigour. Not so for me. Those portraits I deigned to sit for in my later years, kind as the artist may have imagined himself to be, portray too much of these mottled cheeks, lips withered and hair thinned. I had thought to see about sitting for Judith Leyster when I was still in The Hague, but there was no money for it. Upon my return here to London I had hoped to sit for the artist Mary Beale, as I had seen her recent work *Portrait of Lady with a Black Hood* and liked it very much. How gently should my progress into old age have been rendered! Her portraits neither adulate nor misrepresent, and yet the paintings convey a deep sense of the subject's dignity. She should surely have found a way to do as much for me. But now the time for that is passed.

Perhaps I should make one final request of Lord Craven, that he find every portrait painted of me after the age of sixteen and have it taken down and burned. I have little desire to be remembered as an old woman. Let them only see me with hair glorious, torrents of wild curls running in thick red rivers down to my waist, not these grey and meagre strands. Let only those likenesses of me where I sit in youthful beauty, my eyes fresh with promise, be preserved. Naught but the slender waist, the taut and delicate skin upon the cheek. Not this sagging, tired descent into wrinkles. When age looks in the mirror it is with a vinegared vision. I'll leave mirrors to others. Were it my domain I should arrange the world otherwise — that a woman's beauty, rather than diminish, increase, year upon year, and the advent of old age become the harbinger of blossoming loveliness. Justice!

The attendant came in just now and handed me some correspondence — another note from Lord Craven, no doubt, but I see that it is accompanied by a letter addressed to me. The seal is an unfamiliar one, though the handwriting gives me pause to think it may be a person of past acquaintance. In any case I shall put it by for now. Indeed I hardly think I shall bother to read it at all. What good can come from it now, or what ill for that matter? What's left to be said?

It seems to me that in these last days I have become little else but an inconvenience. It is the last thing I could wish for! Must it be the fate of the aged to become a burden? What a sorry lot it is to be a chore. A helpless babe in arms may be malodourous and wrinkled, yet its life is new and so care is given gladly. But what redeems us in feeble age? Why must the road to death be such a trudge? As for the promise of Heaven to come, I say it may turn out to be nothing more than a foolish prank.

It occurs to me that all my life I have been a kept woman. What else does a princess amount to? Or a queen consort? From the time I was a child I was taught that all the considerations of finance were beneath me, and that to even contemplate such matters was unseemly. Money was a vulgar inconvenience relegated to those who lacked the privilege of never having to think about it. Royalty were best to distance themselves from it. Yet looking back, I realize that for most of my life I was not free to indulge in such a dubious luxury.

Far too often it was dirty money I grovelled for from one day to the next.

I draw ever nearer the time when I shall have to stand to my transgressions. But am I the same person now as then? Which self is my truer self: the one in which I am sixteen or the one where I am sixty? Surely over the course of my life every single atomie in my body has been replaced by another, whether it be by skin shed or blood renewed, by endless acts of breath, of eating and drinking and later expulsion, so that there can hardly be one iota of me that has not been exchanged for another in all that time. And so it is for every one of us. That which we are is not that which we were. We are ghosts, and it is memory alone that links us to our former selves.

But what purpose do these late revelations serve? Do they move me forward or draw me back? Where is the victory in discovering some long-sought-after truth at the end of life? It seems but another twist of the dagger. Perhaps I shall wake into death as from a dream, having drifted across a vast sea whose currents carry me at last to that final shore. And having landed, what shall I recall of my life on earth? If time cannot be trusted in life how then in death, where an hour may be an eternity, where what is yet to come may already have passed. All my life I have looked for that which is permanent and found only change. Shall the afterlife convince me of eternity? The next world, be it Heaven or Hell, may turn out to be as transitory as this one.

If Sir Walter were yet alive I could send to him for some of his cordial. There is much I would be cured of. A grey mist swirls about my soul. I did not expect to live to such a considerable age and thought I should surely die in childbirth before I had even reached my twentieth birthday. With each subsequent birth it seemed to me I was playing at the odds, and Death must surely have thought himself cheated. Perhaps it had little to do with luck and more with my stubborn insistence that the midwives wash their hands before they undertake to snatch each babe from my loins. By then I had developed my theory that it is creatomies, unseen and undetected, which cause the trouble. To think I might have written it all up in a treatise, as learned men full of their own importance are wont to do.

The afterlife seems an unwieldy proposition to me. Shall my brother Henry be waiting for me there as a strapping lad of eighteen years, healthy and fit, or will he greet me as he would look now? Perhaps I shall be allowed to choose between the two, though I hardly know which I should pick. The clerics should no doubt think me irreverent for conjecturing upon such matters, and my faith doubtless pales in comparison to theirs, but if the spirit world is to be my next home I can be forgiven a few moments' speculation. For my part I pray there may be some respite from eternal joy, as I have no desire to amble about endlessly in a stupor of silly bliss.

Only the waiting now. Always and forever it seems I have been waiting. I look back and see myself waiting at a banquet table to be introduced to a young prince who will be my husband, waiting in an ornate chapel to be crowned queen of a foreign land, waiting to climb aboard a midnight carriage that will take me into exile. Time and again I have waited, always impatiently, for the child inside me to swell into form and be born. Many a night I waited for the man who was my husband to finish and get off me. How oft even now I hark back to the earliest days of my maidenhood, where I wait yet for Sir Raleigh to undress me and he will not. Must there always be a handsome man in every woman's life who failed to do what she most wanted him to?

But it shall soon be over. The only thing left to wait for now is that which no mortal can deny. Too oft have I been witness to a loved one breathing their last, be it son or daughter, husband or brother, friend or benefactor. Some greeted death with great dignity, and I pray it may be so for me. And yet, I fear it may not. We die as we are born, but once. The clerics would hasten to assure me I shall be born again into eternal life. I cannot say what lies ahead but the chasm awaits. Leap I must, and soon.

The bothersome priests are nowhere to be found and I am glad for it. The same can be said for those physicians who would no doubt advise that I take some laudanum such as they administered to my husband the better to ease his anguish. Was it mercy or manipulation? Somewhat of both, I suppose, but I'll have none of it. To have my end made more bearable by artificial means serves but to rob me of the experience. I will not be cheated. I would know whether it be my finest moment or my worst. As for family or friends, better I should take my leave alone. It will be difficult enough without the added inconvenience of insufferable sociability. What need have I to be hospitable in the face of cold death?

When I consider that the experience of romantic love has eluded me all my life I ask myself whose fault it is. Perhaps I failed to plant those seeds that were needed to bring forth such fruit. At any rate I never tasted it. Yet every manner of fruit will ripen and soon enough thereafter fall into decay. Nothing lasts. It may go to explaining what happened with Lord Craven. Perhaps he sensed that the moment he gave in to his passion would be the moment he started along the path that led inexorably to its extinction.

It draws near, the time when that greatest of all secrets is revealed, at the precise moment I can make no use of it. The very air is precious now, the light, the fading warmth upon my cheek. A stillness final as stone, cold as a star, awaits me. My existence has been a thing borrowed, never mine. We are master neither of our arrival nor our departure. I relinquish all pretense to agency, for I never had any.

I shall take up this latest correspondence from Lord Craven after all, if only to pass the time in these last moments left to me.

Dearest Elizabeth,

The accompanying letter arrived here at Leicester yesterday, and I should gladly have delivered it into your hand personally, but as it is I forward it to you now. I pray you shall yet see fit to grant me a visitation, but until such time, I remain,

Yours in faithful devotion,
Lord William Craven

This letter looks to have suffered somewhat in the passage, and the journey from the writer's hand into mine appears to have been an arduous one. I suppose no harm can come from reading it. And yet, what words herein may serve to bring about one last disappointment? I have torn open too many letters in hopes they might bring me good fortune and change my life, only to have them effect the opposite. But what is one more?

February 4, 1662
Herford Abbey, Saxony

Dear Mother,

I had hoped to write this letter sooner and the reasons for my procrastination are both naive and ignoble, but now there can be no more putting off. News has reached me of your return at long last to London, and of your recent departure from the Earl of Craven's residence. You might as well know that Lord Craven and I have been in correspondence of late, and by such means have I learned you are not in good health. He has told me of your refusal to see him, but I plead you may see fit to relent, or at the very least allow yourself to be attended by a physician.

I write to you from Herford Abbey in Saxony, where I am appointed coadjutrix, and where I shall remain for the rest of my life. There is much work to be done here, and I have dedicated myself to providing refuge for the many victims of persecution who seek sanctuary here, among them the Socinians, Quakers, and also some Mennonites. I find the Mennonites of particular interest, inasmuch as they are a religious sect, but also very much a distinct people. They have about them an air of deference, yet also of defiance, and their fierce humility is tempered by a formidable industriousness.

There is someone here at the abbey who will be of interest to you, a woman of my age who has lived here all her life. Her name is Jane and she was brought here in secret from London as an infant. When I first arrived here I wondered after her more than quiet manner, for I never heard her speak so much as a single word, but soon learned she had taken a vow of silence many years ago. It was not until my appointment to this office that her true identity was revealed to me by the departing coadjutrix, who had been sworn to secrecy in the matter, as had her predecessor, and as I have been. Nearly half a century has passed since the events in question, and so I grant myself permission to break that oath for your sake alone.

There are a lot of things I've never told you, Mother, among them that I used to make a habit of sneaking your old letters out of that supposedly locked chest you kept them in, to read them over and over. I know I always gave off the outward appearance of caring little for matters that concerned you, and I did my best to nurture that pretense, but the truth is very different. I know quite a lot more about you than you might guess. In any case there were a number of letters in there from your cousin Arabella Stuart, including some she wrote while she was being held by your father, the King, at the Tower of London. I remember vividly one that made a cryptic reference to an event whose details she dared not reveal at the time. Now I can tell you what occurred.

Your cousin Arabella gave birth to a daughter there in the Tower, under the most trying of circumstances. On the very night the infant was born into that dreadful cold and damp she was taken from her mother's cell and transported far away to be raised in secret, lest your father learn of her existence and seek to do her harm, as she constituted a threat to his lineage. She was brought here to the abbey in Saxony and raised by the nuns in the convent. The arrangements were seen to by Sir Raleigh, and financed by her father, Lord Seymour. She has lived here all her life and never ventured out into the world. That child is Jane, the woman I have been telling you about. I thought you would want to know.

But that is hardly the reason for this letter. I write because there's something I need to tell you of great importance to me. First, however, I beg that you set aside for a moment my shortcomings as daughter, which are many, and ask that you do the same for yours as a mother. I could never seem to express myself meaningfully to you whenever we were face to face. Being under the eye of your fierce, dispassionate gaze always unsettled me, caused me to lose my composure, and so divided me from my better, surer self. But let me speak frankly to you now, after all this time, from the safe haven of this quiet and contemplative sanctuary.

I want to acknowledge at the outset how grateful I am to you for not forcing me to marry. It would have been perfectly understandable, considering that such was the case for your mother, Anne, brought out of Denmark at the age of fourteen to live in Scotland, and for you, taken away to Bohemia at sixteen. But for you, I should have been spirited away to Poland with that popinjay who came to fetch me, but you spared me that fate, and I thank you for it.

Also, I do not hold it against you in the matter concerning René Descartes. I know you never meant to nurture his affections, or if you did it was inadvertent and not by design. As it is I doubt Monsieur Descartes should have made me happy in the end, though I certainly thought so then. I have come to acknowledge that though we are different in so many ways, in this one thing you and I are alike: that nothing can really make us happy.

But now for the purpose of this letter. It seems we hardly cared to know each other, so much effort did we expend in being at odds with one another. Ours was never a familiar nor an orthodox affection, but as rebellious and intransigent a daughter as I may have been, I want you to know something: I admire you greatly. I always have. I always shall. I think you are the best person I know.

Don't feel the need to write back. In fact it might be better you didn't. With a promise to be always faithful and true to your memory, I am . . .

Your daughter in admiration and respect,
Elisabeth

The letter falls from my hand and I am swept up in a vision of walking at day's end through the wooded hills high above Heidelberg, among forests of oak and pine whose quiet paths are lined with holly and ivy. I run my fingers along an outcropping of granite rock and emerge onto a promontory that provides a spectacular view of the valley below. There lies the town, the great cathedral at its heart, and there overlooking the River Neckar stands the castle walled and moated, its battlements a fiery ochre against the sun's last rays.

I find myself standing next to a tree of staggering girth whose mighty trunk matches the colour of the castle. Its green boughs rise impossibly high into the heavens until they seem to mingle with the clouds themselves. The sovereign leviathan emanates an air of quiet dignity and kindness as I stand in awe of its immensity, gaze up to ponder whether amid the upper reaches of those massive limbs and branches an entire world might yet exist, all unto itself. I grow light, lighter still, until my feet lift away from the mossy forest floor and I begin to ascend into the sweet-scented and rarefied air. Higher and higher I am carried along the length of that great and ancient trunk, witness now to its many scars and indentations, the wounds and markings of age, here the bark scorched by fire, there a great burl where disease sought to take hold, an abrasion where some branch long ago broke away and fell with a great roar and rumbling to thunder onto the forest floor far below. Still I rise while the silent and gentle boughs above me await my arrival.

The End

Afterword

Lord Craven never married after Elizabeth's death. When the Great Plague struck London three years later, instead of fleeing to the country he stayed and helped with the burial of the dead. He saw to it that Ashdown House was completed as planned and that Elizabeth's portraits should adorn its walls, as they do today.

Elizabeth's daughter Princess Sophia of Hanover became heir to the British throne but died two months before her coronation and the title passed on to her son, George Louis. He was subsequently crowned King George I of England, and all succeeding monarchs trace their lineage back through Sophia and ultimately to Elizabeth herself.

Elizabeth's son Prince Rupert financed a voyage of the sailing ship *Nonsuch* to present-day Canada for the purpose of developing the fur trade. The venture turned out to be highly successful, and Rupert went on to become the first governor of the newly formed Hudson's Bay Company. The vast territory of Rupert's Land was named for him.

Elisabeth of the Palatinate spent the remainder of her life in Herford Abbey, where she oversaw the welfare of as many as seven thousand families. She later became known for her correspondence with René Descartes and today she is a frequent subject of academic study in the history of feminist philosophy.

Tobias Hume spent the remainder of his life at Charterhouse in London, where a plaque has recently been mounted in his honour. His music is enjoying something of a renaissance and his compositions for the viola da gamba are featured on numerous recordings, including those of Jordi Savall and Susanne Heinrich. Captain Hume may also have been the inspiration for the character of Sir Andrew Aguecheek in William Shakespeare's *Twelfth Night*. Like Hume, Sir Aguecheek played the viola da gamba, drank and sang wildly, swore profusely, and was generally quarrelsome.

The Hortus Palatinus, the elaborate gardens and grounds Elizabeth undertook to construct at Heidelberg Castle in honour of her brother Henry, was never completed. Much of it subsequently fell into neglect, as did portions of the castle, which has taken on a romantic allure and become a major tourist attraction. The English Wing where Elizabeth lived is presently undergoing reconstruction.

After Frederick and Elizabeth's brief reign in Prague, St. Vitus Cathedral was restored to its former state as the seat of the Archbishop. Caspar Bechterle was commissioned to carve a large wooden relief that depicts the disgraced couple's flight from the palace. It can be viewed along a low wall not far from the altar.

Amalia von Solms, chosen by Elizabeth to succeed Anne Dudley, continued to serve as her lady-in-waiting after they settled in The Hague. She eventually married into royalty herself and started up a royal court of her own, as well as amassing an impressive collection of art and jewellery.

The Great Comet of 1618 was known as "the Angry Star." It boasted a long, ominous tail and appeared red in the sky.

It was visible to the naked eye for almost two months and could be seen even in broad daylight. Elizabeth's father, King James, penned a poem about it, imploring people not to read too much into it.

The cordial concocted by Sir Walter Raleigh while he was a prisoner in the Tower of London continued to be used as a medicine for over a century and became known as "the Great Cordial." Today a liqueur based on the original and named after its creator is available for purchase. It contains over thirty ingredients, but the exact recipe remains a closely guarded secret.

Dr. Theodore de Turquet de Mayerne received part of his early medical education at Heidelberg University, across the Neckar River from the castle. In addition to his duties as physician, Elizabeth's father sent him on a number of diplomatic missions whose secret purpose was to spy for the King.

The failed attempt to blow up the British Parliament in 1605 and install young Elizabeth Stuart as child queen became known as the Gunpowder Plot. Its overthrow is commemorated every November 5th and has become known as Guy Fawkes Night, with celebrations that often include large bonfires and fireworks.

The Charterhouse in London remains an almshouse to this day. Brothers are selected from a variety of professions, including music, art, and literature. In January of 2017 the doors were opened to the general public for the first time since 1348, the year in which it was founded.

The epigraph at the beginning of the book is taken from the writings of Elizabeth Benger (1775–1827), an English poet, novelist, and biographer. She was a child prodigy and composed a remarkable poem at the age of thirteen entitled *The Female Geniad*, which celebrates women's achievements throughout history.

Present-day employees at the Tower of London include a Yeoman Warder known as the Ravenmaster, whose job is to see to the well-being of the ravens that populate the place just as they did in the time of Elizabeth. Custom dictates that should the ravens disappear, the White Tower will collapse into ruin and misfortune must follow soon after.

The compelling anatomical drawings Elizabeth examined in her brother's study are those of Leonardo Da Vinci. The copious notes that accompany them were written backwards for reasons that are not altogether clear. It may be that Da Vinci wanted to obscure them from discovery by the church, or perhaps it was a way of keeping others from stealing his ideas.

King James I abhorred tobacco to the point where he wrote an entire treatise, *A Counterblaste to Tobacco,* against its use. Interestingly, it was Sir Walter Raleigh who brought it back with him from the New World, having been sent there by Queen Elizabeth I. Tobias Hume held quite a different view on the matter and composed a musical tribute entitled *Tobacco*, which sang its praises.

Elizabeth was mother to thirteen children:
Henry Frederick, Hereditary Prince of the Palatinate (1614–29)
Charles I Louis, Elector Palatine (1617–80)
Elisabeth of the Palatinate (1618–80)
Rupert, Duke of Cumberland (1619–82)
Maurice of the Palatinate (1620–52)
Louise Hollandine of the Palatinate (1622–1709)
Louis (August 21–December 24, 1624)

Edward, Count Palatine of Simmern (1625–63)
Henriette Marie of the Palatinate (1626–51)
John Philip Frederick of the Palatinate (1627–50)
Charlotte of the Palatinate (1628–31)
Sophia, Electress of Hanover (1630–1714)
Gustavus Adolphus of the Palatinate (1632–41)

An obscure tomb at Westminster Abbey can be found along the south aisle of the Henry VII Lady Chapel. In the small gap between the monuments to Mary Queen of Scots and the Duchess of Richmond, hidden under a dusty fire blanket, lies a modest stone tablet set into the floor. The shallow inscription engraved upon it reveals that it is the burial place of Elizabeth, as well as her brother Henry and her cousin Arabella.

Acknowledgements

With gratitude and appreciation to all those who had a hand in the development of this novel — for their inspiration, expertise, and support — in particular, the following:

Jack David, David Caron, Rachel Ironstone, Tania Blokhuis, and everyone at ECW Press — for making it possible to tell Elizabeth's story.

Emily Schultz — for making ways to tell it better.

Harold Neufeld, Kimmy Beach, Edna Froese, Marjorie Anderson, and Chris Dirks — for making time to spend in Elizabeth's world.

The Access Copyright Foundation and the Manitoba Arts Council — for making Elizabeth accessible.

Graham Matthews at Charterhouse, London; Wilfried Klein at Heidelberg Castle; the staff of the Rare Books and Music Reading Room at the British Library; the staff at Prague Castle, Westminster Abbey, and the Tower of London — for making it real.

And finally, thanks to my wife, Brenda Sciberras — for making it all special.